"A superb and compelling Regency historical that will keep the reader riveted to the page . . . a wonderful, richly detailed reading experience. Complex, humorous, and sensual, *Vision in Blue* will delight historical fans."

—*The Romance Reader's Connection*

"Ms. Byrd does a fantastic job of balancing the stories of these two couples. Both women are captivating heroines, both men irresistible heroes. Byrd is fast becoming one of the best authors of historical romance writing today . . . I look forward to the next book in this intriguing, well-written series."

—*The Best Reviews*

PRAISE FOR
Beauty in Black

"Delightful . . . witty . . . hooks the audience."

—*Midwest Book Review*

"Another delightful tale by the multitalented Nicole Byrd . . . Heartwarming, humorous at times . . . a well-written page-turner."

—*Romance Reviews Today*

continued . . .

Gilding the Lady

Nicole Byrd

BERKLEY SENSATION, NEW YORK

THE BERKLEY PUBLISHING GROUP
Published by the Penguin Group
Penguin Group (USA) Inc.
375 Hudson Street, New York, New York 10014, USA
Penguin Group (Canada), 90 Eglinton Avenue East, Suite 700, Toronto, Ontario M4P 2Y3, Canada
(a division of Pearson Penguin Canada Inc.)
Penguin Books Ltd., 80 Strand, London WC2R 0RL, England
Penguin Group Ireland, 25 St. Stephen's Green, Dublin 2, Ireland (a division of Penguin Books Ltd.)
Penguin Group (Australia), 250 Camberwell Road, Camberwell, Victoria 3124, Australia
(a division of Pearson Australia Group Pty. Ltd.)
Penguin Books India Pvt. Ltd., 11 Community Centre, Panchsheel Park, New Delhi—110 017, India
Penguin Group (NZ), Cnr. Airborne and Rosedale Roads, Albany, Auckland 1310, New Zealand
(a division of Pearson New Zealand Ltd.)
Penguin Books (South Africa) (Pty.) Ltd., 24 Sturdee Avenue, Rosebank, Johannesburg 2196, South
Africa

Penguin Books Ltd., Registered Offices: 80 Strand, London WC2R 0RL, England

This is a work of fiction. Names, characters, places, and incidents either are the product of the author's
imagination or are used fictitiously, and any resemblance to actual persons, living or dead, business es-
tablishments, events, or locales is entirely coincidental. The publisher does not have any control over
and does not assume any responsibility for author or third-party websites or their content.

GILDING THE LADY

A Berkley Sensation Book / published by arrangement with the author

PRINTING HISTORY
Berkley Sensation edition / August 2005

Copyright © 2005 by Cheryl Zach.
Excerpt from *Seducing the Sage* copyright © 2005 by Cheryl Zach.
Cover art by Leslie Peck.
Cover design by Lesley Worrell.

ISBN: 0-425-20443-X

BERKLEY® SENSATION
Berkley Sensation Books are published by the Berkley Publishing Group,
a division of Penguin Group (USA) Inc.,
375 Hudson Street, New York, New York 10014.
BERKLEY SENSATION and the "B" design are trademarks belonging to Penguin Group (USA) Inc.

PRINTED IN THE UNITED STATES OF AMERICA

10 9 8 7 6 5 4 3 2 1

Prologue

The face . . .

It was the face that haunted her nightmares—but here, in clear daylight, distinct amid the crowd.

Clarissa Fallon drew a deep, disbelieving breath. It couldn't be. A moment ago she had been happily engrossed in the street scene, inhaling the aromas of savory meat and pastry that drifted from a street vendor's cart, as his call of "Hot meat pies!" rose above the clatter of horses' hooves and carriage wheels. She had paused on the sidewalk to relish the sparkle of sunlight off the polished panes of shop windows, which displayed enticing wares like a bonnet trimmed with yellow roses, a pair of elegant ecru kid gloves, and a flowing swath of crimson silk draped artfully across a stand. . . .

And Clarissa herself was free, at last, to consider such once unheard-of luxuries, free to lift her head to meet the eyes of the ladies and gentlemen strolling along the walkway. Free . . .

And then she'd caught sight of the once-familiar face, and

fear pierced her like a thorn lurking hidden amid a nosegay of roses.

Her brother had promised that Clarissa would be safe now. But the face was here. It was turning, and at any moment, those dark bulging eyes would meet Clarissa's horrified gaze, and then—

Clarissa jerked her head aside and fled from the specter that had appeared so abruptly out of the cheerful melee. She pushed her way past two chatting women and ran as if the devil himself waited to snare her soul.

Behind her, someone called, "Miss Clarissa, wait!"

Ignoring the cry, Clarissa rushed ahead. Her heart beat so loudly, the blood pounding in her ears, that she could hear nothing else. Even the noise of the busy London street faded, and she was lost in her worst nightmare.

She ran.

One

Dominic Shay, seventh earl of Whitby, sipped a glass of port. His head was lowered, and he didn't seem to notice when Timothy Galston, standing just to the side of the comfortable club chair, paused.

"Whitby!"

Timothy had practiced his tone of righteous indignation carefully in the privacy of his own rooms, and he was annoyed to observe the other man ignore his greeting. They were old acquaintances, and there was no reason for the slight prickle of unease that the earl always seemed to provoke in the younger man, but there it was. Timothy almost had second thoughts about his rehearsed speech, wishing for a moment he could just slip away, but dash it all, the girl was his cousin.

He cleared his throat and said, more loudly, "Whitby, I'm speaking to you!"

His perfect features set in an expression of arctic disinterest, the earl lifted his face, his deep brown eyes so dark that they could make one shiver. "Oh, hello, Galston. Have some wine; the sutler has just uncorked a quite tolerable bottle."

Timothy waved away such a minor consideration. No, perhaps not minor, but he could not be distracted until he'd aired his grievance.

"How could you do it? Why shoot down a girl in her first Season, who needs all the advantage she can muster, what with those freckles and the habit she has of smirking—" He paused. No, no, he was getting off the track. "I mean, she's a perfectly nice girl, with only a moderate dowry to recommend her, and you had no call to say that she dances like an African giraffe that's drunk too much home brew. The girl can't help being tall, you know!"

The earl frowned, but it seemed more in puzzlement than in anger. "Of whom are we speaking, Galston? Some new infatuation of yours?"

Timothy shook his head. "No, dammit. But she's my cousin, and she deserves better. You dashed her chance of a good Season with one careless bon mot, and you don't even recall? Miss Emmaline Mawper, that's who!"

When the earl continued to stare, Timothy added, "At Almack's last night, don't you remember?"

The earl shrugged. "I was in a bad mood, old man, wishing I hadn't allowed myself to be cajoled into looking into that wretched Marriage Mart in the first place. And I'm sure no one remembers one careless comment of mine."

"You think wrongly, then," Timothy retorted. "I've heard it repeated twice today already, with more jests tacked on, and Emmaline is in tears, my aunt says. Aunt Mary hauled me out of bed—at any ungodly hour, let me tell you—to complain, although what she thinks I can do . . . You're the most eagerly heeded arbiter of the Ton since Beau Brummel took himself off to the Continent to evade his debtors. If you weren't so damned perfect, with your elegant neckcloths and impeccable tailoring, not to mention that flawless Grecian coin of a face the ladies always swoon over—"

This time the earl shook his head, and a strand of dark hair fell back. For the first time, Timothy had a clear view of the ragged scar that marred the earl's left cheek. It started above his temple and ran past his ear and down beneath the erect shirt collar, the jagged line almost—but not quite— hidden beneath the earl's slightly too-long hair, and damned if that shaggy hair hadn't started a new fad among the calflings who aped Whitby's casual elegance . . .

"Flawless?" The earl's voice was icy.

Timothy swallowed. "Oh, that don't signify. It just adds a touch of the exotic, don't you know, romantic war wound, and all that—in fact, the ladies love it," he protested, but he knew his voice wavered. Damn, he always forgot.

"But that doesn't alter my contention," he said, trying to recapture his momentum. "The Ton still looks to you, Whitby, and it ain't right—you misuse your power over Society's opinion."

"If I have any power, as you claim, it is quite unsought and totally irrelevant." Whitby lowered his face again to sip his wine.

Almost tasting his relief, Timothy gulped.

"Not to the persons you cut down, it ain't," he argued. "It's easy enough to put someone down, much harder to build someone up. Why don't you do something agreeable for a change?"

"I assure you, Galston, the next time I see Miss Mawper, I will be charm personified—"

But a new voice interrupted.

"Look, a woman—a lady, I should almost say!"

The earl turned back toward the bow windows of White's, where several younger gentlemen lounged to watch the street. This was male territory, and any respectable lady knew it and avoided St. James Street with utmost care.

So why was a young and very pretty girl dashing down the pavement, pursued doggedly by a stout, red-faced female?

Even Timothy paused to stare. None of the onlookers

could make out the words spoken outside the window, but they saw the older woman catch the girl by the arm and her lips move in what was obviously an energetic scold.

The girl's expression twisted. Was she a lady or not? She was dressed decorously and with obvious expense, but her attitude to the older woman—mother, aunt, governess, whatever—didn't seem in keeping with her youth, nor did she seem abashed by her social transgression. In fact, now she jerked away from the other woman's hold, and while the men watched, entranced, landed a passable left hook into the woman's rounded midriff. The woman staggered back. The girl's hands curled into fists, and her bonnet slid off her fair hair as she waited for the woman to recover.

"Ten pounds on the younger lady!" one of the watchers called.

"Done. But hardly a lady, I'd say," another of the gawkers suggested. He added a comment that made the other men guffaw and offer a few disparaging guesses of their own as to the girl's social status—or even profession.

The earl frowned. One of the men sitting closer to the window looked up to see it, and beneath Whitby's reproving glance, the laughter faded. The other men turned back to watch the mill in progress.

"See," Timothy muttered. "I told you people listen to you. All you have to do is frown or smile, and the Ton obeys. . . ." He paused to stare out the window at the continuing struggle between the two women. He had accomplished what he'd come for, so why did he still feel dissatisfied? Someone ought to show Whitby just how misguided the arrogant earl was, he thought.

Outside, the stout woman—apparently thoroughly out of temper—slapped the girl's cheek, but the younger lady did not give in. She ducked and evaded the next blow. When she glanced up again, her cheek was reddened from the impact, and her eyes were wide with fear.

Timothy saw that the earl had stiffened. He noted, "I say

again, raising people up is much harder than cutting 'em down. For example, I'd bet you a hundred pounds you couldn't make a lady out of—out of—well, whoever that girl is."

"Probably some rich cit's daughter who hasn't heeded her lessons in deportment." The earl shook his head. "Or mayhap some escapee from Bedlam, judging by her barbaric behavior. Can't make a silk reticule out of a sow's ear. Anyhow, we don't even know who she is."

"And if I can find out her name? What about the bet?"

"I can't change her birth, and I'm sure as Hades no damned governess to give lessons in ladylike conduct." The earl's dusky eyes seemed to darken even more.

But this time Timothy, elated to at last observe a chink in Whitby's armor, stood his ground.

"So you admit my point? You can cut down an aspiring miss without a second thought, but you can't lift an awkward girl with, obviously, no sense of propriety, nor expend any real effort in the attempt? Afraid it will be too difficult a task, eh?"

Whitby narrowed his eyes.

Timothy's surge of confidence faded just a little; he tried not to gulp.

"If you learn her name, if she has any pretension to gentility at all, I will see that she is the toast of the Ton. Are you satisfied?"

Grinning, Timothy looked up just in time to see that the matronly woman had finally succeeded in pulling the still-struggling girl back up the street. They were almost out of sight.

One of the men in the window groaned as his mate urged, "Pay up!"

"Oh, very." Timothy tried not to laugh in the earl's face. "I'll let you know her name when I find it out."

And he hurried out of the club to follow the two women.

Clarissa Fallon was sitting in the broom cupboard. Again.

The kitchen cat, a handsome tabby with black and gray markings, had slipped in behind her when she'd darted into her hiding place. Purring, he twined around her feet.

"Shhh," Clarissa told him, rubbing his favorite spot just below his ear. He settled beside her, tucked his paws neatly beneath him and watched her with large golden eyes.

Clarissa rubbed the sore spot on her arm where the governess had pinched her when she had grabbed Clarissa in the street, then hugged her knees and tried not to make a sound. She could hear the heavy footsteps of her frustrated governess, Mrs. Bathcort, as the woman tramped by outside the closed door.

"Clarissa! Oh, where is that wretched girl now?" The woman stomped past the cupboard. In a moment, Clarissa heard the squeak of rusty hinges as the pantry door swung open. She knew that her governess's gaze scanned only barrels of flour and sugar and bins of root vegetables, finding no runaway there. Clarissa had indeed considered taking refuge in the cold pantry, which was larger, but the door was too noisy. Now she thanked her stars that she had chosen the other cupboard nook. But would the formidable Mrs. Bathcort check the broom cupboard, too?

Clarissa held her breath. She'd hidden here two days ago, when the governess's scolding had been too much to bear, and had not been found. Perhaps Mrs. Bathcort thought it not large enough to hold her. The cupboard was narrow and tall and usually crammed with brooms and mops. But the maids had taken most of them away, and until they returned from cleaning the upstairs, there was enough room to insert one skinny female whose petite frame made her look younger than she really was.

And the small space gave her the illusion of safety, of obscurity, of being hidden away from the peril she had thought no longer threatening. In fact, the whole house had seemed a castle when her brother had first brought her home, but today, in the briefest of moments, that comforting sense of security had been shattered. Shivering at the memory of her near-encounter on the street, Clarissa tried to think what she should do.

She must not panic, not again. Her wild flight down London's unfamiliar streets had only gotten her into more trouble. Trying for calm, she drew a deep breath. It was her downfall. The cupboard was not just small, but dusty. As Clarissa inhaled the musty air, her nose tickled. She tried to contain the sneeze, but—despite her best effort—it exploded.

Startled by the sudden sound, the cat bounded to its feet and scratched at the door.

Oh, bloody hell.

The door swung open, and light flooded the narrow cupboard.

"There you are, you miserable girl!"

The cat sprang out, causing the governess to shriek in surprise. Another hiding place gone. Clarissa climbed out reluctantly.

"Stand up straight, my girl, shoulders back—how many times have I said it! But keep your eyes down, a lady does not put herself forward, but at the same time she must look the dignity of her station."

Clarissa tried to obey. She would never remember all the finicky rules that the governess had tried to impress upon her. She wasn't even sure she wanted to!

Now the governess observed Clarissa rubbing her still-tickling nose on the back of her hand.

Mrs. Bathcort scowled. "Clarissa! Where is your handkerchief? You are not six years old, for pity's sake. And as for your disgraceful performance on the street, how am I ever going to teach you how to be a lady if you keep running away from me, not to mention your abuse of my person, and your total lack of ladylike remorse? Actually, I wish you were six—I could just take a cane to you and be done with it! Perhaps that would make you listen!"

Clarissa shivered, but she lifted her chin defiantly.

"I been caned by stronger arms than yours," she said, knowing that her tone was rude. "And it ain't going to happen again, never. For one thing, I'll claw your eyes out if you try. And for another, my brother said so."

"Your brother can take his misguided instructions and—" There was a pregnant pause.

Oh, dear. Clarissa felt just as much chagrin as the woman whose scowl had suddenly been replaced by a totally insincere smile. Her brother stood just a few feet away, and the look he bestowed upon Mrs. Bathcort made Clarissa—almost—feel sympathy for the woman. Matthew Fallon looked as if he were on the deck of a ship again, gazing down on some hapless ensign who had fouled a line. His glance was icy, and when he spoke, his tone even colder.

"That is no way to address a lady, Mrs. Bathcort, and certainly no way to speak to my sister."

The governess drew herself up. Since she came only to his shoulders, that was not an easy accomplishment, but she managed to assume an air of offended dignity. "If you're going to discharge me, Captain Fallon, you can save your breath. I hereby tender my resignation. No one can teach this imp from Hell how to behave like a lady. I advise you to ship her off to some convent school for the mentally deficient, preferably one where the nuns administer only the strictest discipline and feed their charges bread and water. Perhaps that might make an impression on your sister! Certainly, I have not, and I will be the first to admit it."

"I think you should go upstairs and pack your things, Mrs. Bathcort," Matthew Fallon said. His jaw seemed to be clenched. "Both your advice—and your insults—are unneeded."

To Clarissa's gratitude, he said no more as the woman lifted her chin and marched away, her footsteps heavy on the flagstones. When the door to the hallway had swung shut and the sounds of the governess's passage faded, he turned to gaze at his sister.

Across the kitchen, both the cook, who stirred something in a bowl, and the scullery maid, who was scrubbing potatoes, had their backs to their master and his sister as they bent over their tasks. They were very patently pretending the pair were not present. Clarissa was thankful for that, too.

Should she tell her brother what she had seen on the street, explain her fears? She hesitated. His expression was not angry, which she might have borne more easily, but instead disappointed.

"Clarissa—"

"I know," she interrupted. "I'm bloody—I mean—very sorry, Matthew. Really, I am."

"Despite Mrs. Bathcort's offensive manner, some of what she said is true." He took her hand and led her into the hallway so that they had more privacy. "You really must learn to behave like a lady again," he told her, his voice very gentle. "I know it's my fault that you were sent off to that wretched foundling home and then sold into service, but—"

"I don't fault you for going to sea," Clarissa interrupted. "Matthew, you ain't—I mean—you are not the one to blame. You were only trying to provide for Mother and me, and I know that you made a fine captain during the war. If that dishonest solicitor had not abandoned me to the foundling home after our mother died, I wouldn't 'ave ended up working as a nursery maid for that awful man."

"I was the one who chose the solicitor," Matthew told her, his expression darkening. "And between him and that bullying matron at the home, as well as your brute of an employer, you had a terrible time of it."

For an instant she saw again the face in the street and shivered. But in her brother's reassuring presence, her dread had faded, and now she felt less sure. Had she really seen the person she still feared, or was it only a vision out of her nightmares? And how could she add to Matthew's already heavy load of guilt by telling him of her moment of panic?

As she shuddered, Matthew said quickly, "But that is all

behind you, Clarissa. You are safe now, I promise you, and you will never be abandoned again. Please go change your dress. You're covered in dust and cat hair."

Clarissa glanced at the cat, who sat a few feet away, licking one paw and washing its face. No bad memories haunted the cat. It had no responsibilities except to capture any mice that strayed into the house, no rules to follow, no etiquette and code of manners to memorize. She wished for a moment she could trade places with the animal. Sighing, she stood and tried to brush off the skirts of her checked muslin gown. But the dust clung stubbornly. Matthew was right, she would have to change her dress.

She left Matthew and went back into the main part of the house, climbing the staircase and trailing one hand on the carved bannister. She'd had a hard life as a serving maid, rising early, working hard all day on scant rations—at least her brother and sister-in-law fed their staff well! But she hadn't had to change her gown several times a day, or remember to sit up straight at dinner, and as for her speech—she sighed again. Their widowed mother had seen that, despite their penury, Clarissa had been well brought-up as befit their station in life, but during the years spent among the lower classes she had picked up less refined habits, and now she found them hard to break.

On the bedroom landing, she encountered one of the housemaids dusting the bannister. "Ruby, would you please come and help me change?"

"Oh course, miss," the girl, who was hardly older than Clarissa, said readily. She tucked her dust cloth into her apron pocket and followed Clarissa to her bedroom. Matthew had wanted to hire a lady's maid for Clarissa, but she wasn't ready for that, not yet. She still felt *she* should be the one on her hands and knees cleaning out the grate or scrubbing the floor; it was hard to remember that she had been, and was now once more, officially a lady.

Ruby undid the back of her muslin dress, and Clarissa shed the dirty frock. She washed her hands and face in the bowl on her dresser. Then they looked into the clothespress and Clarissa selected a clean muslin dress, this one sprigged in blue. With the maid's help, she put it on.

"Shall I brush out your hair and pin it up again, miss? It's coming down in the back," Ruby suggested.

"Yes, please," Clarissa said, though again, it still felt very strange to sit still on the stool and allow someone else to pull out the pins and brush her thick blond hair with its glints of red. For the last few years, she'd just crammed it beneath a servant's cap and hurried to get on with her work. Now she had the luxury, the opportunity, to be pampered once again. She should have been thankful, and she was, but it didn't feel right. She felt like an impostor.

"There now, miss," Ruby said. "You look very smart."

Clarissa gazed into the looking glass. Yes, she looked well enough, ladylike and trim. The pristine white dress with its sprigs of blue skimmed her petite frame and breasts, the fair hair was drawn up on top of her head, and even the pearl eardrops, which had been her brother's gift on her nine-teenth birthday last week, looked just right. There was no doubt that she *looked* like a lady. Why was it so hard to feel like one?

Clarissa turned her head to take a searching glance at Ruby. The servant was pleasingly plump, with ruddy cheeks and brown hair tucked beneath her cap. Her apron and gown were neat, and her hands strong and slightly calloused from her work.

Clarissa glanced down at her own hands. The callouses were just now fading, after several weeks of ease in her brother's home, and the bruises from her last employer's abuse had also disappeared. She appeared little the worse for her years of exile, except, perhaps, inside her head. The sense of not fitting in, the nightmares that troubled her sleep . . . seeing the ghost of an old nemesis amid a crowded street . . . Had the encounter been real or only her imagination? The more she thought about it now, the less certain she was.

"Are you happy here?" she asked impulsively.

The maid looked surprised. "Of course, miss. Lady Gemma, and the captain your brother, too, are very kind and always fair, though they expect good work, of course. It's the best 'ousehold I've worked for since I left 'ome, and I've been in service since I was fourteen."

"I'm glad," Clarissa said simply. "Thank you for your 'elp—help, Ruby."

The maid curtsied. As she turned to leave, the door opened, and Clarissa's sister-in-law came into the room.

"There you are, and looking very pretty, too," Gemma said with a smile.

Clarissa smiled back as the maid made an unobtrusive exit.

"I heard about the, ah, unfortunate incident with Mrs. Bathcort. We shall inquire for a more patient governess, Clarissa. I'm so sorry you felt harassed. She came with such excellent recommendations, too."

Clarissa made a face. "It was as much my fault as hers," she confessed. "I ran away from her on the street and ended up in front of a men's club, White's, Mrs. Bathcort said. In fact, she said the whole street is not for ladies?"

To Clarissa's relief, instead of looking shocked or angry at her sister-in-law's gauche behavior, Gemma laughed. "That's true, I'm afraid."

"Why?" Clarissa demanded.

"I don't know, it's just how it is," Gemma told her. "But you should not run away from your governess. You might get lost, Clarissa, and there are dangers for a lady alone in the city."

Clarissa nodded reluctantly at the gentle reminder. "I try to remember the rules, but some of it makes no sense. We had been shopping only a few blocks away . . . Oh, Gemma, I don't know if I can do it—learn to be a lady again, I mean."

Gemma came closer and put one arm around Clarissa's shoulders. "You *are* a lady, Clarissa, just as your mother was. That is your birthright. And the habits, the demeanor, that will come back to you. I know it's very hard."

Clarissa thought that Gemma did know, much better than

most. Gemma had once briefly been subject to the harsh rule of the foundling home herself and had met Matthew when he first returned to England and began searching for his lost sister. Clarissa was very glad that Matthew had chosen Gemma to marry—she could not have asked for a more loving or understanding sister-in-law.

But still, she bit her lip. "I don't know, Gemma. I don't feel right, inside. I should be happy. When I was told that my brother had died at sea, I thought I was doomed to a life of servitude forever. Now he's home, safe, and I have him and you and a nice house to live in and no worries—at least, except for the bad dreams that come at night, and, during the day, trying to mind my tongue and remember to behave like a proper lady. But I feel so . . . so confused inside. Why should I feel this way?"

Gemma hugged her again. "Why should you not? Your whole world has been turned upside down, and even though it's a happy change, it takes time to adjust. Don't fret yourself. You'll feel at ease again, eventually."

Clarissa was not so sure, but she didn't argue. It was ungrateful to worry Gemma and Matthew just because Clarissa seemed so twisted inside. And as for her fright on the street, she opened her lips to bring it up, but Gemma continued to speak.

"Get your shawl," Gemma suggested. "Let's take a stroll before dinner. You don't need to sit in your room and brood. Today was the first day you've been out of the house all week."

Nodding, Clarissa rose. "Yesterday Mrs. Bathcort made me parse two dozen sentences because I kept using *ain't,* as well"—she added, determined to be fair—"as a few other words she considered improper."

They headed out together, walking a few blocks and looking into shop windows, then visited a lending library. At least Clarissa's knowledge of reading and writing had not left her, though she had had little chance to use those skills during her years as a servant. She looked eagerly over a stack of new novels and chose a three-volume set to take home.

They returned in time for dinner. Gemma went upstairs to change, but Clarissa simply washed her hands—surely, she did not have to change clothes again!—and came down at the appointed time.

Gemma must have said something to her brother because Matthew said no more about the departed governess. They chatted amicably through the first course.

They paused as the footman and one of the housemaids returned to remove the linen cloth, then an array of desserts was served. Clarissa dipped her spoon into a serving of creamy blancmange—sweets were still a great treat to her unaccustomed palate—and wondered if Gemma, too, had moments of unease in her new role of lady of the house. She had not always known her parentage, Matthew said. She, too, had had doubts about her identity. But Gemma seemed so much the lady. . . . If her sister-in-law could conquer her uncertain past, perhaps Clarissa could, too.

Nose tickling again, Clarissa put down her spoon and, this time, remembered to draw her handkerchief out of her pocket and dab discreetly at her nose.

But even as she congratulated herself on remembering to use her handkerchief, her elbow brushed the table and knocked her spoon off her plate.

It clattered to the floor. Clarissa dived off her chair to retrieve it and bumped into the footman, intent on the same mission.

Red-faced, Clarissa accepted his help in returning to her chair. She sat and stared at her plate, and in a moment, the servant brought her a clean spoon.

She was afraid to look at her brother, knowing that his face would show not anger but the guilt that he would always feel. He would always believe that her years of exile and her current struggle to learn how to act like a lady were all his fault.

"It's all right, Clarissa," Gemma said, her tone soft. "Eat your dinner, my dear."

Blinking back tears, Clarissa obeyed, though the creamy pudding seemed to have lost its sweetness.

"Perhaps," she said, not looking at either of them, "I should wait till next Season to make any appearance in Society. I'm so— I'm not learning very quickly, and I do not wish to disgrace myself, or you."

"You would never disgrace us, Clarissa," Matthew told her, his inflection firm.

And from the corner of her eye, she saw Gemma shake her head. "The Season is still in full swing. You have plenty of time. Even attending a few social events this year will make it easier for you, Clarissa. Otherwise, you will spend the rest of the year dreading next spring. It's confidence you lack, more than knowledge. I'm sure your ease in Society will return to you."

Clarissa took another bite of the sweet and wished she could be so sure.

The next morning in the drawing room Clarissa sat properly, her back erect, doggedly studying a book entitled, *A Gentlewoman's Guide to Proper Decorum*. She would have much rather been deep in her new novel, but, aware of her brother and sister-in-law's faith in her—however misguided she feared it might be—she kept her eyes on the text, trying to memorize a list of titles, and who took precedence over whom in social situations. An earl's wife was a countess, and a marquess's wife was a—she sneaked a peek at the page when the title did not spring to mind—a marchioness. And marquesses were second only to dukes, who ranked beneath princes. . . .

Then the door opened, and Gemma looked in.

"Here you are, Clarissa. Your brother and I have been discussing a replacement for your departed governess. And I have someone for you to meet."

Clarissa braced herself. Whether the next governess was

stout or thin, tall or short, she would—Clarissa had no doubt—soon wear the same disapproving, hopeless expression of the last one.

But when Gemma stepped inside the room, Clarissa's eyes widened. In the doorway appeared, not the middle-aged woman she expected to see, but a young man—a very good-looking young man.

Two

Clarissa tried to compose her expression. But, bloody hell—she shook herself mentally—he was a most seemly young man. He had curly hair so black that it seemed to glisten beneath the sunlight bouncing off the looking glass on the wall, deep-set dark eyes, a thin mustache, and a slim build with somewhat narrow shoulders but a trim waist and erect posture. He was of medium height, so he did not loom over her petite frame as so many men did. His clothing was that of a gentleman, his black coat and neatly tied neckcloth just right, his pantaloons smooth over firm thighs, and his stockings and shoes spotless.

"This is Monsieur Meidenne," Gemma told her. "Monsieur, this is my dear sister-in-law, Miss Fallon."

He gave her a graceful bow. A few seconds too late, Gemma sank into an answering curtsy that was not half so well done.

"Monsieur Meidenne has kindly agreed to add you to his list of dancing students," Gemma explained.

Clarissa felt a flicker of disappointment. Not a gentleman then, exactly, but the dancing master Gemma had promised to find for her. With the Season already begun, it was not easy to find a competent instructor who was not already over-booked with anxious young ladies practicing for the all-important balls and assemblies they would soon attend. Gemma had already obtained vouchers for Almack's for Clarissa, that hallowed institution where rules of propriety were all important, although Clarissa had not as yet had the nerve to even consider attending.

"I am pleased to meet you, Mademoiselle Fallon," he said. He had a slight accent that was hard to place.

"I am happy to meet you, sir," she answered. "You are French?"

His expression slightly affronted, he shook his head. "Belgian," he told her. "We shall begin z'is morning with something simple, perhaps z'e allemande."

Oh hell, already?

"Clarissa is eager to learn," Gemma suggested. "And I will play for you on the pianoforte when you are ready to practice." She rang for a servant, and under her direction, the footman rolled up the rug so they would have a smooth floor to practice on.

Already feeling her feet three times too heavy, Clarissa put aside her book and crossed the room as the new tutor took his place. She wished she had had more experience with the social arts as a child, but her widowed mother had entertained rarely, and there had been few family parties where she might have observed the dancers or followed along on the sidelines.

She stood straight and tried to follow his instructions, still nervous to be standing so near to such an attractive man, and even more intimidated by the thought of having to learn dance steps.

"Z'is foot forward—no, no, mademoiselle, z'is foot, z'e foot on z'e right—"

Blushing, Clarissa tried again. She felt as awkward as—

and her feet as big as—one of the oxen who pulled the farmers' carts.

"Mademoiselle, if you would attend, *s'il vous plait?*"

"Sorry," she muttered, pulling her attention back and thrusting out a foot—again, as it turned out from his frown, the wrong one.

The rest of the hour stretched on for at least a week, until at last Monsieur Meidenne, his smile a little forced, bowed to her again. "I shall return on z'e Friday. Until z'en, mademoiselle, you will recollect all z'at I have said and you will practice z'e movements, yes?"

"Yes, thank you," Clarissa replied, too embarrassed to admit that all his instructions were a jumble in her mind.

But when Monsieur Meidenne had been shown out by the footman, she turned to Gemma and cried, "Oh, Gemma, I can't. Let me just go into the country and hide out in some little cottage for the rest of the Season!"

Gemma came closer and gave Clarissa a hug. "My dear, of course you will be clumsy at first. Do not berate yourself. With practice, you will soon be gliding across the dance floor like all the other young ladies."

"Only if it is greased," Clarissa muttered, thinking of the village festivals of her childhood when eager lads had tried to climb a greased pole to win a prize.

Gemma laughed. "Come along, let's have some tea and cake, and then perhaps we will go out and look into the shops."

Remembering her last disastrous foray into London's shopping area, Clarissa felt a flicker of alarm. "No," she said before she thought, and then, when Gemma looked at her in surprise, added, "I mean, I don't wish to be more of a charge on you than I have already."

Gemma's touch on her arm was gentle. "My dear, thankfully, we do not have to worry about finances. That time is behind you. And your wardrobe must be sufficient for the time when you go into Society."

Clarissa felt even more dismay, but she tried to hide it.

She was not certain which prospect was more alarming, seeing the feared image out of her past rise up out of the crowd once more, or making her bow to the Ton.

*Dominic was sitting at his desk perusing a report of in-*vestment earnings when he became aware that a footman stood in the doorway, a silver tray in his hands. How long had he been there; had the servant spoken? Dominic wasn't sure. At least his servants were accustomed to their master's eccentricities.

"Yes?"

"A note for you, my lord." The footman brought the missive in and placed it carefully on the polished desktop.

Dominic nodded his thanks and, without enthusiasm, unfolded the single sheet of paper. He scanned the scrawled handwriting, and he frowned as he read:

> *The tempestuous young lady's name is Miss Clarissa Fallon. Although her family is not titled, she has every claim to the status of gentlewoman. She lives with her brother, Captain Matthew Fallon, lately of His Majesty's navy, and her sister-in-law, Lady Gemma Fallon, at the address below. She has not yet made her bow to Society but is expected to venture out, soon.*
>
> *I shall hold you to our wager.*

It was signed, *The Honorable Timothy Galston,* and there was an address in the West End added at the bottom, the site of the Fallon household.

Dominic's first impulse was to ball the paper into a crumpled wad and toss it toward the fire. It fell short, and just as well. After a moment, he stood and retrieved it, smoothed the creases he had made and looked again at the address.

He had given his word, and as to why—he had been a damn fool. It was not the lure of a silly wager, but the look he had glimpsed for the briefest of instants on the girl's face—a look of stark terror. He had been reminded of one of his foot soldiers, about to go down beneath the charging hooves of a French trooper's steed.

Dominic put one hand to his brow, resisting the urge to touch the jagged scar at the side of his face. He had dreamed again last night, dreamed of sitting on his horse and lifting his sword to order his men forward, then the shell exploding—red hell opening like some deadly flower and tumult so deafening it was beyond the range of his ears—

He shook the images away. It was not his own injuries that haunted him so much as the memory of the shattered bodies of the soldiers who had paid much more dearly than he . . . men who had been in his charge. . . .

A good commander hardened himself to the loss of his men, did not regard it, or so he had been often told during his years of military service. Wellington had cared, and Dominic recalled that example with relief. Perhaps Dominic was not mad, because even after years away from the battle-field—he had not stayed to see the last bloody struggles, called home by his family obligations when he had inherited the title much sooner than anyone had expected—sometimes the carnage still flashed unbidden into his mind. And his dreams . . . his dreams were barely on the edge of sanity. . . .

He drew a deep breath.

Life went on. With the help of a good agent, Dominic managed his estate, and he was an easy taskmaster for the servants in his employ. The only thing he wanted, desperately longed for, was never again to bear the responsibility for anyone else's life or well-being. That was one of the primary reasons he held himself aloof from any possible entanglements, though it was a habit that drove matchmaking mamas to despair, he was told. And he would be more than happy to be considered a hardened case, he thought, frowning. All the better if the matrons left him alone and stopped nagging him to turn up at every dance or dinner party.

And it was that same aversion that had made this cub Galston's accusations so hard to bear—the charge that he was causing distress to strangers—and that, really, was another reason he had been weak enough, startled enough, not to find a way to evade this insane wager. That, and the look on the unknown girl's face.

But it was done. And she was unknown no longer.

He drew a clean sheet of paper toward him and dipped his pen into the inkwell.

Clarissa had endured another shopping excursion. Although she kept peering into the crowd, hardly able to concentrate on the new gloves and ball slippers that her sister-in-law insisted upon ordering for her, at least no nightmare face appeared out of the mass of people that thronged the streets.

They returned home in time to meet Clarissa's new governess before dinner, although now the official title had been changed to *governess/companion,* since Clarissa was really too old to need a governess, or she would have been if she'd had the proper training in her earlier years, and this lady was not really a governess at all.

This woman was taller and thinner, with a formidable hooked nose and faded hazel eyes, and when they were introduced she gazed at Clarissa with apparently genuine regard.

"This is Miss Pomshack, Clarissa," Gemma explained. "She was kind enough to serve as a companion to my friend Louisa, now Mrs. Colin McGregor, before Louisa's marriage."

Clarissa made her very best curtsy, hoping to show the new companion that she was not, after all, totally unteachable. The woman smiled down at her.

"I am sure we will enjoy a most pleasant time together, Miss Fallon. I hope to do my humble best to assist you as you master the intricacies of social propriety. Even though, as my father the vicar always said, it is the goodness inside one's soul that counts the most, I fear that Society does judge us too often by appearances."

Not sure whether she was supposed to be cheered or alarmed by this statement, Clarissa nodded.

Gemma took Miss Pomshack away to see her room, and Clarissa remembered she was expected to change her dress for dinner. She went up to her room and was struggling to reach the hooks at the back of her dress when Ruby, the youngest housemaid, came into the bedchamber.

"Oh, miss, let me. You should wait for me to help you."

Clarissa bit her lip. She could not get back into the habit of waiting for servants to assist her with the simplest of tasks. Inside, she still felt that she should be the one fetching and carrying, hurrying to answer someone's bidding. But she could not explain that to Ruby. She muttered an answer and allowed the maid to help her out of the gown and into a fresh dress for dinner.

As Ruby brushed out her hair and pulled it back, resetting the pins, she said, "You're very quiet tonight, miss. Do you like your new companion?"

"I suppose," Clarissa told the girl. "I haven't spent much time with her as yet. She can hardly be worse than the last one!" Then Clarissa realized she should not have said that to one of the servants. Bloody hell. "Please don't repeat that, Ruby," she added.

"Of course not, miss," the maid agreed, although she grinned.

It was so hard to remember that she was the lady now, not one of the servants and still free to gossip with the rest of the staff. Clarissa swore again beneath her breath, then bit her lip. Another fault she was trying to break— Oh, it was hopeless!

At dinner Clarissa said little as she concentrated fiercely on her manners, remembering to use—and hold on to—the proper silver, as she listened to Gemma make polite conversation with the new member of the household. Her sister-in-law had come to know the older lady during the time that Miss Pomshack had served as her friend Louisa's companion, although Gemma would always be gracious to anyone, familiar or not. Would Clarissa ever be able to function with the same seemingly effortless poise as her sister-in-law? She couldn't see how.

At least she kept all her silverware on the table this time, although the knot in her stomach prevented her from eating very much. When the ladies withdrew to the drawing room and left her brother alone with his wine, Miss Pomshack favored them with a discourse on the sermon she had heard the Sunday before—"Very well presented, though my father the vicar would perhaps have explained more clearly the concept of Christian charity"—and Clarissa allowed her mind to wander. When her brother joined them, she said her goodnights as soon as she could and went up early to bed.

Once again, Ruby came to help her disrobe. Clarissa thanked her and, catching the servant in a yawn, sent the girl off to her own bed as soon as she could.

"I know you're tired," Clarissa said when the maid protested.

"But I 'aven't brushed out your 'air yet," the girl said.

"I can do it myself," Clarissa insisted.

So Ruby took her leave. Clarissa picked up the silver-backed brush and stared into the looking glass atop her bureau as she brushed out her fair hair. It was only an accident of birth that had one girl doing the chores and the other being waited upon. What gave Clarissa the right to be the "lady," even if she *could* ever again feel entitled to that role?

Her expression wan, the girl in the glass stared back, and no answer presented itself.

It was the way of the world, her brother would say, not unkindly. Why did that answer no longer satisfy her?

Clarissa blew out her candle and climbed into bed. Although she soon dropped into sleep, her dreams were confused and sometimes frightening. Once, she woke and found she was breathing hard, the bedclothes tumbled around her. She had been running, or trying to run, but her feet had seemed enmeshed as if in a bog, leaving her powerless to flee as a vicious face loomed nearer. The figure—larger in the vision than in real life—reached out to grasp at her. . . .

Drawing a deep breath, Clarissa stared into the darkness. The bedchamber was empty. It was only another nightmare. Only . . .

But Clarissa had to rub her damp cheeks on the sleeve of her nightgown, and it was a long time before she slept again.

Clarissa came down to the dining room rather late and found that her brother had already supped and departed. Gemma was still at the table, although she seemed to have finished her breakfast. Miss Pomshack sat on the other side, her attention on her plate and the thick slice of ham it held. A pile of mail sat at the side of Gemma's plate, and she gazed at a letter in her hand.

"Good morning, Clarissa. I hope you slept well?"

"Not 'alf bad," Clarissa lied, then blushed at the cant expression as she paused by the sideboard to glance over the hot plates of eggs and kippers and sausage and ham. After her light dinner last night, she felt very empty. "I mean, tolerably."

"The most amazing thing," Gemma said. "You are invited to a dance."

"What?" Clarissa almost dropped her plate. "Who— I mean, is it your friend Louisa or your brother Lord Gabriel?"

"No, that's what is so astounding," Gemma admitted. "This is a lady—Lady Halston—whom I barely know. Why she has asked us all—most pointedly including you, and not that many people know that Matthew has a sister about to make a late debut into Society—I have no idea."

Clarissa felt a shiver of alarm. She set her plate down, then, knowing that Gemma would be concerned if she ate nothing, took a piece of toast. But when she sat down and the footman poured her a cup of tea, she chewed absentmindedly on the bread and found it as tasteless as a withered leaf. "But I—I don't have to accept, do I?"

To her alarm, Gemma didn't answer at once. "This might be a nice way to break the ice, Clarissa, before we have a ball to launch you into Society. A dress rehearsal, as it were. Mrs. Halston says it is only a small affair."

Clarissa had an unbidden image of a rock being launched into the air, only to sink like the stone it was.

"But I'm— I'm not ready," she stuttered. "And I've told you before, as generous as your offer is, that I don't really want a debut ball."

"The dance is two weeks away. And the dancing master will return this morning." Gemma's tone was soothing, and she ignored Clarissa's last comment. "I'm sure in a fortnight you could be prepared."

Under Gemma's kind gaze, Clarissa found herself unable to argue further. Perhaps Gemma realized that Clarissa was never going to feel truly prepared to run Society's gauntlet.

"I'm sure you can do it, Miss Fallon," Miss Pomshack said helpfully. "And have some marmalade, do, and some butter. That toast must be very dry."

Clarissa accepted the cut-glass bowl of fruit preserves and put a spoonful of the tart marmalade on her toast. The lump in her throat made it hard to swallow. Two weeks!

When they went upstairs, Miss Pomshack assigned her a section of Milton to read, and then they discussed the poet's work together, Miss Pomshack correcting Clarissa's diction when she dropped her *h*'s or used a cant phrase not becoming to a lady. At least Miss Pomshack seemed to have more patience than the last governess! The poetry, as elevated as its theme was, did not hold Clarissa's attention, and the hands on the mantel clock seemed to move too quickly. Before Clarissa was ready to face another dance lesson, the clock chimed eleven o'clock.

She heard steps in the hall and felt her heart sink.

Smiling in reassurance, Gemma came into the room with the dancing master behind her. Clarissa tried to compose her expression.

"I shall play for you when you're ready, Monsieur," Gemma said. They had already had the rug rolled up.

Clarissa made a polite curtsy. Her brief infatuation with the instructor's good looks had faded. There was nothing like treading on a man's foot and feeling like a fool to cure one of a momentary crush. And the Belgian's expression when he bowed and approached her was guarded, his dark eyes wary, so she feared that he felt as little enthusiasm for the lesson as she.

Clarissa was sure she remembered nothing of yesterday's lesson. Apparently, Monsieur Meidenne was of the same opinion. Today, he began with the most basic instructions.

"Now, mademoiselle, we will pretend z'e musicians are z'ere, where Lady Gemma sits at z' pianoforte. Z'e most socially eminent of z'e guests will stand at z'e front of z'e lines, ladies on z'e right in one row, men on z'e left. We shall pretend z'at we are z'e first couple. So if you will take your place opposite me?"

Trying not to blush with nervousness, she obeyed.

He put the book of instructions he always carried on a side table, then returned to his position. He glanced over at Gemma.

"My lady, we will begin today with somez'ing simple, perhaps 'Mr. Beveridge's Maggot.'"

"Maggot?" Clarissa wrinkled her nose. "What does that—"

He ignored her. "Z'e music is a slow three-quarter time, so it should be easier for you to comprehend, no?"

No was all too likely the right answer, but she pressed her lips together and did not make it.

"In z'e first phrase," he told her, "z'e first man and woman—z'at is you and I—cross over and exchange places."

Gemma played the tune, and Clarissa did as she was told, at least today managing not to step on her instructor's toes as he passed.

"Now—ah, we need a second lady. Perhaps you would be so good as to help us, madam?" He nodded to Miss Pomshack, who rose at once.

"Of course," she agreed, her manner gracious. "I do not dance in company these days, but in my youth, I was considered a first-rate dancer." She took her position next in line to Clarissa, and Clarissa had a moment to relax as she watched her instructor pass back to back with the governess. They both performed more credibly and with more grace than she.

"No, no, do not just stand z'ere," Monsieur Meidenne scolded, glancing over his shoulder. "You should be doing z'e same with z'e second gentleman."

There was no second gentleman, of course, but Clarissa obliged by pretending to pass, back to back, with an invisible man.

"Now, observe," the tutor said. He circled by himself and then turned the governess once around by her right hand. "You will do z'e same."

Confused, Clarissa started toward Miss Pomshack, but the tutor exploded. "No, no! You will rotate yourself once and z'en turn z'e second man round by z'e right hand."

"I'm sorry," Clarissa said, knowing that her face had reddened.

"It is noz'ing, we will try again," he said. Gemma, who had paused and looked up in concern, played the tune again. This time Clarissa was able to follow the pattern.

"*Bon*, good," the tutor said. "Now, you and I, mademoiselle, will turn with our left hand halfway, cross over and cast."

"What?"

"Go into z'e second couple's place as we change sides," he told her.

Clarissa tried to obey, but again he stopped her. "No, no, on z'e outside of z'e line! Everyone knows z'at!"

Everyone except Clarissa. She thought wistfully of her days cleaning out hearths and scrubbing floors. That had been easier than this!

"Now z'e first and second men go back to back with z'eir partners." Monsieur Meidenne demonstrated, while Clarissa drew a deep breath, trying to keep it all in her head.

"Next, z'e first and second couples all four take hands and move up six steps and fall back six steps—"

Clarissa found herself a step behind and hurried to catch up, almost colliding with Miss Pomshack.

"And first couple does a figure eight through z'e second couple, first man goes around second man and z'en around second lady, while first lady goes around second lady and z'en second man—"

This time Clarissa did bump into her new governess, and the only way the "second man" escaped her bullish charge was that he did not exist. The music flowed on, but Clarissa paused in the middle of the figure, biting her lip and trying not to burst into tears.

Across the room, Gemma lifted her hands from the keys. "Perhaps we should pause for a moment to get our breaths," she suggested.

The dancing master looked despairing, but he pulled himself together and nodded. "Of course, my lady."

Clarissa turned away from the others and crossed to the window, pretending to stare out although her vision was blurred by tears she tried not shed.

Behind her, she heard Miss Pomshack making polite conversation with the Belgian tutor, and then the door opened. Clarissa turned halfway, enough to see Matthew come into the room, and Gemma rise from the pianoforte. He paused to speak briefly to his wife—Clarissa was glad she could not hear their words—then he continued across the room and paused beside Clarissa.

"A lovely day," he said.

Clarissa had been staring out the window, but only belatedly did she glance toward the cloudy blue sky above the houses on the other side of the street. Not trusting her voice, she nodded.

"You will pick it up again, Clarissa. I used to dance you around the parlor when you were four or five, before I left for the naval academy. You were as light on your feet then as a thistledown."

"I wish I could remember," Clarissa told him wistfully, then wished she had held her tongue. His dark eyes showed his disappointment that the memory had not come readily to her mind.

"Likely you will, my dear. And even if not, you will relearn the dance steps. All you need is practice. Come, let me be your partner this time."

Despite her reluctance, she allowed him to lead her back into position. Gemma returned to her seat at the instrument, and her hands glided across the keys. The dancing master took his place across from Miss Pomshack, and they assumed the role of first couple.

With four people, it was easier to picture the proper form, and this time, Clarissa did a little better. Her brother guided her gently back into place when she strayed, and she didn't actually bump into anyone.

"There, you are making excellent progress," Matthew told her.

Although she thought his pronouncement a gross exaggeration, Clarissa smiled—until he continued.

"In two weeks, you will be gliding about the floor as smoothly as any other debutante at her first ball."

Oh, hell, so he had been told about the dance. Her smile fading, she mumbled, "I'd much rather not."

But he shook his head. "Sooner or later, you must take your proper place in Society, Clarissa."

She would choose *later,* Clarissa thought, but her brother was still speaking.

"I wish you to have your life back, the life you should

have had and which was so cruelly interrupted. I know you may feel some nervousness at your first society event—most young ladies do, I'm told. But you'll do splendidly."

Since Matthew had once faced down enemy ships during perilous battles at sea, she didn't wish her brother to think her a craven over nothing more than a social invitation. How could she explain how her heart pounded and her stomach clenched at the thought of facing a roomful of strangers while she tried to mind her steps and her words? They would all witness how unfit she was, she knew it. Even as she wrestled with the turmoil inside her, for his sake she tried to be brave. She smiled through stiff lips.

"I hope you are right."

Three

*"To assure the good opinion
of the Ton, simply appear
to disdain it."*
MARGERY, COUNTESS OF SEALY

*W*hen the dance lesson from hell finally ended, the
Belgian tutor took his leave, and Clarissa followed
her brother and sister-in-law, with Miss Pomshack bringing
up the rear, down to the dining room. With the lesson behind
her, Clarissa tried to eat. Her middle felt empty, and the airy
souffle, one of the dishes Cook had sent up for them, tasted
delicious. But she had taken only a few bites when Gemma
began to tell her husband about the new gowns they had ordered for Clarissa.

"One is a pale green, which will show off her eyes
nicely . . ." Gemma continued to talk, obviously unaware of
the effect of her words. Reminded yet again of her looming
social debut, Clarissa felt her stomach tighten. Gulping, she
put down her fork.

"They all sound lovely," Matthew said. "I'm sure you will
present a beautiful sight, Clarissa, and dazzle the Ton."

He seemed determined to pamper her, Clarissa thought. It
was so ungrateful of her not to be excited about her upcoming

debut. Obviously, there was no way out. For her family's sake, she must not be such a coward! Taking a deep breath, she accepted a serving of tender lamb and waited while the footman spooned on the mint sauce. Then she cut her meat, took a bite and chewed, and if she tasted the savory meat not at all, at least Matthew and Gemma would not know.

Afterward, Matthew left for his club, and Gemma suggested that Clarissa take a short rest before they went out. "We are invited to Psyche's—Lady Gabriel's—for tea later," she explained.

When Clarissa looked up in alarm, Gemma added, "Just a few ladies, my dear. Nothing to fret about, only some light-hearted chatter."

"How pleasant," Clarissa agreed. After all, she could not spend the rest of her life cowering inside the house and seeing only her own family, she told herself. She went upstairs but found it impossible to lie down. She tried to hold to her newly made resolution, but she felt suffocated. Oh, dear God, if she didn't have a moment to be herself.

Clarissa waited until she heard Gemma go to her own room and shut the door, then she put on her bonnet and slipped down the back stairs.

He would drive by the girl's house, Dominic told himself, merely to take the lay of the land. The wager had been a moment of insanity, and now he wondered if he could simply beg off . . . It really was highly improper to bet on a lady's good name; he could always claim moral scruples.

He told his coachman which street he wished to see, planning to continue on to his club; a game of whist should be starting within the quarter hour. It was simply bad luck that as they passed the row of neat, moderately sized houses, he should see a petite figure making her way along the walkway, a maidservant following just behind her.

Damnation, there she was. What on earth was Miss Fallon up to?

Luckily—or unluckily for the card game that he was not to join—a wagon partially blocked the street. His coachman had to pull up. So, unseen from outside the chaise, Dominic could easily watch as the girl paused at the corner of an alley.

She said something to the maid behind her, and, to Dominic's bewilderment, he saw the maid untie her apron and hand it over, then add her plain cap and take her mistress's fashionable hat in exchange.

A mystery, indeed. Despite himself, Dominic found he was grinning. Was she running away, the little hoyden? But she could be putting herself into a dangerous situation. Had no one warned this girl about the many dangers of London streets?

He knocked on the front of the carriage. "I'm getting out for a stroll," he told his startled coachman. "Wait here."

And he followed the fleeing figure as it turned into a side street.

When she left the house, Clarissa had intended to take a stroll through the park. It would be little occupied at this time of day, and she had a keen desire to be away from censorious eyes. That was quite unexceptional, and she had even taken Ruby with her, just as she should. But as her brother's house fell behind her, she found her steps dragging, and her spirits felt as low as the usual layer of smoke that hung over the city. How would she ever turn herself into a lady?

It wasn't just the discouraging, confusing dance lessons. It was so much more—too many rules to remember, too many nuances, too many lost years when she should have been learning and preparing herself. The whole of Society would think her a fool, and she would never ever feel that she belonged.

Clarissa felt the sting of tears behind her lids and shook her head, trying to throw off her self-pity. She should be counting her blessings . . .

She looked up to see two maids walking side by side, chattering as they carried baskets of produce and foodstuffs back to the household which employed them. They looked so at ease, so sure of their tasks and their place in the world. Clarissa could remember the time when she could have walked up and fallen easily into conversation with these servants. Would she ever be able to do that in "proper" Society?

She had a sudden wild impulse, and she turned and glanced back at Ruby, just behind her. The maid wouldn't walk side by side with her mistress, though Clarissa had urged it.

"It wouldn't be proper, miss," the maid had explained earnestly.

For a little while, Clarissa was ready to be improper. "Here, give me your apron and cap," she instructed. "You take my hat back to the house."

The girl's eyes widened. "What are you about, Miss Clarissa?"

"Only a little joke on a lady I know," Clarissa lied quickly. "I'll be back home very shortly."

"But your brother—" The serving girl twisted her hands.

"Won't know a thing," Clarissa promised. "Please, Ruby."

The maid obeyed her instructions, though she looked bemused. Once the girl had turned her back, Clarissa slipped on the apron and cap and turned up the side street, hastening her steps to catch up with the other two maids. Those two were still deep in conversation and had been paying no attention to her quick and impromptu disguise.

"A good day at the market?" Clarissa asked, coming up behind them.

The stout girl looked over her shoulder. "Not bad. The geese were nice and fat, but I wouldn't touch the cod, if I was you, it's been out of the water too long."

"Unless you want to give your master a good case of the runs," the second maid added, giggling.

Clarissa joined in the laughter. Miss Pomshack would tell her this was disgraceful, she knew, but she felt so much freer here, chatting with girls who would not judge her or wrinkle their noses when she dropped a fork or missed a dance step.

They were curious, though. The thin one looked her over. "New on the street, are you? I ain't seen you in the court-yards or the market."

Clarissa nodded. "I'm at the house down by the end," she said, hoping the two wouldn't ask for more detail. "Just come last week."

The thin maid seemed about to ask another question, but a new figure came out of a side entrance, and the girls paused. A young man with a spotty face and rough clothes eyed them.

"Don't pay no attention to 'im," the stout girl muttered. "'E's the under groom at the colonel's 'ouse, and thinks 'e's God's gift to females. 'E'll have 'is eye on you double quick, 'e will."

"'E's wasting 'is time, then," Clarissa told them. "I've got no use for a man who thinks too 'igh of 'imself."

The other two girls giggled, but the young groom had already changed his path to accost them.

"Lo there," he said, eyeing Clarissa with appreciation. "You're a bonny bit of goods. New to the street, are you?"

"Too bonny for the likes of you, Jack," the thin maid told him.

He made a face. "I ain't talking to you," he told her, his tone sharper. "You can let this un speak for 'erself."

He reached out as if to grip Clarissa's shoulder, but she slipped out of reach.

"You don't 'ave to be so coy," Jack complained. "I just want one little kiss. Welcome you to the neighborhood, eh?"

He reached again, and Clarissa kicked his shin.

He swore, just as a male voice spoke abruptly from behind them. "Here! What you think you're doing?"

Clarissa whirled.

Looking annoyed, Jack turned as if to dispute the stranger's right to interfere. But the handsome man who stood there, his expression arrogant, his clothes expensive, looked him up and down, and the groom's anger smoothed away. "Nothing, sir. Just going, sir."

"Then be on your way."

The two maids had already slipped off, disappearing into one of the back entrances. Clarissa tried to efface herself as well and was annoyed to find the man step in front of her.

"Don't you know it's dangerous to wander about on your own?"

Confident in her anonymity, she raised her brows. "Nothing 'ere I can't 'andle," she told him. "Now, if you'll excuse me, sir—"

"I know who you are," he said, his voice calm, its patrician tones unmistakable.

For the first time, Clarissa felt a qualm pierce her. "What do you mean?"

"You are no serving girl. Why are you playing at this silly—and dangerous—game?"

Of all the arrogant, interfering—Clarissa drew a deep breath. "And who are you, the emperor of—of—Australia?"

He raised a dark brow. "Actually, I don't believe that Australia has an emperor."

"Now you're a geography tutor?" Lord, as if she needed another teacher, Clarissa thought, fuming. Her few moments of escape from the prison of propriety, and this officious stranger had to step in!

In fact, he stepped closer. Before she could stop him, he reached to lift the maid's cap from atop her fair hair.

"Why," he repeated, "are you dressing below your station?"

Arrogant he certainly was, Clarissa told herself, trying to hang on to her anger. But a new and unfamiliar emotion seemed to have replaced it. The stranger was also tall and well built. Standing this close, she could make out the hard muscle that shaped his arms and chest and even his legs, clad in those close-fitting, well-tailored pantaloons. Was she allowed to say *legs*? Or *pantaloons*? Probably not, one corner of her mind thought absently. She could ask Miss P.

But, bloody hell, even without looking at his face, which could grace a statue in the park, the bossy stranger had the most amazing body. It was better than the head groom's at her brother's house, and the groom had arms sturdy with muscle from shoeing horses and rubbing down the carriage team every day.

This stranger . . . She was staring. Clarissa swallowed against the treacherous shiver of feeling that had turned her anger into—something else.

His expression had altered, as well, and she saw something in his dark eyes she couldn't identify.

They were only a few inches apart. The narrow street seemed to have receded, and she could see his chest rising and falling . . . perhaps more rapidly than before. There was a buzzing in her ears.

Clarissa felt dizzy. Did he take a step closer? Was he going to kiss her? One kiss, the groom with the spotty face had said. Clarissa could have evaded the groom's unwelcome advance easily. If this man wanted to kiss her—

But he'd said he knew who she was!

The sudden memory of his words pulled her out of the strange fog that had, for a few moments, befuddled her wits.

If he told her brother— She stepped back.

The stranger drew a deep breath and seemed in control again. The look of restrained arrogance returned—not an improvement—he looked colder now, less appealing.

"I will see you safely home," he told her. "There could be more impudent rascals ready to trouble you."

"You bloody well will not!" Clarissa blurted. Return home under his escort and have the household learn what she had done? She turned and took to her heels, running as fast as she could, and propriety be damned.

Thankfully, he didn't try to stop her. Unhindered, she made it to the back courtyard of her brother's house, slipped through the gate and was soon inside the house. She pulled off the apron—the cap was gone, she would have to get Ruby another one—and Clarissa hurried up to her own room.

The maid was there, and she sighed in relief when Clarissa came into the room.

"Oh, miss, I was that worried. What was you about? If your brother had come asking for you—"

Clarissa saw that the servant's expression was genuinely distressed, and she felt a stab of guilt.

"Just a little joke," Clarissa said. "Forget it, please. I won't ask you to do it again, I promise."

But after Ruby was reassured and the maid left to fetch hot water before Clarissa changed for their trip out, Clarissa went to the window and peeked out, hoping for one more look at the mysterious man who had cut short her masquerade.

The street was empty, of course.

Would he tell her brother what she had done? Matthew would be hurt and angry. Perhaps the stranger had been bluffing. Did he really know who she was? How could he?

She would probably never seen him again, Clarissa told herself.

And if that was in some ways a pity, well, never mind . . .

When Gemma came to fetch her, Clarissa was changed and ready. The two of them took the carriage to the handsome square where Gemma's brother and sister-in-law resided. When they were shown into the house and up to the drawing room, Gemma drew a deep breath as the footman announced their names.

Psyche, Lady Gabriel Sinclair, stood up at once and came forward. "Gemma, how lovely to see you. And how nice to see you again, Clarissa."

Clarissa curtsied and tried not to blush. Lady Gabriel's tone was warm and her smile welcoming. But nonetheless, Clarissa found her a somewhat intimidating figure, so elegant in her blue silk gown. Her fair hair was swept into a simple twist, and her face could have graced a fairy tale. Clarissa had never seen anyone so beautiful.

Lady Gabriel introduced Clarissa to the other ladies in the room. True to Gemma's promise, it was only a small group. Even so, Clarissa had to fight to maintain her smile and to murmur greetings, hoping that her voice did not quaver.

Only after she was safely seated in a brocade upholstered chair and handed a cup of hot tea could she collect her wits and try to remember who was who. She brought the cup to her lips, sipped the hot brew cautiously, and glanced around the circle.

"Have you had any news on the quest for your father?" Lady Sealey glanced at Gemma, who hesitated as she accepted a cup of tea.

This was an enormous secret, Clarissa knew. Psyche's husband, Lord Gabriel, and his sister Lady Gemma, nominally children of a marquess, did not really deserve their titles but could not repudiate them publically without disgracing their dead mother. So they must trust Lady Sealey very much if this lady knew of the siblings' search for the man who had truly been their sire.

Gemma shook her head. "Gabriel is following up every scrap of information he can find," she told the older lady. "But the trail has been cold for years, and I fear that whoever our real parent may be, he may have died, too."

Lady Sealey made a soothing reply. While Gemma chatted, Clarissa could try to sort out the strangers. The exquisitely gowned older woman with the handsome silver hair and straight bearing was a countess, Clarissa recalled. The lady's faded blue eyes were wise and warm, but her bearing had the unconscious authority of one who is accustomed to deference, and Clarissa thought that she would shiver to cross her. But the countess chatted easily with Lady Gabriel and Gemma and the others and often made them laugh with her pointed remarks.

The next woman was younger, her figure more rounded, and she had ash-brown hair and merry brown eyes. Another friend of Lady Gabriel's, though at the moment, Clarissa could not remember her name. She had a vivacious manner and laughed often.

Last, sitting closest to Clarissa was Lady Gabriel's sister. This girl was even younger than Clarissa and obviously still in the school room. She had another odd name—Circe, that was it. Clarissa remembered Gemma mentioning earlier that Psyche and Circe's father had been fond of classical tales. Circe was not as picturebook pretty as her sister, though her heart-shaped face had a certain charm. She had straight brown hair pulled back from her face and vivid green eyes, which made Clarissa think of a cat. Just now, she turned her penetrating gaze upon Clarissa, and Clarissa jumped.

"I hope you are feeling at home in your brother's new house?" Circe asked. "I know you have been away from your family for some time."

Goodness, she did get to the heart of the matter! Clarissa nodded, then said, her tone cautious, "My brother and sister-in-law have been very generous. I'm very lucky that Matthew found me."

"But it must take some effort to readjust to your own class," Circe said calmly. "Psyche has told me of your ordeals when you were forced to work as a servant. You have all my sympathy. By the way, if you hold that teacup any tighter, it may shatter."

Clarissa hastily lowered the china cup to its saucer and drew a deep breath. "Thank you," she murmured. "Yes, it is still difficult for me. I feel so unprepared and—and awkward when I try to go into Society."

Circe's expression was sympathetic. "I can understand that. Your posture is very stiff; I can see that you are ill at ease."

Clarissa blinked in surprise, and the younger girl added, "I didn't mean to offend you. I'm an artist, and I always notice the way a person holds herself. But not everyone would remark upon it, so do not worry."

"I hope they don't!" Clarissa said. What an odd girl Circe

was, but Clarissa found that she liked her. "I don't suppose you are making your debut anytime soon?"

"Oh, no." Her tone firm, Circe shook her head. "I'm not yet old enough to come out, and, anyhow, I have no interest in Society. I wish to travel to the Continent to study under more accomplished teachers than I have located at home. England has many skilled artists, of course, but not everyone will tutor a mere female."

A pity Circe would not be present at the parties that Clarissa would be forced to attend. But she could not imagine anyone calling Circe "mere." Clarissa smiled. "I wish I were an artist, too, and had such a good excuse."

They both giggled, and Clarissa felt almost at ease for the first time since she had entered the elegantly appointed drawing room. So when she was addressed by the older woman, she could turn and face the speaker with only a trace of trepidation.

"I understand you will attend Lady Halston's ball," Lady Sealey said.

Clarissa glanced to Gemma for confirmation. "Yes, I believe she has sent Gemma and my brother a card for the ball."

"And the lady included Clarissa in her invitation," Gemma added. "Though how she knew that Matthew had a sister of an age to come out, I don't know."

"Interesting," the countess said, accepting another small cake from the silver tray the footman bent to offer. "But there are too many Society ladies with little to do but gossip, so every tidbit will make the rounds. Lady Halston is a notable hostess, perhaps she wishes to be the first to showcase such a lovely new addition to the Ton."

Clarissa felt her cheeks turning hot. "You're too kind," she murmured, although the idea that the Ton might be curious about her made her stomach tighten once again. "I hope they will not be disappointed."

"Of course not," Gemma said.

Lady Sealey looked thoughtful. "Lady Halston is a cousin of the earl of Whitby, you know. And although he is a difficult guest to snare, he will very likely show up at her ball—family obligation, and all that."

Psyche and Gemma exchanged knowing glances, but the name meant nothing to Clarissa. "Is he, um, important?"

Although Clarissa had not meant the question as a witticism, Lady Sealey laughed. "Lord Whitby would think so, though he would never admit it. He disdains the social rounds, an attitude that, of course, makes him infinitely desirable to all of the Ton, and his opinion is much sought after by males and females alike."

Clarissa considered this paragon with feelings of dismay. "I shall do my best to escape his notice, then!"

"Any matron would be delighted to have him accept an invitation. Not only is he a social arbiter of the first rank, he is unmarried, and so a prime target for matchmaking mamas," the brunette with the merry brown eyes put in. "I would not run too quickly away from him, Clarissa!"

Everyone else chuckled, but Clarissa frowned. "I have no wish to entice such a hard-to-please gentleman—I mean—lord. And why on earth he should notice me—well, I can't imagine it would happen." Not unless she really muffed her first appearance in Society, Clarissa thought, her heart sinking even further. It must have reached her toes by now.

"But you must not be rude to him," Gemma pointed out, her tone worried. "I mean, he is influential, that part is true."

"Of course not, I will endeavor to say and do all that is proper," Clarissa agreed, muttering beneath her breath, "just as long as he doesn't ask me to dance!"

Gemma hesitated, then pretended not to hear the end of her remark. On the other side of the group, Lady Sealey spoke. She seemed to sense Clarissa's genuine anxiety. "He's not a vicious sort, just a bit, shall we say, detached. I remember him from before the war, a sweet lad, if always a bit aloof in manner. But however much the battles may have marked him, I do not believe he has a cruel heart."

"I agree with your witty—if practical—advice, Sally," Psyche added. "But, truly, Clarissa has no need to rush into a husband hunt." The glance she threw Clarissa was soothing, or meant to be, Clarissa knew.

She took another sip of her cooling tea, this time remembering not to clench the teacup so tightly. Beside her, Circe said nothing, but her smile was friendly. Of course, Psyche's sister had no need to enter the social fray, not yet, so she had every reason to feel at ease.

Clarissa wished she could be that young again, regain the years she had lost when she had been orphaned and alone and thrust into a milieu she was never meant to enter. She had missed years of preparation for just this moment, when all of her class would look her over, inspect her like a horse at Tatler's auctions and pronounce her worthy—or not!

No one here meant her any harm, she knew that, but still, Clarissa felt ill at ease and so very, very unprepared. If she could not even drink tea properly, how would she ever negotiate the complicated seas of a ballroom? She would be as adrift as one of her brother's ships after suffering a damaged rudder, she thought, remembering a story from his days afloat. The guests at Lady Halston's ball, or at any event she attended, would be expecting a gracious and graceful young lady, well drilled in the skills of etiquette and deportment.

A *lady,* it always came back to that. And now Clarissa had two weeks to overcome the bad habits induced by years of living among the servant classes, almost forgetting who she was and where she belonged. Oh, bloody hell.

Clarissa sat quietly during the carriage ride home. Gemma leaned across and pressed her hand. "Did you enjoy the tea, my dear?"

Clarissa tried to smile and avoid an outright lie, while still sparing Gemma's feelings. "Lady Gabriel is very gracious, and they all seem to be very nice ladies."

Perhaps her tone sounded forlorn, or Gemma simply knew her too well. "It will be all right, Clarissa, honestly."

Clarissa wished she could be so sure!

⁓

The next two weeks seemed to go by as quickly—no, much more quickly—than one of Monsieur Meidenne's interminable dance lessons. She had to admit that the man held his temper admirably. No matter how many times she stepped on his foot, her handsome tutor only sighed and suggested that she move with "z'ee other foot, mademoiselle."

Nonetheless, after a week of this torture, Gemma drew her aside one day and presented Clarissa with a neatly bound little book, small enough to fit into a lady's pocket.

"It's lovely," Clarissa said dutifully, looking at the smooth leather cover.

"It's a book of dance patterns, Clarissa," Gemma explained. "I found it at the bookseller's shop. You can slip it into your pocket and take it with you to a ball or party, and consult it quietly between dances, just to make you feel more secure."

"Oh, what a wonderful idea!" Clarissa said, understanding flowing through her. This was similar to the book of dance forms that Monsieur Meidenne always carried with him, only much smaller. She flipped through the pages and felt a renewed surge of hope. Perhaps she would, indeed, be able to survive the upcoming ball. "Thank you, Gemma!"

She gave her sister-in-law an impulsive hug.

Gemma smiled. "I know you're uneasy, and I do understand. But you will do splendidly, and besides, you know that we will love you no matter what transpires."

Pressing the small book to her chest as if it were a talisman, Clarissa nodded. Unhappily, most of the people at the ball would not be related to her, and, she suspected, would not be so tolerant of potential mistakes.

But somehow, having the book safely tucked away inside her skirt seemed to allow the next dance lessons to go a little more smoothly, as if having the instruction book in her pocket also gave her more confidence. Emboldened, Clarissa threw herself into a frenzy of study, reading her etiquette books, enduring daily dance lessons, practicing polite conversation with Miss Pomshack, being fitted for new dresses, and all too soon, the day of the ball was upon them.

That morning, Clarissa woke early with her heart pounding. Had she had another nightmare? It was a moment before she could sort through the confused images that seemed to slip away as quickly as errant butterflies fluttering over a garden wall. The last impression was one of her treading the floor of a ballroom. She had been minding her steps with frantic concentration until she'd looked down and realized with a jolt of panic that she was wearing only her petticoat. Her alarmed consternation had startled her into wakefulness.

That was silly—she would never go out undressed, she tried to tell herself as she rubbed drowsy eyes. At least it had not been the usual and more horrific nightmare. . . . But then the real reason for her anxiety dawned. Oh, hell, it was tonight! The ball was upon them, and Clarissa had no more time to prepare.

Sitting up, she bit back the spate of unladylike words that still, in times of turmoil, rose unbidden to her lips. A glance at the sunlight slanting past the drawn curtains made it clear that the morning was advanced. Gemma must have ordered Ruby to allow Clarissa to sleep as long as she liked. But now that she knew that this was the fateful day, further slumber was impossible. Clarissa reached for the bellpull, then climbed out of bed to tug on her robe and step into her slippers. When Ruby appearing, bringing a cup of tea and an ewer of warm water, the maid beamed.

"Your ball gown is 'ere, miss, and it's ever so lovely. You're going to look a treat tonight."

"Thank you, Ruby," Clarissa said, trying not to shiver. She would be brave, she had to be. Surely, she could muddle through one party, for Matthew and Gemma's sake if not her own. Reaching to touch the cover of the small book of dance forms where it lay on her bedside table, she drew a deep breath. She could do this. She took a sip of her tea, and it was no surprise that it tasted more bitter than usual.

Because she was in no hurry for the evening, the day flew

by. Morning brought one last dance lesson where she seemed to move every way but the right way.

The third time she trod on his foot, even the long-suffering Monsieur Meidenne looked annoyed, and Clarissa herself was close to tears.

At last Gemma called the lesson to an early close. "I believe that will be all today, monsieur."

He tried, not quite successfully, to hide his relief. "*Merci,* my dear Lady Gemma. I wish mademoiselle all the *bon chance* for tonight. I'm sure she will do, eh, *tres bien.*"

Clarissa bade the man a polite good-bye, then when he was safely out of the room and the door had closed behind him, she put her hands to her face. "Oh, Gemma, I've forgotten all I ever learned! Whatever shall I do? I can't go to the ball. Please let me stay home—you can say that I'm ill!"

Gemma smiled at her. "No, indeed, my dear. You have learned a great deal, and it will all come back to you. Just now, you are only having a fit of nerves, quite natural."

"But I will be just as anxious tonight—more so," Clarissa argued.

"I'm told that actors consider a bad dress rehearsal as a good omen for opening night," Gemma assured her. "You get all the mistakes over with before you go on stage, if you see what I mean."

Clarissa did see, she just didn't believe it!

But Gemma called for tea, and Clarissa bit back the rest of her protests. When the tea tray arrived, they sat down around the small table.

"My father the vicar would advise a little calm and solemn reflection," Miss Pomshack suggested as she reached for another scone, "to compose your mind."

After lunch, Gemma urged her to lie down, but rest was impossible. Clarissa read a little of her newest novel and too soon it seemed, it was time to dress for dinner.

The ball gown was lovely. Simply cut of palest jonquil silk, it flattered her pale skin and seemed to elicit the green and gold glints in her hazel eyes. Her golden hair with its faint sheen of red had been well brushed and coiled atop her head, with an occasional curl slipping out along side her face to soften the effect. She wore her new pearl ear drops and a small topaz cross on a gold chain, both gifts from her brother.

Staring into the looking glass, the nervous tremors in her stomach eased just a little. She *looked* like a lady, Clarissa thought. When she came down to the dining room, her brother and sister-in-law were loud in their praise.

"Oh, Clarissa, you look quite beautiful," Gemma declared, herself the picture of elegance in a deep blue gown.

Matthew said nothing for a moment, but the pride and love in his gray eyes spoke more than words. He came forward and took her hand, pressing it and then leaning to kiss her cheek. "You are a picture of loveliness," he told her softly. "And you remind me so much of our mother—she would be so proud, as am I."

Their mother, whom they had lost too soon, when Clarissa had been only a child. Blinking back tears, she managed to smile up at him.

"Quite correct," Miss Pomshack added, more prosaically. "The dress is elegant and becoming, but not too elaborate for a new entrant into Society. Lady Gemma's taste is always very nice."

Society—the word made some of Clarissa's pleasure fade. If she could only dine quietly here at home with her family, she would be content. It was the thought of the strangers who were waiting to stare at her, watch her, that made her mouth seem dry and her stomach full of knots. And the dancing, oh, help—

She pushed her fears aside and tried to eat a little, and to her relief Matthew turned the conversation away from the ball. He told them about his lunch with an old acquaintance, a fellow mariner and ship's captain.

"Since the war has ended, he's gone back into trade," her brother said, taking a bite of his beef. Chewing, he continued after a moment. "This trip he's sailing to the Orient, off to Singapore and Shanghai, lucky devil!"

His gray eyes seemed to look past them, beyond the table with its spotless linen and well-filled silver and china dishes to a vista of endless seas and choppy waves. Clarissa watched him and forgot to think about her own woes. Did her brother regret giving up his ship to stay on land with his family?

"A long trip and dangerous," Gemma suggested.

"Yes," her husband agreed. "But with summer coming, the weather should be constant enough, once they're around the Cape, and James is a good sailor." His gaze still distant, he lowered his knife and fork for a moment, as if remembering. "The taste of salt spray on one's lips, the slap of waves against the sides of a stout ship, the flapping of sails in the wind, now these are the things that make a sailor happy."

Glancing up, he caught Clarissa's eye, and a look of something close to guilt replaced his brief abstraction. Clarissa felt even more to blame. Did her brother miss his former profession? As captain, he could have taken a wife to sea with him, but to drag his sister along—no, Matthew had sworn to provide a safe home for Clarissa and not to leave her again. She was the reason he was stuck here, when his heart still longed for adventures afloat, commanding a tall ship.

"I have bought some shares in his voyage," Matthew added, his tone more businesslike. He motioned to the footman for another serving of the spiced beef. "It's not without risk, but as I said, James is as good a captain as any, and if all goes well, the profit from this trip should be a tidy one."

Talk around the table turned to the teas grown in the Far East, then to the silks from China, the muslins from India, and the wondrous spices from the Spice Islands that would also make up the return cargo. As the others chatted, Clarissa looked down at her plate and resolved that she would put aside her fears. Her brother had done all this for her sake; she must not let him down.

When dinner ended, Matthew called for the carriage. Clarissa went into the hallway to don her gloves and a light wrap, and tried to hide the quivers of anxiety continued to crawl up and down her spine.

Miss Pomshack bade them all a cheery good-bye and waved her handkerchief when the carriage pulled away. Clarissa sat beside her sister-in-law, with her brother across from them, and the ride to their destination seemed, despite the usual London traffic, too brief. When they arrived, they found a mass of vehicles already crowding the street, but eventually they came close enough for the coachman to pull up their team and the groom to put down the steps.

When Matthew helped them down, Clarissa looked up at the imposing house before them. Her stomach knotted, and she had to swallow hard. Lady Halston lived in style. The residence was twice the size of Matthew and Gemma's home, and the footman at the door wore elaborate livery in a deep plum color, his powdered wig sitting precisely on his rather round head, and his expression was more forbidding than that of any nobleman Clarissa had yet glimpsed.

Aware of Gemma's encouraging smile and Matthew's slight pressing of her hand before he released it, Clarissa put up her chin and managed to climb the steps with a more or less steady gait. Inside, the house was full of the smells of fine perfumes and the smoky aura of many candles, as well as the stench of the new-fashioned gas lights. Lady Halston must be wealthy, indeed.

The staircase was crowded with stylish ladies and gentlemen, all heading up to the rooms where the ball was taking place. Clarissa followed Gemma and Matthew up the wide steps, and if her pulse beat fast, she hoped that the matrons who glanced at her with keen eyes, or the gentlemen who gave her veiled but obviously appraising leers, could not tell it.

When they made it to the front of the line, they paused at the entrance to the large room and waited to be announced.

"Lady Gemma Fallon, Captain Matthew Fallon, and Miss Fallon," the footman intoned.

Lord and Lady Halston waited just inside the room to welcome their guests.

"I'm so glad you were able to come, Lady Gemma," Lady Halston declared. "I have been so wishing to know you better." The stout matron's small bright eyes considered Gemma for only a moment, then her gaze darted toward the other members of their party. "Ah, this must be your husband and his sister?"

"Yes," Gemma agreed. Muttering a polite greeting, Matthew bowed. Clarissa tried her best to perform a graceful curtsy, but she felt as awkward as an arthritic goose. Knowing that her cheeks had flushed, she prayed once again that she could just get through this evening without disgracing the people who loved her.

For herself, she had no higher ambition. A glance at the crowded room with its mass of ladies in bright-colored gowns and more sober-hued gentlemen, all equally well-clad and all seeming at ease, and the sound of the clatter of voices and the faint backdrop of music, made her nerves jangle with fear.

She found her hostess still stared at her. "I am delighted to make your acquaintance, Miss Fallon."

"Thank you for the kind invitation," Clarissa answered, hearing the quiver in her own voice.

Then, aware that Gemma and Matthew had moved on, she forced her limbs to move and hurried to catch up with them. As she moved away from Lady Halston, who had turned to the next arrival, Clarissa drew a deep breath. One hurdle down.

Matthew accepted a glass of champagne from a footman passing with a tray full of glasses. He offered it to his wife, and then, after a slight hesitation, passed another glass to Clarissa before taking one for himself.

"Just a few sips, my dear," Gemma murmured in a low tone. "A little wine can help to settle your nerves, but too much could be disastrous."

Clarissa nodded and tasted the sparkling wine. The bubbles were new to her, but the taste was pleasant.

Beyond the crowd, the musicians were striking up a new tune. One couple moved aside, and Clarissa could glimpse the dance floor where a new set was forming.

"Would you grant me the pleasure of your first dance, my dear?" Matthew asked, offering his arm to his sister.

Clarissa felt a shiver of panic run through her. "Oh, not yet," she pleaded. "You must dance first with Gemma, surely?"

Matthew smiled. "Very well, but the next one is ours."

At least she always did better with Matthew's quiet guidance, Clarissa told herself as she watched her brother and his wife go to join the dance form. And if—she took another sip of champagne, and then, her mouth suddenly very dry, drank the rest of the wine in one gulp—she could just slip back against the wall and study her book of dance steps, surely she could survive this. She made her way through the crowd and, glancing about to make sure that no one was staring, pulled the small book from the pocket that Gemma's dressmaker had had orders to put into Clarissa's new ball gown.

Clarissa set her champagne flute down on a nearby table and flipped through the pages of her form book, trying to force her mind to recall the most-used steps. Of course, she did not know which tune the musicians would play next, but—

"Miss Fallon?" someone said.

The voice was mellow and deep and decidedly masculine—and somehow familiar. Caught with her practice book out and feeling as awkward as the most callow of schoolroom misses, Clarissa froze, the incriminating volume still clutched in her hand. She looked up.

Oh, bloody hell. It was the autocratic stranger from the alley! Would he give away her secret, her brief and undignified masquerade? Trying to read his expression, Clarissa stared at him. She could throw herself on his mercy, but the firmness of his jaw and lips did not bode well for that plan. His deep brown eyes held a sparkle of intelligence and perhaps humor, if he would let down his guard, but she had the feeling such moments were rare. Clad in a black evening coat, impeccable white linen, and smooth tan-colored pantaloons, he was just as appealing as he had been in day clothes, but this time, if he made her heart beat faster, she thought it was mostly from fear. Mostly.

While she tried to think what to say, he continued, "Would you do me the honor of a dance? My cousin would be pleased to perform the—ah—proper introductions."

Was he laughing at her? She took back what she'd thought about his sense of humor! It was bloody wicked, it was.

And she still clutched the book. "You're most—most kind, b—but I was waiting for my brother—" Stuttering, Clarissa tried to shove the small volume back into her pocket before he noted it.

"I am Whitby—"

"Oh, dear!" a woman nearby exclaimed, dabbing at a drop of wine on her skirt.

The man turned his head for a moment, and Clarissa saw a scar on the left side of his face. But she noted it absently because she felt jolted with horror. *The earl of Whitby,* Lady Halston's cousin? This was the high and mighty social arbiter whom the ladies had discussed at Lady Gabriel's tea—and the same man who had seen her in the alley pretending to be a housemaid? Oh, bloody hell. Oh, help. She felt numb all over.

She dropped the book. It fell to the polished wood floor with a bang that seemed, to Clarissa's ears, to echo through the whole chamber.

He turned back to her and his expression looked stiff. As any gentleman would, he bent to retrieve the book. No, no—he must not see that she had been studying the forms—Clarissa lunged to reach it first, and somehow managed to trip over her own feet.

She hit the floor with a much louder thud than the book had produced. As ill fortune would have it, the melody dipped at the same moment to a trill of soft notes which did little to mask the unexpected sound.

All around her, faces turned. A laugh rang out, then another, and then came an artificial and awkward silence. And into it, Clarissa spoke clearly.

"Oh, bloody hell."

Four

*T*he *unseemly words seemed to echo across the room.*
Dominic winced. Could the girl neither mind her tongue
nor keep her feet? Whether her birth was respectable or not,
this obvious lack of grace, coupled with the brawl he had
witnessed on St. James Street and the escapade in the alley,
did not bode well for his good intentions. How could he help
her if she did not help herself?

And if it was his scar that had made her so nervous— He
knew his marred face was an unsightly prospect, but he had
never knocked a lady off her feet before! She had made a
spectacle of them both. He drew a deep breath and tried to
control his annoyance as he bent to offer her assistance.

"Miss Fallon?"

She ignored his hand, staring at the polished floor as if she
could not believe her current position. Well, neither could he.

He cleared his throat. "Miss Fallon, are you hurt?"

More people had turned to look, and now even those in
the midst of the dance seemed to notice. Dominic saw a

well-made man with fair hair and a sun-bronzed complexion break away from the pattern of dancers moving smoothly across the floor. Pausing only to wait for his lady to come to his side, he came quickly forward.

"Clarissa, what happened? Are you injured?" When she did not respond at once, the man—it must be her brother, Captain Fallon—turned his suspicious gaze toward Dominic. As if this were his fault!

"I believe she lost her footing," Dominic explained, knowing that his tone sounded stiff.

"Can you rise, my dear?" the lady asked. She bent down and helped the girl at last to her feet.

Her face flushed, Miss Fallon nodded. She still did not speak, although she clutched the small volume in her hand. He wondered absently what she was doing with a book at a dance. Had the girl no concept of what was expected?

Had she had the breath knocked out of her, or was she simply so mortified that she had no words? He found either explanation plausible, though hardly an excuse.

"I will leave you to the fond support of your family, Miss Fallon," he told her. "I hope we can have the pleasure of a dance later in the evening."

Her cheeks still aflame, she nodded. Was she mute? Or had no one ever taught her that she must forge ahead through any mishap? Much of the crowd around them still watched and listened; they would take their cue from her. She should have made light of her fall—as ignominious as it undoubtably was—or at least pretend to swoon. A lady could always get away with a swoon. But he could hardly tell her that now.

Trying to maintain his own savoir faire, Dominic bowed to them all, then watched as the females hurried away toward an anteroom that would give them refuge from the stares of the partygoers. Miss Fallon's brother followed.

Dominic motioned to a footman, who brought him a glass of wine. Taking a sip, he schooled his expression to one of well-bred indifference.

Someone came up; it was young Galston, and the cub was chuckling. Devil take the man!

"I think you have your work cut out for you," the younger man suggested. "Not very light on her feet, is she? The fallen Miss Fallon, in fact."

Standing nearby, a stout man in a green coat chuckled.

"Not so loud," Dominic snapped. "Do you wish to make my task totally impossible? If so, you are hardly acting in a sporting manner."

"Sorry," Galston said, though he sipped his wine and looked totally unrepentant. "A few careless words, amazing the damage they can do."

Dominic frowned.

"I will have you know I have already had a dance with your cousin, Miss Mawper. I was charm itself. Anyhow, she seems to be quite recovered from my thoughtless remark of a few weeks ago."

As he spoke, he glanced to the side. The man in green was speaking to two ladies, and now all three laughed again. The damned jest would go through the whole party in two shakes of a lamb's tail, Dominic thought in dismay. He turned to Galston.

"But I meant what I said. If you deliberately obstruct the Ton's acceptance of the lady in question, there will be more at stake than a silly wager, Galston. I will most surely hold you accountable."

Galston sobered, and his tone sounded uneasy. "I say, old man, when you look like that, I expect you to pull out your cavalry saber. Take a powder, do. Honestly, my lips are sealed."

It was probably already too late, Dominic thought, as Galston murmured a farewell and slipped away to disappear into the crowd. Of course, the girl was likely a lost cause, anyhow. Why had he ever pledged himself to try to make a difference? He knew the answer, but it did little to dissipate his annoyance. Ah well, she was nowhere in sight. Perhaps there was another lady here whose life he could blight. Dominic turned back to survey the partygoers.

He chatted politely with two young women until presently, the hostess herself appeared at his side. He turned to her, letting his mask slip for a moment, but it only earned him another rebuke.

"Why are you wearing such a frown, Whitby? This is a party; you should be merry, Cousin. You will frighten away half my guests!"

Irritated at such nonsense, he glared at her, then forced his expression into a stiff smile. "Is that better? Or perhaps I should simply take myself away so I do not wreak further havoc upon your merry gathering."

"Sarcasm does not become you, Cousin," she told him, her tone reproving. "If you leave early, that will imply that my ball was too boring for words."

"Nonsense. Anyhow, I always leave early," he retorted.

"Which is another reason you must not do so tonight," she shot back. "And what did you do to that poor girl to make her topple to the floor? They are calling her the 'fallen Miss Fallon,' you know, a dreadful jest, if sadly apt. She is going to have a hard time of it."

He almost groaned, but bit back the too-revealing reaction.

"I invited her only because of your request. Why do you have an interest in her? Which she doesn't seem to return, if you alarm her so much that she falls at your feet—and I do not mean in the usual sense." Lady Halston's eyes gleamed with curiosity. Fanning herself, she swept her crimson fan in an arc and awaited his answer.

He could not, of course, tell her about the bet with Galston. For two gentlemen to wager on a lady was a scandalous action—not that it hadn't happened before. But he wasn't about to admit such an ungentlemanly deed.

"I, um, wished to know her better, that is all," he said. "A moment of curiosity that I am now regretting, if you insist on knowing the whole of it."

"Then I have wasted an invitation," she answered calmly. The fan flashed again, and his cousin watched him over the top of it. "You do not have a *tendre* for her? She is not your type at all."

"Of course not. And do I have a type?" he countered. "I didn't realize I was so easily predicted."

"You prefer sophisticated, elegant, often older women who return your casual flirtations without undue emotional involvement and do not expect any lasting commitment, which you have avoided like the plague. Avoided so thoroughly, in fact, that if you do not take care, you will find yourself going unmarried to your grave and your title passing to that idiot nephew of yours," she predicted. "I saw your sister last week, and she told me that her pride and joy had fallen off his horse into a mud puddle in the middle of Hyde Park—"

The fan in her pudgy hand suddenly paused. She stared at him. "Whitby! You are not thinking of setting up your nursery at last?"

"Certainly not," he told her, his tone sharp.

But Lady Halston continued to observe him, and her finely plucked brows puckered. "The family is not particularly distinguished, but they are not beyond the pale, either. Captain Fallon married a marquess's sister, shocking the Ton by reaching so high. You could do worse. On the other hand, you could also do much better," she pointed out. "You, of all people, forgetting your rank?"

"Do not speak of me as if I am a top-lofty moron with no more to consider than a breeder of pugs!"

She stared at him in surprise. "I am very fond of my pugs. But, Whitby! You do have feelings for her."

He looked away. "I have told you, I don't even know her. I simply dislike being lectured to. And I have a perfectly sound understanding of what I owe to my family name."

She appeared unconvinced. Dominic closed his eyes for a moment—why must he have such thick-headed relatives?—and remembered the look of fear on the girl's face, which had first lured him into this mess. And in the alley he had felt a moment of desire that—no, it would be madness. And now all he had accomplished was her further distress. His wartime missions had been simple by comparison! He sighed, then gave his cousin a slight bow.

"You are not leaving?" she asked in alarm.

"No, indeed. Heeding your instructions, Cousin, I shall smile upon your guests and help establish your ball as a rousing success."

"I should chide you for vanity," she answered, her expression conflicted. "Except the problem is, you indeed have the power to do just that."

"You're welcome," he said dryly and turned away to speak charmingly to as many ladies and gentlemen as he could, to even dance with a few of the ladies, so that when he next solicited the hand of Miss Fallon, he hoped it would not cause further remarks from gossipy old cats. He had to try.

*In an anteroom, Clarissa was trying to heed her sister-*in-law's cheering comments and at the same time not reveal she very much wished she were dead.

"You must not waste time contemplating a very ordinary mishap," Gemma was saying, her tone soothing. "I'm sure very few of the guests remarked upon it."

"Ordinary?" Clarissa muttered. "How many ladies fall over their own feet on any given evening?"

Appearing almost as distressed as Clarissa herself, Gemma hesitated. Clarissa felt a surge of guilt. Her family was trying so hard—she could not be so ungrateful.

His gaze gentle but his lips set into a firm expression, Matthew said, "If a young ensign under my command slipped off the mast, Clarissa, I would have, for his own sake, sent him right back up again."

She knew he was right. She had to face and conquer her fear. And anyhow, now that she had embarrassed herself completely, what else could happen? No, she didn't wish to contemplate the possible answers to that!

She took the wisp of handkerchief that Gemma offered and wiped her wet cheeks, blinking back any more nervous tears. "I'm ready," she said.

Matthew offered her his arm, and his expression of approval was reward enough for the effort it took to fix her face into a semblance of serenity. Perhaps she was still a bit flushed, but she had to pretend she was a young lady prepared to enjoy a ball, no more and no less.

And if she felt much, much less . . . no need to follow that thought. She waited for Matthew to give his other arm to his wife, and they all, very much united in both appearance and spirit, strode back into the ballroom.

She gripped her brother's arm tightly. She loved them so much. Clarissa had been alone for all those years, believing Matthew to have died at sea, sure she had no family left. He had come back into her life, found her in difficult circumstances and with Gemma's help had rescued her, and had given her a loving sister, too. Compared to all that, what was one difficult ball, no matter how clumsy Clarissa might be?

And thinking of all she had to be grateful for, she forgot to be so agitated. She found they had passed by the first clumps of people, and yes, several turned to stare at her. For Matthew's sake, for Gemma's sake, Clarissa lifted her chin and maintained her smile.

Watching a footman circulate, refilling glasses of wine, only reaffirmed her resolve. It was too fancy a party to have maidservants working in the ballroom, but Clarissa was sure that belowstairs in the kitchens and pantries, young women labored, their feet and backs aching from long hours preparing for her ladyship's guests. And Clarissa, with no more to do than dance and chat and partake of the delicacies concocted by an excellent cook, was bemoaning an awkward moment? She had so much to be thankful for.

They found seats and sat and chatted quietly until the musicians paused, and a new set formed.

When Matthew glanced toward the dance floor, Clarissa gulped, but she stood and accepted his escort, with Gemma smiling encouragement. Her pulse racing, Clarissa walked out with him and took her place.

For a moment, she could not think at all, then, as the music began again, and Matthew smiled at her, she drew a deep breath. The tune was familiar, this was a dance she had practiced many times. And her brother was here . . . he would not stand by and permit her to commit any truly awful mistake. . . .

She stepped out only half a beat behind the lady to her side, and Matthew guided her surely and easily through the first turn. Step right, turn left . . . It was coming back, just as Gemma had promised her it would.

Even so, the dance seemed to last a lifetime. Clarissa stepped, she glided, she accepted Matthew's discreet and skillful guidance, and she made only a few missteps, all hastily corrected. And perhaps by the end of the dance, fewer people stared at her.

She hoped that the heat in her cheeks had faded, even though her palms were damp inside her gloves. When they turned to leave the dance floor, she uttered a silent but heartfelt prayer of thanksgiving.

Matthew guided her back to a chair, where Gemma now chatted with a matron Clarissa did not know. She sat, and her brother bent over her. "Shall I get you a glass of wine, or perhaps lemonade?"

She reflected. Perhaps gulping down the champagne so quickly might have contributed to her awkwardness. At any rate, better to not risk it. "Lemonade, please," she told him.

Matthew moved away to find a servant.

Clarissa glanced back at the dancers forming a new set, then quickly away—never had she been so happy to sit quietly and watch. And when an unknown young man came up to her, she felt a quiver of alarm.

"Miss Fallon, if the esteemed Lady Gemma would introduce me, perhaps I might beg the pleasure of a dance?"

The gleam in his eyes was too bright. She suspected curiosity or even a touch of malice. Did he wish to learn more about her, only to make sport of her to his friends? "Thank you, but no, I am a bit warm. I believe I prefer to sit this one out," she told him, her voice firm. Was that response polite or not? At the moment, she couldn't remember what her book of etiquette said, and she didn't much care.

"Ah, perhaps another time, then." He bowed and moved on.

She took a deep breath and listened to Gemma chatting with the other woman.

When a young lady of about her own age, rather tall, with medium brown hair and a nose dotted with freckles, drew near, Clarissa looked up again.

"Is this seat taken? The room is becoming so crowded. . . ."

"By all means," Clarissa agreed, and the young lady seated herself with more alacrity than grace.

"I am Miss Mawper," the other girl said. "You are Miss Fallon, is that not so? I heard you being announced. I hope you are all right?"

Clarissa nodded. There was little point in pretending not to understand. She looked at Miss Mawper, whose pale blue eyes were frank.

"I'm fine, Miss Mawper, only my dignity has suffered," she told her.

"Oh, call me Emmaline, do. Listen, you must not repine. At my first soiree I spilled a glass of wine down the front of my best gown. And I danced, one wit said that night, like an African giraffe who had imbibed too much home brew."

"How unkind!" Clarissa said before she thought. Emmaline Mawper's lanky frame did put one in mind of a tall and untamed animal, but still—

"Oh, I'm as clumsy as a cart horse, Miss Fallon," the other girl said, her tone cheerful. "And I think people have forgotten the comment, though I admit, I have not."

"Please call me Clarissa. I hope the gentleman who was rude—"

"Ah, it's the same one who spoke to you before you

tripped, the high and mighty earl, one reason I thought I would offer you my support," Emmaline told her.

Clarissa knew her eyes had widened. "What arrogance! Does he enjoy making sport of nervous young ladies making their debut?"

"No, no, I did not mean to imply that. He has been most attentive tonight, dancing with me very correctly and saying all the polite things," Emmaline told her. "I did not intend to suggest spitefulness on his part."

"I am not so sure," Clarissa declared, her tone dark. "I mean, why on earth would he ask me to dance, anyhow?" She still wondered whether he would reveal her secret.

"You're awfully pretty," Emmaline pointed out, her tone a bit wistful. "Perhaps he admires you."

"You are too generous, but no." Clarissa argued, though she gave the other girl a quick smile. "I have no fashion, no elan. He must be harder to please than that!" She swallowed hard. The lump in her throat had returned, and she found that her nose threatened to drip, perhaps from her bout of tears. She tugged her handkerchief from the reticule hanging from her wrist and dabbed discreetly. "I sincerely think he is quite horrid—"

Emmaline cleared her throat loudly, and Clarissa paused. A tall form had appeared before them. Oh no, not the arrogant earl again! Why, oh why, was he determined to haunt her?

"I promised you that we would have that dance," Lord Whitby told her. Then, before she could find the words to refuse, he turned to Gemma. "Lady Gemma, may I beg an introduction to your sister-in-law?"

"Of course," Gemma answered, smiling at them both. "Lord Whitby, this is my husband's sister, Miss Fallon. Clarissa, Lord Whitby."

"If you would honor me?" He offered Clarissa his hand.

Clarissa found her hand rising automatically to meet his, but she had forgotten the damp handkerchief in her grip. She dropped it hastily and let it fall to the floor, then found she could not meet his eyes. What other disaster could befall her?

The dance floor lay ahead. No, no, she did not wish to consider the possible answers to her unspoken question.

She took a few steps, then hesitated, and he paused, too, to look down at her.

"I—I really do not wish—if you would excuse me—"

"Miss Fallon," he interrupted. "It is my honor on the line, now. Do you wish me to be castigated as the gentleman who knocks ladies off their feet? It hardly does me credit."

"I'm sure your credit will survive first-rate!" she shot back, blinking as new tears threatened to rise and disgrace her further. "But people are staring at me still. I'd much rather retire to the side—"

"Do you always run away from difficult situations?"

"Do you always insult your partner?" she retorted. But the coolness of his tone, not to mention his words, brought anger to the fore, and she was able to suppress her nervous tears. She had no desire to cry, now; instead, she wanted very much to slap him. "You don't know me at all. How can you speak so?"

"I'm trying to give you good advice," he muttered. "And keep your voice down. If we dance and chat and you look amiable and not like the wildcat you do just now, the gossip will die much more quickly. Do not give the hens more to chatter about."

She had more angry words ready to fling at him, but his frankness made her pause. He led her forward again. Unless she planted her feet and made a further spectacle of herself, she was forced to follow.

"But I don't wish to dance," she muttered.

"Why on earth not?"

"I don't—I'm not very practiced at the steps," she almost whispered.

He leaned closer for a moment and spoke into her ear. "Watch the other ladies to see what they do. And when you step out, if you do not remember whether to go left or right, look at me. I will drop my right eyelid if you must lead to the right, or the left for the left."

She stared at him. She had expected more ridicule, not practical assistance. They were in place now, she in the line of ladies, he facing her and side by side with the other men. They were not, thank heavens, the first in line, so she had a moment to observe what the first couple's movements were. And the tune sounded familiar.

Clarissa drew a deep breath and tried to remember all those dance lessons. Surely her brother had not wasted his money, or poor Monsieur Meidenne all his hours leading her through one dance form after another.

She watched the first couple cross and dip and come back to their places, then the second pair step out. When it was her turn, she was ready, and she and Lord Whitby went through their steps without errors. Then Clarissa returned to her place and watched the couple below them take their turn. She found she was breathing hard.

The next pattern was more complicated, but the earl was true to his word. When she hesitated even a moment, he signaled her discreetly, lowering his eyelid, and he was also there to reach for her hand and give her the slightest nudge in the correct direction. And when they held hands and circled, she looked up at his well-made face, with the firm jaw and smooth olive skin and intense dark eyes, and she found that this was not at all like dancing with her brother or even the handsome tutor.

For some reason, her heart was beating very fast, and not with panic this time, but some other just as disturbing but more pleasing emotion. Just now his dark eyes held a light in their center, as if the chandeliers above them glinted a reflection, and when he looked at her, her chest seemed to tighten.

After that, she forgot to worry about the dance patterns and was only aware of his closeness when they held hands and circled, of the dark superfine of his coat and spotless white of his linen and the taut muscle beneath, and how broad were his shoulders and how firm the grip of his hand . . . and she was eager for the moments when the dance brought them back together.

How had she not noticed how sweet was the music or how the candlelight suddenly sparkled? And his firm touch on her hand—he seemed to carry her along on the lilting melody. She forgot to think only of her feet and enjoyed watching the smooth planes of his face instead.

This dance flowed by much more quickly. Suddenly the music was fading, her partner was bowing. She quickly dipped a curtsy in return and swallowed her regret that the dance had ended.

"Now, you thank me sweetly, and I will tell you how light on your feet you are," he told her, his tone low. She was pulled abruptly from her brief reverie.

"Oh, what a cawker!" she exclaimed, forgetting that the slang was not proper speech for a young lady. "When you had to practically drag me through the dance."

"Not at all," he answered. "When you stop fretting about your steps, you are indeed as graceful as any young lady on the floor. But a polite thank-you is always in order."

"I would rather know why you are paying any attention to me at all?" she demanded, looking up at him and determined not to succumb again to that strange and unsettling emotion that had come over her on the dance floor.

"I am trying to guide you," he told her, offering his arm and leading her off the floor. "Help establish you in the Ton."

"Why?" she asked again. "Are you a friend of my brother's? Did he ask you—"

"I regret I am but a slight acquaintance of Captain Fallon's," he told her. "Though I'm sure your brother is a most admirable man."

"He is. But if not—"

"If you are determined to know, I will tell you tomorrow," the earl told her, his expression impossible to read.

"Tomorrow? But I shall not see you tomorrow," she pointed out.

"When I come to call and take you for a drive in the park."

Speechless, Clarissa could only stare at him. But they continued to walk, and fortunately, he kept a firm grip on her arm and this time she did not fall over her feet. When they had safely reached the edge of the room and her sister-in-law, with Matthew now back at her side, the earl bowed and took his leave.

"Well done, Clarissa," Gemma said, keeping her tone low.

Matthew grinned at her and offered a glass of lemonade. "Indeed, you did splendidly."

Clarissa took it and sipped—her mouth felt dry. At least she had made her family happy. And as for herself— She looked around, but found Emmaline Mawper had been taken away to dance by a tall skinny young man with a formidable high collar to his shirt. So when Gemma turned back to speak to her husband, Clarissa had a moment to think.

Why was the earl so determined to be helpful? Tomorrow, he had promised, she would find out. . . .

As the night went on, two more young men requested the honor of Clarissa's partnership, but she made her excuses.

"I'm sorry; I'm afraid I, uh, twisted my ankle in the last dance. I must sit out the rest of the evening. But"—to her annoyance she found herself remembering the earl's advice—"but thank you, anyhow."

The young man made a polite comment, bowed, and withdrew. Clarissa tried not to feel guilty; she could not imagine that he was truly cast down at her refusal. Her ankle felt fine. The truth was, she had survived the almighty earl's escort, and she had no desire to tempt Fate any further on the dance floor—at least, not tonight.

She urged Gemma and Matthew to dance and watched them on the floor, so easy and confident in each other's arms that she felt a tug of wistfulness. But she kept her seat.

Clarissa chatted further with Emmaline Mawper—she found that she enjoyed the young woman's honesty and easy kindness—and also with Gemma and her brother. After a light supper was served to the guests, Gemma and Matthew agreed to her plea for an early withdrawal. It did not seem early to Clarissa, who had been wishing to retreat from the moment she had entered this imposing mansion. It had been one of the most trying nights of her life. Although, perhaps she had enjoyed her dance with Lord Whitby. But her nerves jumped at the thought of doing it again.

On the way home, Gemma said, "You did very well, Clarissa."

"Aside from the small matter of sprawling on the floor in front of the whole party?" Clarissa could not keep from reminding them.

Gemma frowned. "Now, you must put that behind you. You did splendidly after that, and it does no good to repine upon a simple mistake."

Matthew nodded his agreement as Clarissa sighed. But she drew a deep breath when her sister-in-law continued.

"You have no reason to be anxious about enjoying your next dance."

The next? Oh, horrors. Clarissa had given little thought to the future—it had been hard enough to last through the evening. But perhaps in the back of her mind she'd hoped to spend the rest of her life sitting at the side of the hearth like the girl in the fairy story. Clarissa thought of telling Gemma that balls and good-looking men were overrated. She opened her mouth to protest, then recalled how she had felt when she had danced with the earl. Perhaps . . . Then she remembered the earl's promise.

"Gemma," she began.

But when both of them looked at her, Clarissa lost her nerve. She would tell her sister-in-law later about the earl's rash promise. Perhaps he had not meant it. Perhaps it was one of those polite things that gentlemen said to ladies at parties and which did not signify any real intent. She bloody well hoped that might be true!

"Nothing," she murmured. "Except, thank you both for all you've done."

Gemma smiled at her, and Matthew reached across to press her hand. "I promised myself that you would have your life back, Clarissa," he said. "And I mean to see that your hardships are all behind you, and you have the chance to be happy again."

Clarissa smiled at him in return. When he released her hand, she smoothed the silky skirt of her dress. Indeed, Matthew had done so much to alter her life, although the most important change was not the nice dresses or comfortable house, or even no longer having to scrub floors or carry chamber pots. The most important gift had been having her family restored to her.

As for hardships . . . he had no idea how much courage this night had cost her, or how her stomach clenched whenever she had to face her—supposed—peers. It was easy enough to remedy the outer dressings of her life, to thrust her back into her proper social milieu, but as for making her believe it, inside . . .

She would not trouble Matthew by trying to explain her muddled feelings. Clarissa leaned back against the velvet squabs and shut her eyes. When they reached their own home, she was happy to climb down and enter, and after bidding her brother and his wife good night, go straight up to bed.

She did not even wish for any time alone with Gemma, as dearly as she loved her new sister. Tonight, she had no wish to share confidences. All she wanted was to shed her clothes, with the help of the maid, pull on a nightgown, and crawl beneath the bed covers. Yet when she shut her eyes and drifted into an uneasy sleep, the echo of ballroom tunes haunted her dreams, as well as a pair of dark eyes that seemed to conceal secrets in their depths. . . .

It was a Cornish fishing village, like too many he had visited in the last few weeks. The stench of dead fish hung over the place, imprinted its odor into the row of small stone houses and the shingled beach and one small boat tied up to the wooden pier. The breeze was fresh, sticky against his face, and it carried the smell of fish, too, and a cleansing hint of brine.

Lord Gabriel Sinclair slowed his horse to a walk and surveyed the village. There had to be a pub here somewhere, a church and a pub, and sooner or later, everyone passed through one or both. When he saw the inn's sign, cracked and faded from the weather's harsh scrubbing, he dismounted, tied up his horse, and went inside.

He smelled the vinegary scent of ale and the miasma of hardworking men who seldom washed. But the tide was out, and most of the menfolk with it, riding the choppy waves with nets and lines.

The landlord looked up.

"A pint of your best ale, if you please," Gabriel said, and passed over a coin.

The man grunted and brought him a mug full of foamy brew.

"I'm looking for a John Bitterman, who might live in the village. Have you heard of him?" Gabriel inquired, keeping his tone easy.

The man blinked.

Another dead end, Gabriel thought, but before he could frame another question, the man motioned toward the window.

"Happen, ye'll see him there."

Gabriel turned so quickly that the liquid in his mug sloshed onto the wooden table. He set it down quickly and looked through the small window where he could see two stout legs and the wheels of a cart.

He hurried to open the door and mount the steps to the walkway, which wound its way up the hill and onto higher ground.

"Bitterman?"

The man pushing the cart turned to gaze at Gabriel. His face was round, and his brows lifted. "Aye?"

Gabriel felt a quick rush of disappointment. This lad was much too young to be the man he sought. But it might be a family name. . . .

"I am looking for a John Bitterman who worked for my family, years ago in Kent. Might he be a relative of yours?"

The boy blinked. "Me grandpap worked in Kent for twenty-odd years, sir. Worked for a great lord, 'e did, but the man was mean-natured and stingy, me grandpap said, and 'e finally come 'ome again, little the richer for all 'is time."

Gabriel nodded, his voice grim. "That would be the man I called Father."

"Oh, sorry, sir." The boy flushed. "I didn't mean no disrespect."

"It doesn't matter, it was true enough, I'm sorry to say. But I would very much like to speak to your grandfather. Can you take me to him?"

The boy hesitated, and Gabriel drew out a handful of coins.

"It would be to his advantage, I promise you, and I mean no one any ill will. Can you take me to him?"

The lad's expression was twisted. "I can do that, sir, but you'll be none the wiser." And he explained.

Gabriel steeled his expression to hide his discontent, but he wanted to curse.

When she opened her eyes again, blinking at the sun-light that slipped past her draperies, Clarissa felt a stab of alarm. No, no, she told herself, catching a glimpse of her discarded gloves and reticule still lying on the side table where she had left them last night. The ball was over. She had no reason to dread today—

Except for the earl's suggestion that he would call. Clarissa sat straight up in bed. Oh no, surely he did not mean it!

She almost fell out of bed and without even ringing for

the maid, pulled on a dressing gown and found her slippers. She opened her bedroom door—what time was it, anyhow?—then slipped along the hallway to her sister-in-law and brother's room. But the bed was neatly made, and the room empty.

Late, then. Perhaps Gemma was downstairs in the dining room. Clarissa tiptoed down the wide staircase, hoping not to encounter any of the servants. She wanted to ask Gemma's advice about the enigmatic earl.

When she reached the first landing, she heard voices from the drawing room. Visitors, already? Oh, not the earl, it could not be!

She found her heart beating fast, like a fox hounded to its den and surrounded by baying dogs. Not wishing to be seen in her present state of undress, she paused just outside the doorway and listened. No, it was only female voices that she heard.

Clarissa had turned to hurry back upstairs to dress when a comment from inside the room made her pause.

"I was sorry to hear that they were making unseemly jests about her mishap," a woman said. "They are calling her the 'fallen Miss Fallon,' you know."

Gemma's answer was too low to be heard, but the other woman continued, "Of course, I would not tell Clarissa herself. I do not wish to distress her. But I thought you should be forewarned."

Distress her? Bloody hell, she was ruined for life! She wanted to march into the room and shout her anger, but killing the messenger would do little good. Nor would such behavior convince the Ton that she deserved the status of a "lady of quality."

Her fists clenched, Clarissa fled up the staircase. Once safely back in her own room, she paced up and down. What a way to repay her brother and his wife; oh, how had she managed to make such a grudgeon of herself? And the arrogant earl with his abrupt manner—he had had a part to play in her ignominious spill, too. If he had not startled her, if he had never interfered in the alley, she would not have dropped her dance book and she might not have stumbled. . . .

No, she could not assign her guilt or her awkwardness to anyone else. She was the one who had taken a tumble, and she was the one to blame. But her poor brother, who was trying so hard to give her a chance for a normal life . . . But she was not a normal young lady. Clarissa bit her lip.

She was startled by the door opening. It was the housemaid, Ruby, with a tray holding tea and toast. "Oh, you're up, miss. You should 'o rung. Here's some nice hot tea, and I'll bring your some warm water to wash up with."

"Thank you, Ruby," Clarissa said. She drank her tea and nibbled on the toast, aware of the tremors that still disturbed her stomach. She had to get over her nervous qualms, or she would fade away like the lovesick knight in Mr. Keats' poem, she told herself.

So, determined to be brave, no matter what trials the day might bring, she washed and dressed in a jonquil-sprigged muslin and eventually made her way, somewhat hesitantly, downstairs.

Gemma was still in the drawing room, but this time she was alone, staring at the pattern of the wallpaper as if considering its dainty swirls.

Clarissa went in almost on tiptoe. Gemma turned and smiled as she entered the room.

"Good morning, my dear. Have you broken your fast?"

Clarissa nodded. "I'm sorry to have slept so late."

"Not at all, there was no reason to rise early, and I was sure you were tired after the big night. And I did not schedule a dance lesson today. I thought you might appreciate a day off from drills and dance patterns."

Clarissa laughed. "Thank you, that is most kind. Are you all alone?"

"Miss Pomshack has a toothache," Gemma told her. "I have sent her off, with my maid as escort, to a barber to draw the tooth. However, I've already had two ladies call to chat about the ball last night, and, you'll be gratified to hear that we have received more invitations."

She nodded toward the mantel, now adorned with more cards and letters.

Clarissa gulped. Gratified did not exactly describe her feelings. "After I made such a fool of myself last night? What, are they hoping for more sensations—that I will disgrace myself again?"

"Now, Clarissa," Gemma told her. "We must not assume the worst. I'm sure that most of these ladies are trying to be supportive."

Clarissa was not so sure. Gemma was well liked, but she had only resided in London a short time herself; her circle of acquaintances was not large. "I think I am simply the latest curiosity," she argued. "Like a new and exotic beast in a menagerie!"

Gemma smiled. "Either way, we might as well make the most of it. And Psyche has sent us all a card for her next ball. You can be sure that she and my brother mean only kindness toward you."

Clarissa nodded. Yes, but they were family, too, in a way. The other notes and cards she still regarded with suspicion. She thought of the earl's promise—threat?—and again turned to her sister-in-law, ready to explain, but then she heard the decisive thud of the knocker at the front door.

More ladies ready to gossip about the ball—or worse?

Gemma interpreted her change of expression. "Now, do not be distressed, Clarissa. If we have more callers, you only need to sit and make polite conversation. No one is going to assail you in our drawing room."

Considering some of the matrons with their hard eyes and ready criticisms who had stared at her last night, Clarissa was not so sure. But she sat down and folded her hands and tried to present the picture of a proper lady.

At least while she sat, no one could make her stumble, she thought. Except—oh no, she heard a deep voice downstairs, a male voice, and it was not her brother, nor even Gemma's brother, Lord Gabriel.

She swallowed hard, and when the butler came to the door, she felt no surprise, only a sinking sense of doom, when she saw the man who accompanied him.

"Lord Whitby to see you, Lady Gemma, Miss Fallon," the servant said.

They both rose and curtsied as the visitor made his bow. "Please come in," Gemma said. She had hidden her surprise, if she felt it, and surely she did. How did she keep her tone so even and pleasant? "How nice to see you, my lord."

Seen once more in the daylight, the earl was an impressive figure. His riding coat and breeches fit him superbly and showcased his wide shoulders and the toned muscles in his arms and chest and thighs. Surely this man must do more than canter through the park, Clarissa thought, to have such a form.

But she realized she had to speak, too. She muttered a response, not nearly as graciously as her sister-in-law.

The earl did not lift his dark brows at her, as she feared. Instead, he faced Gemma. "I thought I should inquire about Miss Fallon after her mishap last night, and make sure she is not feeling any lasting ill effects," he explained.

"Not at all," Gemma assured him. "It is kind of you to ask, but she is quite well, are you not, Clarissa?"

"Yes, thank you." Clarissa stared at their visitor.

"Splendid," he said. "In that case, perhaps the two of you would do me the pleasure of taking a turn through the park. I have my curricle with me, and I'm told I'm a tolerable driver."

Such a humbug, Clarissa thought. Despite his modest words, the man knew he did everything well—it showed in every line of his assured bearing. What did this paragon know about feeling clumsy or out of place?

But having assured him of her good health, she had done away with any chance of a polite excuse. She threw a beseeching glance toward Gemma, but the other woman smiled. "That's very kind of you, my lord."

Oh, bloody hell. The maid was summoned, and without any obvious escape, Clarissa found herself donning a spencer and bonnet and pulling on her gloves. At least Gemma would be with her, she told herself.

The open carriage was as stylish and well-made as its owner. Lord Whitby helped them both in, then took his place and picked up the leads from his groom, who returned to his place on the back of the vehicle. The earl drove them through the crowded London streets with an almost annoying ease.

At least, since he was occupied with the carriage, conversation was brief, and she did not have to speak to him. But Clarissa found that she stared at him often. Annoyed at her own weakness, she turned her gaze away and observed the handsome team of matched grays.

When they reached Hyde Park, the earl turned the curricle into the park lane and took them around the expanse of greenery. Just as Clarissa had decided that this was not such a frightening expedition after all, he pulled up his horses and nodded to the groom, who jumped down and went to their heads to hold them steady.

"Perhaps you would enjoy a stroll through the gardens?" the earl asked, speaking apparently to them both.

And again, Clarissa had no good excuse. So, with the earl between them, they strolled through the walkways and admired the flowers and scrubs.

When they rounded a corner, Gemma saw another woman she knew and she paused to chat. Clarissa was unsure what to do. She took a few steps and stared down at a bed of bright blossoms, trying to ignore the earl.

He did not seem ready to be ignored.

"Have I displeased you, Miss Fallon?"

Why did he always have to be so direct? No polite chatter for the earl. She looked up at him and frowned. "I am sure you have plenty of other ladies to please, my lord," she shot back, then blushed. Probably not what a well brought-up young lady should say. And if she encountered such a young woman, Clarissa would inform her.

But even so, she looked away from his searching gaze.

"I am trying to help you," he told her, his tone steady.

"Help me? Do what?" If he had in mind more dance instruction, she thought wildly, she would tell him to go to the devil! "Stay off the floor?" Then she blushed even more hotly, glad that Gemma had not heard her mutter such an unladylike expression.

To her relief, he ignored her awkward phrasing. "I simply wish to help you find your place in Society. In fact, I want to do more."

She gaped at him, she could not help it. "Why should you care?"

"I have made a bet," this infuriating man said, his voice calm, "that I can make you the toast of the Ton."

Five

"*What?*" *She drew a deep breath.*

He waited for her outrage, her maidenly shock, willing to risk her wrath and her condemnation, anything that would break through this shell she had withdrawn so unreachably behind.

But to his surprise, she wrinkled her smooth forehead in apparently genuine puzzlement. "Why would you waste your blunt on such a hopeless cause?"

He laughed aloud and, for a moment, felt an irrational urge to hug her. No, he could not do it, of course, in the middle of the park with too many observant eyes all around. And if he did take such a liberty, she would likely box his ears. Whatever her problem, he did not think it was lack of spirit. Anyhow, he was here to save her reputation, not besmirch it.

"Why should that be such an impossible task?" he countered. "You are of good birth and have committed no social sins—that I know of, anyhow."

"Except for tumbling to the floor at your feet," she muttered, looking away.

He frowned at her stubborn tone. "Anyone can make a mistake."

"Seldom in such a public place," she told him. "But—"

"Yes?" he said, hoping she would not pause now, and that her sister-in-law would not end her conversation—which she seemed to be drawing out very kindly—and rejoin them. If he was lucky, he might find out the real reason behind her reticence. He was sure there was more here than another timid damsel in her first Season. This girl had backbone, he was sure of it, and despite her relative youth, something in her eyes hinted at adversity overcome and tragedy survived. If she would only confide in him, his task might be much easier.

She bit her lip.

He tried to encourage her to talk. "You have spent your whole life preparing for this debut," he reminded her. "A stumble or two along the way signifies little."

The glance she gave him was haunted, and it startled him. Yes, certainly more here than met the eye.

"That's the problem," she said, very low. "I haven't . . ."

He waited, but she didn't go on. Perhaps another nudge was in order. "Are you not going to tell me how offended you are, how outraged that I should make a lady like yourself the subject of a wager?"

Her eyes widened. "Oh, yes, I'm sure that's most improper, isn't it? It's not mentioned in my book of etiquette, but—"

She paused in confusion as he was startled into a laugh. Again, not the response he had expected.

"Yes," she went on, her face a little flushed and her eyes bright. "I am most shocked, indeed. Shame on you!"

"I humbly beg your pardon," he told her, wishing he could tell her how her hazel eyes sparkled when she looked at him just so, and how much he longed to trace the delicate line of her throat—no, he could hardly tell her that!

"Then why did you do it? You must call off the bet," she suggested.

"I'm afraid I can't," he told her, keeping his tone as serious as hers. "A gentleman's word, and all that. But I swear to you, Miss Fallon, that I mean no disrespect to you, and I intend to aid you, not harm you."

"I still think you've bet on a losing nag." She pursed her lips as she stared at him.

He wanted very much to laugh once more, but now his luck seemed to have run out. Lady Gemma had finished her conversation and had turned back to rejoin them.

"But give me the chance to help you," he suggested in a low tone. Miss Fallon gave him a doubtful glance, then lowered her gaze. Why were young ladies taught to be so missish? And why did he continue to glimpse the hint of old pain beneath the smooth surface of her eyes?

He liked her much better when she was saying something outrageous, and he was more than ever convinced that Miss Fallon had some mystery in her life. He had not been so intrigued by a young lady in years. He remembered his cousin's suggestion, but shook it aside as he escorted the ladies around the path and back to his carriage.

No, he had no serious interest here, nor was he in any danger of losing his heart. He had no intention of taking on such a heavy responsibility. Incite passion with a marriageable miss? Hardly! He wanted no one's happiness in his charge.

But although it had been Galston's idea, Dominic had rashly agreed to the wager, and he had decided to win it. And if, along the way, he could lighten the burden that this girl seemed to carry inside her, that would not be a bad thing. Since this was only a temporary commission and she was not really his duty, he did not have to fear the consequences of his failure. Even if he did fail and he did not manage to increase her standing in the Ton, she would be no worse off than she was already.

So he drove them back to the Fallon house and showed the ladies inside. And if he held her hand a moment too long when he helped Miss Fallon down, and if she glanced at him with the same mixture of awareness and doubt that he found so intriguing, he managed not to smile.

"Perhaps I may call on you again?" he asked.

Clarissa blinked at him, and stuttered, "Ah, I-I—" And it was left to her sister-in-law to offer a polite response.

"We should always be happy to receive you, my lord."

He bowed to them and took his leave before the younger lady could think of a way to rebuff him. She was not very socially adept, that was obvious, and he meant—in a most ungentlemanly fashion—to take advantage of her lack of skill to further his own ends. And what those ends were . . . No, it was only for the wager, he reminded himself.

Clarissa glanced back over her shoulder as the carriage pulled away. Then the door was shut behind them, and the middle-aged butler and the maid were there to take away their outerwear.

She knew that Gemma was watching her and tried to decide what she should say to any questions about the earl's surprising interest. She could hardly share his confession about the existence of a wager. That really was disgraceful, and she should have realized it at once.

Why had he told her?

The man was so confusing, and if he wished to confuse someone, he should at least have the grace to pick on a lady with more social experience, Clarissa thought crossly. And as to how she felt when he stood close to her— Well, that was neither here nor there, even if it did induce sensations she had never felt before. . . .

"You have a letter, my lady," the butler was saying.

"Thank you, Barrons," Gemma said, accepting the missive but glancing across at Clarissa with an inquisitive gaze.

Fortunately, before Gemma could take her upstairs for a private conversation, they were interrupted. A knock at the door sent the butler back to his post, and when he swung open the door again, a pitiful figure entered. It was Miss Pomshack, returning to the house with maid in tow. Her jaw was swollen and her eyes reddened; the tooth-pulling had obviously been most painful.

"Oh, you poor thing," Gemma exclaimed. She hurried to escort the older lady upstairs to see her put to bed.

"I hope you feel better soon, Miss Pomshack," Clarissa called after them, but then she took the chance to escape to her own room. Once there, she shut the door and flung herself upon her bed. She had to think about the earl and try to sort out her feelings about this blunt, arrogant, and yet appealing man.

Why would he make the wager, she wondered again. Certainly, it was a typically insolent thing to do. Did the man think he could get away with anything? She should feel angry. Instead, she felt a bit wistful. Too bad Clarissa were not such a man, with a title and a fortune to insulate her from Society's judgment. But she wasn't; she was female, with a most loving family of only modest fortune, and such thoughts were useless. Only men like the earl could be so . . . so . . . And yet he thought he could make her the toast of the Ton? He must be insane.

She lifted herself enough to stare across at the looking glass on her dressing table. A tendril of fair hair had slipped out of place, again, and, oh, hell, she had a smudge on her nose. Clarissa wiped at it absently.

Did he really think she could be a success in Society? The idea of someone who was not a relative having so much faith in her warmed her.

Not that he should be betting on it, of course! But, in Clarissa's strange circumstance, it was hard to feel the outrage that a "proper" lady would naturally feel. Oh, the enigmatic earl had no idea what a task he had set for himself.

Once Miss Pomshack was settled and given a soothing dose of laudanum for the pain, which soon sent her to sleep,

Gemma retired to her own bedchamber. She considering checking on Clarissa, but decided to leave her alone for a time. The girl seemed reluctant to talk about the earl and his surprising show of interest. Not that Clarissa wasn't extremely pretty and sweet and certainly worthy of any man's attention, but, still, Lord Whitby could have his pick of the most beautiful, most wealthy, most prominent ladies of the Ton.

Why had he fastened upon Clarissa?

After Clarissa's unfortunate fall at the party last night, Gemma had been very pleased when the man had had the decency to seek out Clarissa and complete their dance. If he had not, Clarissa's case among malicious Society gossips would be even more dismal, although Gemma would not tell her so.

But his call and then his escort to the park today had come as a surprise, as did the suggestion he'd made in parting that he might call on her again . . . mind you, stranger things had happened. A year ago, Gemma would never have guessed that the veils of mystery about her own background might at last be lifted. Clarissa was not the only one who had been restored to lost family.

And finding Matthew as she had searched for her family history . . . that had been even more of an unexpected blessing.

Gemma smiled a moment, then, remembering the letter, sat down and took it from her pocket. She broke the familiar wax seal and unfolded the single sheet of paper. The communication was from her brother, Gabriel, an acknowledgment that still gave her a feeling of warmth and contentment. The message inside was short. She scanned the contents, then read it again more slowly, but the information was still disappointing.

She sat and stared into space, and was still there when Matthew came in and found her.

"Is something wrong, my love?" He leaned over and gave her a kiss.

She returned his caress and reached for his hand, holding it tight for a moment. "No, in fact, we have had a most interesting visitor. But I was just thinking . . . I've received a note from my brother."

She paused, and Matthew looked sympathetic.

"He has had no luck?"

"No, not so far. One former family servant was traced to Cornwall, but the man died two years ago. Gabriel is still searching for his mother's personal maid, but we cannot find any sign of her current address. You'd think the late marquess deliberately tried to obscure any trail back to the truth!"

"Perhaps he did," her husband pointed out, sitting down beside her and putting a comforting arm about her shoulders.

She made a face. "It's not as if affairs among the Ton are not common enough. As long as the wife makes sure her first child, or first son, is truly her husband's, future children who might be the result of a secret affair are not unheard of. Not that I'm advocating such conduct, of course."

He grinned and leaned closer to kiss her neck. "Of course."

She grinned reluctantly. "I would not judge my mother too harshly, however. From all I have heard, the late marquess was a most unpleasant man. I'm sorry I cannot repudiate this silly title, since I don't really deserve it, but Gabriel argues—and I agree—that we would not wish anything malicious said about our late mother. But I do wish we had some idea who our real father was! At least Gabriel remembers our mother. I have no memory of any parent to comfort me."

This time he pulled her completely into his arms, and Gemma laid her head against his shoulder. "You had a most difficult time," he said.

"Not as hard as Clarissa, sold into service," she pointed out, determined to be fair. "But yes, it was hard not knowing who I really was."

"But that is behind you now," her husband told her.

She lifted her head and kissed his cheek. "Thank heaven!

I have a family name at last. Most important, I have you, and a dear sister, as well as my brother and his wife, who are all I could ask for. Even the current marquess, our half brother, has been most kind and welcoming and does not dispute my heritage, even though he knows part of the public version is false. All told, I've never been so happy. And we will make sure that Clarissa also has a bright future ahead of her. But I do wish Gabriel could locate the man who begot us."

"Give him time," Matthew suggested. "It is a hard task, as we know, to track family members who have been lost or gone astray. But Gabriel doesn't give up easily."

"Like you." She lifted her head and accepted his kiss, this time on the lips, returning it with equal vigor. She broke away only to say, "Oh, about our visitors today—"

"Later," he murmured.

And smiling—until he captured her lips again—Gemma offered no argument.

The next morning Gemma was pulling on her gloves when Clarissa came downstairs.

"I shall be back for dinner," she explained, pausing to give Clarissa a quick hug. "Lady Gabriel is picking me up very shortly. It is our day to visit the foundling home and inspect the building, and most of all, to be sure the children are in good health and spirits and the staff doing what they should."

"That's good of you." Clarissa felt a twinge of guilt. She should, no doubt, be accompanying her sister-in-law and spending some of her own time engaged in similar good works.

No one had more cause to be interested in the home than she. Had she not suffered through the abuse and neglect of that institution? Didn't the memories still haunt her? But her recollections were still too painful. Just the thought of rolling up to the big bleak building and crossing the threshold made her throat close up with terror and her body quiver with the need to run the other way.

Her mind might tell her that she was free and that she now had family to protect her, but somewhere inside her a frightened child still recoiled in terror.

Gemma patted her arm. "It will come," she said, apparently reading the emotions that crossed Clarissa's face. "You do not need to reproach yourself for not wishing to return, Clarissa."

"But you spend time there," she pointed out. "I should do the same."

"I had less to forget as well as more years to recover; you will heal, too."

"You're too good to me," Clarissa muttered. Comforted by her hug, she clung to Gemma for a moment.

Then the footman appeared. "Lady Gabriel's chaise is here, milady."

"Thank you, I'm just coming." Gemma nodded. "Have a good day, my dear."

Clarissa waited until her sister-in-law had departed, then went into the dining room and drank another cup of tea. Lost in thought, she was sitting there when Miss Pomshack appeared, looking pale but resolute, her jaw still somewhat swollen.

Today the good lady ate only porridge and toast for her breakfast, and she allowed the footman to bring her some tea. "Good morning, Miss Clarissa. I hope you slept well." She looked a bit heavy-eyed, but she spoke with her usual determined solicitude.

"Yes, thank you," Clarissa answered politely. "How are you feeling?"

"Sore, I admit, but a good deal better. The maid tells me that Lady Gemma has gone out." Miss P took a cautious bite. "This is one of her days for the foundling home visit, I believe. It is most worthy of her, and of Lady Gabriel, as well, to devote time and attention to such a good cause."

Clarissa nodded, but the other woman's comment elicited

more feelings of guilt, so she did not pursue the topic. Fortunately, Miss P was reaching for the strawberry jam and didn't appear to notice.

When Miss Pomshack had finished, they both went up to the drawing room. Miss P picked up her sewing basket and bent her head over an embroidery hoop. Clarissa chose a book from the pile on the side table, but although she turned the pages, she could not concentrate on the words. After a few minutes, she put it aside and found herself pacing up and down the room.

"Would you like to go out, Miss Clarissa?" Miss P looked up from her needlework. "Shopping, perhaps, or a stroll in the park?"

"No, I mean, no thank you," Clarissa said at once. And risk seeing apparitions in the crowd? No, indeed. Yet, she did feel cooped up here, and she— Oh, she didn't know what she wanted, except that the feelings inside her, somehow aggravated by her reflections on the foundling home, seemed rawer than usual.

"Then let us take this opportunity to practice your needlework," Miss Pomshack suggested brightly. "I have an extra hoop and square of linen here, and an ample supply of thread, and you have no dancing lesson today. Come sit beside me, and I will show you how to make a love knot. I'm quite good with my needle, if I do say so."

Without a good excuse, Clarissa was forced to sit down and accept the materials that her companion handed her. Clarissa knew her stitchery was abominable—yet another ladylike skill that she had had little training in, aside from some early lessons from her mother—and within half an hour, she had managed to prick her finger three times and bleed a few drops onto the pristine square.

Clarissa bit back an unladylike oath just in time as she stuck her finger in her mouth and frowned down at the piece of linen.

"Oh, dear," Miss Pomshack said. "However, if I soak it in cold water, I'm sure I can get the spot out."

"You're too kind," Clarissa forced herself to say. She tried to think of a good reason to end the needlework lesson. By this time even Miss Pomshack was looking strained and her forehead showed several new creases. Clarissa considered claiming a headache, but that would only evoke an offer of one of the good lady's tisanes. Biting her lip, Clarissa sighed and picked up her seemingly cursed needle one more time.

A firm rap sounded at the front door. Both ladies looked up, and Clarissa was not sure who was the most relieved when footsteps approached on the staircase and the footman appeared in the doorway. "You have a caller, miss. Lord Whitby."

The earl paused in the doorway to give them both a proper bow. "Ladies, a good day to you."

Clarissa jumped up so quickly that she dropped the embroidery hoop. "My lord! I mean, Lord Whitby, this is a surprise. A nice surprise, I mean." She was annoyed to find she was repeating herself like a lackwit. Belatedly, she remembered to curtsy, making an awkward bob and knowing that she lacked his grace of movement, and even Miss Pomshack's somewhat stiff but totally correct dip was better done. Bloody hell, she would never learn it all!

"This is my companion, Miss Pomshack."

He acknowledged the introduction. They sat down again, and he took his seat across from Clarissa.

"I am pleased to see you both in good health. Lady Gemma is not at home?" Lord Whitby asked, in his usual slightly bored tone.

Clarissa explained about the foundling home. "Lady Gemma serves on the board of governors, along with Lady Gabriel, and they visit regularly to see that the children are properly looked after."

"An excellent endeavor," he noted. "Which brings a thought to mind. Perhaps you would join me in a little good deed of my own, Miss Fallon."

"What?" she stared at him. If she had expected anything from his visit, it was certainly not an invitation to do good works. He hardly struck her as the philanthropic type.

"I am overdue for a duty call on an elderly relative. She is an invalid and seldom goes out. I'm sure she would love to see a new face; it would brighten her day. Perhaps you would like to accompany me, you and Miss Pomshack, of course."

Clarissa stared at him, unable to think of a way to gracefully decline. "Ah, as to that, my sister-in-law—"

What? Gemma would be gone all day, and even she could hardly raise her brows at such a respectable mission.

She saw that he glanced at the embroidery hoop, still on the floor, and to give herself a moment to think, she bent to retrieve it. Unhappily, she jabbed the needle into her fingertip as she grasped the cloth and managed to prick herself yet again. She swallowed the oath that almost slipped out by sticking the sore finger into her mouth. This was a tactical mistake as it gave Miss Pomshack the chance to answer for her.

"I'm sure Miss Fallon would be delighted to spend a few hours in such a laudable endeavor. I shall go up and collect our wraps."

"Thank you." The earl stood as the older lady left the room.

"I'm sure your relation is a lovely person, but I am not very good at conversation—" Clarissa began, trying to find a way out of this visit.

"Oh, no," he interrupted. "She's judgmental, self-centered, and always complaining, aside from not being nearly as ill as she enjoys thinking she is."

"Then why in bloody hell should I suffer her company?" Clarissa blurted, free from Miss Pomshack's constraining presence. She didn't much care, at the moment, whether she offended the overbearing earl or not. Today he seemed to have reverted to his original arrogant self.

"Because she never goes out, and you need the practice." His answer was equally blunt. "If you fall on your face, she will not have the chance to gossip about it. Or not much, anyhow. I thought I could perform two good deeds at one stroke. No need to waste two afternoons, don't you think?"

Unable to dispute the logic of his argument, she glared at him, but she resented it with all her heart. It was one thing to know that she was awkward and lacking social skills, but to have him point it out—

"And you are not incredibly rude to say such a thing to me?" she demanded.

"Of course, but sometimes, one has to be honest," he answered. "Besides, as Miss Pomshack noted, this is a laudable endeavor."

"If you're not the biggest humbug I ever saw—" she began. Clarissa pointed her finger at him, then discovered that her fingertip sported a bright red droplet of blood. She put it hastily into her mouth before she stained her new muslin gown.

"I sometimes do have a charitable impulse," he murmured. He took out his handkerchief and offered it to her.

Unwillingly, Clarissa took it and wrapped it about her finger to stop the blood.

Before she could think of a way to refuse, Miss Pomshack was back with their bonnets and shawls and gloves, and somehow, Clarissa was doomed. He had brought an open carriage again, and it was a pleasant ride, even if the streets were noisy and crowded. Clarissa watched the changing street scene—a stout matron argued with a ragman, a horseman in military uniform rode a handsome dark horse, and a cart full of coal had lost a wheel—and ignored her host, and if he thought her rude, so be it!

She was still seething when they arrived at a large house and were helped down by the groom. Whatever the earl's relation's problems, poverty was apparently not one of them.

When the elderly butler admitted them and took them up to the drawing room, they found a white-haired lady sitting in a Bath chair.

Taken aback, Clarissa thought she should indeed have been more compassionate. She felt ashamed of her sulking.

However, she was further surprised when the lady took hold of the chair's arms and stood, a little stiffly, then came forward to accept their greetings.

"Good day, Aunt," the earl was saying. "I thought you might like some new faces. These are my friends, Miss Fallon and Miss Pomshack. My aunt, Lady Crimshawe."

"How do." Lady Crimshawe gave them a brief nod.

They responded in kind, and this time, Clarissa thought that at least she achieved a credible curtsy.

Their hostess moved to one of the settees and motioned to her butler. "Take the chair away, Hawkins. I shan't need it any longer today. And mind that you don't ram it into the sideboard again."

To her guests, she added, "Those are genuine Ming vases on the sideboard; my grandfather acquired them in France."

God help the servants in this household, Clarissa thought.

"Is your gout acting up again?" Lord Whitby asked as they all were seated.

"No, my back," she told her nephew. Her tone was reproachful. "Did you not read the note I sent you yesterday? I was most stiff this morning when I got out of bed."

"I read it promptly, and I thought sure you mentioned your foot." The earl's tone was pleasant if resigned.

"No, no, that was the day before, and the note before," she argued. "And why did you not call earlier?"

"I was sure that your good doctor would be at your side, Aunt, and I didn't wish to pester you while you were having a bad day."

Humbug again, Clarissa thought, but she managed not to speak her opinion aloud. With a relative such as this, really, could she blame him?

"Hmph," the older lady muttered. "All of my days are bad, as you well know. I suffer from various complaints," she said, turning to her other guests. She proceeded to catalogue them, often offering more detail than Clarissa really wished to know.

"And aside from that, I have a liver that is constantly

failing. Only my good doctor's tonic enables me to enjoy any decent meals at all. Why, yesterday, for example, I was barely able to get down a few bites of gruel."

Her frame was so well padded that Clarissa felt some doubt as to the accuracy of this claim, but she tried to keep her expression compliant.

Miss Pomshack listened closely and made soothing replies, so Clarissa felt it safe enough to allow her own thoughts to wander. She felt some reluctant sympathy for the earl, if he had this termagant as kin. Despite all the symptoms and ailments Lady Crimshawe listed, she looked healthy enough. She was well rounded and her color good, and if she moved a little stiffly, she seemed able to get about easily on her own without the aid of the wheeled chair.

Just as Clarissa thought they would spend the whole visit listening to the older lady's involved detailing of her health, or lack of it—thank heavens a proper social call was only half an hour—she discovered there was worse in store. Lady Crimshawe finally gave over extolling her illnesses and turned her attention to her guests.

"And you, Miss Pomshack, what is your estate?" she inquired.

"My father was a vicar," Miss Pomshack answered, her tone dignified. "He served a large parish in Warwickshire and was most highly regarded by his bishop and all who knew him. I am currently serving as a governess-companion for Miss Fallon. I am an old acquaintance of Miss Fallon's sister-in-law, Lady Gemma Fallon."

Appearing to dismiss Miss Pomshack from her attention—an enviable position, Clarissa thought wildly—Lady Crimshawe turned to regard the younger lady. Lifting the lorgnette that had been hanging on a chain about her neck, she held it to her nose and stared at Clarissa as if she were some weird and threatening insect. "And you, Miss Fallon?"

"I—I—" Clarissa found herself stuttering again. Who did this unpleasant woman think she was—the queen of England?

"Miss Fallon is a lady of good family." To her surprise, it was the earl who came to her rescue. "Do you think I would bring any other such person to meet you?"

Lady Crimshawe shrugged and continued to stare at Clarissa. "You seem old enough to be out."

"I am, I suppose," Clarissa said, struggling not to squirm under the lady's inspection. "That is, I am out."

"And much too old for a governess." Again, Lady Crimshawe sounded disapproving.

"I'm—I'm somewhat behind in my studies, that is—" Clarissa floundered.

"You're not mentally deficient, are you?" their hostess demanded. "Whitby, if you are considering making this girl an offer, I would be very sure of both her and her family's health before you contemplate any commitment. You do not want an incompetent for your heir!"

"Of course he is not making me an offer!" Clarissa hoped her cheeks were not aflame. "I barely know him, and I wouldn't have him if he did!"

"Nonsense, no lady in her right mind would turn down Whitby. He is in excellent health. In addition, he possesses an old and highly respected title, he has wealth and an esteemed family name—my family name, I might add," she said, as if that made all the difference. She stared through the lorgnette. "This is another dubious statement. Do not be coy with me, Miss Fallon; it will not do. If there is any problem with your circumstances, tell me directly."

Clarissa still fumed. "Of all the rude things to say! There is nothing wrong with my mind or my family's health."

"Dreadful lack of manners, too," the old lady continued, apparently undeterred by Clarissa's outburst. "Do you not know to submit gracefully to an older person's polite interest in you?"

"If this is what you call polite—" Clarissa muttered, but the other lady sailed on.

"Why are you behind in your studies? Have you been ill?"

Clarissa eyed the woman and tried to think of what to say.

That she had been sent to a foundling home and sold from there into household service? She hardly wanted to hear the old lady's opinion about that! "I am quite well, thank you," she answered carefully. "And I thank you for your solicitude regarding my health, but it is quite unnecessary."

"My aunt could recommend her own doctor," the earl put in. "In case you ever needed him. Sir Arthur is a man of high reputation."

"Yes, indeed," Lady Crimshawe agreed. "Some may say that Reynold is the most respected physician in London, but indeed, I should beg to differ. No one has shown such sensitivity to my suffering as my good Sir Arthur."

She extolled her own doctor's virtues for several minutes while Clarissa, throwing Lord Whitby a glance of gratitude, thought she had escaped the interrogation.

But in a few moments, their hostess turned to her again. "I still say it is suspicious that you are behind in your studies, and you did not answer my earlier question as to the reason for it."

"Perhaps I think it is none of your concern," Clarissa snapped.

Lady Crimshawe shook her head. "As I said, Whitby. Bad blood here, though she may not wish to admit. Why, look at her pale skin. Probably a faulty spleen. I should look closer at her family, I tell you."

Miss Pomshack opened her mouth, but Clarissa was beyond caring about propriety. "Of all the bloody nerve!" she exclaimed. "My brother is a most excellent man, who served bravely in the war against France. My mother was a perfect lady, kind and well mannered to a fault, and my father a gentleman, although a younger son and not wealthy. I have plenty of faults, but you need not disparage my family!"

"Your brother was in the war, eh? Did he teach you such unladylike language? Perhaps it affected his mind, and he has infected you. Whitby was in the war, and he's never been the same since," the old lady retorted.

"I suppose that should make us well suited, then,"

Clarissa flashed back. "But I am not bloody well interested."

"You may protest, young lady, but I know better. And as for your regrettable choice of words, *my* own dear departed governess would have washed out your mouth with soap!"

"Just try it," Clarissa muttered, but she took a deep breath and tried to contain her anger, although she found herself gripping her hands together in her lap.

"I am older than you, and I deserve respect," Lady Crimshawe instructed, her tone still pompous.

"That does not mean you can be as bad-mannered as you choose." Beyond caring about decorum, Clarissa met the old woman glare for glare.

Lord Whitby cleared his throat. "This has been a most, ah, pleasant visit, Aunt, but I fear we must not overtire you."

Her narrow eyes bright, their hostess had been sitting up very straight. But her nephew's words appeared to remind her of her supposedly invalid state, and she leaned back against her pillowed chair. "Yes, indeed. It is most unkind of you to tax me with such contrary and unobliging visitors."

"I assure you I will not impose upon you again," Clarissa informed her. "I wish you good health, Lady Crimshawe."

Lord Whitby bowed over his relation's hand, which she extended limply as if it were the ultimate honor, and then he ushered them out. Clarissa was still seething.

"How dare you do that?" she demanded as soon as the door was safely shut behind them. "Inflict that old harridan upon us?"

"Miss Fallon!" Miss Pomshack protested, but with somewhat less than her usual conviction. Even she looked a bit pink in the cheeks.

"I told you, it was a good exercise for you. And on the whole, you did quite well, even if you did lose your composure at the end," he told her, his tone quite unrepentant. "Or perhaps in the middle. You managed a few civil sentences, at any rate."

"Lose my composure? You're fortunate I did not smash

that Ming vase over her head!" Clarissa frowned and wished she could kick him in the shin.

And the accursed man was smiling at her! It was amazing how much a smile softened his usually disdainful expression and reminded her for an instant just how handsome he was. Those dark eyes held so much emotion, and the strong chin and well-formed mouth . . .

She found she had forgotten, for an instant, to be angry. Hoping that her expression had not revealed too much, Clarissa looked away.

"Most people who meet my aunt experience a similar re-action. But as I said, on the whole, you did very well."

"I suppose at least I did not fall over my feet," she admitted, and his smile widened.

"As I said."

That made her frown again, but he added as he helped them into the chaise. "Putting a raw recruit under fire will either destroy him or make him stronger. I think you passed the test."

"You have no right to ask me to pass any test!"

To her confusion, he paused and lifted the hand she had reluctantly given him to help her up the step. He brought it to his lips and she felt the whisper of his kiss, even through her gloves. It sent a strange sort of tingle through her. His eyes gleamed, and for a moment she stared into them, and everything around them receded, as it had that day in the al-ley. He moved closer—and then released her abruptly and drew a deep breath.

She looked away. He said quietly, "Touché. You are right, of course."

Which left her nothing at all to say. So, Clarissa climbed into the carriage—fortunately, Miss Pomshack was arrang-ing her pelisse and did not seem to have noticed the moment of intimacy—and sat silently all the way home.

When they reached the Fallon household, he saw them to the door and took a polite leave, but promised to call again.

Why did he bother? Clarissa could not fathom it. He lectured her, tormented her, teased her. It made no sense at all. Was this all about that silly wager?

Even Miss Pomshack was not pleased with their visit. "Upon my word, hardly Christian behavior," she said after they were inside. "I would chastise you for your language, Miss Clarissa, but this time, I must admit you were sorely provoked. Even I— Well, I think I shall go upstairs and read my Prayer Book for a few minutes to settle my mind before I take my afternoon rest."

"Please do, Miss P," Clarissa murmured.

As the other lady left the room, Clarissa walked to the window and watched the earl's elegant chaise pull away. Somehow, she found she was rubbing her fingertips across the hand he had kissed.

Six

O *ne of the misfortunes that accrued from the dance,* from Clarissa's viewpoint at least, was that more invitations poured in. Even without an official coming-out ball, which her brother and sister-in-law still wanted to hold for her, and which Clarissa still pleaded to put off until she felt more at ease at formal affairs, other events were held out for her amusement.

Reluctantly, she agreed to some of the least socially demanding, which was how she came to be sitting in Mrs. Prescott's drawing room the next afternoon and, remembering Circe's instructions, holding her teacup carefully and not too tightly. She wished Circe were here to offer her friendly support, but, Lady Gabriel's sister was too young to be out except for small family parties. Clarissa herself was the youngest lady in the room, and she felt like a kernel of corn thrown out to a flock of hungry hens.

"Another scone, my dear child?" her hostess cooed.

Clarissa smiled and accepted a pastry, but she didn't trust

the matron's narrow eyes, which seemed more curious than kind. She found herself saying little, although Mrs. Prescott had asked several almost too personal questions.

"I understand you are newly come to London, Miss Fallon. Have you been away at school?" She blinked her short lashes and waited.

"Yes, I mean, I have only recently come to the city. For the last few years I was, uh, in the North—" Clarissa hesitated, but it was Gemma who answered smoothly to fill in the awkward silence.

"I was very fond of my school; it was located in the North Country, too, in Yorkshire. Education is important even for ladies, don't you think, Mrs. Prescott?"

Mrs. Prescott frowned for a moment, then perforce directed her steely gaze toward Gemma. "Indeed, Lady Gemma? I should think marriage is the only subject that a young lady needs to study."

Several other women tittered, and their hostess smiled at their appreciation of her mild witticism.

Clarissa drew a deep breath of relief. Thank heavens for Gemma.

"Why fill girls' heads with books and such nonsense?" Mrs. Prescott went on. "Needlework, of course, is a desirable skill, and if one learns to sketch or play an instrument, that will add to one's accomplishments."

"Oh, I don't know. Reading is also of value. I just found a new novel that is quite diverting," Sally Forsythe put in. The handsome brunette, who had attended Psyche's tea party, flashed a friendly glance toward Clarissa. "And although I never went away to school, my governess was quite strict about learning geography and ciphering and French verbs."

Clarissa smiled back but kept her gaze mostly on her teacup. If they only knew how little formal education she had had, the matrons would have no reason to debate the subject of education for females.

"Oh, I leave sums to my housekeeper and butler," another of the ladies said. "Figures do make my head ache!"

"They will steal you blind if you don't watch," their hostess retorted. "That is one area where one must be vigilant. I keep a close eye on my household accounts."

She would not wish to be one of this house's servants, Clarissa couldn't help thinking. She took a deep gulp of her tea.

There was a movement at her side, and, ill at ease, Clarissa jumped. Still holding the teacup, she turned too quickly.

It was the parlor maid, who had come closer with the silver teapot to refill her cup. But Clarissa's out-flung hand hit the pot. The cup she held shattered, splattering Clarissa's blue-sprigged muslin, as well as the maid's white apron, with the dregs of tea. Still holding the teapot, the servant jerked in surprise. Some of the liquid splashed from the spout, as well, showering the woman sitting next to Clarissa, who exclaimed in annoyance.

"Oh, my best silk! This is too bad!"

"Matty!" Mrs. Prescott frowned fiercely. "How dare you be so clumsy! Go away and send in the footman with some dry cloths for our guests."

Her hand visibly shaking, the poor housemaid put down the teapot and hurried out of the room.

"Oh, no, do not scold her, it was all my fault!" Clarissa exclaimed. "I am the one who has been unforgivably clumsy."

"I do have a modicum of manners," the woman retorted. "I should never criticize my own guest."

"No, just your own servant," Clarissa flashed back. "Who is in a much more vulnerable position. But it was not her fault, I tell you. Madam." She turned to the woman sitting next to her, who dabbed at her skirt with a tiny handkerchief. "I am so sorry."

The other guest sniffed. "Perhaps that school of yours should have focused more on manners and grace and less on books and ciphers, Miss Fallon."

"Accidents happen, Mrs. Abbot," Gemma put in, her voice cool. "We should be happy to replace your gown."

"I can afford to pay my dressmaker, Lady Gemma," the

other woman replied. "The point is that a lady should not jump about like that—"

While the two women exchanged polite barbs, Mrs. Prescott rose and went out, her expression still annoyed.

Distressed at what she had done, Clarissa jumped to her feet and followed. A footman met her at the door and offered her a pristine linen towel for her dress, but she waved him aside. Although she could not make out the lowered tones, she saw her hostess exchanging words with the butler, who turned away.

Mrs. Prescott swung back toward the drawing room, then paused when she saw Clarissa. "May I help you, Miss Fallon?"

"I, um, just wished to withdraw for a moment, if you please."

"Of course." The matron motioned to a footman. "Show Miss Fallon to my private salon. And bring her more towels."

Did the woman think she was going to drip tea on the carpet? Her dress was not soaked, and the spots would come out if the muslin were soaked in cold water right away. Clarissa had learned a few useful things while in service.

She waited until Mrs. Prescott had disappeared into the drawing room, then ignored the footman's attempts to show her up the stairs.

"Where is the servants' stairs?" she asked him. "Did that housemaid go up to her room or down to the servants' hall?"

He gaped at her, and she had to repeat the question.

"Uh, down, miss, but you can't—"

Ignoring the protest she knew he would make, Clarissa hurried down the main staircase, and, on the ground floor, located the narrow door that she knew typically led to the kitchen and servants' hall belowground. Despite all decorum, she pushed it open and dashed down the narrow stairwell.

It led into a passage that was less ornamented and hardly as grand as the rooms above, but where Clarissa felt much more at home. She heard the murmur of voices and followed the sounds into a kitchen. She found the maid from the drawing room, her cap askew on her brown hair and tea stains still evident on her apron, crouched on a bench by a plain oak table, holding her flushed face in her hands.

"Oh, please, do not cry," Clarissa burst out. "It was my fault, I would not blame you. I tried to tell your mistress so."

The servant raised her damp cheeks; her dark eyes were flooded with tears. "I didn't mean it, miss. I'm that sorry."

"I know, indeed, I have told Mrs. Prescott," Clarissa assured her again.

"Did no good," an older, angular woman with a North Country accent put in. She had been patting the girl on the back. Now this woman looked at Clarissa with obvious resentment. "Matty's been dismissed, a 'cause of that tea spill. Out on the street with 'ou a reference, and 'ow will she find another post?"

"I can do something about that, at least," Clarissa answered, suddenly inspired. "I am in need of a lady's maid, and I require no references. Would you like the position, Matty?"

The servant stared at her, as if not sure if she was being mocked. "But why would you want such a clumsy girl?" she asked, her voice timid.

"Believe me, we shall suit amazingly," Clarissa assured her. She told the girl the address of the Fallon house. "Can you find the street?"

"Oh, yes, miss," the girl said, blinking hard.

"Then collect your personal things and come as soon as you are ready," Clarissa told her. Her own guilt lightened along with the servant's expression.

Knowing that someone upstairs would soon come looking for her if she lingered, and not wishing to cause the servants any more trouble, Clarissa bade them good day. Leaving the staff staring after her, she hurried back up the stairs.

At least some good could come from being a lady. She felt like singing. For once, to wield the power herself—to do some good. No wonder Gemma went back to the foundling home, Clarissa thought, with a sudden burst of understanding. Someday, she would find the courage to do the same, truly, she would.

When she reached the drawing room, she slipped back inside and took her seat. Gemma glanced at her. "I believe we must make our farewells," she told their hostess. "Thank you for the tea."

Clarissa made a polite good-bye, as well, wishing she could rail at the woman once more for her heartless treatment of her servants, but she knew it would do no good. After they made their way out and were handed into the Fallon carriage, Gemma turned to her.

"Are you all right, Clarissa?"

"Oh, yes," Clarissa said, her tone blithe. "I have hired a lady's maid."

"What?" Gemma stared at her.

Clarissa explained about Mrs. Prescott firing the serving girl. "It was so unfair! And Matthew did say I could have a lady's maid."

"Well, yes," Gemma agreed. "But is she qualified? She must know how to fix your hair and do up your clothes and—"

"If not, she can learn," Clarissa argued stubbornly.

Gemma smiled. "I suppose so. We shall certainly give her a fair trial. Still, please don't hire any more servants without checking with me first."

"Of course," Clarissa agreed, happy that her impulsive decision would not be countermanded. "You are the best of sisters!"

"And you have a kind heart, my dear." Gemma patted her hand.

Clarissa smiled in pleasure, and then fell silent, thinking of what she must teach her new protégée.

The new lady's maid, Matty, turned up at the Fallon house before dinner that same day. Either Mrs. Prescott had been impatient to get rid of the girl, or perhaps Matty herself was eager to leave her former employer, a notion Clarissa could certainly believe. The butler came in to inform his mistress. Gemma, who had been sitting in the drawing room with Clarissa, sent for the girl at once.

When Matty appeared, dressed in a drab dark gown, she looked a little pale. "Ma'am, I mean, my lady," she said, dropping a curtsey to Gemma and to Clarissa. "And miss."

"Thank you for coming," Gemma said, her tone gracious, while Clarissa smiled encouragement. "I understand Miss Fallon has offered you a position as her lady's maid. Have you previously performed any duties in this area?"

"I 'elped out a few times when Mrs. Prescott's cousin visited her, ma'am—milady. And I will do my very best, I swear. I don't usually break things, 'onest!"

"We will engage you for a fortnight, and if all goes well, then consider making the position permanent. And you will be given a fair chance, I assure you."

"Thank 'ee, milady." The girl bobbed another nervous curtsy.

Clarissa stood. "Come upstairs, and I will show you where my room is, Matty. Then the housekeeper can assign you to a room in the servants' quarters."

Once they were out in the hall, she added, "Don't worry, Matty. No one is going to throw you out at your first mistake."

"Oh, I will try so hard, miss, I will," the girl said, her tone fervent. "I do so thank 'ee for the chance."

"I'm sure you will learn all that you need to know, and we will get on very well," Clarissa told her. She showed the girl her own bedchamber, the clothespress that held her gowns, and explained the household routine. "I can tell you a good deal about caring for the gowns, and so on. But as for the hair—"

Clarissa considered, then, with Matty still in tow, went in search of Miss Clemens, the older lady who served as Gemma's personal dresser. Clemens, a birdlike little woman with a habitually stern expression, agreed to give Matty lessons in arranging hair.

Matty expressed such fervent thanks that the other servant looked gratified, and Clarissa could hope that this would work. Then she took Matty to see the housekeeper and left her in that woman's capable hands.

When Matty returned in time to help Clarissa change for dinner, the girl was outfitted in what was almost a proper uniform, even if the apron was a bit too large for her and turned out to be one of Ruby's spares, and her borrowed cap kept slipping down over her eyes.

But she was cheerful, even if still a bit nervous, and listened carefully to all of Clarissa's instructions as she helped Clarissa into a dinner dress. And that night, when she assisted Clarissa in disrobing and brushed out her hair, the maidservant handled Clarissa's fair tresses as if they were attached to a Dresden shepherdess and might break if Matty pulled too hard.

"I'm not made of china," Clarissa pointed out, smiling. "You're doing first-rate."

Over the next few days, Clarissa quite enjoyed seeing that Matty learned the household routine. She instructed her in how to care for her new mistress's clothes, and Matty, under Miss Clemen's supervision, made strides in dressing Clarissa's long fair hair.

As the days passed, Clarissa found that Matty was devoted to her, still grateful for the post and the rescue from her last employer, and the girl's unconditional loyalty somehow gave Clarissa herself more confidence. She did not feel as awkward with Matty as she sometimes did with the other servants.

Lord Gabriel Sinclair rode up to the small *cottage and* looked over the grounds with a thoughtful eye. He owned an estate of his own, which included a number of tenant farms, and he had learned a great deal about agricultural methods since he had given up his wandering and reshaped his life as a responsible landlord and master.

This small plot of land did not seem prosperous. The

garden behind the house was green, but its rows of plants were not as tall as they should have been at this time of year. The goat tethered to a line and nibbling on a clump of weeds revealed the outline of ribs beneath its coarse hide, and the cottage itself was in need of repairs. The thatched roof wanted mending, and the doorstep could use a good sweeping.

A squarely built man of medium height, dressed in rough country clothes, paused as Gabriel rode up. A hoe over his shoulder, he stared at the newcomer with surprise.

"I'm looking for Mistress Molly Goodman? Is this her cottage?"

His thin lips turned downward, the farmer hurumped and made a motion toward the house, then turned and walked on toward the field. Gabriel decided to take the inarticulate response as an invitation.

He dismounted with a fluid, easy grace and tied his horse to the post by the doorway, rubbing its dark nose for a moment, then he rapped with his knuckles on the door frame. The door stood slightly ajar. The day was warm, and the countryside flooded with dappled sunlight as small clouds flitted across the blue sky.

"Nellie, see to the door," a feminine voice called. "If it's a good-for-nothing peddler, tell him we got no blunt to spare."

The door opened wider, and a small girl peered out, then stared with wide eyes at Gabriel's well-cut riding coat and breeches. "Mum? T'ain't no peddler, but a gen'lman."

"What are you on about? Why would a gen'lman— Oh, I beg your pardon, sir." The woman who had followed the child to the door sank into an awkward curtsy. She had a smaller child tucked under one arm and a wooden spoon in her other hand. "Did you mistake the road, mayhap? The turn to the big house is up the lane a good 'alf mile."

"No, I am not seeking the local squire," Gabriel told her, keeping his tone gentle. The woman looked almost as alarmed as the child had done to see such a strange sight appear on their doorstep. "I have come in search of a Mistress

Mollie Goodman. She was once, many years ago, lady's maid to my mother, Lady Gillingham. I have traced her through several addresses, and I'm hoping you can tell me more."

A pause, and the woman's mouth pursed. Gabriel waited patiently.

"I— Why you be seeking her, sir? She done no wrong, surely?"

"Of course not. In fact, I wish to offer my thanks for all the years she offered loyal service; my mother was very attached to her. And I have reason to believe that Mistress Goodman was dismissed abruptly and, likely, unfairly from her post."

The woman blinked, a flicker of new emotion crossing her face. "I think you have the right of that, sir, or should I say me lord?"

"Lord Gabriel Sinclair," he told her, trying to suppress the surge of hope that rose inside him—he had been disappointed too many times already. "Do you know where I might find her, then?"

"Reckon so," she said, with a countrywoman's terseness. She stepped away from the door and nodded to him. "Please come in, sir—me lord—if you would. She don't walk so well anymore, or I would have her come out to you."

His heart leaping—would his long search at last bear fruit?—Gabriel stepped eagerly into the cottage. He saw one big room, neatly made beds tucked into the corners under the eaves, a rough-hewn table holding bowls and other crockery, a small fire on the hearth with a pot bubbling over it, and— again, his pulse jumped—in a chair drawn up to the side of the fireplace, an elderly woman in a neat patched gown, with her graying hair plaited and coiled into a tight bun.

He came closer and gave her as smooth a bow as he would have done to a royal lady. "Mistress Goodman?"

Looking bewildered, she blinked at him, and his hope flickered. Was she senile, her memories and her wit stolen by the passing of time? Was he too late, again?

But the woman who had greeted him came up beside him,

explaining, "She ain't been Goodman for a long time, me lord. She's been Mollie Cutter these many years. After she came away, she married, you see, having a small pittance that her mistress had given her. When me father died, I was the only surviving child. Now me husband runs the farm. It's all ours, what there is of it, though it's a small place to feed so many."

Gabriel saw several other small children peering at him with shy gazes, but he turned back to the older woman. "Mistress Cutter, did you once serve my mother, Lady Gillingham? Do you remember that time in your life?"

"Of course, I do, me lord," the woman said.

Her thin voice revealed her age, but now he could see that her eyes were sharp and aware as she stared up at him. He drew a deep breath of relief.

"You have to be the second boy, Lord Gabriel. Always was a beautiful child, if I say so, who shouldn't. Your mother called you Gabe, and she thought you was an angel, me lord, you gave her that much happiness."

Emotion flooded him, and he pushed it back. Not now, he could not be weak now. He must remain intent on his goal.

"But why you be seeking me, me lord?" she went on.

"I came to thank you for all you did for my mother," he said simply.

The woman smiled. "Does her ladyship still remember me, then?"

Gabriel pressed his lips together, then said carefully, "I'm afraid my mother passed away some years ago."

The flash of pleasure faded, and the old woman's eyes glinted with tears. "Ah, poor lady. Mayhap she is happier in Heaven. She had a hard time of it, you know."

"I do know," Gabriel agreed, pushing back a mosaic of memories, both good—his mother holding him, smoothing his hair and smiling down at him, singing lullabies to him in his bed—and bad, his father shouting and brandishing the whip whose bite the young Gabriel had felt upon his shoulders too often. . . . "So your support must have meant even more to her, and I am forever grateful to you for that. But I have another reason for seeking you out."

He hesitated, and she watched him, wary for the first time. "Did the marquess send you, me lord?"

"The marquess you knew is dead. My brother holds the title now, and he is much more fair-minded, I promise you."

"I'm glad to hear it, me lord, though I know I shouldn't speak about me betters. . . ." She hesitated.

"I need to know, I have reason to believe—" He tried to find the right words. He'd had months to think about this, but it was difficult to ask. "If there was ever a time when my mother withdrew from Society . . ."

"Precious little society she ever enjoyed, if you'll pardon me," Mollie Cutter said, her tone tart. "They called upon the local gentry, in the beginning, went to London once or twice—how me lady enjoyed those excursions!—but then the marquess, the late marquess, grew so jealous, like a dog with a bone he was, if you'll pardon me for saying it. After a few years of marriage, me lady was much a prisoner in her own house, especially after you was born. . . ."

Afraid to stop the flow of words, Gabriel nodded.

"Years later, when you and your brother had been sent away to school, the marquess took himself off to Dover on business. Gone a week or more he was. After he came back, one of the footman—a rat-faced little weasel hoping for a coin or two—told him me lady had gone away for a few days herself." Mollie rubbed her arms as if remembering the blows that had followed this disclosure, and her expression darkened. "It weren't natural, me lord, shutting up the poor woman like that." Her tone was defensive.

"Of course it was not," he said quickly.

But her spate of words seemed to have stopped. She stared into the fire, and her gaze was far away.

"I don't blame my mother or you. I'm glad you were there to support her," he told her again. "Why did my father send you away? I'm sure it was against my mother's wishes."

She hesitated, pushing her thin lips together, and glanced back up at him.

"I wonder," Gabriel prompted, "if there might have been a time when my mother might have been confined . . . by some illness, perhaps, or have gone away to some watering place for her health?"

The old woman snorted "The marquess wouldn't never have allowed her to leave, me lord. But yes, some time after that, she took to her room—was ordered to take to her room, I should say. . . . I was the only one allowed to attend her; even the rest of the servants weren't permitted to see her, and the marquess was such a harsh master, no one dared argue. The marquess made out she had a pleurisy, though he never called a doctor to her." She paused again, and then looked up at him, her faded eyes shrewd.

"Nowadays, these round gowns, they hide a lot, me lord. But twenty-odd years ago, fashions were different, and a lady's condition was harder to conceal. So you know about the babe, then?"

Gabriel felt a tingle as sharp as a fiery spark scorching bare skin, but he kept his expression even. "Yes," he said. "You are not betraying any confidence."

She sighed.

"I delivered her, and I was the one who smuggled her away, me lord. Your mother was afeared what the marquess would do . . . but she cried her eyes out, she did, when she gave the infant into me arms." The old woman's own eyes dampened again from the memory. "I took the poor mite to a lady friend your mother trusted. Did the babe live?"

Gabriel nodded. "I found my sister only this year," he said. "But she is well."

The old woman crossed herself. "Oh, it does me heart good to hear that. I was so afeared. . . . But the marquess— he'd already suspected I had smuggled letters out for your poor mother, and then after I took away the child, he threw me out. I wasn't sorry to leave that miserable household, begging your pardon, me lord, but I hated to leave your mother all alone. The woman who replaced me, she hadn't a flicker of courage in her, and I knew your mother would be left friendless."

They were both silent for a moment, then Gabriel said slowly, his throat aching with the effort to sound as if the answer did not matter, when it so desperately did. "And those letters . . . do you recall to whom you sent them, Mistress Cutter?"

She looked up at him. "I never saw his name. She was afraid to put it on paper, you see, in case her husband— She sent them through an agent, I think."

"I see." The disappointment was overwhelming. To come so close . . .

Then the old lady added, "But they were addressed to Yorkshire, me lord. I'm afraid I don't recall more than that."

The darkness lifted.

Gabriel pulled himself together and thanked her again. And when he walked outside with Molly Cutter's daughter and saw the stout man as he came up from the field, with muddy boots and a still resentful air, Gabriel took out a good handful of silver and handed it to the woman.

"Lady Gillingham would wish your mother to have some reward for all she did," he told her.

The woman's eyes widened. "Oh, thank'ee, me lord. This is most good of ye."

Making sure he spoke loudly enough for the man to hear, Gabriel added, "I will arrange with my man of business to see that a suitable pension is paid to your mother, for as long as she lives. I know that she has earned it."

The woman gave a curtsy and stuttered her thanks.

But Gabriel was sure that it was he who had the most cause to rejoice as he mounted his horse and rode away. Not much, but a hint, a clue, after all these weeks—a step closer to finding his father.

Only a day or two later Clarissa gathered enough courage to venture out, with Matty at her side, for a short errand into the shops. Clarissa found a new bonnet to go with the two new dresses that Gemma had insisted that they order for her, and also purchased a quite fetching shawl, charging it all as usual to her brother and Gemma's account. It was becoming easier to think that she could afford such luxuries and even had the right to wear them.

And, remembering her days in service when she had never had the pleasure of small treats, she made sure to buy Matty some bright pink hair ribbons to wear on her afternoons off, which turned the maid's cheeks almost as pink with pleasure.

They walked out of the shop with Matty carrying the hat box, and Clarissa still holding the forest green shawl, which had such a lovely silky feel. It would go very well with one of the new dresses . . .

And just as she was feeling more throughly at ease than she had in days, they ventured back onto the street, and Clarissa looked up and saw it.

The face . . .

It was the woman whom Clarissa feared most in all the world. And she was here.

Seven

Clarissa froze.

She stopped so abruptly that Matty bumped into her. "Oh, sorry, miss," she said. Then, glancing at her mistress's face, Matty frowned. "Is somet'un wrong?"

How could Clarissa explain that her heart hammered, and her eyes seemed to film over from sheer terror? The stout woman stood a few feet away on the crowded sidewalk. She was speaking to a slightly built young man whose back was to Clarissa, and she was dressed quite respectably in a brown silk gown. She had a nice Norwich shawl knotted loosely about her shoulders, and her bonnet was adorned with bright flowers.

Could Clarissa be mistaken? She had never seen Mrs. Craigmore dressed so well. Perhaps she had been misled by a surface resemblance, and this was not the woman Clarissa remembered. After all, it had been years since she had seen the matron of the foundling home, the woman who had been such a scourge during Clarissa's time in that miserable place.

She tried to still her pounding heart as the woman fin-ished her conversation and turned toward her. If she saw Clarissa—

Clarissa's first instinct was to flee in panic just as she had done before.

No, she would not! She drew a deep breath and gathered all her courage. If this was not the woman she thought it was, she was frightening herself with phantoms. And if it was the same woman— Clarissa would not run away again!

She was no longer an orphan without anyone to sustain her, an unprotected child abandoned to a poorly run foundling hospital. She was grown up now, and she had family about her. Clarissa thought briefly of her brother; she would not let Matthew and Gemma down.

So even though her knees shook beneath her thin muslin skirts, she stood her ground. And when the woman came to-ward her, Clarissa called, "Mrs. Craigmore!"

The stout woman paused, and her smug expression al-tered into something almost like alarm. "What—what do you mean? You 'ave the wrong person, miss."

But by now Clarissa was sure that her first impression had been correct. They stood very close, and she could not con-fuse the face or the form of her old foe, even if the woman's clothing was different and her person more presentable.

Clarissa lifted her chin in defiance. "I'm not mistaken, and I know who you are. How could I forget you? With your shouts and your beatings and your miserly meals, you made much of my childhood miserable."

The matron's eyes narrowed. "You! I remember you, never could 'old your tongue! You witless girl, what are you doing here?"

"I am not witless, and I am not a girl any longer!" Clarissa declared. "I am quite grown up. I survived despite your mis-treatment. In fact, you misused all the children in your charge and mishandled the funds entrusted to you. You ran away from the foundling home, but the authorities are still search-ing for you!"

A few people glanced at them.

"Nonsense!" the matron blustered, but her round cheeks seemed to have paled. "I 'ave no notion what you are saying. You are obviously quite out of your 'ead. Be silent and do not speak so to your betters!"

"You are not my better in any way, not in class and certainly not in morals!" Clarissa shot back. "You are an evil woman, and if my brother or I have anything to say about it, you will pay for your crimes!"

More people were staring, and a handful paused on the pavement to watch the scene. Mrs. Craigmore glanced about her, and her mouth tightened.

"You are raving," she said again, paying strict attention to her diction as if aware of their growing audience. "I will not listen to such drivel, from someone who is probably only a serving girl herself or a clerk from the shops."

"My mistress is a lady!" Matty said from behind them, her tone indignant. "Don't you speak to 'er so!"

But the matron ignored the interruption. "I have better things to do than be insulted by an unbalanced servant." Shaking her head, she tried to push past Clarissa.

With some wild idea about holding the woman until the watch—or Matthew—could be summoned, Clarissa grabbed her arm.

But the woman was more heavily built, and she still had the strength that Clarissa had experienced firsthand, back in the days when the matron had too often struck the children with her heavy rod. At least this time her hands were empty, save for a large embroidered reticule hung over her wrist, and she had no weapon with which to lash out. Clarissa tried to hold her, but the older woman was too powerful. After a few moments of almost silent struggle, Mrs. Craigmore pushed Clarissa aside and disappeared into the crowd.

Some of the spectators muttered, but no one moved to stop her.

The taste of defeat bitter in her mouth, Clarissa watched

the woman slip away. She found that she was trembling now, as much with frustration and disappointment as with fear.

"Are you all right, miss?" Matty asked, her voice anxious.

"Yes," Clarissa said, although she had to lean against the wood railing of the nearest shop front. She felt weak from shock and disappointment as well as the physical effort it had taken her to confront her old nemesis. "I need to speak to my brother at once. If you see a hackney, please hail it."

The street was crowded, but in a few minutes, the maid found a carriage and, waving her arms, was able to flag it down. They were driven back to the Fallon house. As soon as the hackney driver had been paid, they hurried inside.

The butler, who had opened the door, stared at them.

"Is my brother at home?" Clarissa blurted.

Looking surprised at her agitated manner, the man nodded. "Indeed, Miss Fallon. He is in the library—"

At last, a piece of good fortune. Clarissa ran to find Matthew and, her words tumbling out, told him what she had seen.

"The matron—Mrs. Craigmore—I saw her—"

Through another miracle, he managed to make sense of her almost incoherent sentences. When she had stammered out her story, he repeated, "On Bond Street?"

"Yes, in front of the hat shop where—oh, what is the name of it?"

Matty had waited in the hallway, but the study door was open. "Mademoiselle Gray's," she almost whispered.

"Yes, that's it, just along from the bookseller's."

Matthew had already risen. "Stay here," he told her. "Do not, on any account, venture out again. I shall see if I can find any trace of the woman or what direction she may have fled."

The matron was surely long gone, but it warmed Clarissa that her brother would take such immediate action. She saw him snatch up his hat from the hall table and hurry out. Now she could go upstairs to the drawing room and ask the still puzzled-looking butler to bring tea.

Matty watched her anxiously. "I'll put the new 'at away and take up your things, miss. Can I get you some'un else?"

"No," Clarissa said. "Thank you, Matty, for everything."

Clarissa tried to pull herself together. No one could understand how much effort it had taken to face that woman. . . . She stripped off her gloves and untied her bonnet, and gave them to the maid.

"What about your new shawl, miss?" Matty said.

Only then did Clarissa look down and realize that her lovely new shawl was missing. Had she dropped it during the struggle? She actually rose and went to the door, thinking for an instant of returning to look for it, but a shiver of fear made her pause, and anyhow, she remembered Matthew's instruction to stay at home.

"I don't know," she said. "It's gone."

"A shame, and it was that pretty, too," Matty told her, then turned and took the rest of her mistress's things upstairs.

Clarissa sighed over the loss, but it could not be helped. She could send a servant back, but there were too many pickpockets and small-time thieves on the London streets to expect the valuable silk to still lie on the pavement unclaimed. And anyhow, she might have torn it when she had grappled with the matron.

She sat alone for a few minutes. Miss Pomshack must be upstairs, but Clarissa did not send for her, preferring some time by herself. When the tea tray came, she found that her hands were still shaking, but she managed to sip a little of the warm brew. In another half hour Gemma returned from a call on friends and found her there.

"What is it, my dear? You look quite distracted, and you've ripped your sleeve."

Clarissa told her the whole story, and Gemma was so sympathetic that Clarissa began to recover her sense of composure.

"It was brave of you to confront her," Gemma said. "I remember how frightening I found the matron, and childhood impressions linger a long time. I do hope Matthew can pinpoint some clue to her flight. Would you like to lie down, Clarissa, or have a sleeping draught?"

Clarissa shook her head. She had no need for repose, and she wanted family about her. Besides, if Matthew found anything, she wanted to hear about it at once.

But when Matthew returned, he was frowning. "I could locate no trace of her," he told them, his voice heavy. "I questioned all the shopkeepers in the area, and no one admits to knowledge of her."

"You don't— You don't doubt that it was her that I saw, do you?" Clarissa asked anxiously.

"Of course not. Even if you have not seen her in several years, you are not likely to mistake the woman. And despite the fact that we have lost her this time, just knowing that she is in London is a step forward. We have you safe now, thank God, but I still mean to see that the matron pays for her crimes. I will make further inquiries and set some runners on watch."

"I'm most surprised that she would be seen in such an area, shopping calmly amid the most exclusive shops in London," Gemma pointed out. "How has she come up so in the world? We last saw her decamping into the woods with her ill-gotten gains, but she cannot have had ample funds to support herself in such style? Silk gowns do not come cheaply."

Matthew frowned again. "We have no way to tell," he pointed out. "It has not been that long ago that you and I frightened her away from the foundling home, and she might have had more money than we knew. I admit I had expected her to flee farther afield, but it's also true that one can hide amid London's masses—just as easily—perhaps more easily—than in a distant but smaller town."

"She has likely changed her name," Gemma mused. "It sounds as if she was most surprised to be accosted as 'Mrs. Craigmore.'"

Matthew nodded. "I'm sure of it; anyone with any wit at all would think of that. But we have a description of her, and we will not give up."

Clarissa listened to them talk over plans, and she was warmed by her family's determination that Clarissa's mistreatment should not go unpunished. She knew that the odds were against them finding the matron again. But at least they were looking, and as for herself, she had faced her greatest fear. This time, she had not run away. Perhaps her nightmares would ease as a result.

Clarissa took a deep breath; she felt as if something inside her had begun to heal at last.

After Matthew went to his study to write out orders for more investigation, Gemma moved closer. "How are you?"

"Better," Clarissa promised. She still felt unsettled, but she would overcome her foolish fears, she told herself. And if she did ever again come across Mrs. Craigmore, or whatever name the woman now went under, the next time it would be the matron who recoiled in fear!

Clarissa and Gemma spent the afternoon quietly. Miss Pomshack was resting in her room, but Clarissa was still too agitated to sleep. After Matthew had finished writing out his orders, he had put on his hat and gloves and departed to set more inquiries in order. Clarissa changed her dress, giving the damaged frock to Matty for mending, and came back downstairs to chat with Gemma. It was not long after that a knock sounded at the door.

The butler went to open it, and from upstairs, Clarissa heard the sound of a familiar male voice.

Clarissa knew at once who it was. She glanced up and met Gemma's eye.

"Do you feel up to a caller, my dear?" her sister-in-law asked.

Clarissa hesitated. But footsteps already sounded on the stairwell, and she felt it would be too rude to turn the earl aside at this point. Or perhaps she just wanted to see him.

When Lord Whitby entered, he made them a polite bow. "Good day, ladies. Are you of a mind to take another turn around the park?"

Gemma said, "Welcome, my lord. How nice of you to come. Clarissa has a bit of a headache today so I'm not sure if she feels up to a carriage ride." She paused and glanced at Clarissa.

She couldn't decide, so she hesitated. She didn't wish the earl to leave so soon—there was something comforting about his presence—but neither was she sure she wanted to go out into public view again.

She looked up at him, and he seemed to catch some hint of her agitated feelings.

"I'm sorry you are not feeling well. Perhaps I should apologize for intruding and quietly withdraw?" he suggested.

"Oh no," she said before she thought. "I am happy to see you, my lord." Then, fearing that she had been too direct, she blushed.

But Lord Whitby motioned to them to be seated and then chose a chair near her own. "Then we will converse, and I will try to take your mind off your aching head." His smile softened the austere lines of his handsome face and made him seem so much less arrogant and top-lofty, she thought; he should really smile more often.

She grinned back at him, and Gemma went to ring for a tea tray. But now there was another interruption, a loud pounding on the door. Gemma paused in the doorway and Clarissa turned her head. Had Matthew found some clue? Why would he make such a noise?

But when the servant opened the door, she heard a rough male voice demand, "Miss Clarissa Fallon live here?"

What in blazes? The servant's reply was inaudible, but now she heard a thumping of footsteps on the stairs.

Already nervous, Clarissa jumped to her feet. The earl rose, too, and all three looked toward the doorway.

A large man in a rough blue coat stood there. "Miss Clarissa Fallon?"

Bewildered, she nodded.

"I been sent to fetch you to the magistrate."

Clarissa heard a roaring in her ears. Dimly, she heard Gemma protest, and saw the man shake his head.

"But you must wait for her brother to return!" Gemma argued. "She cannot go unescorted to the magistrate! What is this about?"

"Ain't supposed to say," the man repeated stubbornly. "Just to bring her in, as I was tol'."

Lord Whitby spoke for the first time, and his tone was grim. "Take off your hat, trooper. What do you mean by barging into a lady's house with such a demand?"

The man snatched off his hat and straightened his shoulders, as if hearing the note of someone used to command. "Beg pardon, miss, I'm sure. And I'm a Bow Street runner these days, sir. Used to be in the army, did you?"

"I did, and runner or not, I cannot countenance this type of behavior," Whitby said, his voice still stern.

"Only doing what I was tol'," the man said again, but he shuffled his feet slightly on the Persian rug.

"But—" Gemma protested. "My husband—"

"I was tol' to bring 'er now," the runner repeated. He seemed to have only one line to his refrain, Clarissa thought wildly, but he had learned that one too well. "Magistrate goes off at three, 'e does, and I 'ave to 'ave this person back afore then."

"I will escort Miss Fallon, Lady Gemma," the earl said. "Do not be alarmed." Although he spoke to them both, his glance went to Clarissa. "We will sort this out."

She could only nod, as her voice seemed to have failed her. Still frowning, Gemma sent the footman for their hats and gloves, and they prepared to set out.

Since Lord Whitby's carriage waited outside, he helped the two women up, directed the runner to sit up front beside the coachman, and took his own seat across from them.

"I cannot think what this is about," Gemma was saying. "My husband was on his way to see the magistrate after making some inquiries on Bond Street. Could the runner have mistaken his directions?"

"We shall see," Lord Whitby answered. "Do not distress yourself." Again, although he answered Gemma, it was Clarissa whom he glanced toward.

Clarissa felt as if the whole world had turned upside down. She muttered to her sister-in-law, "Do you think that Mrs. Craigmore has lodged a complaint against me for accosting her on the street?"

"How would she dare?" Gemma demanded, her tone indignant.

Clarissa pressed her lips together and said nothing else; they would find out soon enough. But if so—oh, how dreadful to have the whole story about the foundling home come out in court, and what on earth would the earl think?

After a query to the runner, the coachman turned the chaise toward Queen Square and the magistrate's office there.

When they arrived, the earl helped them to step out of the carriage, and the runner jumped down and held open the door. Her heart beating fast, Clarissa clung to Gemma's hand as they entered the building.

Inside, she saw a long room that seemed overfilled with people. A couple of young gentlemen, looking the worse for wear, bickered with some official. One of the young swells had a black eye, and the other held a bloodstained handkerchief to his swollen nose. They quarreled loudly in inebriated voices with a stout, gray-haired watchman and with each other.

"It was entirely his fault. If he had not swung at me when I was not looking—"

"Hardly the act of a gentleman—"

"If you impugn my honor, I will call you out!"

"Sirs, sirs," the older man begged. "Please to remember that dueling is against the law, my good sir. Now, then—"

In the corner behind them, another group awaited the magistrate's pleasure. At the front, two men in rough clothes, their sullen faces unshaven and their eyes vicious, stared out at the rest of the room. Clarissa shivered and looked away.

The only other woman in the room was a female dressed in an overly bright gown with a very low-cut neckline, and she, too, seemed under the influence of drink. She was swearing briskly at one of the runners using language that, had Clarissa had time to consider the matter, she was sure should have caused a delicately reared maiden to blush. However, in her time belowstairs, Clarissa had heard most of it before, and she paid little heed. Gemma frowned and kept a close grip on Clarissa's hand.

Clarissa turned her gaze toward the front of the long room. A railing separated the rest of the space from a large desk. Behind it sat an older man in a gentleman's attire, his expression weary. But when he saw the runner leading them up, he turned an emotionless gaze toward Clarissa.

She trembled again. He looked her over as if she had been a heifer led up to the butcher's block, she thought, as fear carved a cold path down her back. Bewilderment struggled with an increased apprehension.

"This is the female I was sent to fetch, sir, as I were instructed," the runner said. "Miss Fallon."

"This is the *lady* you were sent to fetch," the earl corrected. "And I should like an explanation, if you please! Why have you invaded a reputable gentleman's home in this manner?"

"Her brother will be most displeased," Gemma added, "that you should bring his sister, a respectable young lady, into such a place and expose her to such company as this!" She looked around at the rough-looking criminals who waited their turn at the railing.

The magistrate appeared only mildly impressed at their protests. "Not the usual type of female, um, lady, we have in our charge, certainly," he admitted. "But she was directed to our attention. The shop on Bond Street had her address; the clerk said this lady had charged several items today. So, Miss—" He looked down at his notes. "Miss Fallon."

She nodded, her voice seemed to have failed her.

"First, can you identify this?" He picked up a length of muddy green silk, ripped at its edge.

Clarissa blinked. "Oh, my shawl."

"You admit this is yours?"

"I only bought it today," she said. "But—I—I dropped it, I suppose, in the street. How did it end up here? Did someone steal it?"

The magistrate grunted. "That's your story, is it?"

"I—I suppose," Clarissa said, knowing that she sounded uncertain. "I'm afraid I don't understand."

"Nor do I!" Lord Whitby snapped. "Why are you questioning a lady in this manner over such a minor contretemps?"

"It is not so minor as you suppose, sir," the magistrate told him. "And what have you to do with this?"

"I am the earl of Whitby and a family friend," he answered. "This lady's brother was not at home. I could hardly allow two gently bred females to come here unescorted."

"Ah, I see. Miss Fallon, I'm told by several of the clerks and shopkeepers that you had a loud dispute on the street today with an older woman."

It *was* about Mrs. Craigmore! What lies had that wretched woman told now? Hoping that guilt was not etched across her face, Clarissa swallowed hard. "I did."

"And who was this woman?"

"A— Someone I knew years ago," she muttered.

"I'm afraid we shall need more detail than that," the man told her, his eyes narrowing.

Clarissa bit her lip. To explain to the official about the foundling home in the presence of all the listening ears in the crowded room—such a tale would make her the gossip of the Ton. The scandal would be shattering. And why had that wretched woman raised so much a fuss over such a small quarrel?

"I must ask why you are troubling a lady over a such a trifle," the earl broke in once more, his voice matching the magistrate's in sternness. The two men gazed at each other, and for a moment, Clarissa was not sure who would prevail.

At last, the magistrate frowned. "Very well. You shall see why this is a more serious matter than you know. Come with me."

Picking up a cane, he rose from his chair and, moving somewhat awkwardly, turned toward the back of the room. One of the police clerks motioned them around the railing. Clinging hard to Gemma's hand, Clarissa followed the stout man into a hallway, with the earl just behind them.

The magistrate led the way to another door and opened it. A small room was revealed, and a table, and stretched upon was a woman—a woman whose stout form was all too familiar.

She wore the brown silk gown that had surprised Clarissa earlier in the day, and she seemed unconscious or asleep. Her head was turned away from them. Clarissa held her breath, not wanting the matron to wake and accuse her again. What had happened?

"Is she hurt? But I—I did nothing like this," Clarissa stammered. "I mean, I tried to hold on to her arm—I wanted to summon the watch, or even more my brother, to come to my aid, but she was too strong. She pulled away and vanished into the crowd."

"You acknowledge that this is the woman you fought with on the street?" the magistrate demanded.

"I think so," Clarissa said, even as Gemma interrupted.

"It was not a fight, in any real sense of the word, and you cannot believe that my sister-in-law could do any genuine harm to this person—"

But the older man motioned her to silence and spoke again to Clarissa. "You must be sure, Miss Fallon. Come around and look at her face."

Reluctantly, Clarissa stepped closer. An unpleasant odor hung over the prone figure, and the once impressive silk frock was muddy and disheveled.

Clarissa moved with slow steps around the end of the table. When she got her first real look at the matron's face, which was turned toward the wall, Clarissa gasped. For a moment, the room spun around her.

Mrs. Craigmore's face was swollen and its skin bluish in color. Her eyes, which had always been somewhat protruding, now seemed to bulge even more, and they were open wide, her whole expression frozen into a dreadful parody of surprise and horror. Her lips were parted, and her tongue stuck out between discolored teeth. Her throat was dark with bruises— Oh, it was too horrible a sight to contemplate!

Clarissa trembled. As she swayed, she felt a strong arm around her shoulders to support her.

"How dare you show such a sight to a young lady?" The earl demanded. She had never heard him use such a tone.

Buttressed by his strength, she was able to conquer the giddiness that had threatened to overwhelm her. Still, Clarissa averted her gaze from the awful spectacle of the matron's face and glanced down at the white arms and hands of the dead woman. She saw the scrap of green silk still clutched in the matron's clenched fingers. Clarissa's shawl . . .

"She was strangled with the shawl, my lord," the magistrate told them. "And just now, this young lady, even if she is a lady, seems the most likely suspect."

His tone seemed to echo with the grim note of the gallows. Once again, Clarissa felt the room whirl.

Eight

"I didn't kill her!" Clarissa blurted. "I didn't. How could I? We had a horde of people all around us. Don't you think they would have cried out over a murder done under their eyes? I didn't do it, even if she did deserve—"

She felt the warning grip of the earl's fingers on her shoulders and she paused, trying to collect herself.

"She deserved it, did she?" The magistrate's eyes were still cold. "And why would that be, Miss Fallon?"

"She—she was an evil woman," Clarissa muttered, but she looked away from his skeptical gaze.

"Use your head, man," the earl interrupted, his tone harsh. "The dead woman is—was—bigger and heavier and had to be more powerful. Do you really think she would have stood there on a crowded London venue and allowed a lightly built girl to strangle her, even if Miss Fallon had the physical strength, which is highly doubtful? The shawl was dropped in the street; anyone could have picked it up. That gives you no excuse to harass a respectable young lady."

"I still want to know why the young lady thinks the woman—and what is her name, if you know it?—deserved to die," the older man repeated.

"We knew her as Mrs. Craigmore," Gemma put in, her tone steady, but her glance toward Clarissa also held a warning. "Whether she was using that name recently, none of us could tell you. But if you correspond with the magistrate in Middlesex—I will give you the details—you will find that this woman was sought there for her mishandling of funds at the local foundling hospital where she was, until some time ago, the matron in charge."

"And how do you know that?"

"Lady Gabriel Sinclair now heads the board of directors who looks out for the welfare of the orphans who live in the home. I am also on the board and Miss Fallon and I have spent time at the institution. Since Lady Gabriel undertook her charitable endeavors, I'm happy to say that we have made considerable improvement in the conditions at the home," Gemma said, her tone steady.

That was, more or less, true, Clarissa thought, although Gemma had trodden lightly past the more scandalous details and skated around just how and why they had "spent time" at the home. She fought to make her own expression as unrevealing as Gemma's. But her stomach still clenched, and she fought back nausea. She could still see the dead woman's face. . . . oh, was she to be haunted by that horrible woman's image forever?

The magistrate pressed his lips together, but beneath the earl's stern gaze and confronted by Gemma's controlled and unrevealing blandness, he hesitated. "Very well, Miss Fallon, that will do for the moment, but we shall be speaking to you again, most like."

"You have the lady's address," Lord Whitby said. "And we wish you success in your inquiries. But I trust you will think twice before again dragging a gentlewoman out to such a place." His grim tone added to the warning implicit in his words.

Gemma added, "Yes, and now we certainly need to take Miss Fallon home. She has had a severe shock."

Clarissa bit her lip and said nothing at all. But her thoughts raced madly. Who had killed Mrs. Craigmore? Although he put up no more argument, the magistrate continued to regard her with obvious suspicion.

But the man said no more as the earl guided them both out. The big room was still crowded with people, mostly of unsavory look and smelling of cheap gin or ale, as well as unwashed bodies and clothes. A few runners and several other officials oversaw the mob, and one man with wide shoulders but only medium height seemed to start as they passed by.

"Major, sir?"

Lord Whitby paused for a moment and spoke quietly to the man, then hurried to see them out the door. Not until they were again seated inside the chaise did Clarissa take a deep breath, and she almost regretted it because it made her head spin once more.

"Bloody hell," she muttered.

Gemma looked at her in concern but this time did not scold her for her language. "Oh, I wish I had some smelling salts. Miss Pomshack would, if she were here, but I never carry them."

"Put your head down," the earl said, his tone almost rough. "It will keep you from swooning. Do it."

Clarissa dropped her head into her lap, holding her face in her hands. In a few moments, the distressing weakness passed, and she had command of herself again. She struggled to make her eyes focus and to take deep breaths and not disgrace herself further. After they pulled away from the curb, she raised her head.

"Back to the Fallon home, at once," the earl told his driver, then he turned to regard Clarissa.

She had managed to sit up. Dominic hoped she didn't pass out; she still looked very pale. How dare that officious man allow her to witness such a sight! Dominic himself had seen far worse on the battlefield, but violent death was not a subject suitable for a lady.

Still seething, he sat silently until they reached the Fallon residence. He saw the ladies inside, and although he knew he should leave, he felt a curious reluctance to depart. Miss Fallon still looked so frightened, and he felt the need to do— something! So he said a silent thank-you when Lady Gemma turned to him and asked, her tone quiet, "You have been more than kind, Lord Whitby. If you would stay a few minutes more and sit with Clarissa—Miss Fallon—in the drawing room, I will speak to the footman and give him directions to go out and look for my husband. Captain Fallon must be told what has occurred."

"Of course," Dominic said, more than happy to have an excuse to linger. When he saw Miss Fallon upstairs, she sat down, perching on the edge of the elegant settee, but she gazed up at him with troubled eyes.

"You must not fret," he told her. "There is not enough proof for anyone to seriously suspect you of murdering that woman. How on earth he dared to require you to come and look at the— You must put this out of your mind. It is nonsense to suppose that you might be involved in such a crime. He cannot accuse a lady on such flimsy evidence—"

"No," she interrupted. "It's not. That's why I do worry, my lord. You see, I am not really a lady at all."

He stared at her, not sure how to construe such a bizarre statement.

Still pale, but with her expression resolute, she held up her hand to check any protest. "It's true. Not only will you never win your bet, my lord, but I'm certain that if you knew the truth, you would not wish to be associated with me in any way. And you have been so kind today, acting as my champion, standing by me when the magistrate implied . . . I cannot take advantage of your benevolence any longer without telling you the truth."

Few people had called him kind. Arrogant, dashing, insolent, and overbearing—those and other epithets had been laid to his charge. But not kind . . . Still, he did not dare interrupt her now, when she had at last made up her mind to trust him.

So he listened silently while it all came out. It was a strange story . . . her widowed mother's death, her brother away at sea, the dishonest solicitor who had turned Clarissa over to the wretched conditions of the foundling home so that he could pocket the money her brother had been sending home to support her. . . .

Dominic wanted to reach out and put his arms around her, but, afraid that the halting words would die away if he acted on his impulse, he maintained his control and sat very still.

But when she said, her voice trembling, "I was sent away to serve as a nursery maid when I was fourteen—" He must have made an involuntary sound, because she went, if it were possible, even more pale.

"You were put into service!"

She nodded. "My employer was not a very good man, but I avoided—I avoided his—his . . ." This time she swallowed hard. "I worked very hard, and I learned to survive, my lord, although—" She looked thoughtful for a moment, and some of her remembered pain seemed to be pushed aside. "To be honest, I cannot say that I made a very good servant."

He tried not to grunt again, but she looked at him earnestly, as if bound now to confess everything. "I was not very respectful, you see, and once—once I put rocks in his oatmeal, after he had caned me for forgetting to lay the fire in the schoolroom."

He laughed this time; he could not avoid it. She looked at him in surprise.

"I wish I could put a sword through his heart," the earl told her. "That anyone should mistreat you so!"

She bit her lip. "But you see what they will say, if it all comes out. Mrs. Craigmore beat me many times because I *would* talk back to her, especially when I was first sent there.

I kicked her in the shin once, quite hard, and she never did make me say I was sorry . . . although I bore the bruises from the beating that followed for a bloody se'night."

She sighed, and Dominic tried not to show the surge of anger he felt at the dead woman. Just as well she *was* dead, or he might have strangled her himself!

"Perhaps that was one reason the matron was very ready to send me away. I'm afraid I'm not very good at holding my tongue, even when I know I should. They will say I killed her out of revenge, or even that I've gone off my head after enduring such an unladylike ordeal at the foundling home and afterward." Clarissa wrung her hands together for a moment. "And I think it only fair that you should know the truth, so you can avoid me in the future. Assuming they do not send me to the Old Bailey, that is, or—or hang me."

Her voice quivered, and Dominic put out one hand to grip both of her small ones as she gripped them tightly on her lap.

"No one is going to send you to prison, and you will certainly not be harmed. Trust me, I promise you I will see to that."

Her expression lifting a little, she gazed up at him. "But you cannot want to know me, or claim my acquaintance, after this."

"I am not such a faintheart as that," Dominic told her. "What on earth have you done that you should be ashamed of, or suffer for, now? You were a child. You had no control over what happened to you."

"But you know what the Ton would say if they know—when they know," she argued. "No one will receive me. After all of Gemma and Matthew's efforts, or even yours, I will be forever disgraced."

That, he could not argue with. Even Dominic's so-called influence over Society's elite would not be sufficient to erase such an unusual history. He pressed his lips together. "Then we must be sure that it does not come out, not in court, nor anywhere else."

"But the magistrate—"

He grimaced. "A shame, for once, that the man we saw today is not one of the 'trading judges.'"

She blinked at him. "What?"

"A magistrate who can be bribed," he explained. "No, we will simply have to find out who really killed that repugnant woman. Then you will never have to appear in court, and no one will have to hear the story."

The new look of hope in her eyes was reward enough, even though she demanded almost at once, "But how?"

"I have one ace in the hole," he told her. "And I had better go and see about palming it."

When Gemma returned, with apologies for her delay, the earl made his good-byes. Clarissa tried to express her thanks, but he waved them away. After he bowed to them, she watched him go with real regret.

"My poor dear," Gemma said when they were alone. "Should you like tea or a glass of wine, for the shock? Perhaps you should lie down for a while?"

"No, I think—" Clarissa began, but then she paused as Miss Pomshack came into the drawing room.

"My dear Miss Fallon," she said. "The servants are saying—that is, I cannot credit the stories I am hearing, but I fear you are in some distress?"

Clarissa simply could not bear more platitudes, as good-hearted as her governess-companion undoubtedly was. Clarissa sent Gemma a swift look of entreaty and said, "Yes, it has been a distressing morning, Miss Pomshack. I was just about to lie down, but I'm sure Lady Gemma will explain."

Gemma shot her back a look of understanding. "It was an appalling misapprehension, but it did upset Miss Fallon."

"Ah," Miss Pomshack said wisely, thought curiosity still struggled with compassion on her long face. "Perhaps I should make up one of my tisanes for you?"

"Thank you, that would be most helpful," Clarissa told her. "And yes, I think I will go to my room for a short rest." Anything to escape Miss Pomshack's truisms, she thought, trying not to feel ungrateful for that lady's good intentions.

But once she shut the door to her own bedchamber, Clarissa found herself pacing up and down the room, too restless to lie upon her bed. That dreadful swollen face—had even the wicked Mrs. Craigmore deserved such treatment? Mind you, it was much what one would experience when they put a noose around a condemned person's neck. . . . Would they really convict Clarissa of the murder?

Shivering, she swore briskly, here where no one could hear her and be offended. It was better than bursting into nervous tears! And then she remembered the touch of the earl's hand upon her own nervously clenched ones, and how strong he was . . . how stern he had been in the magistrate's office and how kind when they were alone. One might almost think that he really cared what happened to her. . . .

Some of her fear eased. When Miss Pomshack came up with the tisane, Clarissa was able to thank her sweetly and sip a little of bitter-tasting herbal drink. When her governess had departed, looking pleased to be of service, Clarissa poured the rest into her slop jar.

Then she did lie down briefly upon her bed, wondering what the earl was doing now, and how soon he would return.

When Gemma came up later to check on her, Clarissa explained she had told Lord Whitby about her past.

"And he still wishes to help," Clarissa added. "He is so kind."

Gemma looked thoughtful. "Yes," she agreed. "Very kind."

When Dominic had left the Fallon house, he jumped into his carriage before the startled groom could offer to put down the steps, and directed the coachman to return to Queen Square. There, not wishing the magistrate to see that he had returned, Dominic gave careful directions to his groom and sent him inside the office.

Fortunately, the runner who had spoken to him was still there, and within a few minutes, the groom was able to locate the man amid the crush. Soon they both returned, and Dominic motioned to the runner to climb into the carriage.

"Major, sir," the man said again. "Or is it me lord, nowadays?"

"Lord Whitby," Dominic told him, "When my father died, I had to leave the army and take up my duties at home. Your name is Rubbles, isn't it? I'm glad to see that you survived Waterloo."

The man grimaced. "Oh, they sent me off to that bloody war in the Americas, sir. We fought in a damned swamp in a place called New Orleans, and ol' Packenham made a real mishmash of the battle, he did, not like Wellington would 'ave done. And I missed the excitement in Belgium."

"You're lucky to be in one piece, trust me," Dominic told the ex-trooper dryly. "The excitement, as you put it, was a carnage, even if we did manage to scrape through it and defeat Napoleon once and for all."

The man nodded. "At any rate, not much to do in the army these days, sir—I mean, me lord, so 'ere I am."

"Yes, and I would like to hire your services. Runners are available to private citizens in distress, I believe."

"Indeed, me lord, it would be an honor," Rubbles answered, his tone hearty. "Lost some valuables, 'ave you?"

"I have a young friend who is in danger of losing much more than a few pieces of silver," Dominic told him. "I need to find out more about the woman whose body was brought in today, the one who was strangled. Where did they find her, by the way?"

"In an alley, sir, me lord, not that far from Bond Street. Strangled, she was, with that fancy shawl. Silk is quite strong, you know, when it's of good quality," the man said, with the relish of the professional.

"Do you have any information about her activities? We have reason to think she was involved in criminal activity."

"Is that so? She ain't known in our lists, me lord, not in this parish."

"What about in surrounding districts?"

The runner shrugged. "We only know about the crime what 'appens in our own streets, me lord."

"Make that your first line of inquiry," Dominic suggested. "By then, I'm sure I will have more for you to do. Here's my card. Come round tonight before dinner and let me know if you have found out anything." He detailed a careful listing of the information they knew about her, which unfortunately did not take long.

"Yes, me lord, an 'onor, me lord," the man said, his tone eager. "Good to be working 'neath your command again, if I may say so, me lord."

Dominic acknowledged the tribute and took his leave, but he was thinking hard. If the late unlamented matron had been as harsh as Miss Fallon had said, and he was sure the young lady was speaking the truth, there must be many who might harbor a grudge against that wretched woman.

Of course, finding the real killer amid London's teeming lower classes was like searching for the proverbial needle in the haystack. He swallowed a groan. No, they were only beginning, and he could not relinquish hope so easily. It was necessary to find the killer to safeguard Miss Fallon's reputation and perhaps—even though he would not admit it to her—her life. He could not, would not, rest until it was done, and she was safe.

Lost in thought, he sat in the carriage until a passing coal cart made his team shift nervously at the rumble of the heavy vehicle, then he remembered to tell the patiently waiting coachman to take him home.

It seemed a very long day until Dominic could expect to hear the first report from the runner. However, when the man did return, to be invited into Dominic's study and given a glass of port, which he gulped down in a way that made the butler wince at such mistreatment of fine wine, he had little of importance to disclose.

"None of the surrounding districts reported any criminal

activity as put to this woman's blame, me lord. In fact, I couldn't find a soul who 'eard of a Miz Craigmore."

"You asked for her by name?" Dominic asked.

"O' course, me lord."

Dominic sighed. He remembered now that this soldier had been a resolute fellow, but better at following orders than thinking up any enterprising innovation of his own. Brave of heart but perhaps a little shy of wit, in fact.

"She will most likely not have been using that name any longer," he explained, keeping his tone even with some effort. "You will need to inquire for a woman of her build and general appearance."

The runner looked dismayed, as well he might. "Pardon, me lord, but there's 'eaps of short, portly women who engage in criminal activity. That could take a long time, and then we'd 'ave to sort through the most likely suspects."

"I agree," Dominic told him. "I never said this would be easy. But I don't care how long it takes, or how much it costs, the effort is vital."

"Very well, me lord," Rubbles said, but his expression was still doleful.

Dominic poured him one more glass of wine to cheer him, then sent the man on his way. But when he went into the dining room a short while later, Dominic ate his solitary dinner without much appetite. If Clarissa Fallon's fate depended on the honest but not overly bright runner, she could be in danger, indeed. He would certainly have to take a hand himself. And if Dominic felt uneasy, what was she feeling now?

He would have to go back tomorrow and try to reassure her, Dominic told himself as he sliced so hard at a piece of tender beefsteak that it slid across the china plate and splattered the white linen that covered the table. Of course her family would gather around her, but Miss Fallon might still need someone of influence to stand by her and rally her spirits—merely as a concerned friend, of course.

In fact, Miss Fallon was having the same problem with her own appetite. Clarissa stared at a piece of roasted chicken as if it might turn on the plate and attack her, as unexpectedly as had the strange twist of Fate today. It seemed that Mrs. Craigmore could threaten her happiness even from the grave. Clarissa shivered.

Gemma seemed to notice. "Clarissa, try to put it all out of your mind. We will not allow you to be punished for a crime you did not commit."

"They would not dare accuse a lady on such flimsy grounds," her brother added. Matthew had been shocked and indignant when he had heard the news and had gone round at once to have angry words with the magistrate.

But the magistrate *had* accused her, even if not yet formally, Clarissa thought. She glanced up at them, grateful for their love and support, but unable to share her deep sense of unease. Just as she had been feeling almost restored to what her brother would call her "suitable place in Society," she had once again been plunged into uncertainty, feeling unprotected and at the mercy of those in authority—figures who had, in her previous experiences, proven highly undependable. She had felt just as anxious and frightened when, as a girl, she had been dumped on the doorstep of the foundling home and given into the cruel care of Mrs. Craigmore.

"It would be most improper!" Miss Pomshack agreed as she took a dainty bite of her chicken. "A lady in Newgate!"

Clarissa shivered, but Miss P did not seem to notice that her soothing words were having the opposite effect than she must have intended.

Perhaps that good lady, as well as Matthew and Gemma, believed all the comforting reassurances they were offering her. Clarissa found she could not. So she could swallow little at dinner, and later, after Matty had helped her change and had brushed out her long fair hair, Clarissa climbed into bed but found sleep hard to come by.

And when she did drift off, she dreamed of being caged behind prison bars with the shadow of the hangman's noose falling across her face, and from across the way she saw a group of children who laughed and taunted her. "Cl'rissa's gonna get caned again. Cl'rissa's gonna get hanged again . . ."

They sang the refrain over and over.

She woke to find her face damp with sweat. Shivering, Clarissa found she could not lie still. Rising, she pulled a wrapper about her and went to the window. Pulling aside the draperies, she looked out over the dark, quiet streets, lit only by an occasional streetlight. Most of the houses were dark, all the honest people abed. But out in the darkness, in streets more narrow and littered than this one, another London thrived and stirred and went about its nefarious business. She had had glimpses of that world from her servants' hall and from the foundling home itself.

Why had she dreamed of children taunting her? True, the other girls at the home had made fun of her at first, with her "high class" accent and her fastidious manners. But Clarissa had learned to adapt, and the other girls had not always been unkind. And there had been a shadowy male face in her dream—a boy. There had never been boys at the foundling hospital; where had that image come from? His face had seemed familiar in the dream, but now she found the vision slipping rapidly away.

Clarissa sighed and laid her head against the window-pane, which felt cold against her forehead. As happy as she had been to be restored to her family, to a safe home, she had not valued her rescue enough, she thought. Now that it seemed about to be snatched away from her, she realized just how blessed she had been.

"No," she said aloud, lifting her head and blinking away treacherous tears. "She will not win—she will not defeat me even after her death! I will find some way around this!"

And perhaps, with her brother and Gemma and with Lord Whitby, who so surprisingly had not disavowed his acquaintance even after learning the shocking story of her past, beside her, perhaps, she was not so alone after all.

When the sun peeked over the rooftops of London,

Clarissa returned to her bed and fell into a restless sleep.

She slept late, and when she finally rang for Matty to help her dress, then sipped a quick cup of tea and went downstairs, she found they had an early caller. But it was not Lord Whitby, as she'd hoped, but Gemma's sister-in-law, Lady Gabriel Sinclair, sitting with Gemma and Miss Pomshack.

"I came as soon as I got your note," the elegant blonde was telling Gemma. "I'm so sorry that your brother had already departed for Yorkshire before your missive arrived. Gabriel has found a clue"—she paused and the two women exchanged a speaking glance—"about the man he is seeking, and he was eager to follow up on it at once. Otherwise, I know he would be at your disposal in this matter."

"I do appreciate any help he can give," Gemma answered. "At the moment, we have few facts to investigate, however. Despite that, Matthew has gone out again; he cannot seem to sit still while his sister is so threatened."

"A very natural sentiment," Miss Pomshack declared.

Lady Gabriel nodded in understanding. "But I wished to come anyhow, not only to express my support for Matthew's sister, as of course I would in any case, but to tell you some interesting information that I have come across as I've studied the late matron's books, now luckily restored to us. It's very fortunate that after we thought they were lost, they were discovered in a cubbyhole at the foundling home."

Gemma flushed just a little and seemed to concentrate on pouring out another cup of tea, which she handed to Clarissa.

"I can see why the matron may have stashed them in an out-of-the-way place," Lady Gabriel explained, her gaze on the book in her hand. "During the time that the matron ran the foundling home, her business accounts were very muddled, but it is obvious that not only was she skimming money from the funds that were supposed to go to feed and clothe the children in her charge—"

Remembering the thin, rancid soup that had made up the foundling home's primary meal of the day, Clarissa swallowed, trying not to recall the unpleasant taste.

Looking more serene, Gemma nodded. "I have no difficulty believing that!"

"In order to hide her stealing, I have found evidence in her accounts that she bought and resold food and other goods. This must mean that she had some criminal contacts, ones that perhaps could have reached as far as London. After all, the foundling home lies only a few miles outside the city."

Clarissa gasped. "And if Mrs. Craigmore were connected to such criminals—"

"There could well have been other people who wished her ill—who knows what kind of falling-out they might have had among themselves—and such a lawbreaker would not hesitate to kill," Lady Gabriel agreed.

Gemma glanced from one to the other. "Psyche, this is marvelous! Of course it would be more likely that some falling-out among a gang of thieves would be responsible for the woman's death. But how do we prove it?"

"How do we find the connecting link?" Lady Gabriel agreed. "Yes, that is the question."

Clarissa listened as they discussed the question, and she had a flash of memory. "There was a boy," she said suddenly. "He used to come to the home, to the back door, just as darkness was falling, and collect large bundles. Once he dropped one and I saw flour spill out. . . ."

Setting her cup down so suddenly that the tea sloshed into the saucer, she realized that was the boy she had dreamed about! That was why he had popped up in her dream.

"Yes, yes, what else do you remember, Clarissa?" Gemma urged, her tone eager.

Clarissa bit her lip. "Oh, I can only vaguely recall his image. I saw him only in darkness, and he—he had lank dark hair that fell into his dirty face. He looked ill-fed, and as I recall he wasn't dressed very well. Oh, bloody—I beg your pardon—but if I could just remember more!"

"More of the recollection may yet come back to you," Lady Gabriel suggested. "Often, if you don't strain your mind, the memory will surface of itself."

Clarissa bit back more unladylike words and muttered a polite agreement.

"Perhaps if we went over the lists of goods together," Gemma was telling her sister-in-law. "I studied these books when we were searching for a list of former inmates of the foundling home, but I paid little attention to the lists of household accounts, except to wonder that the matron paid such high prices for food that I do not remember ever seeing on the table. If she were reselling the goods, it all makes more sense."

The other ladies agreed. Gemma summoned the footman, and Lady Gabriel gave him instructions. "Tell my butler to send over the books that are atop my husband's desk in the study," she said.

When the bundle of account books arrived, they all sat down and pored over the accounts. Lists of bread and flour and potatoes and beets . . . Clarissa sighed. It all seemed boring and futile. How was this going to bring them closer to the unknown person who had slain the late matron?

After a time her brother returned. He looked discouraged and weary, but he bowed to their visitor, then put a determined smile on his face when he saw Clarissa jump up as he entered the drawing room.

"Nothing yet," he told them, coming across to give Clarissa a comforting pat on the shoulder.

Gemma rose and touched her husband's hand while a loving look passed between them. They were both worried for her sake, Clarissa thought, trying to push back a tremor of fear.

Gemma explained to Matthew what they were doing, and again, they plunged into the books, turning the ink-stained pages until Gemma exclaimed. "Look, a name!"

"At last," Lady Gabriel said. "Can you make it out? The woman's handwriting is dreadful."

"She obviously needed to practice her penmanship," Miss Pomshack noted, her tone disapproving. "This is hardly a ladylike hand."

Clarissa swallowed a nervous giggle; the list of ladylike virtues the late matron had not possessed would be a long one. They all stared at the page, and Clarissa, who had been pacing up and down, came to peer over Gemma's shoulder.

"Is this a *G* or a *B*?" Matthew wondered aloud.

"I think it's a *G*," Gemma said. "Remember the list of girls we found when we were searching for your sister? This looks like the *G* in my name."

"You're right," Matthew agreed. "*G*, then an *R* or a *K*—"

"Surely, *R* is more likely," Lady Gabriel suggested.

"Very well, *G-R-E*—then what is this last letter?"

He bent even closer to the book. "Grey or Gren, I think. But there is no address."

They turned the pages again, until Gemma exclaimed. "Oh, look, forty shillings, ten pence, and an initial: *G*. And this time a street, as well."

Again they struggled to decipher the matron's cramped writing, arguing over the twisted letters, then at last Gemma pronounced, "It has to be Wren Lane, Whitechapel."

Matthew jumped to his feet. He looked relieved to have something to do. "I shall go to Whitechapel and find this street, and see if anyone knows of this man."

"Can I come with you?" Clarissa asked. She felt as frustrated as her brother, and her heart sank when he shook his head.

"This part of London is no place for a lady, my dear."

"But, Matthew—"

He shook his head, and Clarissa bit back further words of protest. Acting like a lady was all very well, but it was her neck that would be put into the noose if they did not find the real killer!

After Matthew departed, Lady Gabriel also made her farewells. "Lady Sealey has a salon this afternoon, which I had promised to attend. But if you need me, if I can do anything, send word and I will come at once."

The three ladies ate a quiet luncheon, then when they returned to the drawing room, they were discussing a stroll in the park when another caller was announced.

To Clarissa's secret pleasure, it was Lord Whitby.

He mounted the stairs quickly and after bowing to them all, went directly to the point.

"I have had a report from the runner who is collecting information for me."

"Did you find any mention of Mrs. Craigmore?" Clarissa demanded.

He frowned. "Since we do not know what name she was using, it is hard to pinpoint the woman's activities. All I have learned so far is that London holds a great many women of stout build and mature age who are engaged in pickpocketing, petty thievery, and other nefarious activities."

He drew out several papers and unfolded them. The ladies peered at them as he held the lists out for them to see. Clarissa bit back a most unladylike oath. This was worse than the matron's lists of foodstuffs. How could there be so many criminals afoot in the metropolis?

Gemma looked dismayed, as well. "There are so many; how will we ever find which one might have been the woman we knew as Mrs. Craigmore?"

"And this is only two districts; the runner is still collecting names." Lord Whitby frowned. "Some of these women have been sent to gaol, but many are still on the streets, and we have only vague addresses, if that."

"It seems hopeless," Miss Pomshack declared.

Clarissa gritted her teeth. No, they could not give up!

Lord Whitby glanced at her as if he had read her thought. "We are only beginning," he told them. "We will not be discouraged, not yet."

"But there are so many—" Gemma repeated.

"Perhaps—" Clarissa interrupted. "Perhaps we are starting at the wrong end."

Nine

"Never underestimate the power of a curious woman."

MARGERY, COUNTESS OF SEALY

*T*hey all stared at her.

"What do you mean?" Lord Whitby asked, his dark brows drawing together.

"She was very well-dressed when she died—when I saw her on the street the last time," Clarissa said, trying not to see the body in her mind but concentrating on her earlier memory. "A nice silk gown and an expensive shawl."

Since her return to the ranks of the gentry, she had an even greater appreciation for such feminine finery, but her change in social status made her perhaps more aware of the cost of the new wardrobe that her brother and sister-in-law had pressed upon her.

"But why—" Gemma wrinkled her brow.

"I think I see what you mean," Lord Whitby put in. "She was not dressed as we might expect of a pickpocket nor an ordinary snatch-and-run thief."

"Where did she get the money for such a wardrobe?"

Miss Pomshack, who no doubt had practiced her own thrifty habits, put in.

"And for what purpose?" Clarissa added. "What advantage would such a wardrobe gain her?"

"Oh, very good," the earl said, his tone approving.

Clarissa tried not to blush under his glance. When he smiled at her in such a way, it was hard to remember, if she had even wanted to, how much she had disliked his seeming arrogance when they had first met.

"Perhaps she was running some kind of—what is it called?—some kind of flimflam," Gemma suggested. "I mean, who would you be more apt to open your door to? A roughly dressed woman of the street or a middle-class matron dressed in respectable, and by no means cheap, apparel?"

Clarissa nodded. "When I was—" She faltered, then went on, trying to keep her voice steady. "When I was in service, I heard gossip of gangs that would send in one of their members on some excuse, like collecting for charity or asking for direction to a fictional relative's house, to look over the household and see what valuables might be available to a thief. Then later the gang would break in during the night, quickly raid the silverware and other easily looted items while the household was still in confusion, and disappear again into the darkness."

"And then sell the stolen goods," Lord Whitby agreed. "But again, how do we find out just which gang the woman belonged to and where she had been operating?"

"Was there anything in her reticule?" Clarissa asked.

The earl frowned slightly. "According to the runner, no reticule was found with the body, just the shawl that was, ah, on her person."

Wrapped around her neck, he meant, Clarissa shuddered, trying not to remember the swollen face. "When I saw her, she had a large reticule on her arm; it even seemed rather heavy. It bumped my arm as we struggled on the street."

"Interesting," he said. "The murderer might have taken it

or, of course, any chance street thief who saw his chance at easy pickings."

Gemma looked thoughtful. "I think we must search, as Clarissa says, from the other side. While your runner collects more information, we can also do some ferreting of our own."

"How?" Clarissa demanded.

"I will come with you," the earl said, almost at the same time.

Gemma smiled. "I fear you would be a little conspicuous, my lord. I was thinking of the countess of Sealey; she holds a weekly salon where a large group of ladies will be gathered this afternoon. If there is any gossip to be had of housebreakings in well-to-do neighborhoods, there is a good chance that I might hear of it there."

Lord Whitby grimaced. "I see. Very well. I will work on the magistrate's lists of known criminals and any crimes they are suspected of, and you will gather news of domestic thefts. Then we will see if any of the reports match, especially, as you say, in wealthier households."

He took his leave of them, and if, when he bowed over Clarissa's hand, his dark eyes seemed to hold a warmth when he looked at her, she tried not to read too much in to it. At any rate, she had little time to reflect. Gemma had at once called for the carriage. She and Clarissa went upstairs to change into afternoon dresses, then they donned their hats and gloves.

Matty helped adjust Clarissa's bonnet, and Miss Pomshack wished them luck before retiring for her afternoon nap. Clarissa and her sister-in-law set out.

When they arrived at the handsome house and were shown up, Clarissa was pleased to see that today's salon was well attended. Their hostess greeted them with a cordial smile. Gemma drew her aside to murmur in to her ear, and Lady Sealey nodded and flashed Clarissa a quick compassionate glance.

Clarissa drew a deep breath, telling herself that Gemma trusted this woman implicitly. Lady Sealey knew about the search for Gemma and Gabriel's father. The countess would be as discreet with Clarissa's secrets.

Lady Sealey's elegant drawing room was a strange place to search out news of a gang of thieves, but Clarissa was sure that Gemma's idea had merit. So, fueled by the awareness of the importance of their mission, Clarissa plunged, with much less trepidation than usual, into the small groups of women who laughed and chatted and sipped tea.

Across the room Lady Gabriel looked up and saw them. She left the group of friends with whom she had been conversing and came to speak to them. Gemma again exchanged a quiet few words to explain her idea. Lady Gabriel nodded, and they parted again.

At first Clarissa followed in Gemma's wake as her sister-in-law stopped here and there to speak to acquaintances or to listen politely to conversations already going on. The well-dressed ladies around them discussed fashions and parties and Society tidbits, as well as politics and world events and art shows and plays. Lady Sealey's friends were a cosmopolitan bunch. Gemma waited until an appropriate opening and then inserted, discreetly, some comment about a recent burglary in their neighborhood.

London being what it was, this was invariably met with another tale of more audacious break-ins "just down the street, and the whole family upstairs asleep, just fancy! And the servants dozing through it all while the thieves went straight to her mother's best silver, and as for the plate on the sideboard—"

In this way, they collected stories of recent thefts. As Clarissa became more confident, she felt ready to drift away from Gemma and try the gambit on her own. These women, who had seemed so intimidating when she had entered the room, were not that hard to handle, she found. Surrounded by taller, stouter, older women, she was sometimes disregarded, but mostly it was by mischance, Clarissa thought, and she was able to try the opening several times, and again collect stories of recent thefts and house breakings.

When the guests began to take their leave, it did not take a significant glance from the countess for Gemma to motion to Clarissa to hang back. They, and Lady Gabriel, managed to be the last ladies remaining in the salon, and when they were alone with their hostess, Lady Sealey waved for them to sit down.

"Collins, pull the chairs up; my friends and I will have a little chat. And some fresh tea, please."

When the elderly servant took his leave, the countess turned to Gemma. "Now, my dear, did you have any luck?"

"My head is overflowing with tales of lawlessness," Gemma confessed. "I knew crime in London was a problem, but my goodness! Now the problem is to remember them all before I lose track of who told me what."

"We must write it all down," Lady Gabriel suggested sensibly. "Before we forget what we have learned."

"Excellent notion," Lady Sealey said. "There is pen and paper in my desk, Psyche, dear. Why don't you fetch it?"

Lady Gabriel went across and opened the elegant French writing desk and brought back paper, an inkwell, and several quills. Gemma drew up a small table, and for a few moments, all three ladies, Clarissa included, scribbled rapidly.

When at last they paused—Gemma had collected the most names, it seemed—the servant had returned with more tea. Clarissa blotted the ink on her sheet, then accepted a cup, as well as a small delicate cake since she had had little chance to partake of refreshments when she was scouting the salon's ladies, and took a bite as she listened.

"I have half a dozen accounts of break-ins, and at least four of them seemed suspiciously well planned," Gemma said.

"What do you mean?" Lady Sealey asked.

"That is, the thieves went straight to the most valuable and easily portable items, and they were out of the house before the servants or the master of the house could get downstairs to confront them. Sometimes it was done when the man was away and only women and children were at home. None of the four houses had a dog on the premise, and in at least one case, a maidservant was accused of providing information to the gang who broke in, and although she protested her innocence, was discharged."

Pausing with the last of the cake halfway to her mouth, Clarissa wondered if she could find the poor girl and help her find a new post. Matthew might not wish any more servants, but she could ask their neighbors. She would check on the maid's plight.

Lady Gabriel had heard of three more suspicious house breakings, and Clarissa had elicited news of two.

"Nicely done," Lady Sealey told them. "You make clever sleuths, indeed!"

Gemma smiled. "If this is productive, we will accept your praise," she said.

Clarissa sighed and reminded herself not to become excited too quickly. Still, this might bear fruit.

"Lord Whitby said he will come for dinner, and afterward, we can compare our information," Gemma added.

"Really?" the countess answered. "I heard Lady Dobley mention that she was expecting him this evening. She will be disappointed if he breaks the engagement." The older lady turned a thoughtful gaze upon Clarissa.

Clarissa tried not to blush. "He is—he is a very kind gentleman," she said.

"Indeed," the countess murmured. And this time, all the other ladies stared at Clarissa.

On the drive home, Clarissa was silent, and Gemma did not try to make conversation. Was the earl truly breaking a prior engagement so that he could help them examine their newly amassed list of crimes? Was it possible that he had feelings—no, she could not credit it. He could pick from any lady in the Ton. It was only for a good cause, and thank goodness he was inclined to help her. Clarissa was sure she needed all the aid she could find! Gemma had collected all the names and addresses of the thefts and had the papers tucked safely into her reticule.

That turned Clarissa's thoughts back to the murdered

woman's missing bag. Had the matron had anything worth knowing about in her own reticule? If so, it had disappeared.

When they arrived home, Clarissa hurried up to change for dinner, and this time she did not begrudge the effort. If the earl did come, she wished to look her best. Only, of course, because he was being so diligent in trying to secure her safety, she assured herself.

Matty helped her arrange her hair becomingly and tied a blue ribbon to hold back the shorter curls at the front, then Clarissa slipped into a fresh blue-sprigged muslin gown. When Clarissa came downstairs, she felt a small leap of pleasure to see Lord Whitby standing by the drawing room fire, having a glass of wine with her brother.

He bowed to her, and she tried her best to achieve a graceful curtsy. At dinner, the earl was seated at Gemma's right, of course, as his rank demanded, and Clarissa and Miss Pomshack sat across the table with Matthew at the head, but Clarissa had the pleasure of occasionally hearing snatches of the earl's conversation. She was careful to mind her own tongue and to allow no unladylike curses to emerge. Also, by some small miracle, she did not drop her silver nor overturn the sauce boat.

So she was pleased—and her gown unspotted—when dinner ended and Gemma stood and collected the other ladies' attention with a glance. They withdrew, leaving the men to their brandy, but within a short time, Matthew and the earl rejoined them in the drawing room.

"Perhaps we might sit down to a game of whist?" Matthew suggested.

Clarissa looked at him in surprise; her brother was not, as a rule, fond of cards.

But the others agreed, and soon she saw his purpose. Miss Pomshack was not a card player, so she cheerfully bade them enjoyment of their game and withdrew to the other end of the room, near the fire, where she sat down to peruse a volume of wholesome sermons.

Although Matthew laid out a hand of cards, Gemma, who

had taken a seat with her back to the oblivious Miss Pomshack, drew the sheets of paper from her pocket and spread them on the table where they could all see them.

And Lord Whitby reached into his coat and drew out a list of his own.

Clarissa felt her breath quicken. They were all turning into accomplished plotters, she thought, trying not to laugh. But the memory of the dead woman's face, as well as awareness of the lethal penalty that would be inflicted on a convicted murderer, sobered her at once.

While they played the most dilatory game of whist ever, they quietly discussed the two lists and where they agreed.

First, Matthew, his expression dark, told them he had not so far succeeded in locating the mysterious Mr. Grey. "No one on the street will admit to any knowledge of him. But I shall continue the search," he promised his sister.

Clarissa flashed him a grateful smile, though she wondered if he had looked too much the gentleman to easily draw out the denizens of lower-class London.

Then they discussed the other inquiry, on the house robberies.

"We have two that took place in this square alone, and three in the neighboring streets," Lord Whitby pointed out. "Not that far from you."

Gemma shook her head and looked at her husband. "My dear, I think we shall have to get a guard dog. So many, and so close together!"

"I do not think it can be just coincidence," the earl pointed out.

"Not bloody likely," Clarissa agreed, then blushed deeply as her brother glanced at her. Damn, and she had been doing so well, too! Fortunately, the earl didn't seem to notice her slip.

"I know several of these families. I think I should call upon them and make some inquiries," he suggested.

"And not just of the family, but the servants," Clarissa put in. "I had a thought—"

They all looked at her.

Clarissa plunged on. "Gemma said that in one case a servant was suspected of aiding the thieves. My first reflection was that some poor maidservant had been falsely accused, but then I thought many of the foundling home's girls were sent into service when they were old enough. It would be an excellent way to get informants into wealthy houses, if the matron had indeed been connected with some criminal gang."

"But would they agree to help her?" Matthew asked. "Surely they were not all dishonest by nature?"

Clarissa shuddered. "It would be very hard to say no to the matron if you had been accustomed to taking her orders," she pointed out, her tone grim.

Gemma reached across the card table to pat her hand. "I can understand that, as anyone who had spent time under Mrs. Craigmore's control would. You are likely correct, Clarissa."

"And," Clarissa added. "When you go to query the families, my lord, I should go with you. It's possible that I might recognize a servant as a former inmate of the foundling home."

Matthew shook his head. "No, indeed. I do not wish you to risk further danger or embarrassment."

"We are only calling on respectable families," Clarissa argued. "And I would not be alone." She hoped that the earl was not displeased at her suggestion. He had not yet commented, and she carefully refrained from glancing his way.

Happily, Gemma took her side. "I think it is a good idea, Matthew," she said, keeping her voice low. "His lordship will look out for Clarissa. And if there were to be some one among the staff, she is the only one who would recognize a familiar face. I was at the home, too, but only briefly and years ago when I was very young. I'm afraid I would not be much help. I don't remember a great deal from that awful year."

His tone firm, Lord Whitby spoke, "I will most certainly see that Miss Fallon is not in any danger."

"And how will you explain making calls with a young lady by your side?" Matthew asked, sounding skeptical. "It will seem a bit, ah, unusual."

The earl gave Clarissa a glance. "Perhaps I will claim her as a cousin, a fond but distant cousin."

Gemma laughed softly. "If you do, you will have a great many society matrons racking their memories as to who is related to whom, and you must be prepared to explain the sudden connection."

The earl shrugged, with the old arrogance that had once seemed so annoying. Somehow, Clarissa did not find it so any longer. After all, he was doing so much to aid her.

"I will think of a good excuse," he assured them.

Armed with the list of house break-ins, they began the very next day. Lord Whitby arrived just after noon, a proper time for social calls, and he took both Clarissa and Gemma, who had offered to accompany them.

Lord Whitby welcomed them both, and in the carriage, they discussed a story to explain their visit. Whitby knew two of the families slightly, but they would be surprised, he noted dryly, to have him make a formal call.

Gemma suggested saying they were collecting funds for the small foundling home that she and Clarissa had suffered through and that Gemma and Lady Gabriel were now volunteering to oversee. "After all, we may as well get some donations out of this, while we look for information," she pointed out.

"And I have decided to add my patronage to the home, inspired by your and Lady Gabriel's example? Very noble of me," the earl agreed.

But Clarissa knew by now that the gleam in his eye, the humor beneath the wry tone, was as much at himself as anyone

else, and that, when he cocked his head to the side in that familiar way, he was not looking down his nose at her, as she
had first thought, but simply giving her his full attention. In
fact, it was amazing how well she seemed to know him after
what was really such a short acquaintance.

So they approached the first household calmly. The footman did not hesitate to show them in, and if the lady of the
house seemed a little surprised, Mrs. Merdent was also obviously pleased to have such well-connected visitors. Even the
suggestion that they were calling to discuss the foundling
home's needs did not faze her; she was eager to donate a
small sum.

From there, as tea was dispensed, the conversation flowed
into other areas. After a few minutes of gossip, Gemma was
able to mention a burglary in their square, and Mrs. Merdent
was eager to share her own story.

"Oh, we had just such a fright ourselves, only three
weeks past! If I were not such a light sleeper—it's my stomach, you see, and I'd made the mistake of eating lobster
salad for dinner as our cook has this delightful receipt—but
anyhow, I was awakened by a slight sound.. So I got out of
bed and tiptoed down the hall and peeked around the staircase, and there were a positive horde of scoundrels in my
own house!"

"Good heavens, so many?" Gemma asked,.

Mrs. Merdent seemed gratified by their close attention.
"Oh, yes, a dozen at least. We could have all been murdered
in our beds!"

"I woke my husband and ran up the stairs to rouse the servants. The two footmen came down to aid my dear husband—
oh, I was in such a quake that he would be hurt—and then I
ran to the nursery and stayed with my children." The good
lady sighed at the memory.

"Your husband is a brave man," the earl agreed. He had
been sipping his tea and allowing their hostess to chatter on.

"I hope no one was hurt?" Clarissa added.

"Thank goodness, no, except one of the footman got a

nasty cut on his arm—the villains had knives! And they had already cleared the sideboard of the best silver, taken down the clock, which came from Paris, my dear, back before the war began. Even my husband's desk in the study was rifled, but he had only a little housekeeping money there, fortunately, so they didn't get much. But they moved so quickly that all was lost before my husband and the servants could get downstairs to confront them. The footman, the one who was hurt, tried to tackle the last man going out the door, but he was slashed with the blade, and the man got away."

Their hostess fanned herself, and they offered more condolences and asked about the footman, who had recovered, the lady of the house said.

Gemma threw Clarissa a glance. They had discussed another ploy to try. After all, part of the plan was that Clarissa must see the maidservants. "If you would not think it too forward, perhaps my sister-in-law might speak briefly to your staff before we go?"

"Whatever for?" Mrs. Merdent asked, as well she might.

Clarissa tried not to blush. Gemma explained, "Since many of the children at the foundling home are the result of, ah, sad mistakes, we thought it would also be beneficial to remind the servants of the blessings of prudence and modesty."

Mrs. Merdent looked slightly offended. "I assure you, Lady Gemma, my maids are all good girls, and indeed, they always go to church on Sundays."

"Of course," Clarissa agreed quickly. "But they can tell their friends, you know, and a little good counsel from another female can only add to the force of your vicar's sermons."

"I suppose it can do no harm," their hostess agreed. She pulled the bell for the footman. "Peepes, have all the maidservants brought up to the hall; this young lady wishes to say a few words to them."

His startled expression almost made Clarissa giggle, but she was still dreading the "sermon" she must now impart.

As Clarissa followed him into the hall, she heard their hostess say, behind her. "Your sister-in-law is certainly intent on good works, is she not? Is she thinking of going into holy orders?"

Unable to make out Gemma's response, Clarissa swallowed hard. Oh dear, she felt like a total fraud. Worst of all, Miss Pomshack, who had helped her write out her short speech, had thought it an excellent idea! But she would not be harming anyone with her lecture, Clarissa told herself anxiously, even if her motives were not quite what they seemed.

When the girls came up, most of them no older than she, Clarissa looked them over carefully, but no one seemed familiar. She rushed through her short homily, and then added, more practically, "If you know of any orphaned children in your neighborhood, children in want, I mean, who have no relations to support them, the foundling home for girls would offer help, and if there are boys, we will see to their support, too, at another institution. Just send Lady Gabriel Sinclair or Lady Gemma Fallon word, your mistress can give you the directions, and they will see to the children's aid."

To her surprise, one of the younger girls blushed a bright red. When the maidservants turned to go, she avoided Clarissa's eye.

Had she uncovered a former inmate of the home on their first try? One thing was for sure, however, Clarissa could not ask questions under the butler's stern gaze; the little maid would never have the nerve to tell the truth.

The maids disappeared again belowstairs and Clarissa returned to the drawing room. Gemma and the earl stood, and they all made their farewells, with thanks to Mrs. Merdent for her charity.

"Always pleased to help a good cause," she told them. "And be sure to mention my name to your sister-in-law, Lady Gabriel."

"I will, indeed," Gemma promised.

The next house they wished to inspect was only a few yards away, so they did not bother to climb back into the carriage but walked together. When they were far enough to be out of earshot, Clarissa could hardly wait to share her suspicions.

"Did you recognize anyone?" the earl asked, keeping his voice low.

She did the same. "No, not really, but one of the girls colored up when I mentioned the foundling home."

Her expression eager, Gemma looked up. "Did you ask her if she knew anything about the robbery? I must admit, such quick and efficient thievery sounds very suspicious."

"I couldn't, with the footman and the other servants there, lined up in the hall like soldiers," Clarissa explained. "We shall have to question her further later, in private."

The second visit was much like the first. Their titles and the slight acquaintance the earl had with the man of the house—not that he was at home—got them in easily, and though getting permission to speak to the servants was the most awkward part, Clarissa was getting better at her pose of moral instruction. She simply had to pretend to be Miss Pomshack, she thought, sighing a little at the idea of imitating that good lady's always noble intentions.

And this time, when the female staff trooped dutifully upstairs, one of the maids looked distinctly familiar. As Clarissa once more recited, a bit absentmindedly, her lecture on good conduct, she watched from the corner of her eye the thin maidservant with the birthmark on her cheek Did the girl squirm a little at the mention of the foundling home?

And when the staff turned to go, Clarissa tucked the paper into her pocket and managed to snag her fingernail in the lightweight muslin of her gown. She exclaimed in dismay. "Oh dear, I have torn my sash. Could you please render some assistance?" She looked at the servant she had been watching covertly.

The maid hesitated. "Of course, miss. But the 'ousekeeper is better with 'er needle. Mayhap I should fetch 'er?"

"No, no, it's a small tear, I'm sure you can take care of it. If we could just withdraw for a moment?" Clarissa insisted.

The footman showed her to a small parlor, and Clarissa

paced up and down, afraid the maidservant would not return. But the girl reappeared within a few minutes with a sewing kit. She threaded a needle and knelt on the floor to make emergency repairs to the sash of Clarissa's muslin gown. It had taken a good jerk to tear it, but indeed, a few stitches would make it more presentable. While the maid had all her attention on her needle, Clarissa searched her memory, and at last the name came to her.

Hoping that the girl would not stick the needle straight into Clarissa's skin in her shock, Clarissa said, "Becky?"

"'ow you know my name?" Her gaze wary, the serving girl looked up.

"It's Clarissa, Becky, from the foundling home, don't you remember?"

Eyes wide, Becky stared at her. "'ow do you know about that?"

"I had the second bed from the end, and you shared a bed with that girl who snored so loudly, you must remember that."

Becky dropped her needle onto the floor and scrambled to her feet. Afraid she would run out of the room, Clarissa put out one hand. "It's all right, don't be afraid."

"What you doing 'ere dressed like that? Is it some kind of humbug you're playing on me mistress? She's a nice lady and she don't deserve to be done wrong again! This ain't another gang, is it?"

"Another gang?" Clarissa stared at the girl's paled face, the birthmark even more prominent now that she had lost color. "You must tell me the truth, Becky. I promise you that I will see that you are not harmed by it."

"I didn't want to do it." The maid blinked hard against tears. "But it was Miz Craigmore, you know how vicious she could be. She came to the 'ouse collecting for the parish poor 'ouse, and she made an excuse to talk to me. She made me tell her everything, where the best silver was and which plate weren't worth stealing. When the men went to bed, and if my master was out of town any times . . . I didn't want to do it, but she—she said she would palm a piece of silverware and blame it on me if I didn't 'elp 'er. I'd be turned out on the street." The girl bit back a sob. "I been that worried ever since that someone would find out. And I would never do it again, I swear to you."

"I believe you," Clarissa promised. "I don't know if I could stand up to Miz Craigmore, either, when she was at her most bullying."

"She was so 'ard on us when we were in the 'ome." Becky wiped her eyes. "I still shiver when I think of 'er. I just pray she won't come back."

"That you can be sure of," Clarissa told her. "She didn't give you any indication where she was staying in London, did she? She's no longer matron at the home, you know."

Becky looked, for the first time defiant, even if only in retrospect. "She wouldn't 'ave told me."

"Oh," Clarissa said in disappointment.

"But I 'eard her give the 'ackney an address when she left," the maid added.

"Becky!"

"It were Brown's 'otel in Cheapside," the girl said.

Clarissa gave her an impulsive hug. "Oh, that's wonderful, that will be a big help—at least, I hope it will. Thank you, Becky. Are you happy here?"

"Oh, yes, the 'ousekeeper is a pleasant woman, and the mistress so much kinder than Miz Craigmore," Becky explained earnestly. "And the other maids are good to me, too."

"Still, if you ever need help, this is where I'm living now." She told the servant the address of the Fallon house. "My brother was not lost at sea, as the matron told me. He came home and found me, you see."

"Blimey!" Becky looked at her in awe.

After more reassurances from Clarissa, the maid went back downstairs, and Clarissa herself hurried back to the drawing room. The visitors again took their leave.

"Out with it," the earl said when they were hardly off the doorstep. "While we were making boring conversation—

good lord, that woman can talk your ear off!—I can tell that you have learned something much more to the point than how to best roast a peacock, which poor Lady Gemma and I were instructed about in excruciating detail."

Clarissa told them all in a rush.

"Oh, heavens, it is true, then," Gemma said. "How clever the two of you were to suspect such a plot!"

"Clar—Miss Fallon should get the credit," the earl said, just as Clarissa was shaking her head.

"Oh no, I would not have thought of it except for your lists of criminals, compiled with the runner's help."

Exultant over the clue she had uncovered, Clarissa agreed with the other two that their last visit should be as short as possible. And in fact, when they broached the question of speaking to the female staff about proper conduct, instead of looking startled or insulted, the lady of the house threw back her head and laughed.

"All of my maidservants are over forty, so I suspect their courting days are behind them. But by all means, if you wish."

And Clarissa found no familiar faces in the staff, so she kept her homily brief.

Later, in the carriage, they discussed it all.

"And yet, did you note that the robbery here was very much the same?" the earl pointed out. "Fast and efficient. No one woke until the gang was out of the house. Does that disprove our theory, that Mrs. Craigmore helped scout out the houses through her contacts among former foundling home girls now gone into service? If there is no such maid here, how did she know any details about this household? I asked Mrs. Barton specifically if anyone answering to the matron's description had called at the house, and she said she was sure she had not."

"She has two daughters who are out," Gemma noted. "One is in her first Season. They could have gossiped, you know, and another servant overheard it."

"But in so much detail? Surely, they would not gossip

about where they keep the good silver?" Clarissa suggested.

Gemma sighed. "No, you are right. I don't know."

The earl shook his head. "I shall have to check out this hotel. Perhaps tonight—"

"No, tomorrow," Clarissa interrupted. "I mean, if you please. I wish to go with you!"

They both stared at her. "No, indeed—" Gemma began.

Lord Whitby's tone was gruffer. "I will not risk your safety or your reputation."

But Clarissa refused to give in. "I might be needed. You would not know the name of the hotel if I had not come along today! And remember, Mrs. Craigmore was posing as a middle-class matron, so the hotel is likely quite respectable."

"But I am promised to go with Lady Gabriel tomorrow," Gemma said. "I shall see if I can bow out, but—"

Clarissa threw her a beseeching look.

Gemma sighed. "Oh, very well, I have taken some rash steps myself when it seemed important. And I know Lord Whitby will look out for you. Just get her back before dark, I beg of you, and Clarissa, do not tell your brother!"

Clarissa hugged her sister-in-law and threw one quick glance toward the earl. Behind his usual impassive expression, which no longer seemed so enigmatic, he didn't seem angry that she had insisted on coming along. And it was her clue, she had found it! Should she not be there to help unravel it? Besides, it was her neck they could very well put the noose around if the real killer were not unmasked!

Ten

Dominic arrived at the Fallon home the next morning at the appointed time. He had some misgivings about taking Miss Fallon along, but she had a point. She had been quite helpful yesterday, and who knew what they might find today?

If she could just keep her mouth closed—and refrain from swearing—and in other ways not draw attention to herself, no one would likely remark too much upon her presence. And if he, lately, found his days more invigorating when he was in her company, well, she was a singular creature, and quite amazingly lovely.

Besides, desperate times called for desperate measures. God knew, their errand was urgent enough. Miss Fallon was still caught in a most perilous situation, and it must be resolved, especially as he suspected it worried her more than she allowed it to show.

When he stepped out of his chaise and was shown into the house, he was surprised to find Miss Fallon pacing up and down in the front hall, instead of waiting decorously upstairs in the drawing room.

He was also surprised at her appearance. She wore a drab gown and a downright shabby shawl, and her bonnet was plain. And she had a crumpled garment draped over her arm.

She motioned to him. "At last!"

He started to point out that he was just on time, but she didn't pause to listen.

"We must go quickly. I sent Miss Pomshack up to her rooms on an errand, but we must hurry before she returns and tries to stop me. The butler will inform her that I have gone to do more good works."

Dominic couldn't help glancing at the manservant. His expression was impassive, but only, one suspected, with enormous effort.

"And Gemma has asked me to bring along Matty," Miss Fallon continued. "You don't mind, do you? She is quite discreet."

He saw that the girl, dressed today not in her maid's kit but in modest off-duty apparel, stood nearby.

"No, it is an excellent notion to bring your lady's maid, but—"

However, Miss Fallon was already hurrying outside. The butler watched them go, and the footman, who appeared mystified at all the strange goings-on, held open the door. Matty hurried after her.

But outside, the surprising Miss Fallon paused again. "We shall have to hail a hackney, my lord."

"There is a problem with my chaise?" Dominic stared at her.

Raising her brows, she met his glance. "Your carriage screams wealth and privilege, my lord, even if you did not have your crest emblazed upon the door! And, oh, leave your coat inside it."

He bit back a retort. It was undignified to argue with her in front of the house. A small movement of the curtains at a front window made him fear the footman or another servant was watching, and what if Miss Pomshack returned? The thought of facing down that lady's moral righteousness gave even him a qualm. He did as he was told, sliding out of his well-cut coat with the help of his servant, then, feeling ridiculous without his jacket, he sent his groom to hail a hackney.

"Just take the chaise home and wait for instructions," he told his coachman grimly.

"Yes, milord," the man murmured, looking bewildered, but not half so confounded as Dominic himself.

Once a hackney had been procured, Dominic handed the ladies into the hired vehicle. Then he joined them and turned to demand further explanation. But before he could ask, he found that Miss Fallon was looking him up and down, and her gaze was critical.

"I'm sorry about your coat, but you are dressed too richly."

"I beg your pardon?" Dominic raised his brows. He frequented the best tailor in London, and no one had ever complained about his appearance before. And he certainly did not go in for dandyisms or vulgar displays of wealth. He wore no gold fobs or flashy diamond jewelry, just a simple signet ring on one hand that had been his father's. "My coat did not please you?"

"Now, don't get in a huff," she begged. "It is a most handsome coat."

He wasn't sure he had ever engaged in such a ridiculous dialogue. But why should anything about Miss Fallon surprise him?

"I only mean, it says too much about your rank and your wealth, my lord, just as your carriage did. But I think we can disguise you sufficiently. Here you are, I brought this for you to wear."

She handed over the most ill-cut, rumpled coat that Dominic had ever laid eyes on. He touched it with reluctance. It was made of coarse cheap linen, and he would swear that one of the seams was already fraying.

"I borrowed it from the footman. He's about your size, although his shoulders are narrower, so it may be a bit tight. I didn't dare ask him for trousers—" She paused abruptly.

He was gratified to see that even the unexpected Miss Fallon had her limits; she had turned pink.

"You expect me to wear this?" He could not keep his voice from rising. A preposterous idea, they were not going to a costume ball!

Sitting quietly in the corner of the carriage, Matty shivered at his tone. But Miss Fallon regarded him steadily, her expression earnest.

"I thought about this a good deal last night, my lord. There are times when one can impress those who are poorer and of lower social class and obtain the desired results, but there are also times when such a show will only intimidate them. I observed a servant in the first house yesterday who I suspect knew something about the foundling home and the criminal gang we are seeking—I thought of returning myself to confront her—but I doubt it would serve. It was useless to press her at the time. She would never have confided in a lady, and a stranger, to boot."

"I see," he muttered.

"The only reason I obtained any information from Becky, at the second house, was that she remembered me from the home, remembered me as an equal. Gemma tells me that today we are going into a less prosperous part of London. I think we have a better chance of learning more if we look, well, less overpowering."

She really expected him to wear this, this *garment*. Dominic drew a deep breath. He wanted to wither her with a glance, but he had not the heart. And anyhow, it did make a contorted sort of sense.

With great reluctance, he drew on the offending piece of apparel. It was indeed tight through the shoulders, and also through the upper arms and chest—the footman must be a hollow-chested fellow, he thought. Dominic could not quite button it, so it would have to hang open, creating an even more disreputable appearance. He tried not to think what he looked like.

He told himself he had certainly looked worse many a time on the battlefield in a ripped and bloodstained uniform, but he felt, well, undressed, as if he had wandered out of the house in his nightshirt. Thank heavens he would likely see no one he knew, and he was equally grateful his own valet could not see him. He looked up—if she were laughing . . .

"That's better." Miss Fallon nodded in approval. "Of course, the boots are a dead giveaway, but the footman had no extra shoes, and they would likely not have fit, anyhow. Perhaps you can scuff them up a bit and get them dirty, so they will be less conspicuous."

"Scuff my boots?" Dominic stared at her. "My valet is going to resign." As soon as he said it, he remembered that her safety—her life—was at stake, and he pressed his lips together for an instant, angry at himself. "Very well."

She seemed satisfied. "What do you think we will find at this hotel, my lord?"

He wished she would call him Dominic, and that impulsive thought surprised him so much that he forgot to answer until she turned to look at him, her gaze inquiring.

"I—I'm not sure. Whatever information we can about the matron and her habits. I'm particularly interested in learning if she has had any regular callers."

"Of course."

Dominic continued, "If we can trace this gang of thieves, we might identify the real murderer."

Miss Fallon shivered. "I've been thinking about that, too. Even if she were involved in a criminal group, and I would not put it past her, especially after she had lost her post at the foundling home, still, what reason would they have to kill her? If she has been scouting homes to rob, and coercing the girls she once bullied at the home to help her, she must have had value to them."

"Perhaps it was a quarrel over their loot," he suggested.

"And it happened just at the time I had encountered her in the street?" Miss Fallon wrinkled her nose in doubt.

It was an adorable nose, he thought, and her skin was palest ivory, almost translucent, with faint blue veins showing at her temples. If the little maid were not sitting in the carriage— Perhaps Lady Gemma had been wise to insist upon a chaperone. . . .

He pulled his thoughts back to the matter at hand. "That's true, it is a surprising coincidence."

"Surely just what a magistrate would say," she agreed, her tone dry.

"But that does not mean it is not true," he argued, worried about the wrinkle of concern he saw appear in her smooth forehead.

Miss Fallon fell silent, and they rode the rest of the way to the hotel. When they rolled into the courtyard, Dominic looked about. It was a modest establishment, but it appeared perfectly respectable.

A groom appeared, but Dominic shook his head at him. "We are only making a short visit," he told the servant.

The man touched his forehead and turned back toward the stables. Dominic paid off the hackney, then found that Miss Fallon was frowning at him.

"What is it?"

"You still sound like a peer of the realm," she said, her tone reproachful. "Don't be so masterful, my lord. And I will not be able to call you that inside, remember, so please don't take offense. Don't be so quick to stare people down, and perhaps you could slouch a little? You stand very straight. You must not look as if you are so used to command."

Dominic opened his mouth and then closed it again. "You continue to surprise me," he told her, keeping his tone low. "Have you considered going on the stage?"

She seemed to ponder. "I'm quite sure Matthew would not allow it."

He had not meant the comment to be taken seriously, and

he glanced at her again, about to point out her mistake, then he saw the gleam of mischief in her eyes. Imp!

They went inside the hotel. Dominic would normally have hired a private parlor, but if they were not supposed to be wealthy, he assumed that would be inappropriate behavior, too.

Miss Fallon tugged on his sleeve. Normally, he would have frowned, but if she ripped this disgraceful coat apart, he would only be the better for it.

"Go into the taproom," she whispered. "But don't ask any questions just yet. We will join you shortly."

"Why not? And that is likely not a proper place for you to frequent, the company may be low, and—"

She looked adamant. "I have been in such places before, my—sir. Trust me."

She seemed to have taken total control of this expedition. He thought about informing her of the consequences of insubordination, but looking into her hazel eyes, just now full of determination, he knew it would be useless. He felt again a wave of respect for her, and a renewed sense of his own resolve that she would not be allowed to suffer for the death of the late and unlamented Mrs. Craigmore.

Miss Fallon, with Matty at her side, had already whisked away toward the back of the inn and soon disappeared from his view. He watched them go with some foreboding. At least she had the maid with her, but he would feel better if he could keep her in his sight.

Shaking his head, Dominic found the taproom, took a table, and ordered a tankard of ale, passing over his coin to the serving wench. Only a few other men occupied the room, drinking their brews or eating bread and cheese, and the talk was not loud, so perhaps Miss Fallon would not be shocked at what she might overhear. If anything could shock her!

He was nursing the ale, which was not up to his usual standard, when the two women returned. Miss Fallon paused in the doorway, and when she saw him, led the way to his table. As he stood, she sat down and motioned for Matty to do the same.

"Shall I try to obtain some tea for you or a glass of sherry? And what have you been doing?"

"Talking to the women in the kitchen," Miss Fallon said, her tone very low. "Mrs. Craigmore was staying here, but under the name of Livermore."

He blinked at her. "Are you sure?"

"Positive, the description fits, and one of the maids could describe the dress the matron was wearing when I saw her. Now you can question the landlord about her stay here and if she had visitors."

"Well done, Miss Fallon!" he told her, enjoying the glow in her hazel eyes as she brightened at his praise. It would indeed be easier to ask about the woman if they knew the alias she had adopted.

So when he beckoned over the man at the bar, he said, "Perhaps you would share some ale with us, my good man. And some tea for my female relations?" He passed over several coins, and the man took them eagerly.

"Of course, sir." He took away Dominic's half-empty tankard to refill it and presently returned with that, another ale, and two cups of tea on a wooden tray. The tea was the color of mahogany and looked even worse than his own drink, so he did not envy the women.

The man pulled up another chair. "New to this neighborhood, are you, sir?"

"Yes," Dominic told him with all sincerity. "We are traveling through London. I am looking for an aunt of mine, a Mrs. Livermore. I had a note from her a while ago, but the direction was scribbled very ill, so I'm not sure—I don't suppose she has been staying here?"

"Now, that is odd that you should ask. We did have a female lodger 'ere by that name, nice respectable widow, she was, and very quiet about her 'abits, if a bit short at times with the maids, I 'eard—meaning no disrespect to your relation." The innkeeper paused to take a sip of his ale. "But she ain't been back for several days, sir, and I been wondering what to do about 'er room. 'Er things are still in it, and if she ain't coming back, I need the room. And then there's the bill, you see. She was paid up until the Saturday, but after that—"

Dominic nodded. "I am not completely surprised that she has disappeared; we feared as much. She sometimes has, um, fits, you see."

Miss Fallon giggled, then turned it into a cough when the innkeeper glanced her way.

"We shall have to check the hospitals," Dominic continued smoothly. "My poor aunt may have been taken ill. When these bouts happen, she can become confused, not even knowing her own name."

"Mercy," the other man muttered. "Glad she didn't do it 'ere, would have had the maids in 'ysterics. I 'ope they ain't carted 'er off to Bedlam, sir."

"We certainly hope not," Dominic agreed. "It's also possible she might have gone to stay with another friend, of course. Did she have any callers while she was here?"

The man looked offended. "And leave me stuck with 'er bill?"

"She might have become ill, as I said. But did anyone visit her, that you knew of?"

"Only one swell gent, youngish he was. I wondered if he were 'er fancy man—oh, pardon, misses." The innkeeper appeared to remember the presence of the two females. "Or maybe 'e was looking to marry a widow, even one older than 'e were, if she had a bit put by, don't you know?"

"He was a gentleman?" Dominic demanded, surprised.

The innkeeper hesitated a moment. "'e looked it, but, well, 'ard to say. Dressed decent he did, with a fine coat."

Glancing down at his own disgraceful garment, Dominic tried not to shudder. "How fortunate for him. What did he look like?"

"Not as tall as you, sir, thin, dark-haired. The maids giggled over 'im a bit, so I guess you'd say he was pleasing of face."

The man took another drink of ale. Description was not his strong suit, apparently.

"Did you hear his name?"

"Never gave it, sir; she was usually waiting to meet 'im in the 'all."

Dominic tried not to frown in disappointment. "There was no one else?" he asked. "If we could question her friends, it might help us find her."

The innkeeper shook his head. "None that I saw, sir."

No use beating a dead horse. Dominic gave it up. "Very well. Until she returns, or we find her, perhaps we should collect her belongings, for safekeeping and so that you can have the use of your room."

The innkeeper hesitated, and Dominic added, "And I will settle her account, of course."

The man brightened. "That's good of you, sir. I'll 'ave the maid show you and your family up to the widow's room. And I 'ope you find her in good condition, not off 'er 'ead."

Since Mrs. Craigmore/Livermore had already been put into a pauper's grave, that was unlikely, but Dominic saw no reason to point that out. Instead, they all rose and Dominic handed over the amount the innkeeper requested. If he suspected the bill might be a tad inflated, Dominic didn't care. When a maid was fetched, the landlord directed her to take them to the late Mrs. Craigmore's room.

The girl took them up two narrow flights of stairs and showed them a small room tucked under the eaves. There did not appear to be much here, but Dominic hoped for something that might tell them more.

He looked on the one small table, but saw no papers or books. Miss Fallon, with her maid's help, was folding the few clothes that had been left behind. Dominic looked back at the maid.

"Perhaps you could find us a large basket so we have some way to carry this, until my aunt returns?"

He passed over a coin, and she grinned and winked at him. "Thank'ee, gov. I'll find ye something."

Really, this masquerade was a salutary experience for him, Dominic thought, trying not to laugh. If ever anyone again accused him of being high in the instep—

He shook off the thought. Now that they were alone, he set about investigating the room more carefully.

Miss Fallon apparently had the same thought. She was already lifting the mattress to look beneath it, and he went to help her. But they uncovered nothing but a few wisps of dust and a shabby carpetbag.

"What she traveled with, I deduce." He drew it out and glanced inside, but saw nothing.

"She had a secret drawer in her desk at the foundling home—Gemma told me about it," Miss Fallon said.

"But there is no desk here, and thus, no drawer." He looked about them. There was not even a clothespress, just some pegs on the wall and a small chest at the foot of the bed.

The women had already removed all the clothing from it, and Matty was pushing the folded garments into the carpetbag. He opened the lid of the chest and looked inside, but it was empty.

Miss Fallon looked discouraged, and he touched her shoulder lightly. "Don't allow your courage to falter," he told her.

"But we have found nothing, only a vague description of a mysterious man for whom we have no name." She sighed.

When the maid returned with a basket, Miss Fallon asked her about the matron's visitor. The maid giggled. "A very 'andsome man, miss, if I do say so. He 'ad eyes so dark, quite lovely."

"Do you have any idea where he was from?"

The servant looked at him in surprise.

"I mean, did he have an accent that was from town or from one of the shires?"

The girl bit her lip. "I didn't really 'ear 'im talk much, sir, only a word or two and nothing in his speech that seemed to mark 'im. 'Fraid I can't say."

So it was a glum trio that returned to the courtyard.

Dominic sent a servant to hail another hackney. When it came, he helped Miss Fallon and her maid inside and wished he could cheer her spirits.

She looked lost in thought, and the thoughts did not seem to be happy ones.

"I would very much like to know who the 'handsome young man' is," Dominic suggested. "Dark-haired and medium in height, and almost gentlemanly in appearance." He looked down at his own borrowed coat and shook his head, trying to dust off a speck of lint.

But at least Miss Fallon raised her head, and her expression had changed. "The day I glimpsed the matron on the street, before I spoke to her, she was speaking to a man of medium height. I had forgotten!"

Dominic looked at her quickly and ignored his wardrobe's deficiencies. "Did you see his face?"

Looking regretful, she shook her head. "No, nor could I see if he had dark hair. He was wearing a hat, and he looked respectable enough. Perhaps it was someone else, not one of the gang we are seeking."

"I refuse to believe that the woman who has caused us so much trouble had any acquaintances who were not as unpleasant as she was," Dominic told her.

He succeeded in making her smile.

"Not a very scientific deduction, my lord, but perhaps you are right. At any rate, we will keep the mysterious gentleman in mind."

The carriage bounced as it rolled over a hole in the pavement. Miss Fallon paused to catch the side of the seat, then motioned to Matty, who was holding the shabby carpetbag.

"Let me see it, please, Matty. I want to check it again."

Making a face at the stale smell of the clothing and the mildewed odor of the bag itself, she rummaged through it.

Just as Dominic was feeling a pang of sympathy for her, thinking that she was grasping at straws, she suddenly raised her head. Her expression had changed.

"I have found a secret pocket!"

Eleven

"You were searching for it," he charged, even as he shared her moment of exaltation.

"Miss, how clever of you!" Matty said at the same time, then blushed and, glancing at the earl, held her tongue.

Clarissa smiled. "The matron liked secret places to hide things," she pointed out. "And after I thought about it, it could not have been in the furniture, as it was not hers but the hotel's. So I thought the bag was worth a careful look."

"You were brilliant, as usual," he told her, keeping his tone light. "Is there anything inside?"

Clarissa drew out two slips of paper. They unfolded them and scanned the writing. One appeared to be a list of stolen goods—jewels and silverware and clocks, anything portable that could have been quickly taken from a sleeping household—with sums of money written after each one. And the second—

Clarissa frowned at it and passed it to Dominic. "What is it?" she asked.

Frowning, he read it twice. "Another address. I believe this may be a flashhouse or even a receiver."

"A what or a what?" Clarissa asked.

Dominic was glad that, for once, he knew something about the lower classes that Clarissa did not. "I have been getting reports from the runner I've hired," he told her. "Expanding my knowledge of the criminal world. A flashhouse is a pub where petty thieves, or worse, hang out. A receiver is a person who takes the stolen goods and resells them."

"Ah." Clarissa nodded in understanding. "So next we—"

"Next, *I* will go to check out this address," he told her. "It will hardly be a place for a lady to visit."

"But—" she began, but he shook his head.

"No, not this time."

She looked at him in obvious doubt. "I do not think you can pass as a low-born person without my help," she told him, her tone serious.

He threw back his head and laughed. He felt curiously exhilarated, not just at the discovery of another clue, but to see the fear in her hazel eyes replaced by her more usual gritty determination. "If I am found out, I pledge that I will return to you for further instruction. I don't wish to subject you to any avoidable danger."

She eyed him with patent disbelief. "I insist that you keep me fully informed, my lord. It is my neck already well at risk, you know."

"Of course. If circumstances allow, I shall see you before the day ends," he assured her.

She mulled over this, and they rode in silence for a time.

After several more blocks, Clarissa glanced at the maid beside her and saw that the servant's eyes had closed, and she breathed evenly. Was she asleep?

Clarissa turned back to regard the earl. They had so little time alone. On impulse, she leaned forward and touched his hand.

"You have been so kind," she told him in the barest whisper. "I can never thank you enough."

"You don't have to thank me," he whispered back, but he lifted her hand to his lips and kissed it lightly.

She felt his touch even through her thin glove. A thrill ran through her, rippling along her arm.

He didn't release her hand. He turned it, instead, and his lips moved to her wrist. He pushed the glove back so that her skin lay bare, naked, open to his touch. He kissed her wrist, too, and his mouth felt even warmer there.

His lips were supple and strong, and how would they feel if she pressed her own against them? At the thought, she felt goose bumps rise on her skin, and a strange sensation develop in the pit of her stomach.

He was pulling off her glove. Now her hand lay inside his, and he touched each finger, gently caressing. She had never known her hand could experience such sensations. Without her volition, a soft sigh escaped her.

A cart rumbled past them on the street, and the maid jerked.

To Clarissa's infinite regret, he pressed her hand one last time, then let it go. She pulled her glove back on as Matty stirred. But when Clarissa looked up at him again, she saw a light in his dark eyes as he smiled at her.

And when they reached the Fallon household, the earl told the driver to wait, then climbed out first to help them down. When Clarissa emerged, he held her hand a moment longer than necessary and bent to say into her ear, "Don't worry, Clarissa. All will be well."

She nodded, feeling a little breathless still from the interlude inside the carriage. "Shall I tell Lady Gemma to expect you for dinner?"

"I will be here," he agreed.

And she went inside with a lighter heart than at any time since she'd first glimpsed Mrs. Craigmore on the street. How could any peril touch her when the earl spoke her name in that intimate tone?

Dominic watched them until the door shut behind them, then pulled his thoughts—with an effort—back to the business at hand. He returned to the hackney and gave the driver the new address.

The man stared at him.

Dominic reached into his pocket and handed over several coins over and above the required fare. "I'll make it worth your while."

Reluctantly, the man twitched the reins and the tired-looking nag stirred itself to motion. "Not moving loot, are you, gov?"

"Of course not," Dominic said, but he filed the comment away. Did the gangs use hackneys to move their stolen wares quietly about the city? How mundane, and how yet unremarkable that would be to watching eyes.

The streets of Whitechapel were narrower and more littered than the avenues of the West End. Dominic tried not to pinch his nostrils at the noxious smells. He handed over another coin when he climbed down from the vehicle.

"If you wait—"

"Not 'ere, gov. No amount of blunt is enough for a slit throat," the driver muttered, and lashed his horse at once into motion.

That bad, eh? Dominic considered for the first time that he should have gone back and armed himself before coming here. But it was too late for second thoughts. He pushed open the rough door and passed inside.

The air was murky with smoke and smelled almost as bad as the street. Dominic pushed his way through to an empty seat where he could keep his right side turned toward the rest of the pub's patrons, pulled up a stool, and looked about him. The men—and occasional woman—who crowded the tavern appeared blowsy and dirty and most often drunk, and they certainly looked little like honest working folk. Although, he thought as he watched a woman slip a man's wallet covertly from his pocket and into her apron with one hand as she caressed his cheek with the other, perhaps that depended on one's definition of "work."

When a woman of indeterminate age, wearing a dirty apron and a gown with a low-cut bodice, came up, he passed over a coin and ordered ale. When she returned with his drink, he took a cautious sip and tried not to wince. "Who owns this establishment?"

"Huh?" she stared at him and rubbed red-rimmed eyelids, smearing the line of kohl that she had drawn around them.

"Who owns this place?"

" 'Im. Westy." She pointed to a paunchy man behind the bar.

Dominic nodded his thanks. "Do you think you could suggest to him that a few words with me would be to his advantage?"

"Eh?" She blinked.

Not sure if she was drunk, dim-witted, or simply terminally exhausted, Dominic sighed and tried again. "I want to speak to him."

"Why didn't you say so?" she muttered. But she headed for the landlord.

Dominic remembered Miss Fallon's lessons in proper— or improper—deportment and tried to slouch over his drink.

When the man stalked over, he demanded, his tone surly, "What you want w'me, eh?"

"I thought—" Dominic kept his tone low and tried to slur his words a little. "I thought you might know where a man might find a receiver who gives fair price for goods?"

"New at the game, are you?" His eyes narrow with suspicion, the man looked him over. " 'ow I know you ain't some damned police informant, or a runner?"

Dominic knew his brows had shot up. "You must be joking."

"Na, you don't have the look of 'em," the man agreed. "Come down in the world, 'ave you? Lost your fortune at cards and now you're into lifting the odd bit? Maybe I could take it off your 'ands? Or cut your throat and go through your pockets at me leisure."

Without even thinking, Dominic reached out and grabbed the man's shirt. Pulling him down so that they were only inches apart, he met the man's startled gaze.

A mistake; the landlord's breath could fell an ox.

Ignoring it, Dominic said, "I don't think I care for your methods."

Several men at the next table glanced at them, but when Dominic turned his head to meet their gazes, they looked away again. The landlord had paled.

"I didn't—I don't—"

"No, you do not," Dominic agreed, but he released his grip on the man. "Now, answer my question."

"You could try Whitherby, a few doors down, or the Cattery, if she'll let you in," the man muttered.

Not willing to show how cryptic he found these instructions, Dominic nodded.

The man hurried away, and, pushing aside the drink without regret, Dominic headed for the door before the landlord could summon reinforcements.

Outside, he looked up and down the crowded lane and headed away from the tavern. He soon located the man called Whitherby, whose name was inscribed upon a shop front so narrow that there was barely room for a doorway and one tiny window. Behind its dirty panes was a hodgepodge of clothing, household goods, and small valuables, all obviously secondhand, and all without a doubt stolen.

The small withered man who came to greet him gave him a twisted smile; he was missing most of his front teeth. "Wot you need today, gov? I can supply it."

"I need information," Dominic told him. "And if you help me, it will be to your advantage. I'm looking for a woman of middle years, stout of form, dark-haired with a little gray at the temples. She might be using the name Livermore."

The man looked puzzled. "Ain't 'eard of 'er, gov. But if it's a woman you want, I could find you plenty, any age or size you like."

He seemed to be telling the truth. Dominic swallowed a sigh of frustration. "Never mind."

To the little man's obvious disappointment, Dominic left the shop as abruptly as he had entered it. Now what?

He walked up and down the lane, but saw nothing on any building that denoted cats. Was "cattery" a reference to a brothel? If so, in this neighborhood there would be all too many to choose from, and how would he know which one might house a receiver? While he hesitated, not sure where to go next, a girl with a thin face and hard eyes came out of the mass of poorly dressed men and women who crowded the pavement and approached him.

"Like a good time, gov? Only two shillings, and well worth the price! I got a room two streets over, or if ye in a hurry, we can just duck into the alley."

Trying not to show his flash of pity, he gazed at her. Her gown, as well as her person, had seen better days, and her breath reeked of gin. "No, but I'll give you a shilling, anyhow, if you can point me to the Cattery."

Her eyes narrowed for a moment, and to his surprise, she laughed. "Easy nuff, gov, but what good will that do ye?"

"Just tell me where it is," he suggested, drawing out a coin.

She eyed it eagerly. "Only one street over. I'll show you."

Stepping around the refuse and dung that spotted the street, he followed the girl as she hurried up the lane and cut through an alley. Within minutes, she stopped suddenly and pointed to a slightly larger building than the ones that leaned against it.

"That's it, gov."

Hoping he was not being gulled, Dominic passed over the coin.

"'Ope you enjoy it," she said, her tone malicious, then she hurried away and disappeared into the crowd.

Dominic continued to regard the shop. It had *Lady's*

Wares scrawled in uneven letters on the sign above the door. Was it a brothel?

As he watched, a slightly built female dressed in what was, for this neighborhood, respectable dress, opened the door and entered. He tried to watch from the outside, but the glass at the window was dusty. Whatever happened inside the building, housekeeping was obviously not of high concern.

In a few minutes, the girl came out again, glanced furtively up and down the lane, then hastened off.

There seemed little to gain by standing in the street. Dominic went up the door and pulled it open. The girl had not knocked, and he did not, either.

A bell tinkled as he entered. The interior looked more like a shabby tea shop than a den of crime. Several tables and chairs filled the small room, with a bureau or two against the wall, and a lady's gown, its design a bit outmoded but its lace handsome, had been draped over a stand. Frowning, Dominic looked about him.

A woman of middle age and undistinguished mien appeared in an inner doorway and stopped, her expression severe. "Who are you?"

"I'm interested in—"

"Get out," she demanded.

"Wait, I'm looking for a receiver who can—"

"Don't matter, I only deal with females," she interrupted. "The whole street knows that, you lunk'ead. Bloody men can't be trusted!"

"I assure you—" he tried to say, but paused when she drew an ancient but apparently serviceable blunderbuss from a cupboard near the door.

"Out!" she commanded, pointing the muzzle toward him.

Dominic knew when to make a strategic retreat. But outside on the street, he paused and stared again up at the sign. He wasn't sure—

The faintest touch on his borrowed jacket alerted him, and he cuffed the hand that had tried to slip into his pocket.

Someone exclaimed. "Let go o' me!"

Dominic turned to see a boy of middle years struggling to escape the firm grip that held him.

"Your technique needs work," Dominic advised. "Shall I turn you over to the watch?"

"Try and find one round 'ere," the boy taunted him.

"Then perhaps I shall simply give you a good thrashing?"

This time the lad held his tongue, but he directed a resentful look at his captor.

"Tell me about that place and perhaps I will let you go unscathed," Dominic suggested.

"Eh?"

"Without the hiding you so richly deserve," he explained.

"Oh, w'at you want to know?" The boy stared up at him.

"What is that place?"

The lad looked scornful. "The Cattery? It's a shop, so she says, course she's also one of the biggest receivers on the street. But she won't deal with you, gov."

"Why not?"

" 'Cause you're a man, o'course. She hates 'em, men, I mean," the boy said, as if the whole world knew of the woman's aversion to the male half of the species.

"I see," Dominic said. A receiver and slightly demented, as well. But she might know of the late Mrs. Craigmore, who had certainly been female.

"So let go me 'and, already!"

He released the boy, who ran rapidly into the nearest alley and out of sight. Too late, Dominic realized he should have asked the woman's name, but then, she could well have several. At least he knew the location, and he would have to come back. But as to how to get the woman to listen to him . . . He thought for only an instant of donning female clothing, then shuddered. No, not likely, this clumsy-fitting coat was bad enough. . . .

Putting one hand over the pocket with his remaining store of coins to avoid the efforts of more skillful pickpockets than the last, Dominic pushed his way into the mass of ill-clad people on the edges of the street, stepping over a man sprawled in drunken oblivion, and made his way toward the better parts of town, where he could hail another hackney.

When he reached the Fallon house, he told the driver to wait, then went up to the door. The butler opened the door and gawked at him.

With intense relief, Dominic could at last shed the borrowed coat. "Here, return this to your footman with my thanks," he said, and added a coin as more tangible gratitude. "And give him this, as well."

The butler swallowed hard and accepted the coat. "Yes, my lord. Shall I inform Miss Fallon—"

"No need," Dominic pointed out as he looked up to see Clarissa Fallon rushing down the staircase with most unladylike haste.

"What happened? Did you have any success?" she demanded.

He looked around. "Can we speak in private, for just a moment?"

She dismissed the butler with a nod and opened a door. "Come into my brother's study, if you would."

He followed her and, even though it was improper, shut the door gently behind them. It would also be disastrous if the servants overheard any of their plotting. "I have found a promising lead. I hoped it might turn out to be the receiver that Mrs. Livermore used, but the female inside would not speak to me."

He told her quickly what had transpired, and was not surprised to see her face light up. "Then I must go back with you," she exclaimed. "It is obvious."

"It is too dangerous," he corrected. He had feared she would jump to just such a conclusion. "Perhaps your maid could go with me—"

"Matty is an excellent girl and very loyal," Miss Fallon argued. "But you may need me, my lord. We must go back, you know we must!"

He could find no logical argument. Shaking his head, he

muttered, "Your brother will call me out if he discovers I have allowed this. Very well, but I shall take precautions. And bring your maid with you."

Her expression eager, she nodded, "I shall meet you at ten o'clock tomorrow at the bookseller's on Bond Street."

"In drab clothing? Will not Lady Gemma notice?"

"I will try to slip out without her seeing," Clarissa explained patiently, as if he were slow of wit.

"Very well. And please excuse me to your sister-in-law for this evening; I cannot stay for dinner without proper attire."

She glanced at his shirt as if she'd forgotten all about his missing coat. "She's not home yet, so I don't have to, but I will send word to the cook. And, thank you, my lord."

She looked up at him, her clear hazel eyes filled with emotion, and for a moment, he saw beneath the facade of bravado with which she habitually faced the world—a world which, for too much of her life, had been hostile and malicious.

He could not stop himself from taking one small hand and pressing it against his shirtfront. "I will not leave you alone and unprotected," he told her gently. "We will see this through until you are safe, once again."

Her eyes glistened. For a moment, they stood very close, and he could smell the sweet fragrance of her clothing, even the clean scent of her body beneath the thin muslin gown, and despite his best intentions his own body responded. God, she was so sweet, so enticing . . . and courageous to the bone. He could not let her down.

"Thank you," she whispered, her voice husky.

He wanted to pull her into his arms and bend to possess those slightly pursed lips, but he could not abuse her trust.

So he had to content himself with lifting the hand he held to his lips and kissing it—only one brief moment of contact, and so much less than he hungered for. Then he released his hold and was about to turn away before his self-control failed him, when to his surprise, she suddenly stood on her toes and flung her arms about his neck, offering him an unpracticed but enthusiastic kiss, slightly off center.

He was too startled to respond properly, but the brief taste of her only teased him further.

Cheeks pink, she stepped back almost as quickly as she had embraced him.

Dominic found he had to clear his throat before he could speak, and his voice sounded hoarse. "You mustn't do that, my dear—I mean, Miss Fallon."

"Why not? There's no one here to see. And you called me Clarissa in the carriage. May I call you Dominic?"

Oh, God, she didn't understand. She was such an unpredictable mix of worldly knowledge and naive innocence, and he never knew which part would surface—

"If I called you Clarissa in public, people would think we had become too—too intimate. A lady must protect her reputation, most especially a single lady, or tongues will wag, and you could be hurt. And you must not encourage a man because—well, because he may accept the invitation. Like this." He bent and lifted her chin, leaning forward with deliberate slowness and placing a hand on each side of her face. Her eyes widened. She had time to back away, but she stood her ground, pursed her lips and lifted her face to accept his kiss.

This time, he kissed her properly. He touched her lips lightly at first, then more firmly, relishing the sweetness of her, the fullness, the softness. The kiss grew, and he pressed harder as his own passion surged, almost forgetting that his intention had been to frighten her just a little, for her own good. Now he only wanted to possess her, every inch of her. When her lips parted and his tongue slipped into the sweet darkness there, the taste of her was as heady as ambrosia and yet only a faint semblance of more enticing invasions to come.

He felt rather than heard her gasp at the touch of his tongue, and then she responded in kind, and the kiss seemed to consume them both.

And never did she draw away or feign any maidenly coyness or confusion. Instead, she gave herself to the kiss, pressing her body against his until they seemed almost melded into one, and only the thin layers of clothing separated them from a true union. That thought brought a small breath of sanity to blow away the fog that had filled his mind.

Drawing back, he ended the kiss at last. Looking down at her, he tried to control his breathing. "That," he said, "is why you must not encourage strange men . . ." Somehow, the rest of his morally uplifting speech had slipped away.

Her eyes seemed to shine. Her tongue licked her bottom lip, as if she wanted to relish the last taste of him, and at the sight of it, he felt his groin ache. It took great effort not to step forward and pull her close once again.

"But you're not at all strange," she said, her voice low, and she smiled up at him. Her lips were still slightly pink from the pressure of his own.

Oh, God, he wanted her.

He had to get out of the house before he did something even more reprehensible! Striding toward the door, Dominic opened it and waited for her to join him. But as she did, he couldn't help reaching to straighten a strand of fair hair. When she gazed up at him, her eyes full of trust, his heart seemed to lurch.

He couldn't do this, not again.

The footman hailed a hackney to take him home. As it bounced over the pavement, Dominic sat alone in the corner, but the shadows of the carriage seemed filled by ghosts with mournful eyes.

The next day, she met him at the appointed time, having successfully evaded both Gemma and Miss Pomshack. She waited in front of the bookseller's until a dark chaise pulled up.

It was not a hackney, but neither was it the earl's usual elegant chaise with his crest on the door, so she looked at it in surprise. Two burly men hung on to the rear of the vehicle, but the coachman was the same man who usually drove the earl.

And it was Lord Whitby who opened the door and nodded to her. When one of the grooms belatedly jumped down and unfolded the steps, the earl allowed the servant—somewhat to her disappointment—to help her inside. But she realized in a moment that he was deliberately keeping out of sight.

"What—" she began.

"I thought it best to use a somewhat less conspicuous vehicle," he explained. "But I also wanted something more dependable than a nervous hackney driver, so I hired this lumbering but functional carriage."

She nodded, pleased to see that he had dressed down again, if not to the standards of the borrowed jacket she had procured for him yesterday, at least he looked a bit less perfect than usual. And the spark of joy she had felt at seeing him—that had nothing to do with his clothing.

"You had no problem getting away?" he asked, then looked past her. "Where is your lady's maid?"

"She is spending the day at the market; she has a friend who works in one of the stalls. We will pick her up when we are done, before we go back to the house."

He stared at her. "Miss Fallon—"

To her disappointment, he had resumed his autocratic tone, and his expression was once again as haughty as when they'd first met. She swallowed. What had happened to the man who had kissed her so passionately yesterday? *Because I hoped you might kiss me again, you fool,* she wanted to tell him, but, of course, she couldn't. She might not know the finer points of etiquette, but she knew enough not to beg for a man's attention. That could only inspire disdain. She turned her head to stare through the window.

"I thought I explained—" he started.

"Matty is a loyal servant, but she doesn't know my history. I would rather she didn't hear it all," she told him quietly. "I wasn't sure what trickery we would have to concoct today. She might think it odd that I know so much about the working classes."

At least that stopped his bloody lecture. The silence between them was heavy, and the noise outside the carriage, the clatter of wheels on the paving stones, the hollow echo of horses' hooves, the vendors' shouts, all the city's sounds swirled around them. As they left behind the fashionable part of London, the streets became narrower and even more crowded.

Did he think she was trying to entrap him into marriage? Bloody hell, she knew she hadn't money or status enough to marry an earl, Clarissa thought, resting her chin in her hands as she stared out at a passing team of oxen pulling a cart full of coal. When they resolved the murder charge, she had no doubt the earl would bow gracefully and move on to more beautiful, more highly connected ladies. Sharing a few more kisses in the meantime didn't seem too much to ask. Nor did she intend to let their love-making go too far, damn his arrogance. Did he think she knew nothing about men and women?

It wasn't as if she'd been brought up sheltered like a proper lady. Belowstairs, serving girls weren't as protected. She knew what made women's bellies swell with growing babies, and she knew that female servants who were unlucky enough to be caught in such a condition were turned out, to starve on the street or end up in the local brothel. No, she'd never even been tempted, and she'd boxed many a groom's or footman's ear. And as for that slimy employer of hers— he'd been harder to handle, but she was stubborn, and she had a strong voice, and she could pretend to be almost witless when need be, screaming for the whole household to hear. After one or two tries, the man had given up.

But no one had ever made her feel like Dominic had, yesterday. That kiss—it had sparked a flame between them. And now he was back to being the pompous earl. Damn his arrogance, she thought again.

He had been staring at the seat beside her as if his

dark-eyed gaze might drill a hole through the cushion. But he looked up now and glanced outside. "We're almost there. If anything happens, I will blame myself for allowing you to come."

"But you need me," she reminded him, keeping her tone even. "You said yourself, this woman will not talk to anyone except females. And I may struggle to be a lady, but I am certainly female."

"Oh, yes," he murmured. "Certainly, you are."

Wondering if he was jesting at her expense, Clarissa shot him a sharp look.

And indeed, his answering glance seemed brooding, holding some emotion that she could not identify.

She found that she was the one who looked away, staring down at her plain skirt and slightly worn gloves as she clasped her hands together in her lap.

Despite her calm tone, Clarissa found that her shoulders were tense with nervousness. But this had to be done, they must unravel the secrets that the matron—confound her!— had left behind. It was intolerable that she could threaten Clarissa's well-being even after she was dead. Clarissa drew a deep breath and tried to prepare herself for the coming interview.

His voice impersonal, the earl broke the silence, and they discussed what ruse she should use. So Clarissa had her story ready when the carriage drew up a few houses away from the Cattery.

Clarissa got out with one of the groom's help, ignored the stares from others on the street that such treatment—in this part of town—drew, and, squaring her shoulders, walked a few feet to the building and opened the door.

The bell attached to the door tinkled as she went in, and the air smelled musty. The room seemed empty, and Clarissa paused to look around. She felt as taut as the linen in an overstretched embroidery hoop. She drew out the large silk man's handkerchief—supplied by the earl—and rehearsed her speech.

But when a heavy footfall made her turn to see the woman who entered from the inner doorway, Clarissa found that everything she had rehearsed flew out of her mind.

"Wot you want?" the woman demanded. With slightly protuberant dark eyes, she stared down at the handkerchief in Clarissa's hand.

"Lifted a handkerchief, have ye? I can take it off your hands, dearie."

"It—it has a mark on it, the owner's initials," Clarissa said, her voice faint. She struggled to remember her lines.

"I know how to take 'em off, not to worry. What we say to four pence?"

"Is that all?" Clarissa asked, in spite of herself. "This is very good silk."

The woman frowned. "Best price you'll find on the street, I wager. I'm too bighearted for me own good, but I take good care of me girls, I do. And you're new about 'ere, aren't you?"

Clarissa nodded, still trying to find her wits, which had flown out the door at the sight of the woman's strangely familiar face.

"You're too pretty to waste yourself lifting kerchiefs, my dear. You should put yourself under my wing." The woman no doubt thought that her tone was warm. "I can teach you lots of good tricks."

Clarissa shivered. "I—I—"

"Wot 'appened? Some bloody respectable gent'lman try to seduce you and then throw you out on the street when you slapped 'is bloody face?" There was actual sympathy in the woman's voice, Clarissa thought.

She hesitated, and then, to her dismay, the door opened. Looking worried, the earl stepped inside.

The woman who ran the shop bristled. "You! You was 'ere yesterday. Didn't I tell you already—"

"I'm with her," the earl said shortly, glancing at Clarissa with concern.

"You didn't wait," Clarissa answered, her tone low.

"I was concerned—" But he didn't get to finish.

"'Er pimp, are you? Didn't waste any time, did you, dearie?"

The earl stiffened, and Clarissa had a wild desire to giggle.

"Should have come to me, first," the woman complained. "Well, get on out with ye both."

But the earl had conquered whatever outrage he felt, and he said, "No, we need information, and we can pay for it. We are searching for a woman of mid years with dark hair and a generous build. She might have been using the name Livermore."

"Or you might know her as Mrs. Craigmore," Clarissa put in.

They both looked at her, the earl in surprise, the woman of the shop with an expression of disgust.

"She weren't never married. And 'ow you know 'er?"

"From the foundling home," Clarissa said simply. "Are you, perhaps, her sister?"

There was a moment of silence. Lord Whitby's gaze shifted from her to the woman and back, but he held his tongue.

"So you're one of 'er girls, eh?" The woman shook her head. "I always tol' 'er she was wasting her time in that place, stealing pennies when I could 'ave made her pounds, but she liked to bully the girls, I think, and she was too damned lazy to work a real trade."

A real trade like this? Clarissa wondered, but she said instead, "You must be her younger sister." Who had perhaps known the matron's bullying, too, was her thought, but the woman unexpectedly preened and patted her hair, mostly hidden by a lace-trimmed if somewhat yellowish cap.

"Suppose you can tell, eh?"

Clarissa nodded. "Do you know about—"

"That she got 'erself coshed—oh, yeah. What, you the one who did it?" She looked more curious than angry or grieving.

"She was strangled, and I did not do it," Clarissa said

firmly before the earl could speak. He looked grim, but he allowed her to talk. It was obvious that this woman would only respond to a female.

"If it weren't you, it must 'ave been—" Looking suddenly wary, the matron's sister paused.

Clarissa swallowed hard. "Who?" She demanded. "If not me, then who?"

There was an agonizing moment of silence. The woman said, "Why should I risk 'is ire, for naught but a fare-thee-well? You got someone to take care of you—or give you a bloody lip, more likely, when you don't earn your keep. So why do you care?"

"I care if they put my neck in the noose!" Clarissa argued.

And the earl put one hand in his pocket. When he drew it out, she saw the glint of gold. The woman's eyes narrowed.

"Miss Craigmore, if that's your name, too, I can pay you well for the information. I also do not wish to see this lady—this female—hanged for a crime she did not commit."

He held out the guinea, and the woman swallowed, her gaze drawn to the large coin. "Craggity," she muttered. "Me sister was always changing 'er name, thought Craigmore sounded more top-drawer. And if it weren't you, it were the other one, that's all I know."

"What other one? Another girl who had been at the foundling home?" Clarissa demanded "I don't see—"

Miss Craggity shrugged. "Naw, it were a man, o' course. He was in the gang she worked with, after they threw 'er out of the 'ome. I guess she wrangled with 'im. She always said 'e was 'olding out the best part of the take."

"Do you know his name, or where we can find him?" the earl put in, his voice sharp.

The woman shook her head. "Naw, she only called 'im Rudy. And I took a few things from 'er after the break-ins, but nothing big. She said 'e kept the best for 'imself, wouldn't let anyone else enter the study while the rest of the gang went for the silver and the portables. . . ."

"What did he look like?"

Clarissa held her breath until Miss Craggity shook her head.

"Never saw 'im. It was me sister who came 'ere, when she had spoils for me to sell. That's all I know, and all I wanted to know. Not getting my neck snapped for the likes of 'er, thank-ee very much." She eyed the golden coin with open greed.

The earl frowned, but he passed it over. She snatched up the guinea and dropped it into the deep reach of her bosom, while Clarissa blinked in surprise.

"Now, out with ye!"

The earl waited for Clarissa to turn, but she glanced back over her shoulder. "Why didn't you claim her body?"

Miss Craggity shrugged. "Only 'eard about it later, gossip on the street. And why should I waste good blunt on 'er; she never did on me. It's not like we got a bloody family mausoleum, missy!"

Nor any family feeling, either, Clarissa thought. She allowed the earl to hold the door and, after first glancing out, he stepped ahead of her, then waited for her to leave the building.

Outside, eying the carriage, several roughly dressed men loitered nearby. Whether the woman inside had passed some signal, or the vehicle itself had drawn them with its promise of wealth to be made, or simply the aura—and rumor—of well-to-do gents with blunt in their pockets had seeped through the lawless miasma of the neighborhood, she wasn't sure. Clarissa felt her stomach tighten in alarm.

When she and the earl stepped out side, the men closed in.

The man who seemed to be their leader moved forward and confronted the earl.

"'And over your purse, gov, and we might let the girl go," he said, his tone gruff.

Whitby's expression hardened. "Step aside," he warned the ruffian.

"You're outnumbered, gov. What, you don't trust me word? I admit, she's a toothsome morsel—" He leered at Clarissa, and she shivered.

With a neat economy of motion, the earl swung his fist. He caught the man in his flabby stomach, and the would-be thief crumpled.

The other men stepped closer.

Watching them, Lord Whitby motioned, and both grooms jumped down from the back of the carriage. The earl's men drew not one but two pistols from inside their coats. They held them at the ready, and their would-be attackers paused.

The earl opened the carriage door. "Inside, quickly."

Clarissa scrambled to obey. The earl sprang after her, and she felt the vehicle rock as the grooms, or perhaps runners, leaped onto the back of the carriage. The coachman lashed his team, and they jolted forward.

Clarissa braced herself, but she heard only one disappointed shout, then nothing more than the usual clamor of the street. There was no further outcry behind them, and they seemed to be moving steadily. She took a deep breath.

"We did find out a little more," she said, "although a name and perhaps some notion of where to find him would have been better."

The earl was silent for a moment, then he nodded. "You will never, ever go back to that neighborhood," he told her. He had the old ring of command back in his voice, but he looked white about the lips.

"Of course not," Clarissa assured him. "Why should I?"

He didn't answer, and they rolled along the streets back toward home and safety—or as much of it as Clarissa could currently hope for.

Dominic found it hard to let go of his fear. That he had allowed Miss Fallon to put herself at such risk—he had felt the old sickness in his belly—the turmoil he still recalled too vividly from the battlefield. Sending his men into danger . . .

He had taken every precaution, and her presence today had indeed seemed necessary. She didn't seem to blanch at the danger, but he still shivered for her. The face of a young soldier came back to him, young and fresh-faced one day, the next lying shattered on the bloody field . . .

Dominic shut his eyes, but could not block the memories. Not this time, dear God, please, not this time.

He felt her touch on his arm, and he jumped.

"Dominic? I mean, my lord? You're shivering. Are you all right?"

"Only—" She would think him a craven, Dominic thought. The inside of the coach had dimmed as the sun sank lower in the sky. She gazed at him with her usual open glance. "Only that I don't want you hurt. And I remember the men I sent into battle, the faces of the ones that died."

"You didn't kill them," she pointed out, with her usual common sense. "You shouldn't blame yourself."

"But I ordered them into battle. They were in my charge." He couldn't expect her to understand. He shut his eyes again, but she let her hand linger on his arm, then slide up to brush his cheek.

"I don't deserve to be comforted," he told her, even though his skin tingled at the slight touch. "They had sisters, too, some of them, and mothers, wives, babes."

"Who would have been glad their menfolk had a commander who cared if they lived or died," she told him, her voice steady.

Clarissa had never seen the earl look so vulnerable, his dark eyes so shadowed. Was this why he hid behind his shield of aristocratic disdain? She knew about memories, and how they could haunt a person.

"I dream about the foundling home, sometimes," she told him, and recounted the dream about the children chanting and mocking her. "And then I see the shadow of a hangman's noose . . ." Her voice faltered.

His expression changed, and he turned, pulling her quickly inside the shelter of his arms. "God, what a selfish brute I am! Clarissa, you are not going to be tried for a murder you did not commit! You will certainly not be hanged. I will not allow it, I give you my solemn oath. I would spirit you out of England, first. I would die before I let you be harmed. Do you believe me?"

"Yes," she whispered, feeling a surge of joy. How much had to do with his promise and how much to the feel of his arms around her, she couldn't have said.

And at last he kissed her. Kissed her lips, long and hard, touched her earlobes gently, nibbled on the tender edges, caressed the soft skin of her neck until she quivered like a bowl of blancmange. He traced the line of her brows with his finger tips, kissed her hands again, her wrists, her palms, and then returned to her lips and kissed them until her blood seemed to sing in her veins. And although he was careful— she was almost amused to note—not to touch any part of her below her neckline, as if he had drawn himself some private boundary of this much license and no more, still, her stomach quivered and the new and unfamiliar ache inside her grew.

But they could not quench that deeper hunger, and she knew it. So she gloried in his kisses, returned all his caresses with a passion equal to his own, and tried to store up every touch, every sensation, for the barren times ahead when he would have left her, and she would face a life empty and alone.

Twelve

*T*hey picked up Matty at the market, then drove to
the Fallon home. When the carriage pulled up, Dominic got out to help Clarissa down.

"Will you not come in, my lord?" In front of the servants
her tone was formal, but her eyes still held the warmth of
their recent encounter. He hoped he had not made a terrible
mistake, allowing himself the luxury of inciting such feelings in a lady of little experience. Although, the other side of
his mind said, she wasn't exactly shy about kissing him back!

"Of course, if you wish," he said.

They entered the house and found Lady Gemma waiting.
At the sound of their entry, she came down from the drawing
room and greeted them civilly. Still, she took one look at
Clarissa's costume and shook her head.

Dominic braced himself for well-deserved reproaches, but
she seemed more resigned than angry. "Thank you for looking out for her, Lord Whitby. Will you stay for dinner? My
husband sent a note that he has been delayed, but Lady

Gabriel is here, and later we could discuss, ah, recent events."

With the butler hovering nearby, Dominic was circumspect, as well. "Thank you, that's very kind. I'm afraid I'm not dressed for the evening, however."   .

"We have no need to stand on ceremony; you do not need to change," she answered. Although to Clarissa, she looked her drab gown up and down and said, "You, my dear, on the other hand—"

Clarissa nodded, and with Matty behind her, climbed the staircase to don a more suitable frock.

At least he was not in his shirtsleeves, this time! Dominic accepted her offer of wine and followed his hostess to the drawing room, where Lady Gabriel and Miss Pomshack were seated.

With the lady's companion in the room, they had to make small talk until Clarissa returned wearing a pleasing dinner gown, and soon dinner was announced.

Lady Gemma explained that her husband was collecting more facts about the house break-ins, which he hoped might lead them to the real culprit.

Dominic nodded. He still had men on the same errand, but Captain Fallon was a more intelligent sleuth than most of the runners, and besides, he could understand the man's need to do something when his sister was imperiled.

"And my husband," Lady Gabriel told them, her smile twisted, "is combing Yorkshire for a man named Smith."

What that had to do with the current quagmire, Dominic was not at all sure, although Lady Gabriel and Lady Gemma exchanged glances.

At dinner, he was seated between his hostess and Lady Gabriel, as his rank demanded. Across the table, he was glad to see that Clarissa ate a decent dinner, even if she looked a little distracted. Both the ladies near him made witty small talk, but he was still glad when the time came for the ladies to withdraw. After only a few swallows of his port, he rose and followed them to the drawing room.

There, they used the same stratagem of a card game to

withdraw a little way from Miss Pomshack, leaving that good lady to her book, so that they could discuss what progress they had made.

Dominic gave them a brief version of their foray into Whitechapel, leaving out the absence of Clarissa's chaperone, and although he omitted many of the more ominous details, Gemma shuddered.

"I know it was most improper—" he began.

"So is being hanged," Clarissa interrupted, sounding impatient. "Improper, that is. Gemma will not scold us, and anyhow, we are home safely. I am more concerned that we did not discover more."

Lady Gemma sighed. "Let us think about what you did learn. We were right about the late matron's connection with a gang of thieves and housebreakers, at any rate, although we are not much further along with finding them, or their ringleader."

"Who is surely the best suspect for her murder," Lady Gabriel agreed, keeping her voice low as she pretended to check the cards in her hand.

"But we have to find him!" Clarissa said, too loudly, then with a quick glance toward Miss P, lowered her voice again. "I'm sorry, it's just so frustrating."

Lady Gemma pressed her sister-in-law's hand in sympathy. Dominic wished he could do the same, and for more than to just express compassion, although he certainly felt that. But the touch of Clarissa's soft skin was so . . .

To distract himself, he frowned and tapped his cards. "Yes, and Miss Craggity implied that there had already been some dissension between them, which is even more suggestive. She said that her sister claimed that he was 'keeping the best for himself.' "

"Yes," Clarissa agreed. "She said he was the only one allowed to enter the study."

Lady Gabriel frowned for a moment, then nodded in understanding. "Of course. My husband keeps his cash box in his desk."

"And that would be the best bounty of all," Lady Gemma agreed. "Money. No need to resell it to a receiver and get only a fraction of its worth, like the household silver and other valuables."

"So perhaps she demanded more of the results of their criminal acts," Dominic suggested. "And that led to their quarrel and her death."

"But how can we find him?" Clarissa bit her lip.

"If there were some way to know which house they were targeting next—" Lady Gabriel said.

Dominic shook his head. "London has many gangs and even more houses. If I hired every runner in Bow Street, and there are not that many, we couldn't possibly cover every house, not even in the West End. And without the matron's connection to her past, the foundling home orphans now in service, we would have no way of knowing which residence they might target next."

"And my husband says, from his survey of the magistrates' offices, that household robberies have dropped off a little," Lady Gemma put in. "Perhaps the gang is lying low for a time. It's possible that the hue and cry over the matron's death has alarmed even them."

For a moment, they were all silent. Dominic looked at Clarissa's face and said, "We will keep working, Miss Fallon. You are not alone."

She nodded, although she still looked grave.

"And we have made progress," Lady Gemma put in, her tone also encouraging.

They finished the card game, and Psyche took her leave. While Lady Gemma said good-bye to her friend, Dominic turned to look again at Clarissa. They had all risen when the game had ended, and now he stepped closer to her.

"Do not lose heart," he told her, keeping his voice low.

She smiled up at him suddenly, and, glancing around to see that the other ladies had stepped into the hall, rose on her toes and gave him a quick kiss.

His hunger rising unbidden to the surface, he pulled her

close and returned her kiss. Then he released her as abruptly and drew a deep breath. "Enough, you vixen," he said beneath his breath. "We will be discovered."

Ignoring the rebuke, Clarissa smiled. Her eyes were bright. "Thank you, my lord, for being there for me," she said. "And for everything you said. And for—just for being you."

He was so shaken he could barely mutter his good-byes when he moved to the doorway. Lady Gemma looked a little puzzled at his unusual lack of suavity, but she thanked him, too.

"I do not lay the blame for the trip to Whitechapel on your shoulders, my lord," she said quietly. "I know Clarissa too well. But I appreciate your care with her safety."

"I only took a few logical steps to protect her," he told her, knowing that even that, had the foray into Whitechapel gone wrong, might not have been enough.

Although she must have had the same thought, he was grateful that Lady Gemma did not remark upon it.

Under her sister-in-law's eyes, not to mention Miss Pomshack's, who hovered in the background, Clarissa gave him a prim curtsy as he made his leave. But he saw the glimmer of mischief—and more—that lingered in her bright eyes.

When he left, he climbed into the nondescript carriage and found that his whole body ached for her.

It was very late when Matthew returned. Clarissa had retired to bed, but when she heard his voice in the hall, she threw on a wrapper and went out.

She saw him on the landing below, speaking quietly to his wife. His face was gray with fatigue. She leaned over the bannister.

"Matthew?"

He came up to her and kissed her forehead. "I've been out all day, my dear. I did find one case where a woman I believe to be Mrs. Craigmore was had up before a magistrate in a nearby parish. She was charged with theft, but unhappily, she got off with a small fine. I have reason to believe that the magistrate—his name is Donaldson—may have been bribed. It often happens, I hear. But I will not give up until we find the villain who did this and see your good name and your safety no longer threatened."

"Matthew—" It made Clarissa hurt to see him look so exhausted and discouraged. "This is not your fault."

He looked away. "Of course it is my fault. If I had given you a better guardian when I went to sea, if after our mother died you had not been sent to that foundling home and into that woman's clutches—"

"Matthew, you didn't know! You did the best you could. You are not to blame. I love you, and you must not shoulder all the responsibility." She threw her arms about him, and he sighed and hugged her.

"You are too forgiving, Clarissa. But I will not stop until we find the real killer."

"I know that, and I am appreciative." She didn't point out that they were all working for the same end. She suspected that he needed to do this, needed to spend long hours combing London's courts and records and the city's seamier side.

His expression lifted a little, and he said good night to her. "Sleep well, my dear."

"I will," she promised and watched him return to where Gemma waited, saw them go arm in arm to their own room. At least Gemma could comfort him, would be there for him.

For herself, Clarissa shut her door and crawled into bed. But after some times worrying about her brother, she reached to the table near her bed and took out of her reticule a man's handkerchief. The earl had forgotten to reclaim it after their adventure today.

She stroked its soft folds and held it to her cheek. Those kisses in the carriage—bloody hell, she'd never suspected a man's touch could feel so good. If the earl were not such a gentleman, perhaps she could experience it again. Perhaps she could convince him that being proper was not always such a good thing. . . .

Smiling, she blew out her candle.

But when she slept, despite Dominic's promise, she dreamed again of the hangman's rope, and of ragged children who watched her from the shadows and chanted in shrill voice's and uneducated accents.

"Cl'rissa's gonna get caned again, Cl'rissa's gonna get hanged again."

The next morning, Clarissa woke late and heavy-eyed. When she went down to breakfast, she saw Gemma observe her with some anxiety. No doubt her sister-in-law thought she was exhausted from yesterday's foray into the poorer side of London.

Clarissa knew it had more to do with her restless night and alarming dreams, but she didn't want to discuss them. Talking about the visions seemed to give them too much weight, so she simply sipped her tea and tried to eat a little breakfast.

When a note was delivered, Clarissa looked up eagerly.

However, the footman took the missive to Gemma. With an apologetic glance toward her, Gemma broke the wax seal.

She skimmed the contents quickly, then looked up. "The earl sends us word that he is returning to Whitechapel today to make further inquiries and will visit later if he has any new findings, today or perhaps tomorrow."

"Why didn't he—" Clarissa began, then paused. He could have taken her along! And he certainly could at least have told her directly. Oh, no, gentlemen did not correspond with unmarried ladies, Clarissa recalled, her spirits dropping again. Damn all this bloody propriety, anyhow!

Gemma wrinkled her brow. "He's quite right; it's too dangerous a place for you, my dear. And you did what you needed to do yesterday, identifying"—she paused, glancing at the servants in the room—"identifying that person, so you need not fret. And besides, you missed a dance lesson yesterday. Monsieur Meidenne was annoyed. I paid him anyhow, of course, but I also promised that you would be here today when he comes."

Dance lessons! Oh, heavens, just what she did not need! Clarissa wanted to argue that, with her life hanging—oh, dreadful word—on this investigation, it was much more important to find the killer than it was to polish Clarissa's still rough society manners. But she knew what her sister-in-law would reply: Life had to go on, they had to believe that Clarissa would be exonerated and all would be well. And perhaps Gemma truly believed that. After all, she did not suffer dreams in which she saw the noose's shadow or heard chanting children. . . .

Miss Pomshack came in and filled her plate, and Clarissa let the argument pass. When the dance instructor arrived, promptly at eleven, they went into the drawing room so that Gemma could play on the pianoforte and provide accompaniment.

Unhappily, Clarissa found that, not having given any thought to her dance forms for several days, today she appeared to have even less grasp of the proper steps than during the last lesson.

Her lack of practice soon became all too obvious.

"Mademoiselle, if you will attend, *s'il vous plaît!*" Monsieur Meidenne commanded, his tone sharp, after Clarissa had once again trod upon his foot.

Clarissa blushed and muttered yet another apology.

"Perhaps a short respite would be welcome," Gemma suggested. "Let me call for tea." She went outside to speak to a footman, and, perhaps in the hope of soothing his much-tested patience, motioned to the tutor to follow her for a word.

Clarissa knew that her cheeks must be flushed. She reached into her pocket and discovered she had forgotten to put in her small book of dance forms. Damn! She looked about her and saw that the tutor had left his larger volume sitting on a table nearby. If she could only scan the pattern and refresh her memory of the more complicated steps. . . .

She lifted the cover. Yes, it was a listing of dance forms, much like her own smaller book, and Clarissa skimmed the pages, looking for the steps she sought. But something was not quite right—she stared at the words in front of her.

Then, hearing the tutor's voice, she let the book fall close and took several steps away, not wishing to draw more censure. With Gemma at his side, Monsieur Meidenne came back into the room, and Clarissa turned away, afraid she was blushing even harder. She walked across to gaze out one of the drawing room windows and avoid meeting his eye.

What was wrong with the forms in his book?

The tea tray came, and Gemma poured tea for everyone. Miss Pomshack helped make polite conversation, and by the time they returned to the lesson, Gemma tried grimly to keep her mind on the steps.

This time, the tutor chided her for watching his feet instead of meeting his gaze, but at least she did not tread on his toe, and if she had another reason for not wishing to catch his eye, she hoped he was not aware of it.

When the seemingly unending dance lesson at last wound to a close, Clarissa muttered polite thanks, but her thoughts were still elsewhere.

Gemma said, "You are improving, Clarissa."

Unwilling to debate such an optimistic but loving assessment, Clarissa nodded and went upstairs to find her own dance book.

She was still puzzling over what she had seen when the earl was announced. By this time, Miss Pomshack had retired for her usual mid-afternoon rest, and Gemma and Clarissa were back in the drawing room. She looked up eagerly when Lord Whitby came into the room.

"Nothing new, I'm afraid," he told them. 'There is no doubt that Miss Craggity is a noted receiver, even if very eccentric about whom she deals with, and I found two people who admit to having seen her sister visit her, but I cannot trace any more of the late matron's contacts. Whoever was in the gang she was connected to, I'm not sure we have any way of finding them."

"Perhaps we should set up a trap and lie in wait for the gang to break in?" Gemma suggested.

"How would we make sure they came? And that it was the right group of thieves? There are many operating in London," the earl pointed out.

"But we must do something," Gemma said, sighing. She turned to gaze at Clarissa. "My dear, do not be downhearted."

Clarissa realized she had been sitting silently for several moments. She tried to pull her thoughts together.

"What is it?" the earl said.

He always seemed to read her moods.

"It is probably nothing," she said slowly. "But—" She explained how she had come to glance inside the dance instructor's book of dance forms. "It was not accurate."

"Perhaps it was only a slightly different version of the steps," Gemma suggested, looking puzzled. "There are variations on many dances, you know."

The earl waited, and under his encouraging gaze, Clarissa found the nerve to shake her head. "It's more than that. I have been studying my own book of dance instruction," she said. "At least, not recently, as was all too apparent from my performance this morning, but I have scanned it often, and I examined it carefully after the lesson. Monsieur Meidenne's volume was wrong. I noticed one line that should have said, 'Two steps back and cross over.' Instead, several words were crossed out, and *twenty g.* written in."

"G?" The earl wrinkled his brow.

"And a few lines down, I saw the name, *Davidson,* and more numbers. My brother Matthew has, after much searching, come across a magistrate named Davidson, who might have had contact with the matron. He is also a magistrate whom Matthew suspected might be open to taking bribes," Clarissa pointed out.

The earl put down his teacup and sat up even straighter. "Magistrates who have been convicted of bribery can go to prison. Or at the least, lose their position."

Her expression puzzled, Gemma looked from one to the other. "I don't see what this has to do with our dance instructor?"

Clarissa found her heart beating faster. She looked at the earl. "What did the matron tell her sister? When they broke into a house, the gang's ringleader always took the master's study for himself, to ransack without the others watching."

Whitby nodded. "I don't know about your brother, but I keep more than money in my desk. It holds papers, both private and business."

"But why would an ordinary housebreaker care about that?" Gemma asked. "Papers would have no value to him."

"On the contrary—" the earl began.

"Perhaps this thief is not so ordinary after all," Clarissa said at the same time. "Perhaps he found something even more priceless than the household silver."

The earl gave her a quick smile. "Yes, information. A letter from a lover, business deals that were not totally honest, even perhaps a list of bribes taken. In a word, material for blackmail."

Thirteen

*"The slyer the fox, the more cunning
the hunter must be."*

MARGERY, COUNTESS OF SEALY

"*B*lackmail?" *Gemma looked from one to the other.*
"So it is more than simple household theft?"

"Information, embarrassing or incriminating, could pay
for itself time after time, in contrast to a few valuables soon
sold for much less than their original worth," the earl pointed
out.

"But, Monsieur Meidenne—a thief? Surely not, he came
so highly recommended!" Gemma looked aghast.

Clarissa was still thinking. "Remember the households
where there were no servants we could connect to the
foundling home? One of them, you mentioned, had daughters
who were out. What do you wager those young ladies had
a dance tutor?"

"Most of them do," Gemma agreed, her expression still
doleful.

"It would be another way for someone to check out a household," Clarissa pointed out. "And he's quite good-looking.

I'm sure he would have no trouble flirting with the maidservants or even the young ladies themselves."

The earl gave her a quick look, and there was something in his eyes she could not quite identify. But he turned to Gemma.

"Have any of the tutor's other clients had break-ins at their homes?" Lord Whitby inquired, and he had smoothed his expression.

She nodded, but added, "Yes, I have heard of several. Still, not all of Monsieur Meidenne's patrons have been robbed. Certainly, we have not."

"Perhaps he was simply being careful, wary of inciting suspicion," the earl said. "If all his clients had their households invaded, it might occur to someone to connect him to the burglaries. His position—and his ability to go in and out of prominent homes—has value only as long as he is not suspected of any nefarious motive."

Gemma sighed. "This is dreadful. I will terminate his services at once."

"No!" Clarissa objected. "We must go on just as usual and not let him know we suspect him."

"I agree," the earl said. "We shall have to do more investigation of this Monsieur Meidenne."

"I suppose so, but how on earth shall I greet him now without showing my suspicions?" Gemma fretted.

"You can do it; you must do it," Clarissa urged. "We must not alert him that we suspect that he is any more than a dancing tutor!"

Gemma nodded.

Lord Whitby looked thoughtful. "However, we can make use of this very valuable information. Perhaps now we can try some of your earlier ideas—plant an enticement for a break-in."

Clarissa knew her eyes had widened. "Here?"

"Probably not here; it might be too obvious, but if we can find a friend willing to help—"

They discussed the matter at some length, and when the earl departed, his step quick with purpose, Clarissa felt a thrill of expectation.

At last, they could take real steps toward catching the man in the act and proving that he, not Clarissa, might be the one guilty of murder!

The next day was a long one. The dancing tutor was not due back until the following morning, and while they all had tasks to perform, Clarissa knew that the earl was the one who had the most to do. Still, she and Gemma could call on Lady Gabriel and share their ideas.

When they arrived, they found another caller, too, sitting in the Sinclair drawing room, and Lady Sealey seemed most interested in their plan. Since she was a trusted confidante of both ladies and had already aided them once, they did not hesitate to discuss the situation in front of her.

"No, the trap should not be laid here, Psyche," she said, putting down her teacup. "You are a close connection because of Lord Gabriel and Lady Gemma's family bonds. The man might be suspicious, and unless he brings his gang of thieves when we wish it, nothing will be accomplished and it will all be for naught."

"We could not ask anyone else to take such a chance," Gemma began, as if suspecting where this was leading. "The risk—"

Lady Sealey shook her head. "Bosh, we will be prepared, obviously. And I will not, as much as I shall hate to miss such an exciting event, be in the house. That's the whole point, to announce discreetly that I am going out of town for the weekend to attend a house party. As indeed I am, this coming weekend."

"Is there enough time to put everything in motion?" Gemma looked around the circle at them all.

Clarissa felt a glimmer of impatience. "We must try!"

"I think you are right," Lady Gabriel said, her tone thoughtful. "But, my dear Lady Sealey, you must take thought to all the dangers."

The countess chuckled. "I shall leave unsecured only the ugliest of my silver. And perhaps, if I'm truly lucky, they will take the epergne that my great-aunt insisted on leaving to me, the one with the Gothic carvings and engraved gargoyles."

Clarissa laughed, and she felt a surge of optimism. "We must inform the earl," she pointed out.

"At once," Gemma agreed, stirring her own tea, which she seemed to have forgotten to drink. "I will send him a note."

Clarissa felt a flicker of envy. Protected by her married state, Gemma could do what Clarissa could not.

She felt the countess's glance. "I am hearing gossip, my dear. The Ton has noted that the earl is spending much time in your company, and many ladies are seething with jealousy behind their fans. Half of Society has you already engaged."

Clarissa flushed. "Nonsense, he is only being helpful. He is very kind and very, very brave!"

"Indeed," the older lady agreed politely. Her lips seemed to want to smile, although she controlled them.

"At least it is better than—you have not heard any hint of talk linking Clarissa to an involvement with the dead—the late matron?" Gemma lowered her voice as the footman left the room, taking out an empty tray that had held small delicious cakes and fruit tarts.

"No, thank heavens," the countess told them. "Not a word."

"If you have not heard it, then it has not been said, and Clarissa's reputation is still secure," Gemma declared, and the others nodded.

Clarissa wanted to ask if the Ton were still calling her the "fallen Miss Fallon," but knew the countess would hesitate to confirm her fears, even if they were true. And compared to her neck in the noose, she thought, what did a slip on a dance floor matter? She did not care if the farcical title lingered.

The once-painful nickname now had little power to wound her.

So their plans continued, and that night, Clarissa could hardly sleep as she braced herself for the next morning; she must betray no hint of her suspicions about the tutor. As a result, her dreams were even more confused than usual, but still menacing. She went down to breakfast with heavy eyes.

When the dancing master was announced at eleven o'clock, she found her heart beating fast. Bracing herself and forcing her expression to remain bland and unrevealing, Clarissa dipped a polite curtsy as Gemma spoke her greeting.

As it turned out, Clarissa found she hardly needed to worry. Her performance this morning was so bad that she had every excuse for looking flustered.

Fortunately, Gemma very soon asked Miss Pomshack to join the lesson, and that good lady was even more chatty than usual, so it helped to cover Clarissa's silence. Between watching her own feet and biting her lip over yet another misstep, Clarissa found the lesson crawled by.

And it seemed natural, when they took a break for tea, for Gemma to share with Miss Pomshack the news that Lady Sealey had been invited to attend a large house party for the weekend and was, as usual, taking her elderly butler with her, as well as several of the other house servants.

"They're having a dance on Saturday night and a concert with a visiting Italian soprano on Sunday afternoon, so I'm sure Lady Sealey will find it a delightful interlude," she explained.

"What a shame you were not also invited," Lady Pomshack said, happy to gossip. "I know that family; they are distantly connected to the Viscount Henley. I once spent two years chaperoning his younger daughter when—"

Clarissa let her thoughts wander. Miss Pomshack sounded quite natural, and since she had no reason to know their secret agenda, there was no reason she should not. Was the tutor paying attention, stowing away the tidbit as he sipped his tea? Even more essential, would he and his gang take the bait?

All Clarissa and her allies could do was wait and see.

Gemma allowed Miss P to ramble on for a few minutes, than glanced at the clock on the mantel. "Perhaps I should return to the pianoforte and allow Clarissa and Monsieur Meidenne one more dance before our time is up."

"Of course." The governess prepared to take her place, and Clarissa followed more slowly. At least he had no reason to know just why, today, she was reluctant to touch his gloved hand, and he could put her clumsiness down to her usual awkwardness on the dance floor.

Clarissa thought of dancing with the earl and how very different it had been from these sessions with her instructor, and tried not to feel wistful. Would she ever have the nerve to step out onto a real dance floor again?

And now the earl would be placing himself in peril, for her sake. . . . Was it possible that the countess's hints were correct? Could it be that he felt something more than pity at her difficult circumstances, that he felt real emotion for her? She recalled the kisses they'd shared, but caresses were easy enough to give, and he was a man of the world . . .

She stepped on the tutor's foot and muttered an apology. But at least, she had forgotten for a moment how strange it was to stand so close to a man who might be the murderer they sought.

Monsieur Meidenne seemed as relieved as she when their hour was over, and he could bid them a polite good-bye.

Clarissa dipped a curtsy and allowed Gemma to walk him to the door. Clarissa went to the window and watched the instructor's slim frame as he strode rapidly away from the house, soon moving out of her view. Would he take the bait? Would the thieves come?

That afternoon, the earl called, and they had a rare stroke of luck, at least as far as Clarissa was concerned. Not expecting company, Gemma had gone out, and Miss Pomshack had accompanied her, so Clarissa was alone in the drawing room when Lord Whitby was shown up.

He hesitated in the doorway. "Am I intruding upon your privacy?"

Having achieved a credible curtsy, Clarissa straightened and shook her head. "Not at all. My sister-in-law will be back very shortly; please sit down."

Taking care to be on her best behavior, she bade the footman bring up a tea tray. Keeping her voice dignified, she tried to imitate Gemma's calm certainty and seemingly effortless poise. When she turned back to him, she found the earl smiling at her as if he detected her efforts, and she grinned back at him. Would he kiss her? But today he seemed unwilling to take chances.

"I came to hear how the dancing lesson went," he told her.

"Tolerably well," she answered. "At least, I was dreadful during the lesson, treading on the poor man—no, if he is who we think he is, he deserves no pity!—several times. If he is a murderer, I shall be sorry I didn't break every bone in his foot! But I don't believe I gave him any cause for suspicion. Heaven knows I've been clumsy enough from the beginning, as you well know, so hopefully he did not realize why I was so awkward today."

He leaned over and reached to take her hand, pressing it lightly. "You underrate yourself, Clarissa."

She doubted the truth of his statement but glowed that he should contradict her. She was sorry when he drew back his hand. "At any rate, Gemma chatted with Miss Pomshack about Lady Sealey's departure on Friday, and they gossiped at length about the house party, so he has all the pertinent information."

"And we must hope that he acts upon it," the earl agreed. "I hope it was not too trying a morning. You look rather tired."

She touched her temple. She did have a headache although she was loathe to admit it. "I didn't sleep well. It was not the lesson so much, but perhaps the dread of it that brought on one of the nightmares."

"You are still suffering from the dreams?" he asked, his tone concerned.

She tried not to wince.

"I promised you—"

"I know," she agreed. "And I do believe you, really, I do. When you're with me, I feel quite safe. But when you're gone, the fear creeps back in, as well as the dreams."

Dominic looked grim. "Perhaps you should talk about it, rid yourself of some of the fears. What was the foundling home like?" he asked her. "Do you have any good memories of the place?"

She shrugged. "Some of the girls were good to me. Others made sport of me and my 'uppity' airs. But I learned to fit in. I suppose we do what we must."

"If we have the courage, and you have a great deal," he told her.

She flashed him a smile.

What about—" She paused as the footman brought in a tray laden with a teapot and china and cakes and scones and jam. "Thank you. I will pour."

After the servant had left, she very poured out two cups of tea, aware that the earl was grinning at her, not unkindly, and handed him one. "If I drop this on your lap, it will serve you right," she warned him, then added, more soberly, "Tell me about your dreams. At least, if it will not pain you."

She looked up at him, seeing shadows in his face that he usually kept hidden. She wanted to ask him more, but she hesitated.

He took the cup, then looked away from her gaze. "I dream of the battlefields, but mostly I don't see the whole panorama, it would be too much, even in memory. So my visions show me one wounded soldier lying drenched in his own blood or one horse trembling with its foot blown off—"

She must have made a sound despite herself, because he shut his lips firmly together.

"I'm sorry, I didn't mean to distress you."

She shook her head, still appalled, but also sorry she had

stopped the flow of his words. "I'm sorry, but you should not be. You went into battle to serve your country, and save us from Napoleon's threat of invasion. You make me realize that my own suffering was mild in comparison."

"Not in the least," he objected. "I was a soldier, a grown man, and most of all I regret the fact that I might have done more to avert the carnage, the suffering of my men. You were only a child, and had no one beside you to protect and comfort you. This was a very different circumstance. You have every reason to feel what you feel."

For a moment, they sat in silence, and she clung to his hand.

"Does it get any better?" she asked, her voice quiet.

He gazed at her, as one wounded soldier to another. "I think so, in time. Perhaps it never departs completely. But if you face your fear, it will not overwhelm you."

"How on earth do you do that?" she demanded. "When the hurtful times are in the past, when your foes are long departed, how do you go back and face them down?"

His glance at her held meaning, but she could not read it. "You will discover a way," he told her. "When you are ready."

There was too much pain in his eyes. Perhaps she had no right to encourage him to revisit his own visions of struggle and loss. Had he not done enough for her already, risked himself enough?

He still held one of her hands between his own. She lifted the other and touched his cheek very softly.

His eyes lightened, and he put up his left hand to hold her palm against his cheek. She felt the warmth of his skin beneath her palm, the slightest prickle of barely visible facial hair. He was so overwhelmingly masculine, and the way that he looked at her made feelings stir again inside her. She moved her hand slowly across his cheek, down to his mouth, to trace the outline of his lips beneath her fingers.

He drew a deep breath, pressed her hand to his lips and kissed the palm.

Clarissa felt the thrill run through her whole body. It was

a small gesture, but so intimate, and the touch of his breath made goose bumps rise on her arm. If only—

Then there were footsteps in the hall, and to her great regret, he released both her hands and turned.

She drew a steadying breath. When Gemma and Miss Pomshack appeared in the doorway, Clarissa tried to find her voice.

"Lord Whitby called to see—" she said, then paused, remembering that Miss P did not know about their plot.

"To see how you all are," he finished for her. "I fear I must be going; I have some business to set into motion."

He sounded quite controlled again, but as he made his bow, the glance he threw her way made her quiver.

Clarissa clasped her palms together and tried to hold on to the warmth their two hands had shared.

Two nights later, Dominic found himself, as planned, sitting quietly in the shadow of the large bookcases in the countess's study. He was prepared for a long night of tedium. They had no way of knowing if the gang would come— assuming they came at all—on Friday, Saturday, or Sunday.

But he had to be here, just in case. He glanced around him. The large house was very quiet, and the darkness broken only by slivers of palest light where the draperies were not quite closed. A clock ticked from the mantel, and he could hear the large clock in the hall striking the hour. One o'clock. The house creaked, a faint sound, but it made him stiffen and listen hard. But after a few moments he decided it was only the floorboards settling a bit as the air cooled.

Outside on the front door, the brass knocker had been removed, and the drapes were drawn mostly shut. He had allowed a few cracks at the windows in order to filter in the light from the street lamps, so the interior of the house was not completely black. They could do no more to announce that the house was empty except paint a sign on the front! He only hoped that the wrong thieves would not appear.

It was all a gamble, and it might all be for naught. He would have given up three nights of his usual boring social rounds to sit in an empty house . . . and Dominic found he had no regrets at all at the notion. Until Miss Fallon returned to Society, there was no one in anyone's drawing room or ballroom that he wished to see. . . . The thought brought a flicker of surprise with it. When had her presence become so indispensable to his happiness? No, more than that, his satisfaction, his contentment, his—

Another creak broke his train of thought.

Where had the noise come from? The attics were currently empty; all the female servants who had not gone with her ladyship had been sent away for their own safety, in case Dominic's ruse was successful.

There—it came again. Someone was forcing a window, somewhere toward the back of the house, he thought. The door to the study had been left open, and Dominic strained to hear the small noises. Yes, now there were footsteps, stealthy but detectable in the hush of the apparently vacant house.

The other men who waited in the darkness had been given strict orders not to interrupt the burglary until Dominic commanded it; he hoped no overzealous law officer would forget his instructions.

Now he heard people moving about the house, their footsteps muffled, but the occasional creak of a floorboard gave them away. And now he made out clinks of metal as silver was shoved into bags. He hoped this did not go wrong and the countess did not lose a good part of her household goods. Despite her brave words, she could not put too much away, or the gang would be suspicious.

Dominic felt his nerves crawl with impatience. Where was the ringleader? Was this even the right gang?

At last, a shadow appeared in the doorway. It was a man's form, slim and only medium in height. Stepping into the room, the figure paused to get his bearings.

Dominic sat very still, knowing that, in his far corner, he was effectively hidden in the deep recesses of the wing chair he had chosen for the purpose.

The man in the doorway crossed to the desk, and without fuss, pulled open a drawer, then another. He found the cash box and made a small grunt, likely in disappointment. They had left some money inside it, but not a great amount. There was the jingle of coins as the thief slid them into his pocket and replaced the box, then a pause. A sudden burst of light appeared, like a solitary firework breaking the inky darkness of a smooth summer sky.

Dominic blinked, and the light, dazzling in its first flare, resolved itself into one small flame. The intruder had lit a candle, and with its light, he began to search the desk and scan the papers inside.

Dominic lifted the pistol he had been resting on his lap and stood.

The thief's head jerked; he must have seen the motion from the corner of his eye.

"Stand very still," Dominic commanded.

Instead, the man moved his arm in one swift, fluid motion.

Some instinct left over from the battlefield made Dominic twist to the side before conscious thought could move him. A slim, lethal blade sank deep into the leather cushion of the wing chair. It had missed him by only inches.

He muttered a few succinct words and lifted the pistol, but the thief was moving again, diving for the doorway.

It would do little good to have the man dead; they could not prove that he was the one who had murdered the matron if he were unable to speak! Cursing, Dominic ran into the hallway after him.

"He's making for the street! Come out!" he shouted.

At the agreed upon code words, the men who had been carefully hidden sprang out of pantries and anterooms and from beneath curtained tables. The hush of the house was broken by curses and the sounds of blows and a crash as some small piece of furniture was sent flying.

Dominic hardly noticed. He pursued the fleeing thief, who made a beeline through halls and doorways retreating to the open window in one of the back kitchens where the pack of scoundrels had entered. With apparently not a care about the rest of his gang—loyalty among thieves, my ass, Dominic thought cynically—the man ran for his life.

Dominic ran after him.

He scrambled through the window only a few seconds behind the other man, who was smaller in frame and made his exit more swiftly. Dominic had to squeeze his own shoulders through the opening, but at last he made it, dropping to the alley below.

He got his balance and listened. The sound of muffled footsteps led him on. Dominic kept a firm grip on his pistol and pelted after the escaping thief. After all this, he could not lose him!

The alleyway was dark, with no streetlights. But by the smell, it ran along the stables behind the big houses. In the darkness it was hard to keep his eye on the slim shadowy form that by now had gained a few yards on him. Keeping his pistol ready, Dominic settled into a hard run. In another block, he had narrowed the gap between them.

Then the man darted around a building and disappeared from sight.

Swearing beneath his breath, Dominic followed, but he had enough caution to duck slightly as he rounded the corner, hoping the man was not carrying another blade.

The air exploded.

Fourteen

For an instant, the blast seemed to blind him. Dominic felt the sting on his shoulder and fell back a step, then he lifted his own weapon. Even though he still blinked against the detonation of gunpowder discharged at such close range, he fired, too.

At first he thought he had missed, then he heard, despite his ringing ears, a muffled thud as a body fell. Hoping he had not hit the heart or any vital spot, Dominic hurried forward, tucking the now useless gun into his waistband.

The man lay chest down at the edge of the grass, one hand folded beneath his body. His face was toward the dirt, and it was too dark to make out much about him. But he was the right size and form to be the dancing tutor. . . .

As Dominic knelt to turn the thief over and see how badly he was wounded, he heard footfalls behind him as another man ran into view.

"There you are!"

Dominic had twisted and raised his fists, but now he

lowered them and drew a deep breath. "I have shot him, I think, but have yet to see his face. He has fired at me and thrown a blade, so he's a dangerous bastard."

"Let's see him!" Matthew Fallon said, his tone eager. "We have taken most of his men, though a couple slipped from our net."

He reached to turn the body, but beneath his touch, the fallen man twisted of his own volition. The arm that had been hidden rose, and it was not empty.

"Look out!" Dominic shouted. As the gun barked, he grabbed Fallon's arm and jerked him to the side.

The bullet hit the captain, anyhow, and he fell back against Dominic. Dominic tried to support him, but swore again as he saw the thief jump up and take to his heels once more.

"Damn and blast!" Dominic lowered Fallon to the ground.

"Go after him!" the other man said.

But as Dominic patted the wounded man's chest, he felt the wetness of blood. He could not allow Clarissa's brother to bleed to death in the darkness, just as he would not have abandoned one of his soldiers.

"No, we must take you back to the house and staunch the bleeding," he said, hearing the defeat heavy in his own voice. "There will be another time for Monsieur Meidenne."

But he felt the same deep chagrin that he knew Captain Fallon was experiencing. Damn and damn again! To come so close and yet lose him—

Frowning, forcing his frustration and anger into icy resolve, Dominic helped support the captain as they slowly made their way back to the countess's house.

Clarissa had been unable to sleep, knowing that all the men she cared about were risking their lives for her sake. She had gone up to her room when she was bidden but had not bothered to undress. She picked up a book and tried to read, but when at length she cast the volume aside and found herself pacing up and down her bedchamber rug, she gave up and went downstairs.

As she had suspected, Gemma was awake, too. Clarissa found her not in the drawing room but in Matthew's study, as if closeness to her husband's books and papers was somehow comforting during this long night of waiting.

Gemma jerked when Clarissa appeared in the doorway, then drew a deep breath. "Oh, it is you."

"I'm sorry to startle you," Clarissa told her. "I could not sleep, either." She crossed to where Gemma sat behind the big desk and bent to hug her sister-in-law. "I suppose I'm unsettled, as well."

"I know," Gemma said simply. For a moment, they shared an embrace.

It was comforting, but still— Clarissa straightened and swore briskly for an instant, making her sister-in-law jump again. "Bloody hell, why must women be forbidden to do so much?"

"Such as risk one's life in the middle of the night facing a gang of murderous thieves?" Gemma's tone was dry. "I would be happier if no one felt constrained to do such a thing."

"If it weren't for me, no one would," Clarissa pointed out, her tone grim.

Gemma shook her head. "Not you, too! Matthew is almost drowning in his guilt, and you cannot start, as well. Sometimes we face a difficult fate; we must face it well and overcome it, that is all. Recriminations do no one any good."

Gemma's tone was severe, but then, she had not exactly had an easy life, herself, Clarissa recalled. Gemma had spent years not knowing who she was and who her real family might be. Clarissa flushed at the recollection. "I'm sorry."

Gemma nodded in understanding. "No, I am the one who should be contrite for speaking harshly. I didn't mean to lose my temper." She reached out again and clasped Clarissa's hand, and they sat for a few minutes in silence.

Presently, Gemma suggested. "Should I wake a servant and ring for some tea?"

"No, don't trouble them," Clarissa said. "They work hard; they need their sleep."

Gemma's glance softened, and Clarissa looked away. When a light knock sounded at the front door, both women jumped to their feet.

Clarissa ran more swiftly and was the first to reach and pull open the big door. She paled to see her brother, his shoulder bandaged, supported by the earl and an unknown man.

"Oh, Matthew!"

Behind them, Gemma gasped.

"It is not as bad as it looks," Lord Whitby said quickly. "We need to get him upstairs and in bed, however."

Gemma guided them up to the main bedchamber and supervised as her husband was put to bed. Clarissa followed and hovered in the doorway, looking away as her brother was efficiently stripped and clothed in his nightshirt.

"He has seen a doctor and had the wound dressed," the earl assured them, his voice as calm as always. "The villain's bullet grazed a rib and scored his side; it could have been much worse."

Looking pale but composed, Gemma nodded.

"And it would have been, except for Whitby," Matthew told her. "He pulled me away from the villain's line of fire. Really, it's only a slight graze. I will be fine."

"If he stays in bed a few days," the earl added. "The worst part was that he lost a good deal of blood."

"I will see to it," Gemma said, clasping her husband's hand. "Thank you, my lord, with all my heart."

The glance she exchanged with her husband made Clarissa's eyes fill. She blinked against the tears and said a quick prayer of thanksgiving that both the men she cared so much for had returned safely.

The earl sent his man back to the waiting carriage, and

Clarissa had a moment to come inside and press her brother's hand. "Thank you, Matthew," she told him.

He twisted restlessly against the pillows, wincing as the movement pained him. "The devil is, the man got away. But we will find him, Clarissa."

"I know you will. Just rest now," she urged him. To Gemma she added, "I will see the earl out."

And thank him, too, she thought, although when she tried, Lord Whitby waved aside her words.

"They are premature," he said. "I am deeply disappointed that, although we captured four of his men, Meidenne and two other of his henchmen escaped. He was the one responsible for the attack on your brother, so that is another debt he owes us."

"Are you sure that it was him?" Clarissa asked.

To her disappointment, he frowned. "I could not swear to it, I fear. The scene was dark. I never got a clear look at his face, but the shape of the man fits his height and form, from what you have told me."

She wrinkled her nose. They had gone down the stairs together and now she paused in the front hall. "Did he smell of pomade?"

The earl looked at her in surprise. "Yes, in fact, now that you ask, I remember that he did. I could detect the odor in the study before he fled."

She nodded. "I have danced with him, and it's impossible not to smell it. He wears so much of it on his hair, to keep his curls in place, I suppose. I think he's rather vain about his looks."

To her surprise, he took her hand and lifted it to his lips. "You are quite brilliant, Clarissa. Your quick wits will yet see us to the end of this quest."

Flustered, she did not know what to answer. "I think your courage and initiative have been much more significant," she said after a moment. His touch on her hand, the soft brush of his lips—she found her heart beating fast.

There were no servants in the hallway, and his own man

had gone out to the carriage. Gemma was upstairs and un-likely to leave her husband's side. Such a moment should not be missed.

Clarissa stood on her tiptoes and kissed him.

He responded with a passion equal to her own. He put his hands on her shoulders and drew her to him, and she threw her arms about his neck.

His mouth was firm against hers, and the pressure only sent her blood pounding more loudly in her temples. Feeling rushed through her, a river of sensation, taking her once again to exotic and delightful territories. She returned the kiss with all the fervor inside her.

Time seemed to have stopped. She pressed herself against the hard form of his body, the firm chest, thighs—and more! Startled for an instant, Clarissa relaxed her hold, then tight-ened it again. She wanted to become one with him, wanted the heat inside her to rise and consume them both, like a mythical phoenix reborn through flame. Through this grow-ing new passion, this wonderful rush of sensation she would be reshaped, changed forever. . . .

And still they kissed. She felt the touch of his tongue and allowed her lips to open, savoring the sensation. Her body was almost aching now, and she felt stirrings inside her that seemed to come from her deepest level of being.

Suddenly, he pulled back, and she stared up at him in disappointment.

"My dear, you are too innocent— I have been selfish— we cannot do this."

For an instant, she felt as if she had been slapped. Then she realized that the earl was breathing hard, as if he had been running. He was not unaffected, rather the opposite. Had she not felt the firmness of his body responding to her own? Nor was his expression revolted, as he could have been by her boldness.

"Too hell with propriety," she said. "I want—"

"I want the best for you, and this is not the wisest choice," he told her, his voice this time under better control. But his eyes betrayed him; the flame simmering inside them matched the fire inside her own soul. She smiled up at him.

"Are you so sure?" she whispered, taking a step closer.

She put out one hand to lightly touch his mouth and traced the outline of his firm lips with her fingertip.

He drew a deep breath, and she felt the rush of air against her fingers, but to her regret, he did not weaken. He took her hand, kissed it quickly, then relinquished it. "Yes. If you do not know it, I must be resolute enough for us both."

Then he turned and left quickly, before she could even ask him when they would confer again about the dancing master and the gang of thieves.

As the door shut behind him, Clarissa touched her own lips, still hungering for his contact. Sighing—she had meant to set limits, too, she remembered belatedly—she knew he was right. She had to focus on the baseless charge of murder. She still had to safeguard her life and liberty, and if her heart ended up empty—best not to think of that just now.

The next day, Gemma called for their own physician to visit and check Matthew's condition.

He told the women that he found the patient doing well, on the whole.

"Most surgeons would advise bleeding him, but since, to my mind, he suffers now not just from the shock of his wound but from the blood he has already shed, I will not, unless he becomes feverish," the man told them. "I will return on the morrow and check on his condition."

He added admonitions to her brother to lie abed and drink plenty of beef broth and red wine to restore the blood he had lost. Gemma promised that she would see to it that Matthew did so.

By the time the doctor had taken his leave, a note had come from the earl.

It was addressed to Matthew, but Gemma took it from the

footman and carried it up to their bedchamber. Clarissa followed and waited to hear the contents.

Sitting up in bed, his arm in a sling, Matthew broke the wax seal and quickly scanned the letter. "They have had the gang members up before the magistrate at Queen Square. One of them has admitted to dealings with the late Mrs. Craigmore, but no one will confess to any connection to or knowledge of her murder."

Clarissa frowned, and he looked at her.

"Do not worry, my dear. This is more evidence that you are not involved, it must be seen as such! I am almost sure that the magistrate would not now dare to bring you up on charges, when we have given him a more likely suspect."

"I would be happier without the 'almost,'" Clarissa admitted. "And if we could produce Monsieur Meidenne for the magistrate to see."

Gemma nodded, but she added, "We will find him."

Clarissa thought of the rabbit warren of streets and alleys that made up the poorer areas of London and could not be so sanguine. But she did not wish to trouble Gemma or especially Matthew, whose expression was twisted.

"We will," he agreed. "I just wish I could be up and about! Drat this stupid wound—it's really nothing. I'm sure I'm strong enough to get out of bed."

Gemma put one hand out to stop him. "You know what the doctor said! The earl will keep searching, my love; we will waste no time. It's a pity that Louisa and Colin are still on their honeymoon trip. I know he would help, too, if he knew what was happening at home."

Matthew grumbled a little more, but his wife stood firm. Clarissa thought it better to leave them alone to argue the point, so she went downstairs to think.

She found Miss Pomshack in the drawing-room.

"Your poor brother," the lady said. "I have heard the news of his injury. So much crime in London this season! It's really dreadful. I blame the government."

Clarissa agreed absently and allowed the good lady to

ramble on until Miss P suggested that she go to the kitchen and make up a healing tisane of her own invention for the invalid.

Unwilling to subject her brother to Miss P's famed, if ill-tasting, herbal remedies, Clarissa looked up. "I'm not sure that is wise, Miss Pomshack, although I know he appreciates your concern. The doctor left orders—"

"My healing draught will only aid his recovery," the governess declared and took herself off to the lower floors.

She could mix it, but he didn't have to drink it, Clarissa told herself. Her thoughts drifted to the thieves her brother and the earl had entrapped, now no doubt crammed into crowded cells with other felons, and she shivered. It could have been her, if her family had not been so determined to clear her, if she had not taken steps to help herself. . . .

The next afternoon Gemma was upstairs with Matthew and Miss P had retired for her afternoon repose, so Clarissa was sitting alone when Lady Gabriel Sinclair was announced.

"Oh, do come in," Clarissa said, rising and dipping a curtsy. To the butler, she added, "Please inform Lady Gemma that we have a caller, and bring tea."

Lady Gabriel came in and pulled off her gloves. "I received Gemma's note. How is your brother?"

"He's doing well. The physician returned this morning to see him, and he says there is no sign of infection. The injury itself was slight, thank God," Clarissa told her. "Although I think our villainous tutor intended otherwise! But Matthew is very impatient to be back on his feet, even though he knows that Lord Whitby will continue his efforts on our behalf."

"Does Monsieur Meidenne know that he has been unmasked?" Lady Gabriel's blue eyes were, as usual, bright with intelligence.

"We're not certain," Clarissa admitted. "And would much

like to know. He sent a note excusing himself from our lesson today, claiming an illness. Is that because he knows we know he is a thief and the mastermind behind the break-ins, or does he only suspect that we might have suspicions? Or is he, in fact, not well? The earl fired at him that night, but we don't know if the bullet hit its mark in the darkness."

Lady Gabriel nodded, and then greeted her friend as Gemma came into the room. They discussed the situation at length.

"With your husband confined to bed, I think I shall have to ask Gabriel to put aside his own search until later and return to help us," Lady Gabriel told them.

Gemma looked torn, but then she agreed slowly. "I suppose we must, although I know how important his quest is to him."

And to Gemma, too, Clarissa thought, feeling a tinge of guilt. Must everyone's life be disrupted because of her peril?

Gemma looked over and patted her hand. "It is only a temporary setback," she said. "Gabriel can return to Yorkshire and continue combing the North Country after we have found and have arrested our elusive tutor."

Clarissa nodded, but privately she wished she could be so certain of such a happy outcome.

Lady Gabriel had news of her own, which she broached with some hesitation. "I have had a note from Lady Sealey. I sent her word yesterday that her house was safe, and that, except for a few pounds from the desk, her belongings have been recovered."

Clarissa waited; that news could not be why their guest looked so grave.

"Today she summoned me to her house. She has returned early from her house party, using the robbery as an excuse, and she told me—"

Gemma raised her brows. "What is it?"

"The countess has heard the first glimmerings of gossip, perhaps after the arraignment yesterday of the criminals.

The earl's presence was noted in the magistrate's court, and a few people are whispering about Clarissa. The link is not yet firmly made between the matron's murder and any connection with Matthew's sister, but—"

But it might soon be. Clarissa felt her heart sink. In some ways, her reputation seemed a small thing besides her life. But if her good name were tainted, it must surely make the earl hesitate about pursuing any real connection, assuming he had any interest in her as more than a good deed he had committed himself to. She swallowed a few words of which neither of the other ladies would approve, but she knew that she had grimaced.

Gemma drew a deep breath. "Then we must fight back."

"How?" Clarissa asked.

Lady Gabriel arched her fair brows and waited.

"We must go ahead with your formal coming-out party, Clarissa."

"But I don't want to face the Ton, especially not now, with this rumormongering about to begin—" she started.

Gemma shook her head. "No, that's exactly why we must do it now, not wait for it to be too late. We must face them down, Clarissa."

Clarissa stared at her. Gemma had had her own experience with social rejection, she knew. And her tone was resolute.

Clarissa nodded. She must be brave, as well. "Very well," she agreed. "I will do it."

"We shall plan a dance, a ball," Gemma said. "Within two weeks, I don't think it can be done properly more quickly. But we will get the invitations out at once, and that will divert people's attention a bit, or so I hope."

"If you would permit me," Lady Gabriel put in. "Would you allow me—my husband and I—to host the ball? We are family, after all, and we wish to support Clarissa, too. We could have it at our country home, which is not a long journey from town, and it is larger than the London house. In Kent, we have a spacious ballroom, as well as rooms for overnight guests. We could make a weekend party of it, and be really festive. If you wish to make a splash in Society, let's make it a big one!"

"Oh, Psyche, that is very good of you," Gemma exclaimed. "That would be lovely. Don't you think so, Clarissa?"

Clarissa swallowed her trepidation and repeated Gemma's thank-yous. "Very generous, indeed."

And if the thought of a weekend party was even worse than one night of merrymaking—and how merry could one be when one had a habit of tripping over one's own feet on the dance floor and was awaiting rumors accusing one of being a murderess?—she tried to put on a brave face.

Matthew had taken a bullet for her; the earl had risked his life, as well. Before such sacrifice, how could Clarissa do less? She could damn well risk the less mortal but almost as painful on-dits of malicious Society matrons.

"We will do it," she agreed, and managed to keep her voice from quivering.

To her annoyance, Clarissa had to leave the sleuthing to the earl while she threw herself into helping Gemma with frenzied preparations for her coming-out ball. They had lists to make, invitations to write out and send, ideas to discuss about decoration, and the all important ball gown to design.

Clarissa tried to look appreciative of all the effort her family and friends were devoting to this event. It was certainly very kind of Lady Gabriel to offer her country estate so that the ball could be put on properly. Matthew and Gemma's London house, though perfectly comfortable in most respects, was only of moderate size and didn't offer scope for anything more than a few couples and a quiet dinner dance.

On the other hand, having a genuine ball simply made Clarissa more anxious about her performance. And now that she genuinely wanted to perfect her dancing skills, her elusive dance instructor was nowhere to be found.

"Probably departed hastily for the Continent," Lord Whitby told her. "Afraid that we are on to him."

"Do you think he knows that we know?" Clarissa asked.

"Impossible to be sure. On the night of the robbery at Lady Sealey's it was too dark to see him clearly. Still, he seems afraid to show his face here, and that tells us something!" the earl pointed out.

To her relief, despite his vow to avoid any further intimacy, the earl still came to see her and share any tidbits from the reports given to him by the runners he hired, and on his own investigations, although his conduct was depressingly proper.

"The rest of the gang have been convicted of robbery," the earl told her a few days later. "Two have been sent to prison, and two others deported. They were lucky not to hang."

She shivered.

"Two that we know of got away, in addition to the ringleader. But eventually, we will ferret him out, so do not worry. In addition, I believe we've convinced the magistrate that he is the one to blame for the matron's death, or at least given the court enough evidence that they will not pursue a case against you."

Clarissa nodded a little absently. At the moment, the criminal charge was not the main subject on her mind, though she was sure it should have been.

"What is it?" Lord Whitby asked. "Are you still troubled about the courts? You should not be."

She grimaced. "It is a small thing compared to my neck, but—but I still don't know all the dance steps, and my brother is not yet allowed up—"

He grinned at her, but said, "Perhaps I could stand in for your errant tutor?"

She blinked. "I can hardly make you into a dancing master! The great earl of Whitby—whom all the Ton look up to? That would be too bold a request even for me to make, my lord."

He laughed out loud. Across the room, Gemma looked up in surprise, and he suggested that they should have some dance practice.

Looking startled at the suggestion, Gemma agreed and called for a footman to roll up the rug. She sat down at the pianoforte and played for them, and the earl took Clarissa's hand and led her to the center of the room.

As a dance instructor, the earl was much superior to her departed tutor, Clarissa thought. True, he made her whole body tingle from his touch, and passing so close to him made her aware of his nearness in every inch of her being. But he guided her surely, caught her missteps before she could make them, and induced such a sense of well-being that dancing was, for the first time, a genuine pleasure. She felt as if she could float off the polished floor, and under his sure guidance, she could bask in a delightful illusion of competence and grace.

"Oh," Clarissa exclaimed impulsively. "If I could dance only with you, this would be no problem at all!"

Something in his eyes made her pause, and she felt her cheeks grow hot. She struggled for the proper words. "That is, I mean, I hope we will have the honor of your company at the ball, my lord. I know your presence is much sought after . . ."

"Of course I will be there, goose," he told her, leaning closer to speak into her ear. "I have my bet to win, you must remember."

But the gleam in his eyes lingered, and she did not think he was concerned about a trifling wager. By this time, she knew she should be most insulted that two gentlemen would bet over her ladylike conduct, or lack of it, but she didn't care. Just knowing that he would be at the ball stilled her nervous qualms, and she breathed again.

"I will do what I can," she whispered back, and didn't care that across the room, Miss Pomshack frowned to see them share such intimate conversation.

*That afternoon, they went, not to Gemma's usual dress-*maker, but to a couturier that Lady Gabriel had recom-mended. Although Clarissa protested at the extravagance, her brother and sister-in-law were determined to spare no expense when it came to her coming-out ball.

"No, we shall go back to Madam Lovalle for the other dresses, but this gown must be perfect."

So they went together to sit in the exclusive dress-maker's parlor and look over designs for the gown, while the great woman, in her turn, looked Clarissa up and down. Clarissa soon found herself in her shift, being measured for the ball gown. When she was released, she was able to dress and rejoin her sister-in-law. She found them examin-ing fabrics.

But although Gemma fingered the delicate swathes, the dressmaker shook her head. "No, Lady Gemma, these are well enough, but they will not do."

"But—" Gemma was not allowed to finish.

"Most young ladies making their debut wear white or pale pink or another pale color, but your young lady, with the so-fair hair with its glint of reddish gold and such an ivory complexion and clear eyes, ah, she deserves more than yet another ordinary white dress," the modiste continued.

"We don't want to be too ostentatious," Gemma pointed out, her tone polite but a little dubious.

Clarissa nodded. It was going to be hard enough to be the center of all eyes at her formal presentation. If on top of that, she suffered any doubts about her dress, she would likely die of anxious qualms.

"Of course not—we do not wish the *scandale*—"

Clarissa had to press her lips together to hold back a ner-vous laugh. No, a scandal was indeed what they did not want!

"—but I have a cloth *particulier* in mind," the couturier said. She conferred briefly with her assistant and the younger woman left the room. She returned shortly with a bolt of fabric in her hands.

Clarissa drew a deep breath. She had never seen anything quite like it.

It seemed to be a lustrous white silk, but it was woven through with a fine gold thread that made the whole fabric seem to shimmer. Anyone who wore a dress made of this would look like a princess from a fairy tale. Who could deserve such a gown—certainly not Clarissa, who did not, even now, feel like a genuine lady. . . . But she gazed at the fabric entranced by its beauty.

"Oh," Gemma said, obviously spellbound as well. "It is lovely. You don't think it will be too much for a young lady making her coming-out?"

The couturier looked affronted. "I would not have suggested it, else!"

"Of course not," Gemma said quickly, her tone soothing. "Oh, it is certainly beautiful. What do you think, Clarissa?"

"It's lovely, but surely too much?" she answered, her voice faint.

But Gemma seemed to make up her mind. And when the dressmaker's assistant held up the fabric to Clarissa's face, the other ladies gazed at her in open admiration.

"Quelle effet!" the couturier muttered.

"Breath-taking," Gemma agreed.

How could Clarissa argue further? She glanced across at the tall looking glass in the corner and sighed in appreciation of the lovely silk.

They made an appointment for the fitting, and not until they had been handed back into their carriage did it occur to Clarissa that the fee for such a gown must be exorbitant.

Conscious-stricken, she turned to her sister-in-law. "Oh, with such fabric, this will cost much too much. We should go back to the other dressmaker, instead!"

Gemma smiled at her. "First of all, your brother would never hear of it. Second, when I made discreet inquiries about what the final cost would be, I was told that Lady

Gabriel has insisted on paying for the ball gown, as her and my brother's gift to you."

"Oh," Clarissa said faintly. "This is very, very kind of them."

"Yes, you must write them a thank-you," Gemma agreed. "And, Clarissa, don't mention this part to your brother just now. His first impulse may be to dispute the gift, and that would sound ungrateful, indeed."

Clarissa agreed. When they reached the house, she sat down in the drawing room to write out both the thank-you note and the final invitations, and she worked until her fingers were stained with ink. By the time dinner was announced, she had finished the list that Gemma and Lady Gabriel had compiled between them.

The next day the invitations were put into the post, and they were committed. Lady Gabriel came to discuss the decorations with Gemma and Clarissa, and Matthew, as soon as he was allowed out of the house, his arm still in a sling so as not to strain his wound, departed in the carriage to make a purchase of his own.

He returned with a velvet-covered box and presented it to Clarissa. "For the ball," he said simply.

She opened it to find a circlet of pearls, lovely and simple and elegant, just right to match the pearl ear drops he had given her for her birthday. "Oh, it's beautiful, Matthew," she said. "Thank you!"

He smiled at her delight. "The jeweler assured me that this is just what you need for your first Season. And Gemma tells me your dress will be white with gold trim, so this will do nicely."

Feeling a flicker of guilt at the mention of the dress, Clarissa nodded and allowed him to fasten the clasp of the necklace. When it was in place, she glanced at herself in the looking glass on the wall and then turned back to hug him gently, remembering to avoid the still-healing gunshot wound.

"Thank you, Matthew," she said again. "For the necklace, and for everything! You are much too good to me."

"I could never be that," he told her. "And considering that I was not there for so many years when you needed me—"

She shook her head at him. "You must not say that, ever again. Look, I am here, and I am safe and happy. You must put away your regrets."

He sighed. "That is harder to do than to say, but I will try. I thank God for the happy outcome, and that you are indeed safe. And I know this is not easy for you, either, Clarissa. You are brave to face the Ton and any lingering gossip; I pray it will not turn out to be a difficult task. You know we are always beside you."

"I know," she said, and rose on her tiptoes to kiss his cheek. "I am very fortunate."

A true statement, and it appeared that as part of her great good fortune, she was not, despite all their fears, likely to be charged with murder, Clarissa told herself later, when she had gone upstairs to show Matty the lovely necklace.

While her maid exclaimed over the gift, Clarissa answered absently, still thinking. Was there going to be a happy end to her struggles with propriety's demands, after all? Could they really make a silk purse out of a sow's ear? Or a social success out of an awkward former serving girl? Could she make sure the earl won his bet?

Could she win his heart?

One thing at a time, she told herself. First, survive the ball.

Fifteen

*A*fter the earl's promise and the arrest of most of the gang of thieves and the disappearance of Monsieur Meidenne, her nightmares had subsided. But, perhaps because of her tensions over the fast approaching dance, Clarissa was chagrined to find them returning. She woke more than once to brush aside the visions of the children watching her from the darkness, their malicious chants ringing in her ears.

But she was safe, surely, from a false charge of murder. Was this the late matron's curse on her, the woman's final revenge? Was Clarissa never to be free of these terrifying visions? Perhaps it was true what the earl's abhorrent aunt had said, that Clarissa was mentally deficient, scarred by her unusual and painful experiences.

Clarissa rubbed her eyes and tried to ease the tenseness of her muscles so that she could sleep again. She had told Matthew to put aside the past and its bad memories; she must do the same. The earl had told her she would know how to face her fears, but she had done all she could, surely. Was there something she had missed?

Sighing, she closed her eyes and prayed that the nightmare would not return.

Gabriel slowed his horse to a walk as he entered the village and looked over the small street lined by shops and houses. He noted only one tavern at the middle of the street's length, and it would likely be the center of most gatherings. Sighing a little—how many villages of small stone houses and just this appearance had he visited in the last week?—he slipped off his horse and tied up the reins.

Giving the beast a pat on its neck, Gabriel went into the taproom.

A stout man in a spotted apron came up. "A pint of ale, sir?"

"If you please," Gabriel agreed. He looked about the small room, which smelled of a smokey fireplace and lingering odors of long past meals of mutton and home-baked bread. "And perhaps some bread and cheese for a hungry traveler."

The man filled a tankard, then called to the kitchen for the foodstuffs. He returned and leaned on the wooden counter. "Not from these parts, are ye, sir?"

Gabriel shook his head. "I'm from Kent, originally," he agreed. "What about you?"

"Ah, I been 'ere these twenty years, sir. But yes, I was born and bred in Londontown. My wife's father had the inn, you see, and it seemed worth coming north for, when 'e died."

Gabriel motioned to the drink. "Will you not have a drink with me, landlord?"

"Thank'ee kindly, sir," the proprietor said, and promptly filled another mug.

This was a stroke of luck, finding a gregarious innkeeper, Gabriel thought. He had found, to his frustration, that the usual Yorkshire inhabitant tended to be close of mouth and suspicious of mind, especially when it came to strangers.

"What brings you into the North Country, sir, if I may ask it?"

"I'm looking for a man named Smith, on a matter of old but pressing business," Gabriel explained, choosing his words with care. He had found that if he made the matter sound too urgent, people pulled away. Even now, the man glanced at him, his brows knitting.

"Owes you money, does 'e?"

Gabriel grinned and pushed across coins for their drinks and the food that was coming. "No, that's not it. But he has some information I am seeking. Are there any men by that name in the village?"

A young girl brought out a pewter plate holding a round brown loaf, still warm from the oven, and some hard cheese. Gabriel broke the loaf and took a bite, schooling his own expression to one of patience.

The landlord chuckled. "Lor', sir, how many do you need? Old Jamie Smith, at the farm on the North Riding, for one; 'e has two sons, and they have a bunch of little uns, too. And then there's Thomas, at the smithy. 'E's only got a bunch of girls at home, but there's 'is nephew, who left to go to sea during the war and came 'ome with a wooden leg, poor sod."

Oh, hell. Gabriel would have to speak to them all, except the children, of course, and they would all know nothing useful; he would bet upon it.

It was going to be another fruitless few days wasted, and still he had not found any link to his unknown father.

Trying not to show the raging frustration he felt, Gabriel drew a deep breath. "Have any of them ever acted as a receiving agent, or held a position in which they might have received and forwarded letters?"

"Eh?" The landlord looked confused.

Gabriel tried to explain. While he was speaking, he glanced outside the somewhat dusty panes of the front window and paused. A girl walked by along the grassy edge of the dirt street. She was dressed in modest but respectable garb, and as she looked over her shoulder to call to someone out of sight, something about her face sent a shiver of recognition through him.

He jumped to his feet. "I believe I see someone I know." Gabriel took long strides for the door.

But when he plunged through the low doorway, he was frustrated to see no sign of the nicely dressed young lady—surely she was a lady? She had shown, even in his brief glimpse of her, not just a respectable appearance, but an indefinable something in her bearing that denoted an assurance of social class, even in this tiny hamlet.

Gabriel walked past several houses, but the girl seemed to have vanished off the street as effectively as if he had dreamed her.

He returned to the front of the tavern and retraced the young lady's steps. She had come from this direction. Either she had come out of a private home, or—the only other possibility was a small shop.

Gabriel opened the door and went inside. The shelves that lined the walls were crowded with an assortment of merchandise, from boxes of salt to bolts of muslin. A middle-aged man came up.

"Can I 'elp you, sir?"

"Was there a young lady just in here? Do you know her name or where she lives? I saw her on the street, and I—I think she may be someone I know," Gabriel said.

This man seemed much more like the usual taciturn Northerner who had hindered Gabriel's search for days.

"If you knew her, you wouldn't need to ask her name or where she lives, would ye now?" he pointed out, his words slow and his logic infuriating.

"Yes, but—"

"We donna care to see our young ladies hassled by strange men, if you'll pardon me for saying so," the shopkeeper concluded, his expression stern.

Gabriel bit back an angry retort, which would not help the situation, and bowed, instead. When he was back on the street, he muttered quiet curses on all tightlipped Northerners.

But she was a lady! And perhaps he would not leave the area just yet, after all.

Gabriel rented a tiny room above the taproom and spent the next few days combing the countryside. But although he spoke to numerous men laying claim to the name of Smith, he found no one who would admit to any knowledge of having at any time received letters for a mysterious man whose name Gabriel could not supply. It would have been easier to ask questions if he'd had more information to start with, Gabriel thought for the hundredth time. Nor did anyone open up to him when he tried to bring up the question of young, blue-eyed ladies of good birth. . . .

He began to feel as demented as the sturdy countryfolk seemed to think him. He was searching for any wisp of a clue, and like the faint smoke of a dying fire, every hint of real information seemed to slip away whenever he came close enough to grasp it.

He had sent a note to his wife letting her know where he was and how his search was progressing, or more accurately, not progressing, and he received an answering letter from Psyche shortly after.

My darling, it read. *I know how important this pursuit is to you, but I need you home for a few days. Then you can return to your search. I have offered to host Miss Fallon's coming-out ball, and it will look very odd if the master of the house is not in attendance.*

His brow knitted, Gabriel read the rest of the letter, sighed, and penned a short answer, promising to be home in time for the festivities.

He spent two more days searching, and then packed his saddlebags again and paid his bill. He had left the village behind and was making his way south along a back road when he heard a commotion coming from a short distance away.

Hesitating, Gabriel glanced at the sun, which had cleared the top of the tallest tree. He had a long way to go today.

But the voice was feminine and sounded as if its owner might be in some distress. He turned his horse and trotted down into a shallow vale, past several clumps of trees.

The greenery had hid the young lady's predicament. Until he was almost upon them, Gabriel could not make out her form. He heard only a running commentary of annoyed and sometimes slightly improper rebuke.

"You are the most irascible, stubborn, hardheaded, *stupid* bloody animal in the entire kingdom. Get up, Lucifer, get up, do!"

The beast she addressed was sitting on its haunches in a small bit of bog. At first startled glance, Gabriel thought it was a small horse, but when he looked closer, it appeared to be another type of equine.

Gabriel bit back a chuckle. "Excuse me, do you need some help with your, um, donkey?"

The young woman whirled.

Gabriel no longer had any desire to laugh. It was the young woman he had glimpsed on the street! She wore an ancient riding habit, whose cut Psyche would have observed was many years out of date. Gabriel simply noted absently that it was heavily coated with mud. The young lady wiped a smudge of mud off her cheek and regarded him with distrust. When she spoke, she sounded educated, and her voice lacked the heavy accent of the villagers.

"He is quite a good donkey, normally, but occasionally—" She paused.

"And this is why you have named him Lucifer?" he suggested, his tone bland.

Her eyes flashed—blue eyes the color of deep ocean waters—eyes such as Gabriel himself bore, and his sister Gemma . . .

He drew a deep breath.

"Perhaps I can be of assistance?" he suggested, keeping his voice under control with some effort.

"It is kind of you, sir, but I'm not sure anyone can move Lucifer when he is in one of his sulky fits," she explained, in an apparent burst of candor.

"Then perhaps I can give you a ride home?"

"Thank you, but no." She looked at him with apparent return of her suspicions and pushed a tendril of dark hair back beneath her hat, adding yet another smudge of dirt to her face.

"I cannot leave you stranded in the wilderness," he pointed out.

"Thank you, but my home is not far away, and I cannot just abandon him. He's quite a useful beast, you know, especially when the horse is lame yet again—not that it's his fault—the horse, I mean. My sister would insist on jumping him over the hedge, and he's much too old for such antics."

"Nonetheless, I cannot just leave you here," he repeated. "Are you sure you cannot budge him? Have you tried a touch of your riding crop?"

She looked at him aghast. "I do not carry a crop, sir!"

"I see. Then if I cut a short branch and just gave him a flick of the switch on his flank— I would inflict no serious harm, I promise you."

She shook her head, and he sighed.

"In that case, I don't suppose you have a carrot about your person?"

She pursed her lips. "No, I fear I did not leave home with any vegetables in my pocket."

"I just wondered," he pointed out. "With a recalcitrant donkey, it might be a wise habit to take up."

A bird called in the brush, and Gabriel tried to think. He not only wanted to help, but he had to find out this girl's name before he departed, or she might disappear again into thin air—or the boggy heath.

"Is there anything you know of which might tempt him?"

She considered. "He's quite fond of sugar lumps."

"Ah." Gabriel shook his head. "If I had known, I would have been sure to bring some with me."

She was going to think him mad, too. But she regarded him quite kindly. "That is understandable. You had no reason to think that you would need them. One does not generally encounter errant donkeys—"

"Or ladies," he murmured, trying not to smile.

"—along the way. Are you married?" she suddenly demanded.

"Yes," he told her. "I am."

"Oh, good," she said, explaining, "My sister always said that if I ever actually met an eligible gentleman, I would be in just such a scrape as you find me, and I would rue my unfortunate habits. So, as you are obviously a gentleman, I am most glad you are not eligible."

Gabriel nodded, not ready to point out that, married or not, he might be extremely ineligible as far as she was concerned. But he had to find out if they might be related, and as long as this confounded beast sat in the mud—

But even as he thought it, the brush behind them rustled as an unseen rabbit or fox or other small animal ran past, startled by something outside their view. His horse snorted and tossed its head, and he tightened the reins without even thinking, keeping it under easy control. In front of him, the donkey suddenly brayed and clambered to its feet.

Gabriel pulled on the reins and backed his own steed to avoid the flying dirt. The young lady was showered with bits of mud, but she said, "Oh, good boy, Lucifer!"

Despite the animal's muddy coat, and before Gabriel could offer his assistance, she managed to scramble back up into the small lady's saddle on the donkey's back. "Thank you for your concern, sir," she told him. "But as you see, I shall be just fine now."

"As long as your mount does not decide to rest his haunches again," Gabriel noted. "I shall see you safely home before I continue my journey."

No way in hell he was letting her out of his sight now, Gabriel thought, although he smiled pleasantly at her.

"I suppose—I mean, that's kind of you," she said. Once more atop her somewhat unreliable mount, she seemed more assured. But then, she had never seemed really disturbed, only annoyed. So much for rescuing the damsel in distress. Gabriel could have laughed again, partly from pure excitement, but he maintained his composure and motioned for her to lead the way.

She nudged the donkey's side with her heel and guided it back up out of the slight vale and through the trees until they reached a narrow but recognizable country road, even smaller than the one Gabriel had been following.

While they trotted along—the donkey could maintain a respectable speed, it turned out—Gabriel tried to make conversation, though it was awkward. He had to ride just behind her, and he was several feet above her.

"Is your family an old one?"

She looked back over her shoulders, her expression puzzled. "I beg your pardon?"

"You seem quite at home in the countryside," he tried to explain.

"Oh, yes, I've lived here all my life," she agreed.

That told him very little.

"I am from Kent, originally, though I also have a home in London," he told her. "Do you ever get to London?"

She didn't answer. Whether she had not heard or was ignoring inquiries she thought too personal or impertinent, he didn't know. Perhaps she thought he was flirting with her. And now she was turning into a drive that led half a mile or so up to a pleasant-looking if hardly opulent country home, the type that a local squire or gentleman farmer, not too flush in the pocket but not beggard, either, might inhabit.

She pulled up her donkey for a moment. "I am quite safe now," she pointed out, as if to a crotchety grandfather who made a habit of worrying over nothing. "And I thank you for your concern."

"You're most welcome," he told her. "Not that I was very

helpful. Next time I will remember to bring along that sugar. May I ask whom I had the honor of escorting?"

She hesitated, then appeared to see no harm in answering. "Miss Dapplewood, sir."

"Good day to you, Miss Dapplewood," Gabriel said. And most incorrectly, he did not offer his own name, but turned his horse back toward the main road. "I hope we shall meet again."

Looking puzzled, she nodded.

Gabriel rode until he was out of sight, then pulled up his horse and hesitated. He took a watch out of his coat pocket and groaned at the time. But he couldn't leave, not just yet. . . . Nor did he have time to confront the man of the house . . . but he had to at least confirm his suspicions before he rode on to London and beyond.

He tied his horse in a quiet thicket and then made his way on foot back to the house, circling the grounds and coming up at the side of the building. He slipped around a shed and a small henhouse, staying out of sight of anyone inside. At last he reached the house itself and could slide along the wall until he could see through the windows.

One room was a small parlor, neatly if not richly furnished and presently unoccupied. The next— Gabriel found his breath catching in his throat.

The next room was a small library or study. Books lined the cases on the wall, and a desk sat near the window. Behind the desk was a man, bending over the desktop with a quill in one hand and a pair of spectacles in the other as he peered at the papers in front of him. He was writing a letter or perhaps adding up a list of figures.

But it was the face that Gabriel stared at, gazed at as if he were transfixed.

It was Gabriel's face.

Older, yes, with slight wrinkles about the eyes, a touch of gray at the temples, but the same well-made and good-looking countenance that had stared back at him from looking glasses all his life. The face that had elicited many a lady's smile, many a welcoming flick of the fan, and ensured him all too many easy conquests, before he had met Psyche, his soul mate, the keeper of his heart, and given up such meaningless encounters.

His face—his father?

It could be no other. He had a name at last: Mr. Dapplewood . . . A gentleman, by the look of it— Would Gabriel's mother have loved any other? He had never expected the man to be a servant or a peasant. A gentleman, not rich, and apparently married, if he had other children besides the ones he had sired outside of wedlock and had never, could never have acknowledged.

Gabriel felt his first rush of exultation fade, and a certain grimness replace it. He had so many questions, and this man could finally answer them.

He wanted to pound on the door, go inside and shake the man by his throat until he answered them all. To have to leave now, when he had waited so long, searched so far and with such effort—

But he was already late, and to embarrass Psyche by not appearing for the ball—no, he would not—could not be so unthinking, and anyhow, she would worry if he did not appear as he had promised.

Gritting his teeth, Gabriel watched as the man lifted his head, as if in answer to some call from farther inside the house. As the man turned his face away, Gabriel eased back from the window and made his way around the outbuildings and to his horse. He untied the reins and sprang into the saddle. He walked his steed through the uneven countryside until he reached the road and then urged his horse to a faster pace.

He had a long way to go, and not much time in which to cover the ground. But when the coming-out ball was over, Gabriel would be back.

And then at last, he would uncover the secrets behind the biggest mystery of his life.

⟨≈∕⟩

The next day, Gemma accompanied Clarissa to the final fitting of the ball gown, and it was truly a dress to take one's breath. When the skirt had been eased over her head and the bodice buttoned, Clarissa gazed at herself in the mirror.

Who was this glittering vision? Surely not a former servant who had almost forgotten where she belonged, who for years had barely remembered her true name. Blinking in disbelief, the face in the looking glass stared back at her.

"You look amazing," Gemma told her. "As beautiful and elegant as any young lady could wish, and you look—it suits you, Clarissa, in truth, it is perfect."

The couturier agreed, and accepted their compliments on her skill with calm demeanor. "I always know best," she said.

Clarissa was too awed by the dress to have any desire to giggle at the woman's assurance.

After a few more moments of admiring the image in the glass, she took off the gown and returned home to more mundane tasks. The days were flying by, and tomorrow, the dress packed carefully in tissue paper, they would drive down to Lady Gabriel's estate. On Friday night there was a relatively quiet dinner for the early houseguests; on Saturday there would be shooting in the morning for the men, while the ladies prepared for the big event; then the ball Saturday night; and on Sunday there would be a concert by a noted pianist invited for the occasion and then the guests would begin their departures.

Some guests would stay the weekend and many more would drive down on Saturday, Clarissa had been told. The acceptances were already pouring in; a pile of them sat on the desk in the study right now. Considerable curiosity about Gemma still lingered among the Ton. After all, Gemma herself had burst onto Society's awareness not that long ago. In addition, Lord and Lady Gabriel were both very much sought-after. As a result, almost no one they had invited was

declining the invitation to either the ball or the whole weekend. The house would be packed!

Trying not to think about a crowded ballroom with all the
guests' staring eyes turned toward her, Clarissa directed
Matty as they packed up her new dresses—she had to have
more than just the ball gown, of course—put her pearls into a
small jewelry case, which her lady's maid would carry, and
tried not to think about the nervous shivers inside her stomach. Then, somehow, they were being handed into the carriage, their cases lashed to the back. Matthew, who usually
rode but was still forced to nurse his wound, joined them in
the chaise. Another carriage had been hired to hold the accompanying servants, and she and Gemma and Matthew rode
at ease as their chaise headed out of town.

What a short time it had been since she had been returned
to her family, Clarissa thought as the streets of London slid
past the windows of the chaise. Only a few weeks, yet in
some ways, an eternity. Despite all her doubts, she had been
more or less transformed from a rebellious serving girl to a
young lady on the brink of her coming-out. She had met an
earl, been accused of murder, gone into London's most
criminal neighborhood, and now she was going to a ball, her
own personal ball.

Surely, nothing would surprise her again. . . .

When they rolled into the grounds of the large and well-
appointed home in the Kentish countryside south of London,
Clarissa looked about her, enjoying the sight of the rolling
lawn and the handsome stone house, its many windows
sparkling in the sunshine.

Footmen hurried out to help them down and to take off
the luggage. In a moment, Matty came to help her mistress
smooth the creases in her new green traveling outfit, and
then Gemma and Matthew crossed the gravel to greet their
hostess, and Clarissa followed.

Lady Gabriel smiled at them all. "Come in and we will show you to your rooms. After you've had time to rest, we'll have tea in the drawing room."

"Thank you for all your hospitality, Psyche." Gemma took the hand that was held out to her and returned the other lady's smile. "Has Gabriel returned?"

"Not yet, but he should be on his way," the lady of the house assured them. "He promised to be here for the ball. And we will have more guests arriving at anytime."

At this hint, Clarissa hurried inside. A few more minutes of peace was a much-desired prize; she would have days of being on display, and she dreaded it.

One of the maidservants showed them up to two adjoining guest rooms. In the chamber allotted to Clarissa, she and Matty unpacked her clothes. After being sure that her mistress had no immediate needs, the maid took the gowns away for a final pressing, before, as she said, "The whole 'ouse is full of servants trying to get last-minute chores done, miss."

Not at all averse to a few minutes alone, Clarissa nodded. She walked across to the draperies and peeped out. Yes, she thought she had heard the crunch of wheels on the gravel drive as another carriage arrived, as well as horses stamping and people calling greetings. Oh, dear, could she really handle a whole weekend of this?

She bit her lip. She must not let her brother and Gemma and Lady Gabriel down, and all their kind friends, too. She could do this, she tried to tell herself, willing her stomach to stop its fluttering.

She threw herself across the bed, rolling over to stare up at the ceiling. For some reason, she had a flash of memory— the matron berating her—"Stupid girl, what do you think you're doing? Put that book down and get back to work! Fit for nothing, you are!"

Clarissa drew a deep breath. That voice had been quieted forever; she could not allow it to live on inside her head. Then, strangely, a picture came to her of the departed dancing master, and he seemed to peer at her with a hint of disdain in his eyes. She had been clumsy enough during his instruction, but she refused to allow that silent criticism to linger. She refused to think of herself as lacking. . . .

She could do this! No one would yell at her here, even if she took a misstep, and the earl would be here, and her brother, two partners at least who did not wish her to fail. She blinked, forcing the images away. Perhaps the memories of those who hurt us can be as persistent as happier recollections, she thought. But she would not allow old foes to blight her final steps into a new world, the world the lucky accident of her birth had always entitled her to.

She had been lucky, twice. Fortunate enough to have been born into the gentry, and even more blessed to have a brother who had never given up until he had found her and reclaimed her from her accidental abandonment. She was once again surrounded by the security of her family's love and protection.

And now there was the earl, who also engendered strong feelings inside her, but emotions very different than those of sisterly affection. Just thinking about Lord Whitby cheered her. Dominic, she said inside her head, then she whispered the name aloud. "Dominic."

What did he feel for her, and would he ever say it to her face? And if he did care for her, why would he hesitate; he was no shy calfling afraid to own his feelings. Of course, he had been the target of marriageable young ladies for years; what made her think that she could win his heart? He could choose from ladies much more impressive in rank and wealth. She shouldn't expect—

A knock sounded at her door. "Clarissa?"

"Come in," Clarissa answered, pulling her thoughts together and sitting up.

Gemma entered and closed the door behind her. "Good, you're taking a rest. Psyche has had a messenger from Lord Whitby, so I thought I would tell you privately."

"He's not coming?" She heard the dismay in her voice and swallowed hard.

"Oh, no, he will be here, but he has been delayed; he said you would understand. He will arrive tomorrow for the ball, so you should not fret," Gemma told her quickly.

"Oh." Clarissa drew a long breath in relief.

Gemma came closer and sat down on the edge of the bed. "I've been meaning to talk to you about that, Clarissa."

Clarissa looked at her in surprise. "What?"

"Only that the earl has spent so much time with us, for the best motives, I'm sure, but it is causing gossip. You know how Society is—or, at least, you soon will know."

Clarissa shivered at the thought of acid-tongued matrons scrutinizing her conduct, but she shook her head.

"He only wishes to help," Clarissa pointed out, for some reason feeling defensive, even with her sister-in-law.

"I'm sure his motives are good," Gemma agreed. "I'm not sure about his feelings, however. Nor do I know what yours may be?" She hesitated.

Clarissa found herself looking away.

"We have seen that the earl can be most kind, but he does have a reputation for being arrogant and sometimes even rude—"

"Oh, no," Clarissa interrupted without thinking. "He is never unkind. If he was heedless, it would be quite un-planned, an oversight, I am sure. I've noticed that when he is thinking, he sometimes does not hear one speak, but he means no slight. And even if he sometimes might make a thoughtless remark, there's no real malice behind it. He has the kindest heart you could imagine!"

She stopped as her sister-in-law gazed at her. Some of the worry in Gemma's blue eyes had faded.

"You do care for him, then."

Her comment was gentle, but Clarissa flushed. "How could I not, when he's been so kind and so dedicated to help-ing and protecting me . . ." Belatedly, she remembered the wager the earl had admitted to, but she was not inclined to share that nugget of information with Gemma. Anyhow, the earl had no real need of a few pounds, nor was his pride fragile enough to be threatened by its loss.

"But you must not confuse gratitude for love, Clarissa. I know he has a title and wealth, and he is certainly pleasing to look at, except for the scar on his cheek and he cannot help—"

"It is barely noticeable, and anyhow, why should I—why should anyone care about that!" Clarissa interrupted again.

Her glance amused, Gemma went on. "I was about to say, the disfigurement was earned honorably in battle for his country and must have our respect."

"Oh," Clarissa muttered, aware she had betrayed herself again.

"Very well, I shall say no more, and I shall not worry that you will be led into any commitment against your deeper feelings. In fact, if the earl should choose this weekend to speak to your brother about his intentions, I shall assume you are amenable."

"Oh." Clarissa felt her cheeks flame. "I'm sure you're making too much of his kindness. I don't know that the earl—his rank is—you mustn't assume . . ."

"Don't think about it now," Gemma told her, patting her shoulder. "Just enjoy the weekend. This is your party, and Matthew and I wish you to relish every moment of it."

"You're both too kind," Clarissa answered, knowing she could never convince them that she would be happiest when the weekend was ended. And as for the earl, no matter what her private feelings might be, she was not at all sure of what the earl thought of her, and she did not wish to be publically humiliated—again!

It was bad enough that the first time they had officially met that she had fallen at his feet for much of the Ton to see. She did not wish to repeat the action metaphorically if not—please heaven!—literally.

Which reminded her of the important matter of the dance, the forms and the steps that she must be able to remember. She went to the bureau and dug through a layer of nightgowns until she located the book of dance forms that Gemma had given her, then sat down to study it.

Sixteen

When Matty returned with her arms full of freshly pressed frocks, she put away the dresses carefully, then helped Clarissa change for dinner.

The meal was elegant, the food delicious, the company pleasant. But with the earl absent, something was strangely lacking. Even the well-appointed table with its white linen, its silver dishes piled high with skillfully-wrought concoctions of meats and puddings and side dishes and sauces, the glasses filled with carefully chosen wine from their host's cellar, even as delicious as the dinner was, it did not totally sate her appetite. Somehow, she craved something more than well-cured ham or roasted pheasant. . . .

The company was agreeable, too, but somewhat lacking in elan, she thought. The young man on her left engaged her in conversation on carefully chosen topics, nothing that would disgust a well-bred young lady.

"Lady Gabriel says that there will be fireworks tomorrow

night at midnight," the young man was saying, "in honor of your coming-out ball."

Clarissa pulled her wandering thoughts back. "Yes, that will be lovely."

"I do love a first-rate display of fireworks," he said. "Noisy, but such a good show. And our hosts are going to great trouble to make your weekend special. You must be gratified to have such eminent friends to sponsor you in your coming-out."

"Lord and Lady Gabriel have been more than kind," Clarissa agreed, remembering the expensive ball gown that waited upstairs for her debut tomorrow night. "I am most grateful for all their efforts."

At this moment, she was also heartily bored, she realized. Clarissa was forcefully reminded that she missed the earl's occasional bluntness and his ability to laugh when she said something not at all ladylike. With the earl, she never felt, as she did now, the necessity to pick her words with care, to watch the subjects she introduced so that she did not appear unseemly.

With the earl, she felt freer, more real, more herself, she thought, wondering that she had not realized it before. What other man could compare to him? If he had no long-term interest in her, no personal interest, she faced a bleak future indeed. Clarissa felt her heart sink and tried not to dwell on such lowering thoughts.

When the diners had finished toying with the last bites, Lady Gabriel glanced up and down the long table and collected the ladies with one practiced look. The men stood as the female half of the company withdrew, then settled back to another round of wine.

In the drawing room, the ladies settled themselves for a little feminine chatter until the men rejoined them.

Gemma sat next to their hostess. As she walked past, Clarissa overheard Lady Gabriel saying, "I'm sure Gabriel will be home tomorrow. He would not miss the ball."

Clarissa took a seat a few feet away and chatted with

Emmaline Mawper, who seemed delighted to have been included in the weekend.

"It was so kind of Lady Gemma to invite me. This house is so lovely, and Lady Gabriel has so much planned. I am having a marvelous time! This will surely be one of the events of the Season," she told Clarissa. "My cousin Mr. Galston is coming down tomorrow, so he will dance with me, and I might dare to think that Lord Whitby would solicit my hand for one dance. The earl has been most kind, ever since our first meeting. I'm sure he did not mean that unfortunate comment. It may even may been misreported, you know."

"I'm sure he didn't," Clarissa agreed. It had been so long since she had thought of Lord Whitby as arrogant and unkind that it was jarring to remember her first impressions. Nonetheless, she made a mental note to make sure that the earl did indeed dance with Miss Mawper, then blushed a little to realize she expected him to heed her admonitions.

Clarissa looked up to see Gemma excuse herself and slip quietly out of the room. She looked a little pale. Was something amiss?

Clarissa also made her excuses and went out to find the lady's withdrawing room. She waited for Gemma to come out. Yes, she did looked a bit strained.

"Are you all right?" Clarissa asked, keeping her tone low. She hoped that her sister-in-law was not concerned about her ward's behavior. "You are not anxious over my deportment, I hope? I am trying very hard to behave like a lady, I promise you. And I'm studying my book of dance forms—"

"Oh, it's not that, Clarissa," Gemma assured her. "I have the utmost confidence in you, believe me. You are going to do just fine. I'm only a little unsettled in my stomach. It's not nerves, truly, most likely something I ate that did not agree with me."

But she didn't quite meet Clarissa's eye, and, in an almost protective gesture, she lay one hand over her flat stomach.

Clarissa's eyes widened. She was more informed on some

topics, which were more freely discussed belowstairs than the average young lady. "Gemma! Is it possible—"

Gemma blushed. "It's possible," she agreed. "I'm not totally sure, I'm only a week late. Don't say anything to Matthew just yet. He has enough on his mind right now. He's determined to put aside his sling for the ball, no matter what the doctor says, so that he can dance with you. And anyhow, if I am increasing, I will not start to show until the Season has ended, so you don't have to worry that I will not be able to go into Society with you, or that your social life will be curtailed just as it begins."

"Oh, I don't care about that!" Clarissa assured her. "Oh, Gemma!" She hugged her sister-in-law quickly, thrilled at the thought of a niece or nephew to cherish, but feeling some anxiety, too, about the always present dangers of childbirth.

Gemma seemed to read both her pleasure and her unease. "Don't worry, my dear. Psyche assures me she and my brother have the best doctor in London, and I am going to talk to him next week."

Trying to picture only a happy outcome and not cloud Gemma and soon Matthew's joyous anticipation of a baby, Clarissa nodded.

They went back to the drawing room together, and soon the men rejoined them. Card tables were set up, and those, like Clarissa, who were not interested in cards, gathered at the side of the room and played a lively game of charades.

And if she still missed the earl, Clarissa tried not to make it obvious.

She woke early to what seemed to be the distant sound of a gunshot. She had been dreaming again, and to be pulled from the chants of her nightmare by such a sound made her heart beat fast.

She sat abruptly up in bed and looked about her for a bell pull.

Presently, Matty appeared in answer to the summons, carrying a tray with a tea pot and cup and a plate of food. "You're up early, miss."

"I thought I heard a gun fire," Clarissa said, aware that her voice sounded tremulous.

"Oh, the menfolk went out early for some target practice," Matty told her. "Nothing much to shoot at this season, so they have set up straw targets to show off for the ladies, silly gents." She giggled. "I brought you some tea, miss, and toast and ham and such, in case you're feeling peckish. And I'll be back with warm water soon."

"Thank you, Matty," Clarissa said, feeling foolish that she had been so apprehensive. She was as safe here as she would be in her own house, and it was silly to be so nervous just because the menacing dreams would not leave her.

She took a sip of tea, then turned her head again at a new sound. It must be a carriage on the drive. "Is someone arriving?"

Matty pushed the draperies back and peered out. "Yes, miss. A lady and gentleman in a nice carriage; I don't know their faces but they is dressed very fine."

More guests for the ball, but not, as she had at once hoped, the earl, who would come alone and whose form Matty would recognize. Clarissa put down her cup. She realized she was not hungry, and she also felt a qualm about the swelling number of guests she would soon have to face.

"Don't fetch bathwater just yet," she told her maid. "I think I will dress and take a walk about the park before I start preparing for tonight. I feel the need for some fresh air, and perhaps some exertion will quiet my restiveness. If Lady Gemma inquires for me, be sure to tell her where I have gone. She will understand."

"Yes, miss," the maid agreed.

So Clarissa donned a walking costume and, telling Matty to finish the food on the tray if she wished—Clarissa still well remembered her time as a servant and how often she had been hungry—she slipped down the back staircase and out a side door.

She wanted to put off as long as possible the time when she had to put on her Society manners and play the role of well-bred young lady. And in the open air, she felt less confined and hedged about by rules and expectations.

As she left the house, she picked up an unexpected escort. One of the family's dogs, a big shaggy retriever with long ears and a tongue that hung out the side of his mouth, came up to greet her, his tail wagging. She petted him and when she turned away, found that he was inclined to follow her.

"Very well," she agreed. "Perhaps you are in need of a stroll, too."

With the dog trotting ahead of her, she skirted the formal walled garden, where other guests might be taking the air and she would be forced into polite greetings. At the edge of the lawn she walked past men assembling wooden forms, which she guessed were for the evening's fireworks display.

Soon she passed the field where the menfolk were playing with their sporting pieces, with servants at hand to reload after each shot, and much joking and wagering on each other's aim. Her brother, who had only one functional arm at the moment, was not there. But several of the female guests had come down to watch and admire from a discreet distance the men displaying their skill, so Clarissa did not linger here, either.

She walked on into the edge of the park itself, admiring the rolling hills and dells and the trees heavy with green leaves. A pleasant breeze cooled her cheeks, and it was true, after tramping through the extensive grounds, she felt more at ease and less apt to jump at the slightest sound.

And yet, once when she paused on the top of a knoll to look out over the pleasant Kentish countryside, she felt a strange sensation as if someone or something watched her.

His hackles rising, the dog suddenly whirled and growled.

"Here, sir," she instructed. "No chasing after foxes, if you please."

With obvious reluctance, the retriever, who had run a few steps toward a nearby clump of trees, returned at her command. Whining a little, he gazed wistfully toward the forbidden and unseen lure.

Clarissa looked up at the sun and decided it was time to return to the house. So, with the dog at her heel, she avoided the grove that had excited the animal's interest and retraced her steps.

She slipped quietly back into the house and climbed the staircase to her room. This time she submitted to her maid's ministrations, bathed, and then dressed. After her walk, she was more than ready to eat, and even the larger crowd at the long dining table, which had had several more leaves added since last night to lengthen its expanse, did not totally kill her appetite.

She had a different young man on each side of her this time—Lady Gabriel was doing her duty as a good hostess and making sure that Clarissa met plenty of eligible young men. Again, she made polite and uninspired conversation with one or the other. And once, when she had taken a good-sized bite of roasted chicken, she remembered her first, and now departed, governess's admonition that ladies must eat only small portions.

Oh, hell. The chicken had a wonderful sauce, and she was hungry. If the young man beside her, who was busy telling her with great detail about his morning's shooting and how well he had done, was not impressed, too bad.

But still, she ate less of the second course, and some of her nervous qualms seemed to have returned. Why did she have to suddenly remember the obnoxious governess's many criticisms of Clarissa's deportment. *Take small steps. Glide, do not clump like a plow girl. Keep your shoulders back and your head up, but don't stare. . . .*

The list had seemed endless, and Clarissa had never been

able to remember—or carry out—all the admonitions. She sighed.

Afterward, most of the ladies retired to rest or to begin their extensive preparations for the evening's festivities.

Clarissa went up to her room, too, and allowed Matty to put up her hair in rags to create pleasing curls about her face later on. But she felt no need to nap, and her mind was all too active. She had begun to envision new disasters on the dance floor, and to counter those awful thoughts, she took up her book of dance forms and studied it earnestly.

Her new ball gown had been pressed and was laid out on a chaise, awaiting the appointed time for her to don it. As beautiful as it was, Clarissa found she did not want to gaze at it; the sight of so much elegance and so much implied expectation made her stomach roil. Oh, she needed more time! All her newfound confidence seemed to have evaporated while her worst anxieties had all returned.

So when Matty came in after an errand and said, "You are wanted in the library, miss," Clarissa looked up sharply.

"What? Who wants me? Is it Lady Gemma?"

Looking mysterious, Matty shook her head. "But I think you will wish to go, miss. Trust me."

Biting her lip, Clarissa put her book aside. "We must take these out," she said, patting her hair.

Matty removed the curling devices and brushed out her hair. Clarissa left her room, shutting the door quietly behind her. Gemma and Matthew were in the next guestroom, and if Gemma was napping, Clarissa did not wish to disturb her. And, to be truthful, neither did she wish a chaperone.

Following Matty's instructions, she reached the ground floor and located the large library, then she slipped inside.

Lord Whitby was waiting.

Dominic turned when Clarissa came through the door. Her smile lighting her face, she looked up at him.

"My lord, you are here!"

She came forward and Dominic bowed. "I wanted to apologize for not making it yesterday. I had a report from one of the runners I've hired saying that a man had been detained at Dover who matched the description of our missing dance instructor. So I posted down, but it was a wild-goose chase. I found only a clergyman with his wife and four children, all agitated about missing their boat to France."

"Poor man," she said, but she continued to smile.

"Are you looking forward to tonight?" he asked, and was at once sorry he had reminded her of the coming festivity, as her expression clouded.

"Not really, though I could not confess as much to Gemma or my hostess. I keep thinking of all the mistakes I could—and well may—make. I'm not sure I shall ever be able to act like a perfect lady, my lord," she told him, as if confessing some dreadful sin.

He smiled tenderly at her. "Don't try."

"What?" She looked startled. Her delicate brows rose.

"No matter what all the old biddies tell you, being a lady is more than insipid manners and meaningless conversation. You have so much more, Clar—Miss Fallon."

"But what about your bet?"

He had all but forgotten that meaningless wager. Her eyes on his face, she waited, and he made a gesture as if waving away such a trifle.

"It doesn't signify."

She had endured so much, this plucky girl with the beautiful face and the amazing spirit, gone through such hardship and yet emerged with her spirit still shining bright. And now, she should worry about social solecisms? Ridiculous!

He continued, watching his words more carefully. "You have such courage, such life, such fire inside you. Anyone who knows you will admire you, Miss Fallon."

Her eyes had widened. "You really think so?"

"I know so. Just be yourself."

"But I always say the wrong thing or—"

"A little fresh air can do wonders for a stuffy room. If you shake up the Ton's staid propriety, so be it. They will be the better for it."

He was rewarded with one of her flashing smiles. He couldn't resist taking her hand and lifting it gently to his lips. Her skin was soft and her hand so small inside his. He wanted to pull her into his arms, but that—in the privacy of the empty library—could lead rapidly to another session of lovemaking, and this time, he might not be able to stop at a few kisses. He was accustomed to self-control, but every man had his limits. . . .

Her expression changing, she looked away. He turned his head and heard it, too, voices in the hallway.

They both stood without speaking, in silent collusion, until the people outside walked past, then he told her, keeping his voice low, "You should go now. I don't want to incite gossip. I just wanted to let you know my progress, or lack of it, and to wish you good fortune. I will see you tonight. I hope you will grant me several dances?"

"Of course," she murmured, but her lips lifted again.

He pressed her hand one last time, then released it with reluctance and watched her go quietly away.

And if he ached for her, she was too innocent to know, and just as well.

Clarissa made her way back to her room, but this time, her heart was light. If the earl approved of her, admired her, to Hell with the rest of the Ton. Of course she still did not wish to disappoint her brother or sister-in-law or the friends who had been so kind, but just knowing that Dominic—Lord Whitby—believed in her made her feel stronger and less anxious. So she put aside her book of dance steps and dressed for dinner with an easier mind.

Because she did not wish to spill a drop of soup on her amazing ball gown she had decided earlier that she would change after dinner, not before. So she donned a different frock for the meal and went downstairs when the time dictated, feeling a little guilty that she had not been in the drawing room with the ladies earlier.

But Gemma did not scold, and even though at dinner, Clarissa did not have the luxury of sitting beside the earl, who was seated farther up the table as his rank demanded, she knew that he was there, that he sometimes glanced her way without being obvious about it, and that he always had a special look in his dark eyes when she managed to casually meet his gaze.

Compared to the earl, the young men beside her were so boring that she struggled to keep up an appearance of polite interest in their conversation. But out of pity if nothing else, she managed to maintain an air of attention that caused the young baronet on her left to babble on what seemed like forever about his home in Dorchester and his new methods of agriculture. Only as dinner wound to an end did it occur to her that he might have been trying to impress her, and perhaps he was nervous, too, an amazing idea. She was glad she had listened and answered him politely.

When the ladies withdrew from the dining room, Clarissa was not the only lady to retire to her room or to the lady's withdrawing room to change her dress or repair her hairdo before the ball began. Matty was waiting in her bedchamber, and this time, Clarissa gathered her nerve and put on the ball gown. Her maid buttoned up the back and helped arrange the sash, then fastened her pearls about her throat. Her hair had been put up in the back, with soft curls about her face, and a handsome pearl comb that Gemma had given her adorned the coil of fair hair.

"Oh, miss, you look that lovely," Matty told her.

Clarissa finally had the nerve to stare into the looking glass. Bloody hell! Or rather, goodness, who was this stranger?

No one could deny, at least at first glance, that this golden vision was indeed a lady. The dress was a marvel, its alabaster-hued silk with glints of gold and gold-trimmed lace made her skin appear almost translucent and her hair a matching shimmer of gold. Her hazel eyes were bright with excitement.

She looked, well, downright pretty!

Clarissa gazed at herself with astonishment. No grimy face today, no dusty gown, no rips in her sleeve. How had this happened? She looked elegant and poised and sure of herself.

Was it only a facade? She thought for a moment about fairy changelings, beings who were not what they appeared. What was a fine dress with no substance behind it?

Then she remember the earl's amazing assertion. She had spirit, he'd said. No empty shell after all.

A knock sounded at the door.

Taking a deep breath, Clarissa took up her gold-trimmed fan and licked her suddenly dry lips. "Yes?"

The door opened, and it was Gemma. "Are you ready, my dear? Oh, you look quite beautiful!"

Clarissa smiled at her in gratitude. She thanked Matty and went into the hall, where her brother made her a solemn bow. "I am dazzled, Miss Fallon."

She laughed at his formality. "Thank you, sir. I only hope I don't trip over my feet this time."

"Never," Gemma predicted. "You will have an enchanting evening."

In such a dress, she could indeed feel that she had strayed into a fairy tale. Uplifted by her wave of self-assurance, Clarissa was only slightly daunted when they made their way to the ballroom where she learned she had to stand in the receiving line with Lady Gabriel and Gemma and Matthew and greet all the guests.

She had noted at dinner that Lord Gabriel had not yet arrived. When they entered the ballroom, Clarissa saw that Lady Gabriel looked a little worried, although she shook off her frown and greeted them cordially. "Clarissa, you are a vision. You will indeed be the toast of the evening."

"Thank you for everything," Clarissa told her. "You've been so generous. I should never have expected such an amazing dress, and the ballroom looks wonderful."

"This is a special night, my dear," their hostess said. "I'm so sorry my husband has apparently been delayed. I expect him at any time."

"I hope his journey hasn't been difficult," Clarissa said, then gave way to Gemma and Matthew, who also greeted their hostess, while Clarissa looked around her.

The big room was festooned with greenery and bright flowers from the garden. So many candles burned that the crystal chandeliers above them glinted and the looking glasses that lined the wall reflected soft halos of light. The sky outside was still layered with lavender and rose as the sun sank behind the trees, and the air through the open windows was soft and sweet with the scent of growing things. It was going to be a magical evening. Even she could not destroy such a mood.

Buoyed by this sudden burst of confidence, Clarissa took her place in the receiving line and the party began.

The stream of guests seemed endless. Clarissa smiled warmly at Lady Sealey and blushed when the earl appeared, wearing his aloof Society expression, though his dark eyes met hers with a private smile tucked deep in their depths.

The rest of the company blurred into an unending stream of faces, polite smiles, silk gowns and well-tailored evening wear. It was a relief when she heard the musicians hired for the event tuning their instruments, and at last her brother, who had as he'd threatened put aside his sling for the evening, bowed to her.

"May I have the first dance, my dear?"

He led her to the dance floor. Clarissa's heart beat quickly, but it was a familiar tune that the musicians struck up, and with Matthew's comforting guidance, she was able to follow the dance form without difficulty.

"I hope your wound is not paining you?" she asked, a bit anxiously.

"Never mind me, I'm quite well," he told her. "I want the ball to be perfect for you, Clarissa."

"Oh, Matthew, you are a wonderful brother," she told him. "I am so lucky to have you."

He smiled down at her, and tonight his mood seemed easy. And when the set ended and they walked off the floor, she saw that the earl was waiting to claim the next dance.

He made her heart beat faster, too, but in quite a different way. He looked incredibly good-looking in his perfectly cut coat and well-fitting pantaloons, his spotless linen and his white neckcloth tied just so. Even the slightly too long dark hair suited him, and she had long ago ceased noticing the scar on his left cheek. She pitied the rest of the young men, who paled to insignificance beside him. And it was not just his attire, of course, nor even his handsome face, but the intelligence in his dark eyes, the character and decision that firmed his jaw, the dry wit and irreverent comments that always made her laugh.

"Yes," he told her now, nodding at her expression as he led her onto the dance floor. "This is how you should be. At ease with yourself, then the rest of the world will worship at your feet."

She laughed at such nonsense, but didn't try to argue.

The music rose and fell about them, and she felt as if she were skimming the clouds, not just the polished floor. Her earlier fears and doubts seemed to have evaporated, like early morning mist touched by warm sunlight. She glided through the dance without hesitation, and if her feet felt light and free, her joy seemed ready to spill over. The warmth and surety of his touch on her hand, the intimate glance that he shared with her, the intoxicating sense of being near him as they circled and met and turned and met again was heaven. How had she ever thought otherwise?

The music seemed to fill the room while the ever-moving dancers created a mosaic of graceful pattern, and the bright colors of the ladies' dresses, the elegant dark and white starkness of the gentlemen, only added to the effect. Clarissa felt dazzled, and she gave herself to the moment, to the lyrical tune, to the rise and fall of the violin's trill, and most of all, to the delight of the earl's closeness.

They danced two sets, and when the last note faded, she almost protested when he led her off the floor, then remembered to hold her tongue. More than two dances would cause comment, of course. He was only thinking of her, as he always did.

The earl bowed over her hand. "Are you overwarm, Miss Fallon? Your cheeks are flushed."

"Only with pleasure," she murmured.

He smiled at her. "We will dance again later," he promised. "And I have secured your sister-in-law's permission to take you in to supper."

With that to sustain her, Clarissa was able to smile at the next young gentleman who came to claim her hand.

And if this time, the music was less sweet and the dance itself less intoxicating, the poor man couldn't help his fatal flaw of not being Lord Whitby. To compensate for her private disappointment, Clarissa smiled at him so sweetly that the young man flushed and stuttered and seemed quite captivated. For her part, Clarissa, once more keeping one part of her mind on her steps, answered his polite stammers absently.

Her next partner looked familiar, and after a moment, she realized it was Mr. Galton, the young man who had made the ungentlemanly wager with the earl.

"I hope you are having a pleasant time?" she asked politely, while she considered stamping on his foot.

He nodded. "Of course, wonderful country seat Lord Gabriel has, and his wife throws a smashing good party. And you look quite the thing, downright dazzling in that get-up, and perfectly ladylike, too. Didn't think you had it in you, I must confess."

She laughed at his candor. "You're too kind," she told him, her tone teasing. "I shall consider dropping my plate at supper, just to save you your wager."

Looking appalled, he reddened. "Whitby told you? I do beg your pardon. I should never have—that is—I mean—"

"No, you shouldn't. But don't fret, Mr. Galston; I forgive you. Although, I retain the right to make a wager about you, you know."

"Quite right," he agreed. "And one good thing if I've lost, Whitby's so rich he'll never notice if I pony up. Just as well, as I'm quite out of pocket till the end of the quarter."

She shook her head at him, and they finished the dance in a state of amicable accord.

Gemma came up after Mr. Galton had bowed and taken his leave. "Are you having a good time, Clarissa? I have heard only the most glowing remarks about you."

Clarissa chuckled. "That is the most amazing thing yet. But yes, it is a wonderful party, Gemma. I'm glad you persuaded me to submit to such pampering!"

Her sister-in-law laughed, too.

Then there was another young man waiting, and Clarissa took a quick sip of wine to sooth her dry throat, then accepted his hand and returned to the dance.

By the time supper was announced, she was glad to have a respite, and even happier to be able to rejoin the earl.

They sat at Lady Gabriel's table, and although their chance for private conversation was limited, she still found his closeness almost as thrilling as on the dance floor.

"I hope Gabriel has suffered no mischance," she heard Gemma say to their hostess, and Clarissa noticed the empty seat at the table.

"As do I," Lady Gabriel agreed, her brow wrinkling. "But no doubt he has only been delayed by a sudden rain storm or a problem with his horse."

Matthew agreed and offered a reassuring comment as Clarissa turned back to meet Lord Whitby's glance.

"You are quite the triumph," he told her. "Beautiful, graceful, and poised—undoubtably the belle of the ball."

Flustered, she dropped her napkin, but remembered to

wait as he bent to retrieve it for her. And it gave him a pretext for pressing her hand as he returned it. Clarissa knew her cheeks must be glowing again.

"Then you must inform Mr. Galton that you have won your wager," she told him, keeping her tone low.

"That puppy? I saw him dancing with you. I hope he did not dare to be annoying because if so, I will have a few words with him!"

"Oh, no, he was most, um, complimentary," she assured him.

To her amusement, Lord Whitby frowned, and she thought she detected an acrid note in his voice. "Flirting with you, was he? Impertinent calfling!"

She laughed.

Clarissa was sorry when supper ended and their table broke up, but she took the opportunity to slip upstairs and ask Matty, who was eager to hear about the ball, if she would tuck up a straying lock.

Matty picked up a brush and carefully adjusted her mistress's curls.

"Oh, I knew you'd be a success, miss. And all the other maids are so awestruck by your gown, it's a marvel."

Clarissa grinned. "I'm glad they approve."

With her hairdo restored, she visited the necessary and was on her way back to the ballroom when a footman approached her.

Bowing deeply, he said, "Lord Whitby asked you to meet him outside for a moment, miss, if you would."

What was this about? She had left the earl only a few minutes earlier, and he had said nothing about a meeting, except that he would claim another dance soon. Had something untoward occurred?

"Of course," she said, but the servant was already turning away. She hurried after him.

They went down the hallway and out a side door without seeing anyone she knew, then on past the lanterns hanging on the wall of the garden. The footman unhooked the last one to carry with him to illuminate the path. Past the garden wall, Clarissa saw there was only shadowy darkness.

"Where are we going?" she called to the footman.

"There's a gazebo just ahead, miss," he answered, but he didn't turn.

All at once the set of his shoulders looked strangely familiar. Clarissa paused.

"But—you—it can't be!"

The man wheeled. Now she saw that while he held the lantern in one hand, he had retrieved a blade, silvery in the lantern's flickering light, which he held in the other hand. Beneath the powdered wig, his face, even shorn of the mustache he had always worn before, was recognizable at once now that she had her first good look at it.

"Come along now, no screams—unless you wish your throat cut!"

It was the dancing master.

Seventeen

S taring, she blurted, "What happened to your accent?"

He sounded like one of the barrow men, she thought, who called outside her window early in the morning. She had known servants, and girls at the foundling home, too, whose voices held the same intonations.

His lip curled. "Fooled you, did I? Quite the foreign gentleman I was. Come along now, and keep your trap shut, or you'll be the one sorry."

He grabbed her arm and jerked until she gasped, but although she tried to pull away, she could not evade his grip. He had always had a strong clasp, she recalled, and now there was no semblance of polite behavior. He had given up more than his accent and his gentleman's costume.

As he dragged her along the path, the shadows fell in laddered patterns across his face. Free now of the small moustache, its truculent expression was also unveiled. And something in her memory clicked, and Clarissa was so surprised that for a moment she went limp in his grasp.

He paused to frown at her.

"You're the boy in my dream," she said, her voice trembling. "You're the boy who used to come to the foundling home and smuggle away the matron's stolen foodstuffs. I saw you there. That's how you first knew her!"

He raised his brows, his expression almost comical beneath the powdered wig, which in her struggles against his hold had been knocked slightly askew.

"Come a long way, 'aven't I, love? And would have gone further without your interfering. Think you're such a fine lady, now you 'ave money? I was going to 'ave money, too!"

"I didn't kill anyone to get it!" she retorted.

He cuffed her almost casually, then pulled her along again, despite her attempts to slow him down, to somehow make him release his grip. They didn't stop again until they reached a small stone outbuilding with a low doorway and no windows.

The door was ajar, and from inside the structure, a lantern showed its wavering light.

"Help!" Clarissa shrieked, kicking in vain at the man who wrestled her along and hoping for a friendly face.

No one answered her cry.

The tutor—she had no idea what his real name might be but she was certain now it was not Meidenne—twisted her arm painfully and pulled open the door. His blade still at the ready, he pushed her ahead of him into the building, keeping his grip on her arm and his knife at her throat.

"Clarissa!"

The earl gazed at her in horror.

Clarissa tried to push back her own fear. She had thought that the earl's request was only a plot to get her outside and leave her vulnerable to attack. But apparently, her former tutor had delivered a similar message earlier.

"I was told that you requested my presence," Lord Whitby said slowly. "I see that we were both misled. Is this man who I think he may be?"

Feeling somehow to blame, she bit her lip. "Beneath the servant's kit, this is my, ah, former dancing instructor," she agreed.

Lord Whitby did not look surprised.

From the corner of her eyes, she saw her captor smirk. His knife felt sharp against her neck. When Clarissa swallowed, she winced as the point dug painfully into her skin.

"Let her go, and I will give you what you want," the earl offered, his tone remarkably steady.

The man who held her gave a high-pitched laugh. "And 'ow do you know what I want, your bloody lordship? You and 'er 'ave messed up the best deal I ever thought up. Bad enough to 'ave to deal with that whining matron, but I got 'er out of the way before she could foul up me plans. But you, blimey, just wouldn't stop, would you? Got most of Bow Street on my tail, don't you?"

He jerked Clarissa in emphasis as he spoke, and the knife jabbed her again. She felt a drop of blood run down her throat. Trying to control her fear, she drew a deep breath. The man still smelled of pomade, though now the scent was overlaid with the odor of sweat.

Her lips felt stiff, but she pressed them together, refusing to allow her captor to see how terrified she was. But she suspected the earl could read the fear in her eyes, and she saw Lord Whitby's expression tighten.

"Just let her go. I will make it worth your while," he repeated.

"Not likely. So she can go and call out the dogs on me? You and 'er are staying 'ere for the big show, gov. And don't think you'll escape easily."

Without warning, he pushed Clarissa heavily toward the earl. She stumbled, but Whitby caught her, and she clung to him for a moment.

When he thrust her away, she knew why, but she had to bite back a protest. The earl jumped toward the door, but not in time. The slight delay she had inadvertently caused had given her former instructor time to slam the door in their faces. She could hear a bolt slide, and then more shuffling sounds as of something being dragged. What else was he up to?

The earl looked as if he were about to throw himself bodily against the door, but to her surprise, he paused and reached inside his jacket. From some inner pocket, he drew out a small but sharp-looking dagger.

She gazed at it with wide eyes.

"Our adversary has a habit of going about with weapons," he explained. "I didn't really expect to meet him this weekend, but nonetheless, I have recently adopted a habit of being always prepared."

"You did better than I," she said. "I should have paid more attention. You didn't know his face; I had every reason to." Of course, the tutor had kept it out of view as much as he could, she thought while the earl went to the door and slid his blade carefully along the crack between the door and its frame.

"What are you doing?" she asked, keeping her voice low just in case the villain should still be within earshot. Although, surely he was making his escape and well on his way out of England by now! But they had thought that before, and look where it had gotten them—trapped in this garden shed, which might have been small but seemed all too sturdily built. It was quite empty, the air smelled musty, and even the exposed beams above them had nothing hanging from them. She wondered what it was used for? Perhaps winter storage.

She heard the earl swear beneath his breath, and she picked up the lantern to see what he was disturbed about.

"Don't bring it too close!" Lord Whitby warned, his tone urgent.

"What is it?"

He drew back his blade, and she saw a few grains of black powder on the sleek blade. "He has piled boxes outside the door. They are filled with gunpowder; I made a small crack in one. I think he has been rifling the fireworks display. If I force the door, the impact might well cause the powder to explode."

"How on earth did you guess?"

"His comment about not missing the show . . . and throughout his career, he has displayed a devious mind."

She imagined the stone walls flying apart, spewing stones at them, and she shuddered. "Then don't touch the door, by all means. We must simply stay here until someone finds that we are missing," she said. "They will notice, sooner or later."

It seemed a sensible suggestion. Why did he look so grim? She raised her brows in inquiry and waited. In a moment, he answered slowly.

"If it is later, it may be too late, indeed," the earl pointed out. "I fear that our master villain has not left our fate to chance. I suspect he has a fuse attached to the boxes."

"A fuse?" She found that her voice squeaked and tried to clear her throat. "I don't understand. I fear I've never seen a fireworks display. I was quite looking forward to my first one."

He looked away for a moment. "They put the fireworks on long fuses, my dear, so that one leads to another. Think of it as a rapidly burning candle, though it is usually only wick. One firework ignites, then another, then a cascade of explosions will follow. Unless the men who set up the display are very vigilant—and they arranged it all this morning in the daylight—I'm not sure anyone will remark on what he has done."

"But surely they would have left someone to watch over the display?" she argued.

The earl didn't answer, and she had a vision of the tutor, with his wicked blade and his servant's disguise sidling up to the workman with an offer of food or drink. Did another victim lie bleeding somewhere in the dark?

"I see," she said, again controlling her panic with some effort.

"Let us call for help," the earl suggested. "See if we can gain anyone's, attention."

They shouted as loudly as possible for several minutes, but no one seemed to hear.

"Could we pound on the door?" she suggested, when they paused to take breath.

"With several boxes of gunpowder outside, leaning against it?" he reminded her. "I think not."

Sighing, Clarissa recalled that they had walked a fair ways from the house to this place, and the stone walls of the outbuilding were thick. Music still played in the ballroom, and even the kitchen and the servants' hall belowstairs, she knew from experience, would be noisy, people chatting as they worked, pots clanging as the scullery maids washed and dried.

When she stopped again for breath, she felt a little weak. The shed held nothing to sit on or even lean against, so she folded her legs and sat down upon the stone floor, which felt cold beneath her. The earl came to kneel beside her and tried to pry up one of the flagstones. But the stones were thick, and his knife small.

"Can you dig a tunnel?" she asked hopefully.

He tried to slip his knife beneath a stone but could not get it to move. "Maybe, in about two months," he answered, his tone grim.

After several minutes and a nicked blade, he put the weapon aside—it made a poor substitute for a spade—and groaned.

"I was going to protect you. I would have given my life to protect you, and I have failed again."

"It's not your fault," she protested, then a sudden memory made her pause. "Although, did you not know it was me when I called for help?"

"When?" he demanded.

"Just before we came inside," she told him. "When I saw the light of your lantern through the doorway."

He sat down beside her and dropped his face into his hands for a moment; she had never witnessed the arrogant earl looking so defeated. His voice sounded muffled, and he would not meet her eye. "I did not hear you, my dear. The cannonshot that gave me this"—he touched the scar on the edge of his face—"also took away the hearing in my left ear."

"Oh!" she said, filled with both sympathy and an urgent need to banish his look of despair. "I didn't know."

"My stupid pride," he told her, his voice rasping. "I hated to admit such a weakness, so no one except the men I once served with knows my deformity."

She thought of other times he had not heard her, and how she had assumed he was only lost in thought. Clarissa put up one hand to touch his cheek, ran her fingers lightly over the thick scar at the side of his face, then reached beneath the shaggy dark hair to touch the ear itself. It was effectively hidden from view, but beneath her gentle touch, she found it slightly misshaped. He winced, and she lowered her hand.

"You have nothing to be ashamed of. I am only glad you came back from Napoleon's battles at all," she told him. "I'm thankful you were here to make your silly bet and to stand by me when I needed you. Without you, my attempt at entering Society would have been a most miserable fiasco, and besides that, I should likely be in gaol right now accused of killing the matron. What would I have done without you?"

"Probably better than this," he said, shaking his head and springing once more to his feet. "I have failed you, Clarissa, and I will never forgive myself as long as I live or as short as that time may be, dammit it all. Nor would I care, if I could just get you safely away!"

"I would care!" she protested, but he paid no heed. He paced up and down the small area of the shed.

Bloody hell, she would not inflict guilt on another man she loved! How could she divert his thoughts?

She shivered again and looked down at the stones beneath her. Her lovely gown was going to be ruined from the dirt and damp. Not that it mattered.

They were really going to die.

Surely Gemma would soon notice that they were missing, but she might assume they were enjoying a quiet tête-à-tête in an anteroom. Improper, yes, but she would hardly call anyone's attention to their absence, for fear of starting a scandal. By the time any of Clarissa's family was alarmed enough to search for her in earnest, it would be too late.

"The fireworks were to take place at midnight," she recalled. "Do you know what time it is?"

He shook his head. "I do not carry a pocket watch in my evening dress, but it was after ten when I left the house."

Bloody hell, they had not much time.

They were going to die.

Matthew and Gemma would be so upset. Clarissa hoped her brother wouldn't blame himself again.

She thought of all the things she would never get to do. She wanted marriage and babies, she wanted to see her children grow up—and she hadn't yet learned to waltz. It was quite unfair! And she was freezing.

"My lord," she said, looking up at him as he paced up and down the flagstones—a sad waste of energy, although she knew he was trying to control his anger and frustration. "I'm cold."

"My dear, I'm sorry." He came quickly and pulled off his evening jacket, draping it around her shoulders.

She accepted the coat, but she gazed at him and repeated, "I'm *very* cold."

"The floor is clammy," he agreed. "What can I do?"

"Come and put your arms about me," she suggested. "If we're going to die in an hour, we can spend it more happily than this!"

He made a sound between a laugh and a groan, but he dropped to the stone floor and put his arms about her. "Dearest Miss Fallon—"

"I like Clarissa better," she told him. "Dominic." She rolled the word on her tongue and liked it exceedingly. "I have seldom call been able to you by your given name, not aloud, anyhow. Dominic," she repeated and she reached up to touch his cheek. "If that is improper, I don't care."

He caught her hand and kissed it. "This is all highly improper, you know."

"I know, but at this point, why should I—or we—care?" she argued.

There was no doubt a good answer to her question, but Dominic couldn't think of what it might be. She looked up at him, her eyes so clear and so unflinching, and she said, "Make me forget, Dominic."

"What?"

"All of this." She glanced about them. "Make me forget. If I have one hour left to live, make it a splendid one."

He looked at her in astonishment. "Do you know what you are asking?"

"Oh yes," she said, lifting her face to smile at him, her eyes shining with that mischievous sparkle he loved so much. "I do know. I did not have a sheltered childhood, my darling. I know what I have not had, and I want it all."

She put her hand to his cheek, ran her fingers across his lips, and he felt the need inside him surge, despite their danger, despite his guilt over not averting this quandary.

It was true. If they died here at midnight, it would be sufficient scandal when their mangled bodies were found together amid the rubble. Surely her brother would realize it was not just an accident with the fireworks, Dominic told himself. Fallon would have to realize that his sister would not have been so brazen.

Although now, her hand had dropped to his throat, and he thought perhaps that was not quite the right word.

She began to untie his neckcloth. He stopped her for a moment, then pulled it off himself and used it to dab at her neck. "You're bleeding a little, dearest heart."

"Oh, I like that title," she said. "And yes, I know. It stings a bit. Would you kiss me, Dominic?"

She was the bravest person he had ever known, and he had witnessed courage often enough on the battlefields. But surely even his soldiers' rugged valor could not top this petite woman who had a heart as sturdy and as true as any trooper's.

And if she wanted to forget their current danger, their almost certain doom, then by God, he could give her that!

He pulled her into his embrace and leaned closer to touch her lips with his. She met his kiss eagerly, and when he pressed more firmly, she matched his need with a hunger of her own. She had surprised him before, but she continued to amaze him. No other young lady he had encountered had been so honest about her own desires. . . .

Dominic tightened his grip and allowed his tongue to slip between her lips, probing, tasting the sweet warmth of her mouth. She met him once again with equal fervor, passion meeting passion. And she pressed herself against him until the buttons of his jacket squeezed into his chest, and surely hers, too.

Cold or not, she pushed the coat away. He lifted his head, and she smiled up at him. "Would you unbutton my dress, please? I cannot bear to rip it, even though—"

He thought of exploding shards of stone tearing silk and skin alike and thrust the image away, glad that she had turned and did not see his face. Make her forget . . .

She slipped out of the gown and put it carefully aside, then pushed her petticoats down and he untied the light stays that had held up her small well-shaped breasts. They were quite alert on their own, he thought, trying not to smile as she pulled her shift over her head. Parade ready, the soldiers always said. . . .

"Well?"

He realized he had been staring and too idle for her liking. He shed his own clothes as quickly as possible; she was rubbing her arms again.

He rubbed them for her, and Clarissa's lips lifted. "You have wonderfully strong hands, my lord—I mean, Dominic."

"I'll show you strong hands presently," he murmured into her ear, then nibbled on its perfect lobe.

She shivered, but this time with pleasure. He kissed her neck, pressed his mouth against the top of her breast, and then lay her gently back against his coat.

Clarissa felt the coldness of the stone seeping past the too-short coat, but now he was lying on his side, close to her, and the warmth and nearness of his body was more than sufficient to distract her from the floor's discomfort. His skin was very warm indeed, and now he put his well-shaped hand—she must tell him soon how much she enjoyed the symmetry of his form, she thought absently—on her breast. And then she forgot everything else as he stroked the sides of one breast, then the other, teased the nipples with the barest whisper of touch until her skin seemed afire, and then, just as she moved restlessly beneath his hand, he leaned forward and put his lips around a nipple.

This time she did gasp, then sigh in delight at the flashes of feeling that his tongue and mouth elicited. Her nipple strained against his tongue, and deep in her belly, other fires flamed. He gentled her nipple, stroked it, sucked and kissed it, and the flashes grew and the pleasure deepened. Then he lifted his mouth and before she could protest, he moved to the other nipple and coaxed it into the same fiery feelings. His mouth was firm against her breast, feeling just as wonderful as it had felt against her lips . . . and again her thoughts floated away.

He was stroking her belly now as he suckled one breast. The rivulets of fire spread, and her whole body seemed to glow from his touch. Her legs trembled and fell apart quite naturally so that he could run his hand down and find the soft places between her legs that had developed their own ache.

And now she found that he, indeed, had strong hands. His fingers stroked the inside of her thighs until she groaned from pleasure and need, and then at last he moved his hand to the heart of that strange yearning, found the soft folds and moved his hand in just the right places till the pleasure was so intense it almost frightened her. She arched her back against him and found herself making small sounds that could not—must not—be ladylike at all.

But he looked up to smile at her, and Clarissa reached for that dark shaggy hair and pulled his head closer so she could kiss his lips eagerly, hungrily.

"Don't stop," she whispered against his cheek, kissing it, too, kissing the rough scar that was part of him and thus as beloved to her as every other inch of that incredible body.

So he moved his fingers up and down and then, to her shock, slipped them deep inside her. And again a ripple of need flowed through her, and every movement of his hand seemed to both satisfy and inflame her, delight her and tease her into wanting more. He stroked and gentled and probed the recesses of her being, and she enjoyed every moment.

And she wanted more.

"Oh, Dominic," she whispered. "I need you, my love."

He turned and lifted himself over her, and she felt, rather than saw, in the flickering faint light of the lantern, the firmness of him against her thighs. Then he moved slightly and put his hands beneath her hips to lift her just a little, and she felt him slide inside her.

Bloody hell, she thought. He felt as big as a mountain, and yet just right, just what she had yearned for, the right puzzle piece when she hadn't even known what space was empty and needed him to fill it.

He waited a moment, then moved gently further into her, and there seemed to be something wrong, an obstruction.

She frowned, and then he pushed forward and there was a brief ripping pain.

"Oh," she said.

Dominic leaned forward and kissed her lips. She returned

his kiss eagerly, loving the feel of him against her, his whole body pressed onto her, her breasts pressing against the hardness of his chest. And she relaxed again and forgot to tense herself against the unexpected pang. Then he lifted himself once more, and before she could brace herself, he pushed again. And this time, instead of pain, she felt a rippling wave of pleasure so deep and pure that she groaned.

He paused and looked at her, and she managed to smile. "Don't stop," she whispered. "My love."

"My own dearest heart," he murmured.

Then he moved again, up and down, in and out, and the waves of delight flowed together, lifting her onto a crest of joy that infused her whole body as if she were a small pale fish caught in a current of pleasure. She was swept along with no control at all, only her body responded to his motion, and when he paused to kiss her breast, touch her lips, run his mouth along the curve of her neck, she felt white-hot from the heat of the passion they shared.

Then he lifted himself a little and moved again inside her, and she was swept back into the river, but now the feelings were so intense, the passion so scorching that she felt it must be a river of lava from some exotic volcano. He moved and she was swept along, the heat running through her, over her, cutting her to the bone with the deep joy of their passion. At last she felt as if her body had slipped into the molten waves at the center of the maelstrom, and the flood of pleasure impelled her, captured her, body and soul, her whole being rising and circling as it swept her to the peak of the bursting mountaintop—

When the joy exploded, she cried out, and he held her close and kissed her again and again, and she held him tightly, curled into him, wanting to be nowhere on earth but here, in his arms.

And if they died together—the thought seemed distant and far away—she would perish in a moment of sheer happiness, and how many of God's creatures were granted that boon?

She shut her eyes for a moment, then opened them again

and gazed at his beloved face, so close in the dimness. "Thank you, my love," she said.

"Dearest heart," he answered, his voice faint from spent passion. "You are the most amazing, most precious, most incredible woman I have ever known. If we should happen to live to see daybreak, tell me you will marry me, sweetling."

She knew her eyes widened.

"Oh," she said. Perhaps she had dreamed of this, in some distant corner of her soul, but she had never put the thought into words—it was too far-fetched, the earl and the former serving girl, the aristocrat and the not-quite lady . . . Did she deserve such a husband? She only knew that no lady, no matter how highborn, could ever love him more.

So she smiled and nestled closer, if possible, inside his arms. "I will marry you, Dominic. And if we don't see sunrise, then I proclaim it now, for the heavens to acknowledge. I love you, and I take you for my husband, Dominic Shay, earl of Whitby."

"And I claim you for my wife," he answered, his voice stronger but still husky. "For better or for worse, indeed! For the rest of our lives—whether minutes or years, we will spend them together."

She smiled at him, and the fear that had colored the beginning of this tryst was a distant memory.

But then, just as she was about to shut her eyes and await their fate, she looked up at the flickering shadows cast by the lantern—was its fuel fading?—and her eyes widened.

Eighteen

"*What is it?*" *he asked*.

"Dominic, there is a window, after all! There, just under the eaves."

He rolled over swiftly and stared at where she pointed. "Yes, very small, and very, very high up. If you stood on my shoulders, do you think you could reach it?"

She looked at the window and, with regret, shook her head. "I always wanted to be taller, you know, just a few inches. It's most unfair."

He grimaced. "Normally, I would tell you that I would not change one hair on your head, but just now, a few more inches might be helpful."

She nodded, and he went on. "Still, if we could get you to the rafter, there, I believe you could reach it, my love."

He sat up, and with his coaching, she was able to sit with her legs about his neck and balance herself as he stood carefully. Having his head press against her naked stomach was an interesting sensation but, just now, not one she could savor.

"I can't reach it," she said in acute disappointment. Even when he stood close to the wall so that she could stand, with its support to keep from slipping off his slightly damp shoulders, she could not quite reach the rafter. A few more inches . . .

"If I had a rope to throw over it," she suggested. "Put me down, Dominic. Where is your knife?"

He found it quickly and she took up her wonderful ball gown, sighing at what she was about to do.

He stared as she held out her hand for the blade. "Silk is quite strong, you know," she told him. "And this is heavier than my petticoats, which would rip too easily."

She used the knife to rip apart her dress, refusing to show the pangs she felt. Time was short, had to be short. Had someone outside lit the first firework yet?

She worked as fast as she could. She ripped the dress into short lengths of fabric, and Dominic tied them together until they had a roughly made rope that looked long enough to serve their purpose. The irony of it was that the gold threads in her gown that had given it such a magical, simmering beauty seemed to strengthen the fabric. The couturier's whim might yet save their lives, if the time did not slip away from them.

As soon as they could, she was balanced on Dominic's shoulders again, this time trying to throw their rough lifeline over the rafter. The first time she tossed it, she swung too hard and lost her balance. Shrieking, she slipped from his shoulders and fell. But as the stones rushed up at her, Dominic grabbed her waist. Although the shock of his catch jolted her, and they both ended up in a heap, he had stopped her fall and taken most of the impact so that she did not hit the stone floor with full force, which could easily have splintered a bone.

It took a moment for her to catch her breath, then they started again. First, balance on his shoulders, lean on the wall, scramble to her feet, catch the rope when he passed it up, then, more carefully, try to toss it over the rafter.

The first throw fell short.

The second touched the beam but slipped away too soon.

The third attempt went over the beam.

"Knot it twice," Dominic instructed, his voice a little tight from the strain of supporting her.

Now another scary moment. She had to swing on the rope, find a toehold in the rough stone and try to make it the rest of the way. She took hold of the rope and tried to work her way up.

She made it a few inches, half a foot.

But her fingers were damp with sweat, and her hands slipped on the rope. Clarissa gasped and dug her nails into the silk, hoping she wouldn't shred it.

She stopped her fall, clung desperately to the line, and tried again. She reached up, inched a little farther, dug her feet into the stone wall beside her and tried to find a crack wide enough to support her. Reached a hand up to take another grip.

Inch by inch, she fought for every handhold.

Gemma felt her stomach clench with fear, but she forced her expression to remain composed. Where could Clarissa be? The air was cool, and she shivered.

"I cannot find her, Matthew," she whispered. They had joined the other guests in front of the house as everyone waited for the fireworks to be lit.

Lady Gabriel had suggested, with the greatest courtesy, that the guest of honor should have the best spot for viewing.

Except that the guest of honor seemed to have disappeared!

Gemma bit her lip. "I blame myself," she said. "I should have paid more attention to my duty and not have ignored your sister."

If they had not danced two sets with each other, if she had not briefly forgotten everything except the pleasure she felt when she and Matthew joined hands, and how they might have something new to celebrate . . . But now she chastised herself all over again. "Oh, it's my fault. I am her chaperone. I should have made sure she understood, but I don't believe it. Clarissa cannot have slipped away—unless they are together and she has forgotten the time—but no, surely she would realize that she cannot vanish from her own ball!" Her mind was going in circles, and her thoughts made as little sense as her words, she told herself, but she was beyond caring.

"And I am her brother!" Matthew said, also keeping his tone low, although she detected the note of alarm in it.

"You don't think—surely, there can be no dangers here?" Gemma protested, even as she felt a coldness in the pit of her stomach, and this time, she thought it was undiluted fear, not the evening air at all.

She had looked for them, for Clarissa especially, once already, but it was hard to search the whole house without alerting the other guests and starting gossip that nothing would quench, and that Gemma was not yet willing to do.

Psyche had been understanding, and she had sent word to delay the start of the fireworks, though one rocket had gone off before the servants received her command.

Now, the guests around them muttered and shivered a bit in the cool air, as they waited for the rest of the display.

"Is there a problem?" a stout older man inquired.

Psyche hurried off to pacify him, offering some excuse, which Gemma did not hear.

"I shall go through the house again," Gemma said, when suddenly Matthew turned. "What is it?"

"One of the dogs has slipped out."

"I thought Psyche had them put up; they are always frightened by the gunpowder and the lights," Gemma said. But now she heard the barking, too.

"This one seems to have escaped the pen. And what is he snarling about?"

"It may be only the fireworks, my love," she told him, but he had already turned. She saw him hasten forward, and some premonition sent her hurrying to find a footman to send after him.

≈

"You're almost there," Dominic called. *"Hang on, love,* hang on."

She felt as if her shoulders must be on fire. Not the delightful fire of their shared passion, but a deep pain as she swung on the makeshift rope, supporting most of her own weight on arms unaccustomed to such exertions. Still, she was likely stronger than the average young lady. Clarissa remembered the pails of water and hods of coal she had toted during her time as a maidservant, and thanked heaven she had not totally lost the muscles she had built up as a result. Biting her lip, she reached higher.

And suddenly her fingers brushed the rafter! Emboldened, she scrambled for a new toehold and tried again. This time, she got one hand around the rough wood, and although a splinter stung her hand, she gripped the beam hard. Between the wood beam and the support of the wall beneath her scrambling feet, she got one arm over it, then another, then, not daring to rest, her whole body trembling with fatigue, she pulled herself over.

Balancing again—she could not fall now, she would never be able to make this climb again—Clarissa braced herself against the wall and, knees wobbly, managed to stand and reach for the window itself.

It was partially blocked by a wooden shutter that, to her fury, did not want to budge. She had not come this far for nothing!

She pried and pushed with no result, then lost her temper and struck the ancient piece of wood with her fist. It came to pieces beneath her blow. Wincing—she had collected more splinters, but there was no time to worry about small pains— she pulled apart the remnants.

"Get through it if you can," Dominic urged from below.

She looked down at him. "I will not leave you!"

"You can bring back help, beloved, but go, if you can squeeze through. Use the rope to slide down."

But although she shoved the last pieces of broken shutter aside, she saw very soon that escape was impossible. The opening was too narrow.

Now she could see the black sky outside, and oh, God, was that a flash of light? Yes, and she heard a bang. The fireworks had begun! How long till their own lethal fuse was lit by other explosions, and the building came down on top of them?

She tried to push her head through the window's space, but it was so small she could barely get her face into the opening, and her shoulders would never fit.

"Quick," she called down. "Throw me my shift."

The lantern would be better, but she did not trust herself to catch it if he tossed it, and, anyhow, the motion might put out the flame.

He tried to throw the thin garment, but it was so light of weight, it was hard to get it high enough for her to catch. After several futile pitches, he wrapped it around one of her slippers and tossed both.

Swaying on her perch, she grabbed the bundle. She unwrapped the shift and pushed the fabric through the square to wave like a flag.

"Help!" she shrieked, and Dominic added his yells to her own. She fluttered her undergarment out the opening, and they made as much racket as they could.

And every second she expected to feel the building tremble and the final explosion come. But still, they shouted.

Until she heard a sound outside and motioned to Dominic to leave off. "Wait." Then she put her mouth to the window. "Is someone there?"

"What's wrong?" a male voice called. "Who's there? Did you get locked in?"

"Yes, we need help," she shouted toward the outside.

Below her, Dominic turned toward the door. " 'Ware the gunpowder! There is gunpowder outside the door. Look for a fuse and pull it loose, then move the boxes very carefully!"

She repeated the warning, and after a few breathless minutes that seemed to stretch for years, she heard a reply. "Yes, I see it. Get away from the door. I will take the fuse off, and then get help."

"Oh, thank God, it worked." She felt suddenly so weak she feared she would fall from her narrow perch.

"Here, love," Dominic called. "Come down, and bring your shift with you."

"What?" With a start, she realized she was still quite naked. Dominic, her lover, her husband-to-be, grinned up at her.

"You might want to face the world with something on," he suggested.

"Oh, bloody hell," she muttered. She pulled her now somewhat tattered shift back inside and started to lower herself from the rafter, only to fall—her exhausted limbs and shoulders seemed to have no strength left—into Dominic's strong arms. He lowered her to her feet.

She leaned against him, and he kissed her forehead, sweaty now and with her hair pasted to it. What she looked like, she hated to guess.

"Well done! You are a marvel, my dearest. If we had had you in France, Napoleon would have been defeated in half the time."

She smiled weakly at his jest, then he helped her pull the shift over her head, and he wrapped his coat—also much the worse for wear—around her shoulders.

Presently, they heard voices outside the door, and the sounds of boxes being moved. There had been no more explosions, she noted. Clarissa had been listening anxiously, still not totally reassured about their situation.

She had thought she had resigned herself to dying together, but, strangely, the hope of rescue had brought back all her fears. Now she shivered inside Dominic's arm until she heard the bolt slide back and saw, at long last, the door open.

The face she saw at the door was a surprise.

"Lord Gabriel!"

"At your service," he agreed. "Miss Fallon?"

He looked from her to Dominic. Clarissa blushed and pushed a strand of hair out of her face. Her hand was bleeding, she noticed. It stung, too, but she had not yet had time to think about such minor details.

"It's a long story, and not what you think," the earl said, his tone steady.

Clarissa added, "We tore up my dress to make a rope so that I could climb to the window to get help. The man who locked us in and put the gunpowder at the door of the shed is a murderer!"

"And came close to being successful at his killing once again, it appears from the boxes at the door," Lord Gabriel agreed. "I have just now arrived home. My horse went lame, and I had to walk to the nearest village, then hire a total plodder who could amble along barely faster than I. As a result, I am much delayed, and I offer my apologies for missing your ball. Believe me, I have cursed every lost hour. Still, if I had not been on my way to the house from the stable just now, I would never have heard your calls. Everyone else is in front of the house waiting to see the fireworks go up."

Clarissa shivered, not sure if she would ever again find any enthusiasm for such a spectacle.

"We need to get Miss Fallon inside and away from censorious eyes," Dominic suggested.

Lord Gabriel nodded. "I summoned two of my menservants to help, but my staff is discreet and well-trained. Ah, allow me to offer my coat, Miss Fallon. The one you are wearing has a slit in an unfortunate location."

Surprised, Clarissa glanced down at her breasts and found he was quite right. Blushing again, she accepted the new donation and wrapped it around her shoulders in place of Dominic's ripped and torn jacket.

At some point while she'd clambered on the beam above his head, Dominic had put on his shirt and pantaloons and was not quite as disreputable-looking as she. He put one arm around her now and with Lord Gabriel in front of them, they went as quickly as possible back to the house, in through a side door and then up the steps to Clarissa's guestroom.

To her great relief, even the visiting servants all seemed to be gathered outside waiting for the fireworks, and they met no one on the staircase or in the halls. And truly, she needed Dominic's support. Now that the urgency of their peril had passed, her body had rebelled, and she felt so weak and trembly that she could barely stand.

"I will find your sister-in-law and your maid," Dominic told her. "You must have your hands dressed, and those splinters removed."

She nodded, too tired to argue though she winced at the thought. Suddenly, every part of her body seemed to hurt.

"You were very brave, my love," Dominic told her, bending to kiss her forehead gently. "You saved us, you know."

"I couldn't have done it without you," she protested, but she smiled at him, and her aches seemed to ease just a little. "Are we still betrothed? Since we are going to see the sun rise, after all?"

"You must be jesting." For moment, she heard the old arrogant aristocrat in his tone, and she narrowed her eyes at him, then blinked as he lifted one grimy, bloody hand so he could gently kiss her battered fingers. "Do you think I would risk losing the most incredible woman I have ever had the good fortune to find? We will marry as soon as is decent, and I shall never let you out of my sight again, or God knows what adventures you will lead us into."

"Good," she said simply. Then he lay her back against her bed and went to find assistance.

Lord Gabriel must have already alerted Gemma because her sister-in-law appeared very shortly afterward in the doorway.

"Clarissa, thank goodness you are safe! I was out of my mind with worry. Oh, my dear, you are covered in blood!"

"Some of it is only dirt," Clarissa argued. "I'm all right, for the main."

"Oh, and you'll never suspect whom your brother has just caught lurking in the underbrush. Of all the strange things, how he should turn up here—" Gemma began.

Clarissa was so shocked that she found she could sit, after all, although she grimaced at the pain in her shoulders as she pushed herself up. "He found our villain?"

"Yes, Monsieur Meidenne. Why, oh, heavens, is he the one, tell me, Clarissa, what happened?"

"He lured me outside with a fake message and locked us in the shed," Clarissa said. "But tell me about Matthew."

"One of the dogs kept barking into the brush, and Matthew followed and found the man hiding there. He seemed to be waiting for something, but why—"

Clarissa shivered. "He wanted to be sure," she muttered. "He wanted to see us die in the explosion!"

Matty arrived now, and she exclaimed in alarm when she saw her mistress's condition.

Gemma pulled herself together. "Bring warm water and bandages, and ask Lady Gabriel to bring up the powder she was using to dress Matthew's wound," she told the maid. The serving girl departed again, but Clarissa put out one hand.

"Is Matthew all right?"

"He has injured his shoulder again in the scuffle with the tutor, but he's so pleased to have caught the villain—and will be even happier he did so when he finds out what that ruffian did to you tonight!—that I couldn't reproach him," Gemma explained. "Psyche was helping me see to him when Gabriel found us and explained that you needed me. Oh, Clarissa, thank God you are all of you safe."

"Thank heaven, indeed," Clarissa echoed, but she winced when her sister-in-law hugged her. "Oh, ouch, sorry. I ache everywhere."

Matty brought up warm water. Between them, they bathed her and doctored her wounds. The splinters in her hands were removed, though painfully, and all her scrapes and cuts dressed and bandaged before she was put into a clean night-gown. If Gemma had any thoughts about what else might have happened inside the stone shed, Clarissa was thankful that she didn't voice them. And Matthew was not allowed to see her until she was once more tucked into bed, exhausted but clean, and as limp as a wilted celery.

"My dear girl," he said, looking alarmed at the bruises that were beginning to show on her face and at her bandaged hands. "I shall wring the man's neck myself for this, even before he goes before the magistrate!"

She shook her head.

"To be honest, I think I did most of this to myself," she explained. "Trying to climb up to the window and find a way out of that building before the gunpowder blew up."

Matthew gritted his teeth. "It was still his fault, the villain, since he put you there!"

"That's true. And I am so glad you caught him, Matthew," Clarissa assured him. "I shall heal, and now I can sleep easily again, knowing that he is no longer at liberty, free to hurt someone else or to threaten us again."

Smiling, her brother nodded, even though his eyes were grim. "If I have anything to say about it, the man will hang."

She shivered, and her brother leaned closer to kiss her forehead. "Try to rest, my dear. I will see you in the morning."

She was too tired to argue, but as he turned away, she opened her eyes and added, "Matthew, I believe that Dom— that Lord Whitby might wish to speak to you tomorrow."

"I rather thought he might," her brother answered calmly. "Sleep well, Clarissa."

Perhaps, she thought, the nightmares would stop, at last, and she truly would sleep well. Although, perhaps there was one more thing she needed to do. . . .

She shut her eyes and allowed her slumber to claim her.

Epilogue

They rode up to the building in Lord Whitby's ele-gant chaise, and Clarissa found that, even with Dominic sitting close beside her, she had her still lightly bandaged hands clasped tightly together in her lap.

"There's no need to rush," he told her. "You don't have to do this today, my love."

"Yes, I do," Clarissa contradicted, even though she smiled up at him, loving the concern she saw in his dark eyes. "It's time, past time. You said I had to face my fears."

The carriage rolled to a stop, and she heard the horses stamp their feet and their harness jingle.

Now the groom was at the door to help her out, and Dominic seemed to sense that she wished to step out first and be alone for just a moment.

Bracing herself, she stared up at the large building in front of her. It was the same—and yet not at all what she remembered.

Oh, it was still large and somewhat stark in its design, but where there had once been hard-packed dirt in front, now flowers bloomed. Rosebushes grew, adorned with pink and white blossoms, and ornamental grasses lined the walkway.

The building's glass windowpanes shone with polishing—when had she ever seen the windows clean? Amazed, Clarissa took a step forward, then another.

The front door had been painted, and a new brass knocker installed. She walked slowly closer, then paused at the door itself, and found that Dominic had come up quietly behind her. He waited for her to make the last commitment.

Her hand felt heavy, but she lifted the knocker and rapped at the door.

Almost at once, it seemed, the door opened.

A young woman in a neat uniform smiled at them. "Good morning, miss. Are you Miss Fallon? Lady Gabriel said you would be coming to visit."

Feeling a little numb, Clarissa acknowledged the query and greeted the girl. Her voice sounded faraway to her own ears and a little shrill. Still, she tried to smile normally and managed to introduce Lord Whitby, then she took a few steps into the hall.

The old stench of rancid pork and boiled cabbage was missing. She smelled beeswax and soap, and the walls were clean, and the floors shining. It seemed quite a different place from the dark and gloomy interior of her memories.

"Shall I show you anything in particular, Miss Fallon?" the girl asked.

Clarissa shook her head.

"Perhaps we might just look about us for a while," Dominic suggested.

The girl dipped them a curtsy. "Of course, my lord, miss."

Clarissa turned toward the stairs, and she knew that Dominic followed. But she was lost in her own memories. The third stair from the bottom—here was where she had stumbled and twisted her ankle most painfully while fleeing the wrath of the matron. Of course, the woman always caught her, but she'd run away, anyhow.

She didn't realize she had spoken aloud until Dominic gripped her shoulders. "That must have been very hurtful, my love."

"Yes," she said, looking down at the now clean steps, remembering the small girl who had sobbed and sworn and cowered from the matron's blows, but who was always defiant inside, and often muttered words that elicited further beating. Clarissa felt her eyes dampen, in sympathy with that child who had hurt so often, been abused and alone.

But she was no longer a child, no longer weak and defenseless. The matron she remembered was dead. And she would not be alone, ever again.

Dominic offered her his arm, and this time, she leaned on it, taking comfort from his nearness. Together, they climbed the rest of the flight.

She found the attic room where she had once slept and was amazed to find that the room had been whitewashed, the beds were clean and made up with thick blankets, and the air smelled pleasant with the scent of lavender.

She paused long enough to touch one of the beds and caress the thick wool blanket, comforted to know that children were no longer shivering here in cold darkness.

Dominic watched her but held his tongue.

The next room was obviously a schoolroom. She didn't wish to go in and interrupt the lesson so she paused to the side of the doorway and glanced in. Sitting before long tables, the benches were full of small children, girls who bent over their slates and books as a hum of youthful industry hung over the room. The girls she could see were dressed neatly, their faces scrubbed and their hair brushed, and they looked well fed and quite unafraid.

She stepped back out of sight, and again, she rubbed her cheeks, feeling the dampness as tears escaped her control.

"My darling, this is too hard," Dominic whispered.

She shook her head. "No," she said. "They are happy tears—for happy children, don't you see?"

"I see," he agreed.

"Lady Gabriel and Gemma and the other ladies on the board, and the new matron and teachers, have done so much, it is so changed, so much better. I would not have known this place," she told him. "Oh, I am so glad. I will come back and help, too, truly I will."

"I know." He held her close in the quiet of the empty hall. She clung to him for a few moments, then took the handkerchief he offered and wiped her cheeks.

"And the nightmares will not return," she predicted. "I will make new memories to replace them."

He smiled at her. "Courageous to the core," he said, his tone caressing. She gave him her widest smile.

They descended the staircase, and this time she saw no lingering ghosts.

On the ground floor, Clarissa paused long enough to say good-bye to the young assistant who had greeted them and to promise to return soon.

Then they walked outdoors, away from the tall front of the foundling home, and Dominic helped her back inside the chaise. The coachman flicked his whip, and the team pulled the carriage forward.

"I believe you have a fitting this afternoon for your wedding dress," he reminded her.

"Oh, bloody hell, yes," she said, holding his hand again as she leaned to take one last look as the big building fell behind them. "I thought a coming-out ball was difficult to plan, but a wedding is even worse."

He laughed, and she laughed with him, and, turning in the seat to face London and her future, lifted her lips for his kiss.

Note to Readers

Obviously, this book continues the story line begun in *Vision in Blue,* when Matthew Fallon searched for his lost sister, and we first visited the foundling home. Readers may like to know that this small and ill-supervised institution is not the same orphanage as the much larger London Foundling Home, which dates back to the eighteenth century.

Next, behind the glittering facade of Regency London, crime was indeed a serious problem. History buffs can read more at our www.NicoleByrd.com website. Look under Writing Tips for a short piece on Law and Order in Regency England.

This book continues the Sinclair family saga, but can also be read separately. A list of Nicole Byrd books and how they connect is also on the website.

And last but not least, a big thank you to Kris and Bill Litchman, international experts on folk dancing, who shared some of their knowledge and helped me with details on the dances Clarissa struggles to learn. Any mistakes are mine alone!

Happy reading!
Nicole Byrd

Continue reading for a special preview of
Nicole Byrd's next novel

Seducing the Sage

Coming soon from Berkley Sensation!

Miss Juliana Applegate had one arm around the top branch of a gnarled oak tree when she saw him. Her bare toes clinging to a lower branch, she wavered, almost losing her balance.

Before she spotted the solitary horseman, she had been playing a determined game of chase with a red hen, but so far, the blasted fowl was winning. It had evaded her first in the thicket. When it had flown to the lowest branch of the tree, Juliana swore and grabbed for the bird, but it fluttered to a higher fork and out of her reach. Still swearing briskly, Juliana kilted up her skirts and unlaced and pushed off her boots so that she could climb, too. This meant displaying an unseemly amount of limb, but she knew that old Thomas was safely occupied in the east pasture mending the last of the gaps in the fence, and there was no one else to see her.

The fence should have been mended earlier, but she had thought the temporary switches would hold until the hay was in—if it rained before the hay was cut and dried and stacked, the animals would starve during the long Yorkshire winter. So the hay had been harvested, but in the meantime, the cows had gotten out of the pasture. One had gotten mired in the bog, and although they'd pulled it to safety, the poor thing had broken a leg and had to be shot. It was the second cow they'd lost this season. The other had succumbed to some ailment that even Thomas did not know how to treat.

"You stupid bird, do you want to be next?" Juliana demanded, glaring at the hen. It watched her with beady eyes.

"If I don't get you inside the coop before sundown, a fox

will snatch you, and then we'll have no eggs for Father's breakfast. Do you want to be fox food?" She reached toward it, but the irascible fowl flew to the next higher branch.

Juliana swore and prepared to follow, holding on tightly to the tree so that she didn't tumble to the hard ground beneath. The bark felt rough beneath her hands, even though her fingers were calloused from her daily chores.

Absently, she rubbed a healing blister on her palm, still tender from the hard work of haying. She tried so hard to be the son her father hadn't had, tried to tend the estate since he had become unable to walk his small acreage, but she always seemed to come up short. Despite spending her whole life in this remote part of the shire, she wasn't wise enough about animals or crops or weather. Nor was she strong enough to do the haying without extra help—she had hired two lads from the village—and old Thomas was so bent with rheumatism that he was not very effective, either.

The awareness of her shortcomings burned inside her, and for a moment, her view of the hen blurred. Juliana rubbed her eyes. Every year seemed harder than the last. With their income from the estate shrinking, they had sent away the servants, all but Thomas and his wife, Bess.

When Juliana's older sister, Madeline, had tried to explain gently that there was no longer money for salaries, Thomas had exchanged a glance with his wife and then, his expression stolid, turned back to them. "Wages or no, nowheres else to go," he'd said. "No family left, and too old to be hired some'wheres else."

It was true. Even in this remote part of the kingdom, Juliana had heard how, in recent years, towns teemed with displaced farm workers, turned out by landowners converting crop acreage to sheep pastures in order to produce lucrative wool for the new machine-driven looms. And most of those now idle laborers, unable to find work in the cities, were driven to crime, begging on the streets, or quietly starving.

The elderly couple had stayed, and Juliana and her sisters—the always responsible Madeline and even the

twins, Ophelia and Cordelia, in somewhat sporadic bursts—
had redoubled their efforts to stave off their creditors and
hold on to the land her father's family had owned for gener-
ations.

So when she saw the man on horseback approaching this
small, out of the way house, Juliana's pulse jumped. Waving
aside a bee hovering near her head, she narrowed her eyes to
focus on his face.

He was not one of their neighbors; she knew them all by
sight. Was it a courier, bearing dire messages about overdue
debts? The man looked too well dressed for that, and he rode
too well to be a habitually desk-bound clerk.

Then the stranger rounded a bend, and she got a better
view of him. Juliana gasped and almost lost her hold on the
branch. She had seen this man before! Surely, this was the
traveler who had come across a mud-soaked Juliana as she'd
tried to coax her donkey out of the bog? That had been days
ago, and the man had insisted on seeing her home. But—

She stared harder. It was the same man, she was sure of
it. He was tall and dark-haired, amazingly good looking, and
dressed very fine. But why on earth was he here?

She felt a sense of foreboding and tried to thrust it aside.
There had to be some simple explanation. Maybe the man
had lost his way. But her heart pounded as the horse and its
rider drew steadily nearer.

As if aware of her lack of attention, the hen sidled a few
inches closer along the branch. Juliana reached out and
clutched the errant bird. "At least," she said, "I have you!"

Burdened by the squawking hen, she climbed down as
quickly as she could, scraping an elbow in the process, then
slipped into her boots and hastened to put the hen safely into
its pen with its sisters. She had just tossed several handfuls
of grain inside the coop and barred it for the night when she
turned to see her older sister rushing towards her.

"Jules! A stranger has come. Oh, and you are a sight!"

Madeline herself looked as neat as usual. Even though
Juliana had last seen her sister in the kitchen, rolling out

dough for shepherd's pie as she helped Bess prepare dinner, Madeline had shed her apron and showed not a hint of flour on her face. Every curl of her soft brown hair was in place, and only a small crease in her forehead revealed her anxiety. Whereas Juliana herself—she looked down and shook her skirts back into place, then brushed at her faded muslin dress. A leaf clung to her bodice and a stray chicken feather adorned her collar. Tendrils of her own darker hair clung to her face, which was—she shut one eye and rubbed the tip of her nose—grimy after her struggle with the runaway hen. At least she had donned her boots.

"Come quickly—you must wash your face and straighten your hair and your collar," Madeline told her.

"Why?" Juliana stared at her sister even as she followed her rapid pace toward the back of the house. "He didn't ask to see us, did he?"

"Of course not, Bess took him in to see Father. And they have the door shut—but—but I'm worried, Jules. I heard shouting."

"Shouting? At Father? How dare he?" Juliana broke into a run. Was Father in danger? But the stranger—when Juliana had met him before, he had seemed reasonable enough, even polite and helpful, insisting on coming to her aid and seeing her safely home. And from his speech and his dress, she had judged him to be a gentleman. So why would he yell at a man older and weaker than he? It made no sense.

She had passed her sister, and it was Madeline this time who hurried to catch up. "Where are you going? Wait!"

"We must help Father!"

But when they entered the kitchen door, and Juliana ran to the hallway to listen, she could hear only the faintest murmur from the study.

Her sister insisted that Juliana wash her face before going any farther. She obeyed, but with haste, splashing the water in the bowl and scrubbing her cheeks with a threadbare linen towel, then she dashed down the hall to the sitting room. Madeline followed at a more ladylike pace.

Still, the study door remained shut. The interview inside seemed to stretch on for an eternity. With the heavy door firmly closed and the voices inside well muffled, Juliana could detect little of what was said.

"I should go in to Father," she muttered.

Madeleine shook her head. "No, if he wishes us, he will ring. We have no idea what this is about, Jules. He may not—may not wish us to know the business between them." Her tone was resolute, but she appeared pale.

"Then why do you look as if your whole world—our whole world—is about to come crashing down?" Juliana demanded. "What is it you suspect? Tell me, Maddie!"

Her sister shook her head. "I don't know. Only that I glimpsed the man as he walked down the hall, and he—he looks so much like Father."

Baffled, Juliana stared at her sister. When she had first encountered this man, he had seemed strangely familiar, but she hadn't thought—

"Perhaps he's a cousin that Father has never mentioned." She did not care for the expression on her sister's face. "A distant cousin."

"Or perhaps more," Madeline murmured.

"What are you not telling me?"

Juliana felt a surge of frustration when her sister shook her head.

"I can't. I promised."

"Then I am going to see for myself!" Juliana bolted into the hall before her sister could stop her. But although she strode toward the door which led to her father's study, though she reached for the door knob, she hesitated.

The voices inside were still low, and perhaps her sister was right. Would her presence aid her father or only make this worse? But why the shouting earlier?

As she lingered, not sure what to do, she heard footsteps from inside approaching the doorway. Unwilling to be caught in such a compromising position—the man might think she was trying to eavesdrop!—Juliana rushed away from the door and around the next corner. Breathing hard, she paused there and leaned against the wall.

Was he going into the sitting room? No, she heard the front door shut, and, faintly, the patter of hooves on the gravel drive. He was leaving.

She heard Madeline's voice. "I'm coming, Bess. Did you find Miss Juliana?"

"No, Miss," the elderly servant answered. "I'll look upstairs for her."

Juliana gave the maid time to disappear up the staircase, then turned the corner to meet her sister in the hallway.

"Bess says that our father wishes to speak to us," Madeline explained. She was still pale, but her tone was resolute.

Feeling almost sick with fear, as well as a dreadful curiosity, Juliana nodded. She waited beside her sister when Maddie knocked on the study door.

A pause, then from inside, their father called, "Come in."

He sounded defeated. What was this all about? Had the bank called in their debts? Surely that handsome, fashionable gentleman had not been an ordinary bank clerk, come to deliver the bad tidings?

Her head whirling with unlikely ideas, Juliana followed her sister inside the room.

Behind the desk, Father stared at the bookshelf on the wall and didn't looked up. When he raised his head, his expression was grimmer than she had ever seen it.

"Shut the door," their father said. "I have a complicated story to tell you."

Lord Gabriel Sinclair rode up to a smallish country house built out of gray stone, bigger than the cottages the local farmers inhabited but smaller than the seat of the local squire. He discovered that his heart was hammering as if he were going into battle. Perhaps in a way, he was.

How long had he searched to find the man who dwelt

here? In some ways, he thought, all his life. There had been long empty years when he would have bartered his soul to find the missing part of himself, even before he'd understood exactly what was lacking. So why did he feel icy cold, now?

He pulled up his horse and dismounted, tying the reins to a convenient post. No servant had yet appeared. The household seemed neglectful or perhaps understaffed. No matter, as long as the man Gabriel wished to see was at home.

He rapped the brass knocker. It gleamed from a recent polishing, and the doorway had been swept.

He felt as tense as if the door opened, and he pushed the thought away. An elderly servant in a faded gown gazed at him in inquiry.

"I wish to see the gentleman of the house, Mr. Applewood," Gabriel told her.

She nodded. "Yes, sir. If you'll come this way. Who shall I say is calling, sir?"

"Just tell him Mr. Smith." She would not understand the irony of his lie, but the man he was about to see should.

She led him down the hall to a room toward the end and opened the door. He stood back a little while she announced, "A Mr. Smith to see you, sir," and then made her departure.

Taking a deep breath and trying to control his expression, Gabriel stepped inside the room. Getting his first good look at his host made Gabriel's chest tighten. It felt like a blow, seeing how similar to his own were the man's features, only a little blurred and softened by several decades of time passing. But he had the same dark hair, the same unusual deep blue eyes and firm chin . . . all the features that women had so often deemed pleasing in Gabriel.

The man behind the desk looked up now but did not stand, and his expression of polite welcome froze as he took in the newcomer. For a moment, the air seemed charged with sudden emotion.

Yes, Mr. Applewood deserved an unpleasant surprise. Gabriel had had enough of them in recent years.

Gabriel met the man's astonished stare with a hard look

of his own and waited. At last, the older man broke the silence. "Your name is not Smith, I think," he said slowly.

"No." Gabriel heard the curtness of his answer, but did not try to soften his tone. He had expected many feelings on seeing this man for the first time, had imagined he might feel affection or relief. But now, most of all he felt anger blossom inside him. He found his hands curling into fists and tried to relax his fingers.

"Society knows me as Lord Gabriel Sinclair. But you, of course, know that is not really a valid designation."

The older man's mouth twisted for a instant, then he had himself under control again. "I think the marquis owed you—and your mother—that much," he answered, his voice level. "My acknowledgment of paternity would have helped neither of you. In fact, it would have ruined her in Society's eyes, as you well know."

"How dare you even speak of my mother!" Without conscious choice, Gabriel found that he was shouting. "You have no right!"

"I loved your mother, and she loved me," the man with his face said. The calmness of his tone only stoked the fires of Gabriel's long repressed anger. "I hardly think you can judge. You have no idea what the situation was."

"I know you—by your involvement with a married woman—made her life hell!" Gabriel snapped.

"Her life was already hell. She told me so, and she swore that I gave her the only solace, the only happiness she'd ever had the chance to grasp. I—I hope she spoke the truth." His tone remained even, though bleakness darkened the familiar hue of his blue eyes.

"If you had not taken advantage of her unhappiness, perhaps—" Gabriel paused, knowing too well what his titular father's character had been, and how unlikely it was, under any circumstances, that his mother's condition would have improved.

"If I had been older and wiser, I might have been more prudent. Yet, how could I not have come to her aid? My involvement—as you call it—with your mother began the night I found her weeping, hiding in the corner of a London garden. The marquis had struck her, and she was afraid to go back inside to rejoin the rest of the party until the flush of the blow had faded from her cheek."

Gabriel winced. Growing up, he had suffered similar blows often enough, and he had no trouble crediting this tale, though it pained him to admit as much. He swallowed hard against the lump in his throat. "But—"

"I was aware of the dangers our association held for her. But I loved her from the moment I saw the tears on her cheek, from the first time I touched her hand . . ." The man behind the desk looked away, and his forehead creased. "She was a gentle spirit, your mother, beautiful and good to her core. She deserved a better life. The marquis had been charming and solicitous before the marriage, and not until she was his wife did she learn his real nature. She'd tried to run away once, before I met her, but he found her and brought her back. He threatened to kill her if she left again."

The words pounded him as a fist might. Gabriel found his chest constricted. Trying to push away the fog of pain that slowed his thoughts, he shook his head.

"She could have applied to Parliament for a divorce, but that is a slow and uncertain process," Applewood continued, his tone dogged. "She was sure the marquess would slay her long before the decree could be granted. I offered to take her away to the Continent—Napoleon had not yet tightened his grip over Europe—but again, she feared her husband too much. The marquess had wealth and power, and I—well, you see my situation." He gestured vaguely toward the neat but small room with its book-lined shelves and plain desk.

"I was a small landowner with barely enough resources to support a family. I would have given it all up for her, I swear to God I would have, but she was afraid to risk it. And besides, something else held her back. You know, of course, that she already had a baby. If she had left her husband, she would never have seen him again."

Gabriel pressed his lips together to hold back a groan. His older brother, John, the current marquess. Yes, it all made a dreadful sort of logic. Yet he held on to his anger, which he had nursed for so long. It was an old friend and had comforted him for years. How could he so easily accept this facile explanation?

But the older man was still speaking. "In the end, the marquess became so suspicious she told me we must part, forever. I did as I was bade, though it pained me more than I can tell you."

"And married very soon afterward, I see, and fathered more children." Gabriel knew his tone was accusing, but all his life he had lacked a father who cared for him. And this man had just walked away?

Applewood winced. "Yes."

"And you felt no responsibility? If not for me—enduring the marquis's hatred all my life, disinherited and sent into exile when I was barely grown—what about the other child you sired upon my mother?"

Applewood looked away. "That was not planned. I was in the south of England, and your mother had escaped the estate for a few days during her husband's absence. We met unexpectedly. I—it was not wise nor right, no. But I take the blame."

"As you should," Gabriel muttered. But despite his attempts to nurse it, his anger was ebbing. "The marquis threatened to kill the child, you know. My mother had to send her away. And then later my sister Gemma was left all alone, what about your duty to her?"

The other man's expression was contorted. "Yes, I failed her for a time. There were complications, circumstances which distracted me. But I sought her out as soon as I could and saw to her well-being, from a distance. So you have found her, then? The solicitor I engaged to issue her allowance wrote that she had gone to London and was searching for her family. I'm pleased that you are reunited."

"No thanks to you," Gabriel told him. "And why, after my mother died, after the marquess died, did you not come forward? Did you plan to ever tell me? Can you not face the consequences of your actions? I call you a coward, sir!"

Applewood's features tightened, but instead of jumping to his feet or calling him out—could one morally, even with the direst justification, fight one's own father?—the man lowered his face to his hands.

Gabriel's anger leaped again. He would not allow the man before him to evade—yet again—an accounting for all the suffering that his actions had caused. Gabriel took two quick strides and rounded the desk, ready to pull the man to his feet and shake him until his teeth rattled in his head.

And paused just as suddenly.

The chair Applewood sat in appeared to be specially made. Wheels had been added to allow it to slide smoothly, and a rug covered the man from his waist down. Despite the covering, Gabriel could now make out that his father's legs were wasted and strangely twisted.

Looking up to see Applewood raise his head, Gabriel saw for the first time the veneer of pain that dulled the once handsome features. Stunned, he met the older man's gaze.

"As I said, there were complications," Applewood said, his voice low.

"Come in, girls," their father told them.

Juliana drew a deep breath. The situation could not be as bad as she feared—surely, it could not. But the expression on her father's face, the sound of his voice, flattened with anguish just as if he were having one of his worst days—oh, dear heaven, what could this be about?

For a moment she hated the good-looking stranger who had disrupted their peaceful, if impoverished, lives, hated him with an intensity she had not suspected she was capable of. How dare he come here and say—say what, exactly?

Her father was speaking, slowly and almost painfully, and she pulled her attention back to his words.

"Perhaps it is natural to wish to spare the ones we love knowledge of our darkest sins," he said. "I told myself I wanted to save you the pain of knowing—perhaps I was really thinking of myself."

Juliana shivered. Without thinking, she reached for her sister's hand as they stood side by side and clung to it as if it were an anchor. Madeline's fingers were icy to the touch; she must be as cold with fear as Juliana herself.

"At any rate, I had hoped to avoid telling you—what I must tell you now. But perhaps it's better that all secrets are out, at last. I can only say at the start that I am sincerely sorry for all the sins I have committed," he continued, his voice rough with pain.

Juliana felt an answering ache deep inside her. "Father—" she began, but he waved her to silence.

She felt Madeline press her hand, and she heeded the unspoken admonition and was silent. Every word seemed to cause her father distress—better to allow him to say what he felt he must say, even though she both wanted desperately to hear it and feared the revelation.

"When I was a young man, I spent some time in London, among Society more elevated and more wealthy than I." He paused and sighed.

Juliana bit back the reassurances she wanted to offer him. Her father had always been a most good-looking man, and he was charming and intelligent and had a kind heart. Just because he was not rich . . .

"I had not enough fortune to make an advantageous marriage, and I always knew I would end up coming home again, but I was young and ready for adventure. I found it when I chanced upon a lovely young lady weeping in a garden. She was a remarkable person—and I fell in love, even though she was already married. We met secretly for a time, and there was a child born . . ."

Juliana bit back a gasp. The stranger who had looked so like their father—

"Yes, the man who came here today is your half-brother, although no one but his mother and I knew the truth. But her husband the marquis suspected, and after that he kept a tight watch on his wife."

He paused, and Juliana knew her eyes had widened.

A *marquis*? This was lofty heights of Society, indeed. Even though her father had been born a gentleman, such rank was far outside their usual social sphere. And a secret affair—for an instant she tried to picture her father as young and impetuous—then he was speaking again.

"At that point we agreed that we must part, both for her sake and the child's. Deeply unhappy, I returned to Yorkshire and tried to focus on running my tiny estate. A young lady I had known all my life appeared to notice my malaise and was kind and soothing. We fell in love, married, and had wonderful daughters . . ."

"So you never saw her—the marchioness—again?" Madeline asked, her voice gentle.

He winced. "Only once. Some years later, traveling to Dover to purchase a bull, I encountered her unexpectedly. She had come south to visit a lady friend while her husband was away from home. It was totally unplanned, but I regret to say that our scruples and our resolutions slipped away. We had two days together, only, but another child was the result, this time a girl. And it was almost the marchioness's undoing. After that, her husband kept her a virtual prisoner for the rest of the years she lived."

He stared into the distance, and his expression was so grim that although Juliana wanted to rail at him on her mother's behalf, she held her tongue.

"I know you will find it hard to forgive me—" His voice faltered.

Juliana forgot her outrage. She hurried around the desk to kneel beside his wheeled chair and take his hand. "We love you, Father. We will always love you."

He rubbed his eyes and swallowed.

She wanted to ask, *Did our mother know?* But she didn't have the courage.

It was her sister who spoke.

"So the stranger who came to see you today—" Madeline's tone was amazingly even. Was she not as shocked and astounded by these revelations as Juliana?

"He is Lord Gabriel Sinclair," their father said. "Your half-brother."

"Did you write to him? How did he find you?" Madeline persisted.

Juliana felt a stab of guilt. After coming across her and her donkey in the bog, he had escorted her home . . .

Their father shook his head. "He says he had been searching for me for some time. He and his brother, the current marquis, found some clues in their late mother's effects that made him suspicious. He is angry at me, too, with reason, just as you have every right to be. But he also—well, he told me I had been lax in my responsibilities, and I agreed. I will live with those sins all my life, as well as other transgressions on which God will judge me. But I suggested that having sought out the knowledge of his kinship, he has, in effect, invited additional obligations. Blood is still blood. I suggested—and he has agreed—that he invite one of his half-sisters to come visit in London."

"What!" Juliana forgot herself totally. She found she had jumped to her feet. Trying not to shriek like a fishwife again, she lowered her voice, but it still sounded strange, even to her own ears. "This man—this lord—probably hates us, and we should pay him a visit? Why should he—or we—wish to do such a thing, Father?"

"He is family, and blood ties matter, even when they are not to be—we have both agreed—acknowledged openly."

"But—" Madeline protested.

Their father shook his head. "Girls, look about you. As much as it grieves me to admit, I cannot provide for you properly, you know that. Since my accident and despite our best efforts, the estate has gone downhill. It was never terribly prosperous to begin with. With no real dowry and so few eligible young men in the neighborhood, you have no hope of a good marriage. Your sister Lauryn was extremely fortunate to fall in love with the squire's son, and he with her, and lucky as well that his father allowed him to offer marriage."

And the fact that their father had made over their best and largest pasture for the new bride, for her husband and father-in-law to make use of, had no doubt nothing to do with it, Juliana thought, then pushed away the cynical notion to pay close heed to her father's amazing words.

"But what about you two or the twins? No, if I have to face the results of my youthful transgressions, and rightfully so, at least some good should come of it. Lord Gabriel—"

"If what you say is true—I mean, I know it is, but—he's not really a lord," Juliana muttered, rebellious, but her father ignored her and continued.

"Up to now, we have had no closely connected kin able to sponsor you and allow you to meet a wider range of suitable nuptial candidates. For your sake, I will not waste this chance. Lord Gabriel has agreed to take one of you back south with him in two days' time. It really should be Madeleine, since she is the eldest—"

"I am not leaving you, Father!"

Their father tightened his jaw. "One of you will go to London," he repeated. "You can talk it over between the two of you and decide who it shall be. But I shall not pass up this chance to allow you an opportunity to look about you; you deserve a decent marriage."

"But if we cannot even acknowledge that this man is our brother—our half-brother—how will it help?"

"He can still sponsor you," their sire said. "We have agreed to say that we are distant cousins." His moment of firmness seemed to have passed, he had turned his gaze toward the ledger on his desk. "Now, I have some work to do, accounts to balance if we are to pay our bills this quarter, and the harvest was meager enough. You may decide between yourselves which one shall journey to London."

"And the twins?" Madeline asked.

"You can tell them when—when you think they're ready." Their father sighed. "They're very young, and it may be a shock to them."

Since Juliana knew that little short of a volcano's eruption or a badly made dress—on the rare occasions when they could afford new clothes—would alarm the twins, that was the least of her present worries. But she saw that she and her sister had been effectively dismissed. Her father picked up his quill, and her older sister motioned to her.

Wishing she could stay and argue, Juliana reluctantly followed her sister out into the hall.

"I am not going to London with that man!" she snapped.

"Hush, don't let Bess hear you," Madeline said. "Come back to the sitting room."

So Juliana pressed her lips together and hurried back to the front room, where they could shut the door—although not before their maid appeared in the hall, her expression inquisitive as she rubbed her hands dry on her apron.

"Would you like a tea tray, Miss?"

"Not yet, Bess," Madeline answered. She shut the door firmly and turned to face her sister. "You see, she is curious. We must not allow this news—"

"Is it news?" Juliana interrupted. "How can you be so calm, Madeline! Tell me the truth, did you know?"

"That we had a half brother—and, heavens—a half sister, too. No!" Madeline dropped down into one of the chairs.

Juliana could not sit calmly. She paced up and down the threadbare rug. "But you knew something—tell me!"

Her sister rubbed her temple. "I only know what Mother told me once, when she was ill and a little out of her head with fever. Later, when I asked her if it were true, she made me promise not to tell anyone else, not even you, dearest. Besides, you were very young at the time."

"Barely two years younger than you!" Juliana snapped, irritated by her sister's long held tendency to assume a maturity beyond her years. She shook the old exasperation away so she could concentrate on the present thunderbolt. "But what did she tell you? She knew about the other woman?" Horrified to think that their sweet patient mother had had to live with such knowledge, Juliana bit her lip and stared down into the fireplace.

"She knew that Father had been in love with someone else before they began their courtship. He had told her as much, though not the details. I didn't know that it was a married lady, or that her rank was so high." Madeline paused. "If she knew about the transgression, she never told me."

"I hope she did not," Juliana muttered. "When she could do nothing, it would have been a dreadful blow. How could he do such a thing!" She drew a deep breath, trying to calm herself. "What else did Mother know?"

"That was all she remarked upon. And she told me, later, when she was more coherent, that it didn't matter, really. She said she loved Father so much she didn't mind being his second choice, as long as she had him to sit across the dining table from her every day, as long as he was the one who fathered her children. And he was always an attentive husband. I do not believe she was unhappy, Jules."

"Oh!" Juliana had to blink hard and look back at the hearth. Their parents' marriage had seemed so serene and so loving—no, she must not allow all her memories to be destroyed. Her mother had loved her father, and he had loved her. Despite the other relationship. She had to believe that was true. And yet—no, she shook her doubts away.

"Life is complicated," Madeline muttered. She seemed to be thinking much the same. "And it's not for us to judge."

"I don't see why not!" Juliana retorted, turning to glare. "We are certainly suffering the consequences of it, just as much as Father. At least Mother did not have to see a stranger with Father's face ride up the drive! Oh, Maddie, what if people guess? I mean, you did, right away. If they look at this—this Lord Gabriel and then at us—"

Madeline rubbed her temple again, and Juliana knew that she was not the only one pained by these revelations. But she was too distressed to think beyond her own inner turmoil.

Her sister said, "I only suspected because of Father and the resemblance this man bears to him. No one in London will have seen our father recently, and I doubt few remember him visiting the city over thirty years ago. And you look more like our mother, really, except that you do have Father's eyes."

"Mayhap, but—" Then she frowned. "You are assuming that I shall go to London? No, Maddie, I refuse! I need to be here to keep an eye on the estate and help Thomas. And you're the eldest, you should go and look over whatever marriageable men our new half-brother can introduce you to. Though without a dowry, and I cannot believe this—this stranger—is going to provide dowries for four hither-to-unknown and quite illicit connections, I don't see how a visit to London is going to help us!"

Her sister sighed. "No, nor do I, but our father is grasping at any straw, I think. He is much concerned about our future and has been ever since his accident. And as for the estate—" She looked up to regard her sibling as if she guessed how much their father's comment about the estate going downhill had wounded Juliana's feelings. "I know how you have labored, far more than you should have. You have tried hard to be the son he didn't—or we assumed he didn't— have. But it's not fair to you, Jules. You should go. I remember you used to talk of seeing London."

"Years ago," Juliana argued, looking away from her sister. "And certainly not under these conditions. It's not as if I have any great beauty or charm to compensate for my lack of fortune! No, you should go, Maddie. I should be here. There's the south pasture to be resown, and—"

"The hay is in," Madeline pointed out. "The grain reaped, and most of the garden harvested. Thomas can dig the potatoes and beets and tend to the animals. There is little to do for the rest of the year. You've done your best. It's not your fault the estate is not more productive."

Juliana bit her lip. How could it *not* be her fault? She should have been able to do better, she should do better . . .

"But I need to be here to help out!"

"You will help by not being here. With your absence, we will have one less mouth to feed," her sister noted.

Startled, Juliana looked up. "Is it as bad as that, now?"

"Close enough," Madeline said. "Father does not tell me the details, but I have seen how closely he watches the household accounts. And he insists that someone accompany this—this so-called cousin. I will not leave Father. I promised our mother I would look out for Father, you know that."

The curse of being the oldest child, the oldest girl, Juliana thought. "That is hardly fair to you," she argued. "You are six and twenty, Maddie. If any one of us should go—"

"No." Madeline's voice was firm, and her chin set stubbornly so that she looked quite like their father. "I am an old maid already and quite resigned to it, Jules. No, I promised I would look out for him, and he has no one else."

"He has other daughters. Do you think I care any less than you?" Juliana shot back. She folded her arms.

"Of course you care. But I swore to our mother, Jules, on the day she died. I cannot break such an oath!"

"So you, who are the most beautiful of us all, are allowed no other purpose in your life? I cannot believe Mother would have wanted that," Juliana tried to protest.

Her sister shook her head. On this matter, she had never listened to her sister's counsel, and Juliana feared she never would.

"And you can hardly wish to send one—or both—of the twins, to London, without us to keep them in check."

"Oh, good God!" Truly aghast, Juliana put a hand to her mouth. She had not even considered such a possibility. The twins—or even one of them, though they were seldom separated—abroad in a big city? When they could get in enough trouble in the countryside?

"Of course not," she agreed. "We are lucky they are visiting Lauryn at the squire's home and not here to see the—our half-brother—appear out of the blue. I don't even want to tell them, not yet."

"We shall have to tell them something. Father is serious, Jules. You must go. And anyhow—"

Her sister's voice wavered, and without thinking, Juliana braced herself. "What? Not more bad news?"

Her expression hard to read, Madeline looked up at her. "I didn't wish to tell you, but you will find out soon enough. Mr. Masham is coming home."

"Oh, hellsfire!" Juliana sank down, at last, upon the closest chair. What other disaster could befall her?